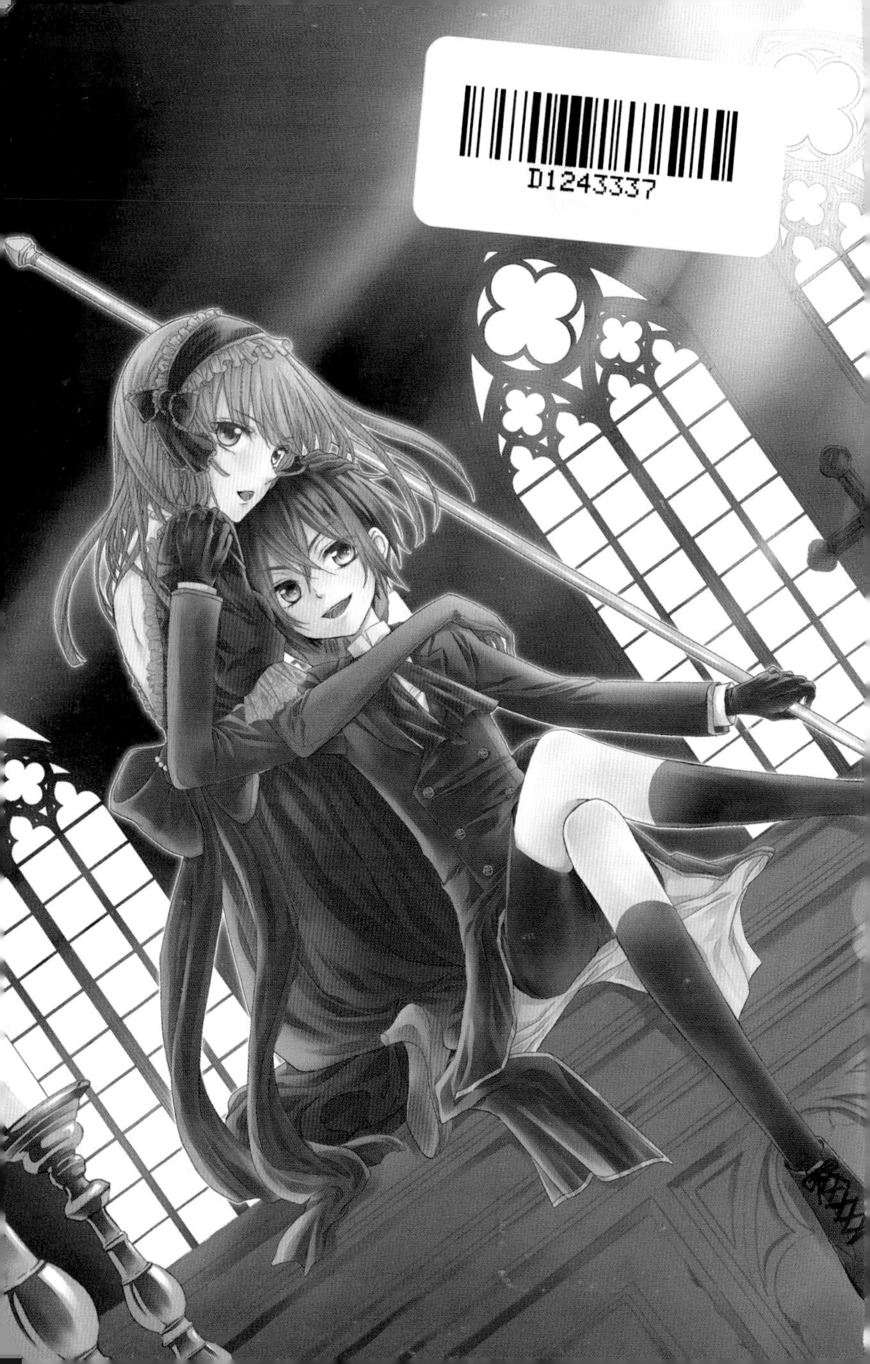

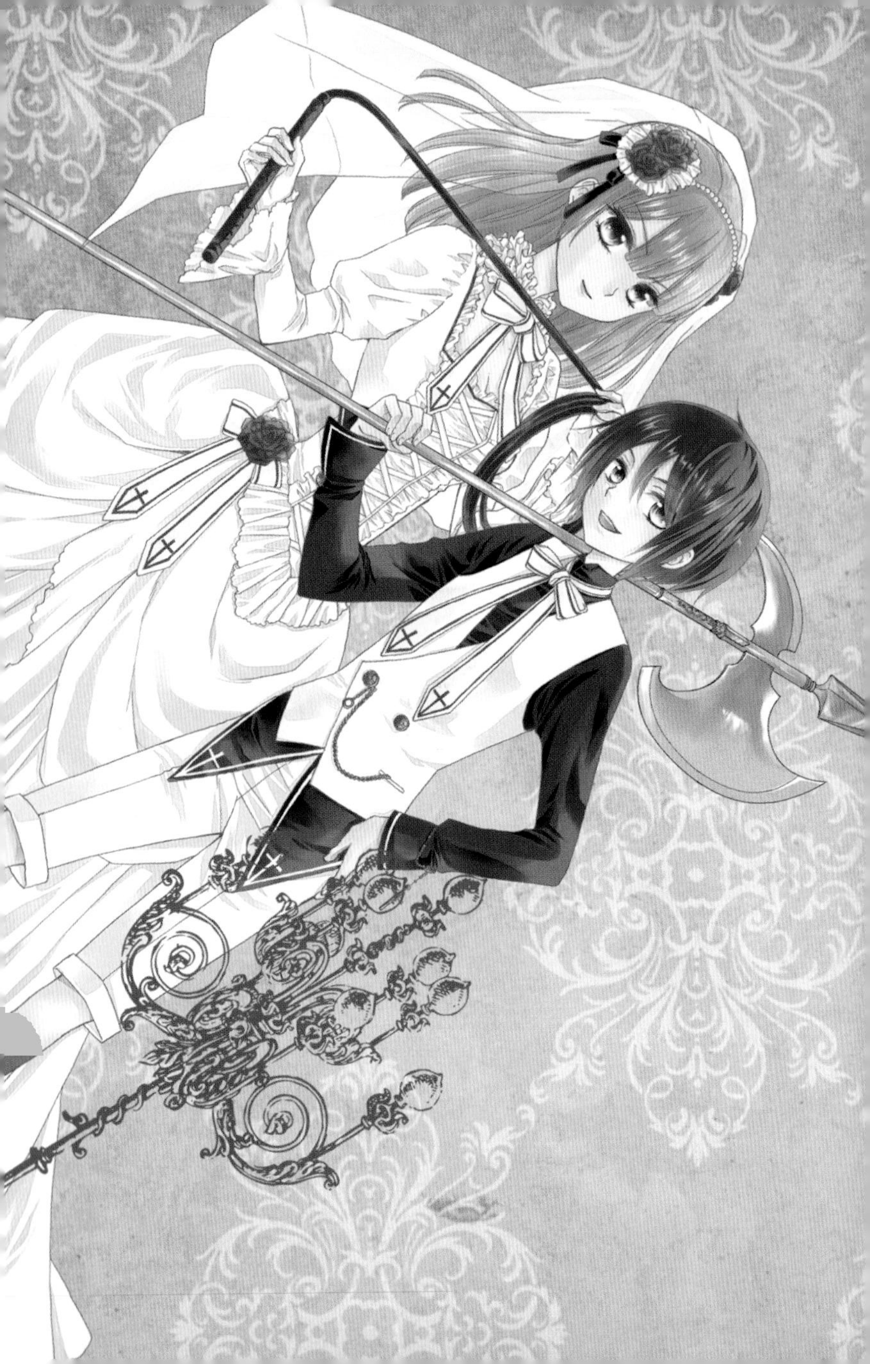

The Bride & the Exorcist Knight

III

CONTENTS

The Bride & the Exorcist Knight

3

Keiko Ishihara

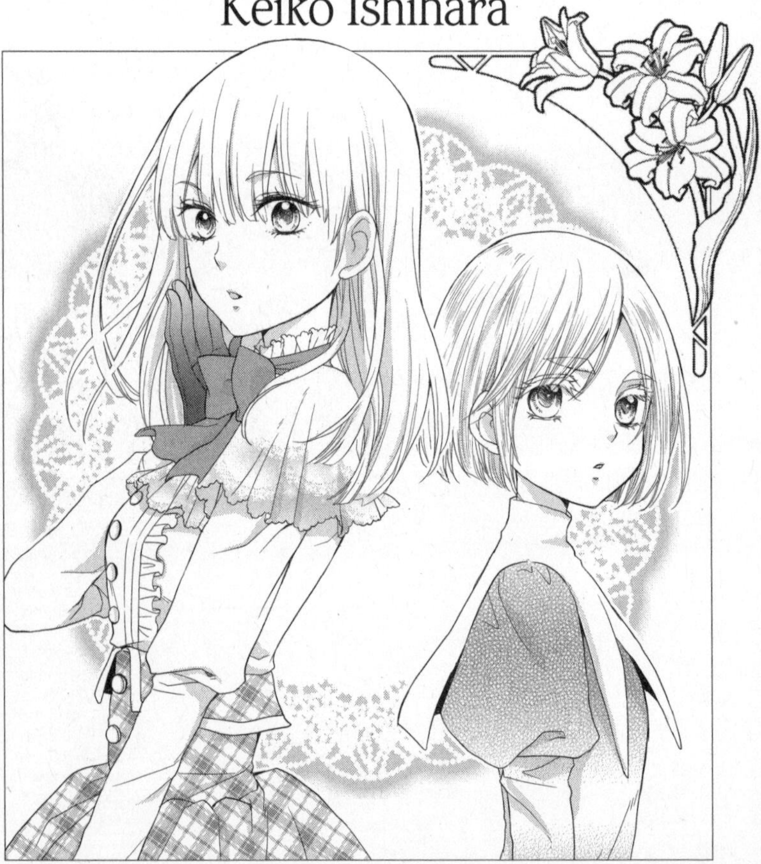

Our Story...

Anne was doomed to become the bride of the great demon Mephisto, but she was saved by boy genius exorcist Haru! Five years her junior, the talented Haru repeatedly asked Anne to marry him, but she turned him down every time. However, after a battle with Mephisto, Anne has decided to accept Haru's proposal and become his wife.

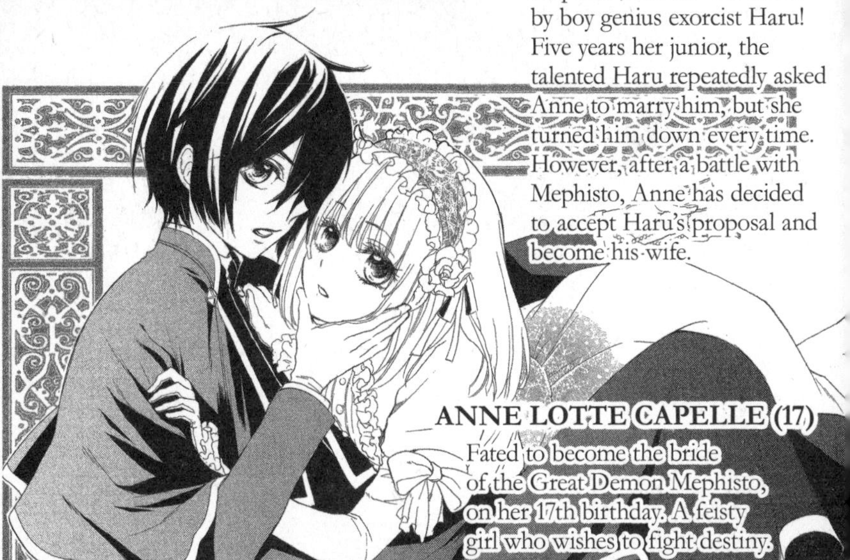

ANNE LOTTE CAPELLE (17)

Fated to become the bride of the Great Demon Mephisto, on her 17th birthday. A feisty girl who wishes to fight destiny.

HARU VELLMAN (12)

Next in line to be the head of the Vellman family of exorcists. Anne saved him when he was young, and that moment inspired him to become an exorcist to protect her.

LITTLE DEMONS

Anne's servants. Low-level demons.

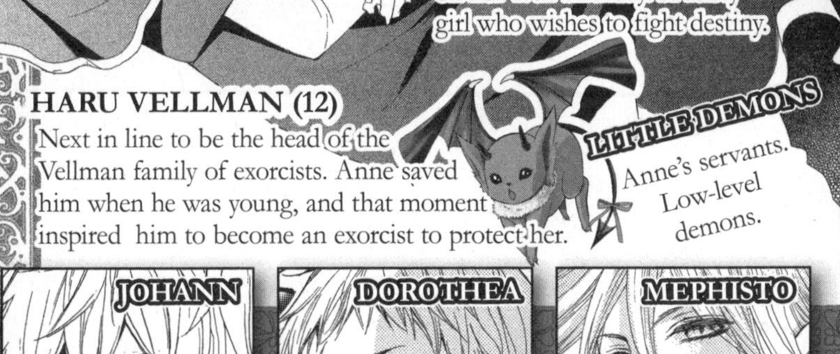

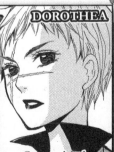

JOHANN

One of the Vellman family exorcists. Unmotivated and likes to mess around.

DOROTHEA

Current head of the Vellman family. A tough, no-nonsense woman.

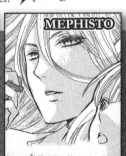

MEPHISTO

A powerful demon. Determined to make Anne his bride. Escaped Haru once, but he hasn't given up on Anne just yet...

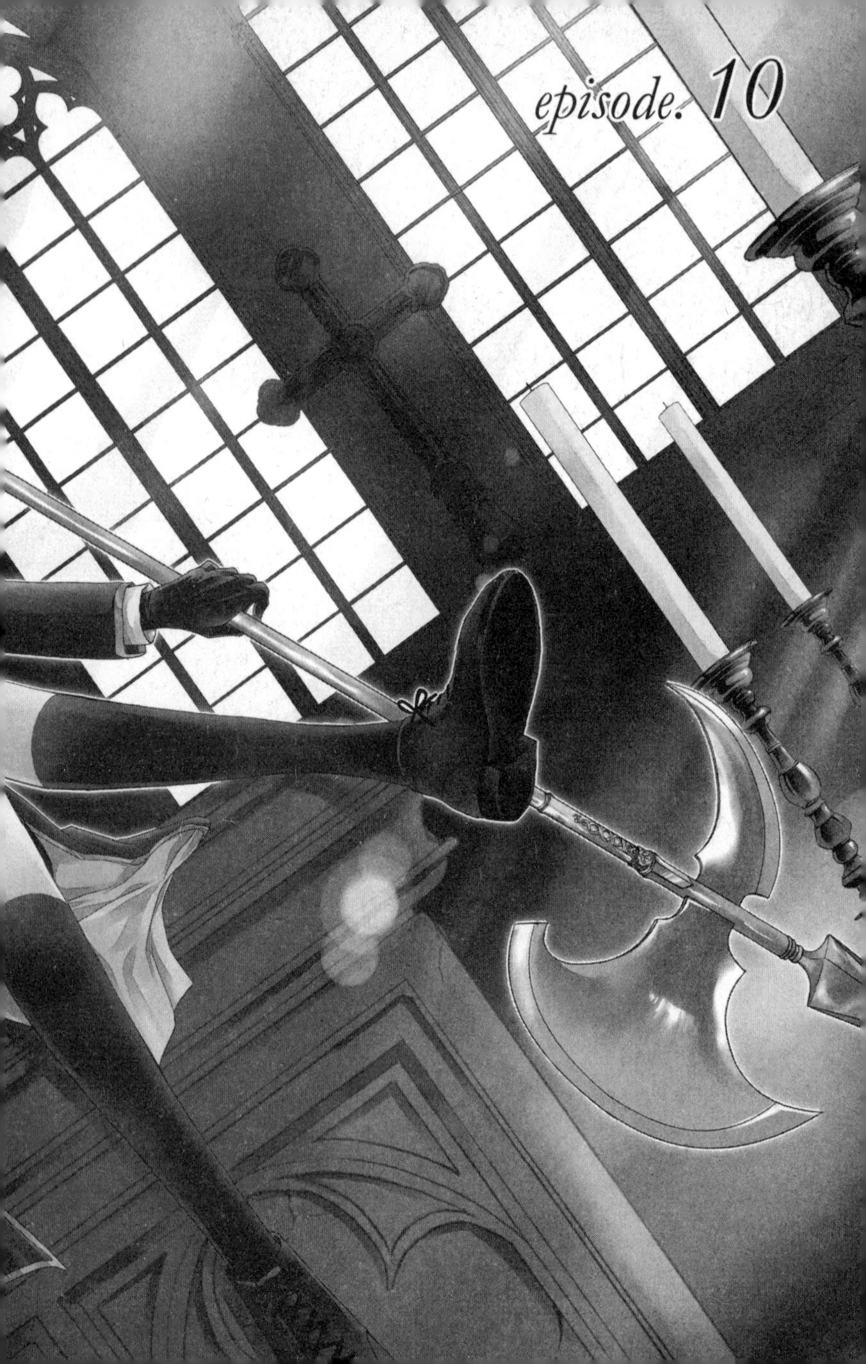
episode. 10

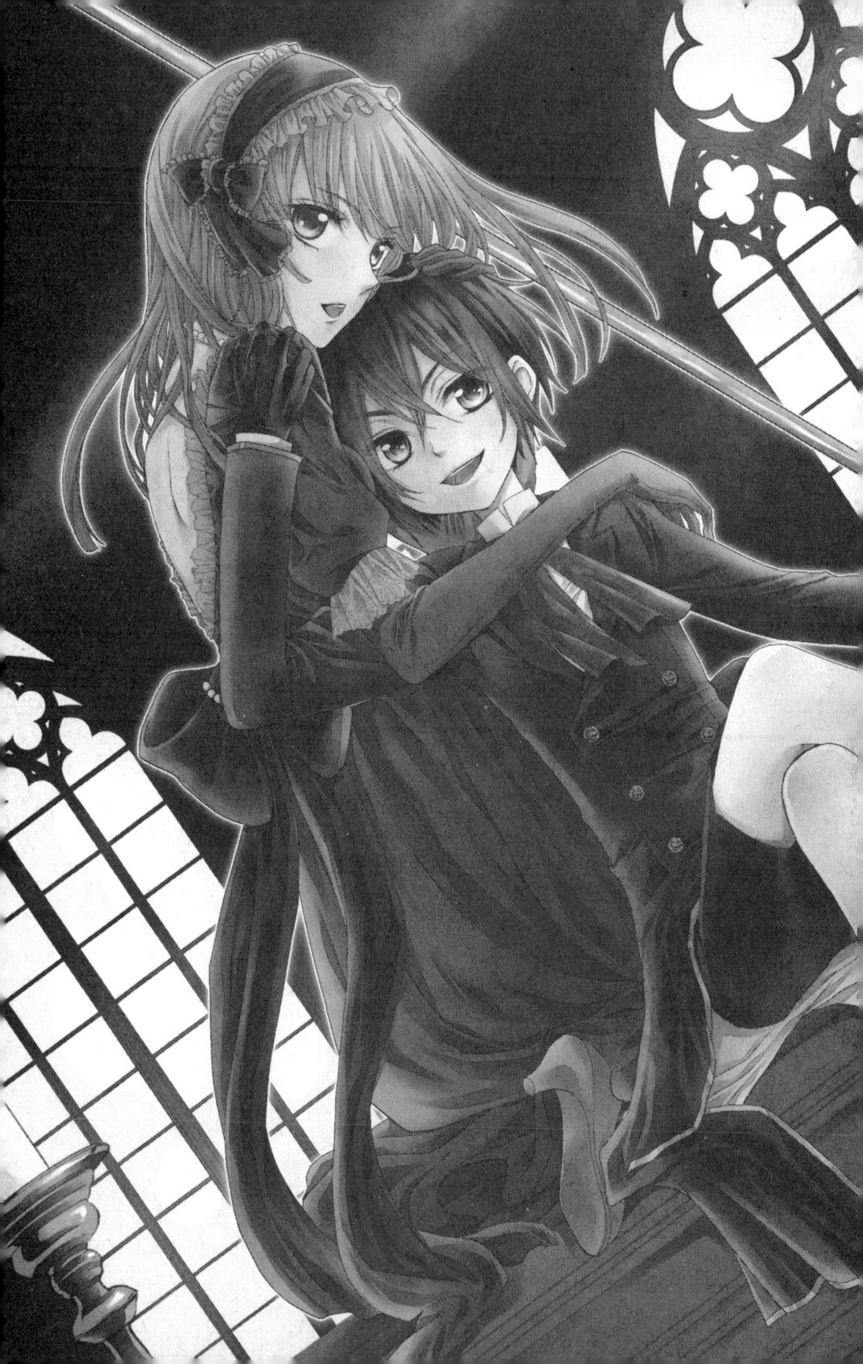

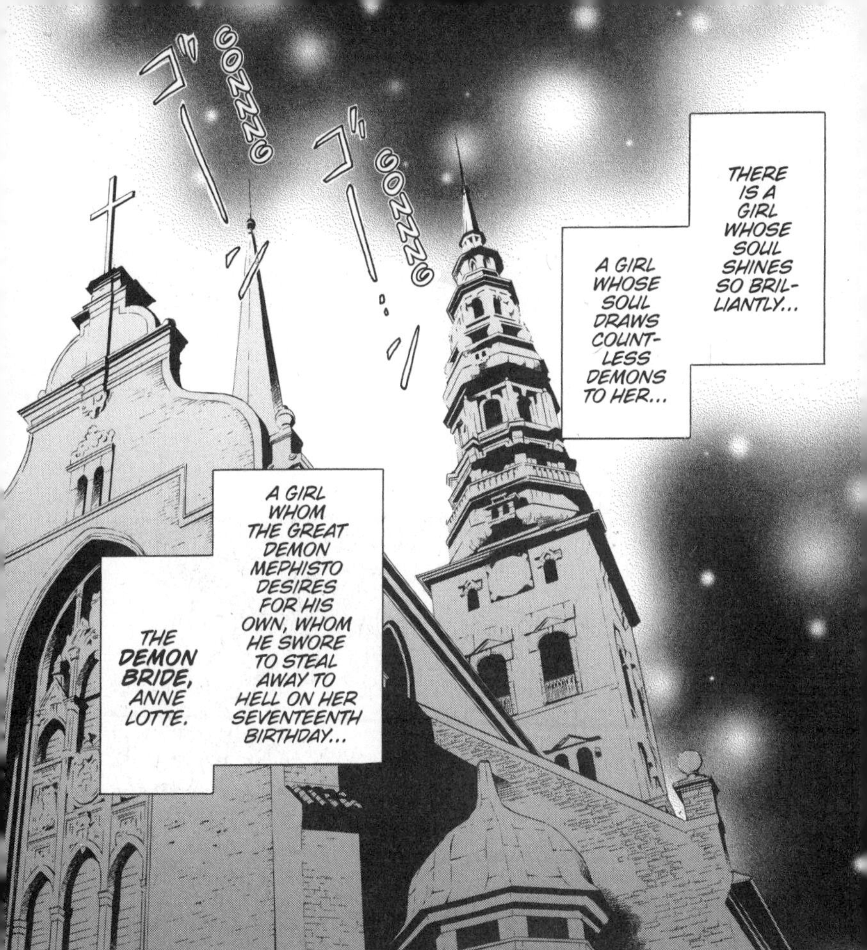
GONNNG
GONNNG
THERE IS A GIRL WHOSE SOUL SHINES SO BRIL-LIANTLY...
A GIRL WHOSE SOUL DRAWS COUNT-LESS DEMONS TO HER...
A GIRL WHOM THE GREAT DEMON MEPHISTO DESIRES FOR HIS OWN, WHOM HE SWORE TO STEAL AWAY TO HELL ON HER SEVENTEENTH BIRTHDAY...
THE DEMON BRIDE, ANNE LOTTE.
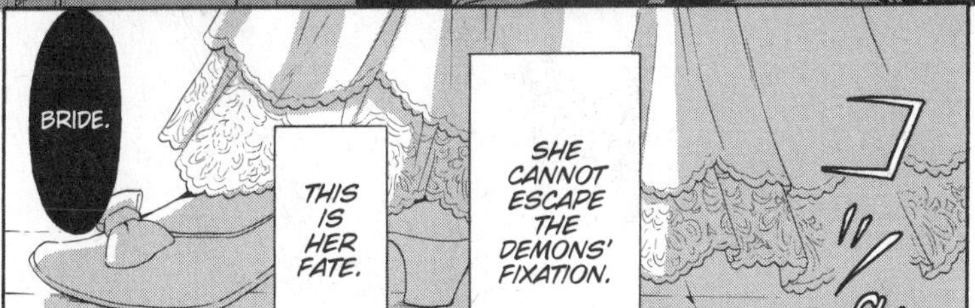
CLACK
SHE CANNOT ESCAPE THE DEMONS' FIXATION.
THIS IS HER FATE.
BRIDE.

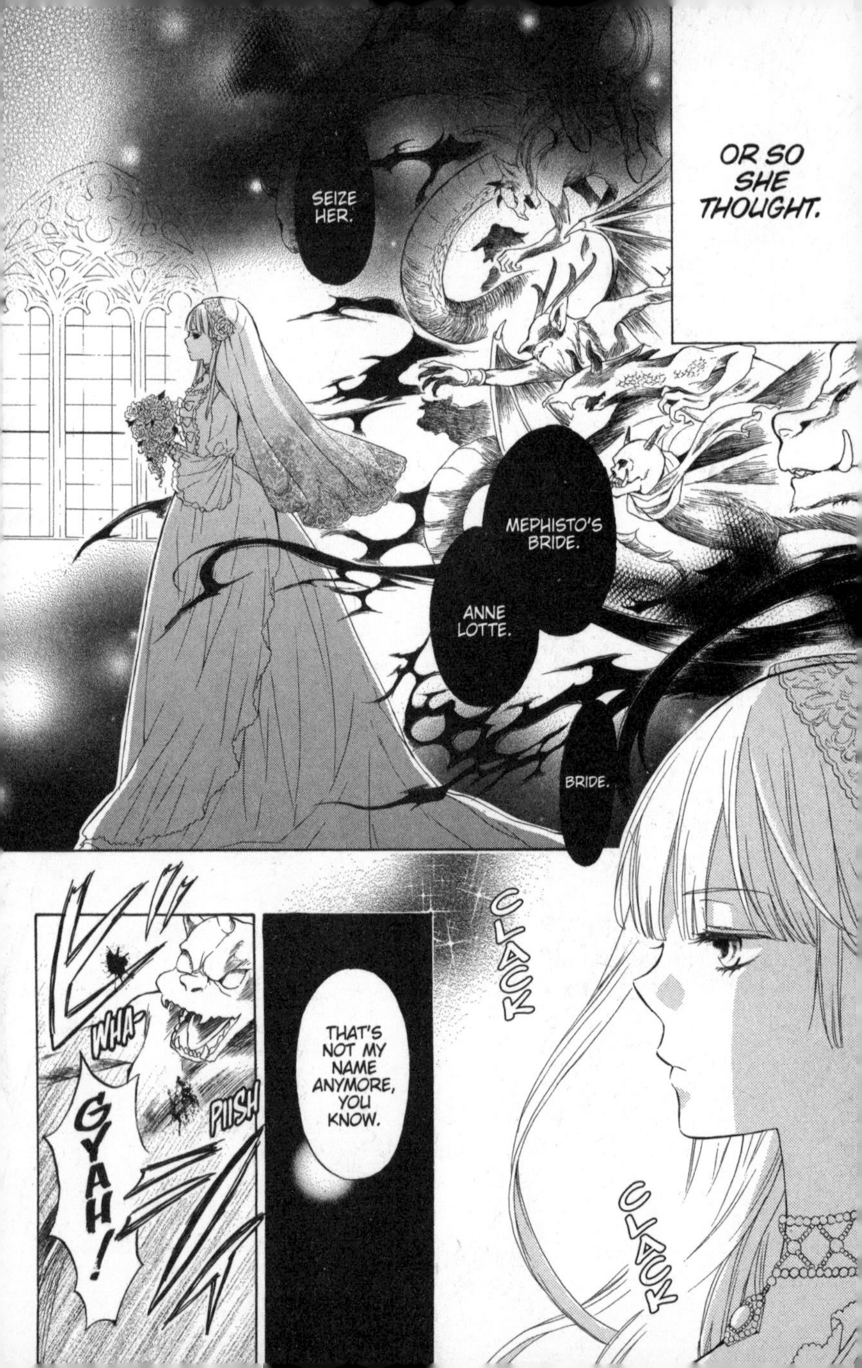
OR SO SHE THOUGHT.
SEIZE HER.
MEPHISTO'S BRIDE.
ANNE LOTTE.
BRIDE.
CLACK
CLACK
THAT'S NOT MY NAME ANYMORE, YOU KNOW.
WHA-
PIISH
GYAH!

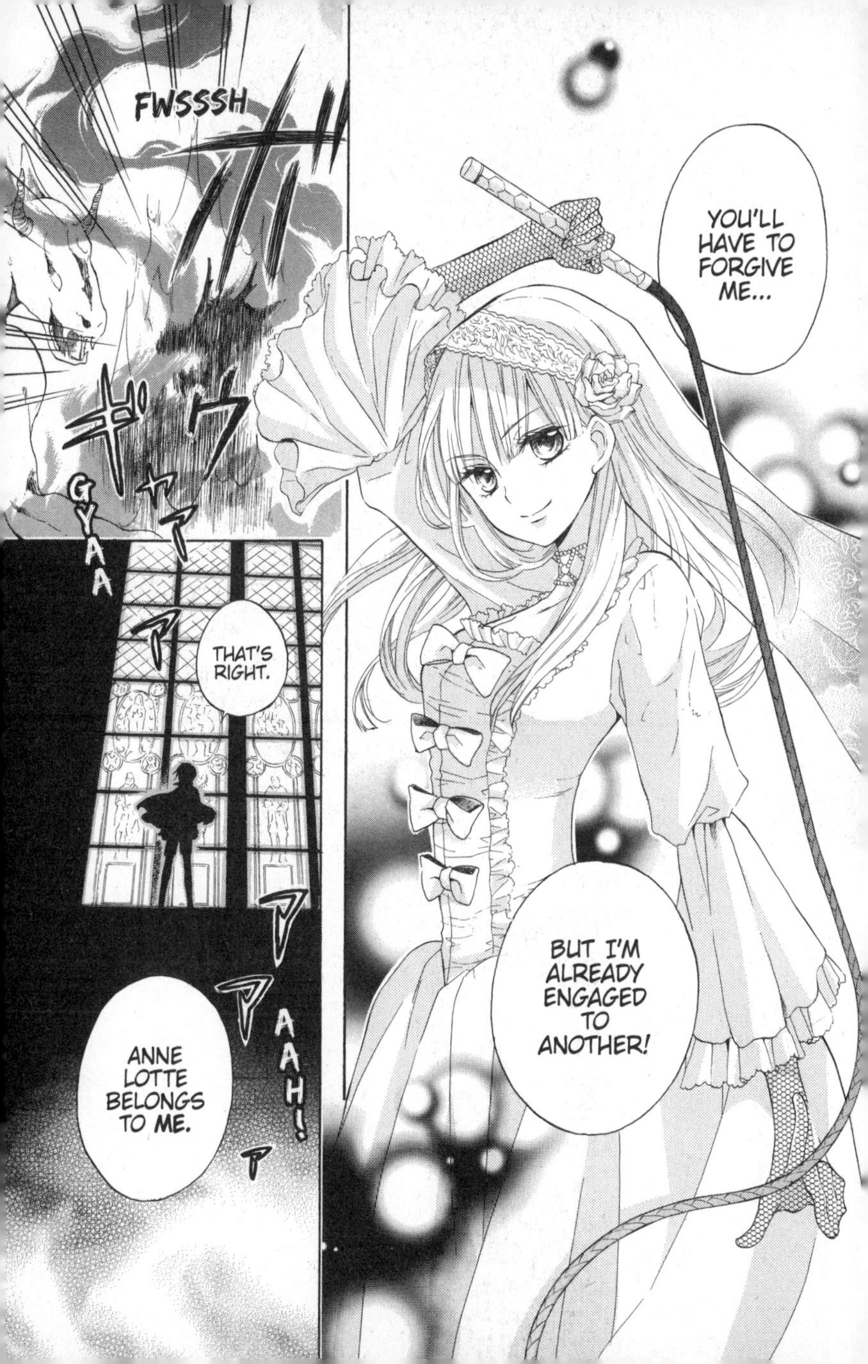
YOU'LL HAVE TO FORGIVE ME...
BUT I'M ALREADY ENGAGED TO ANOTHER!
FWSSSH
GYAA
THAT'S RIGHT.
AAAH!
ANNE LOTTE BELONGS TO ME.

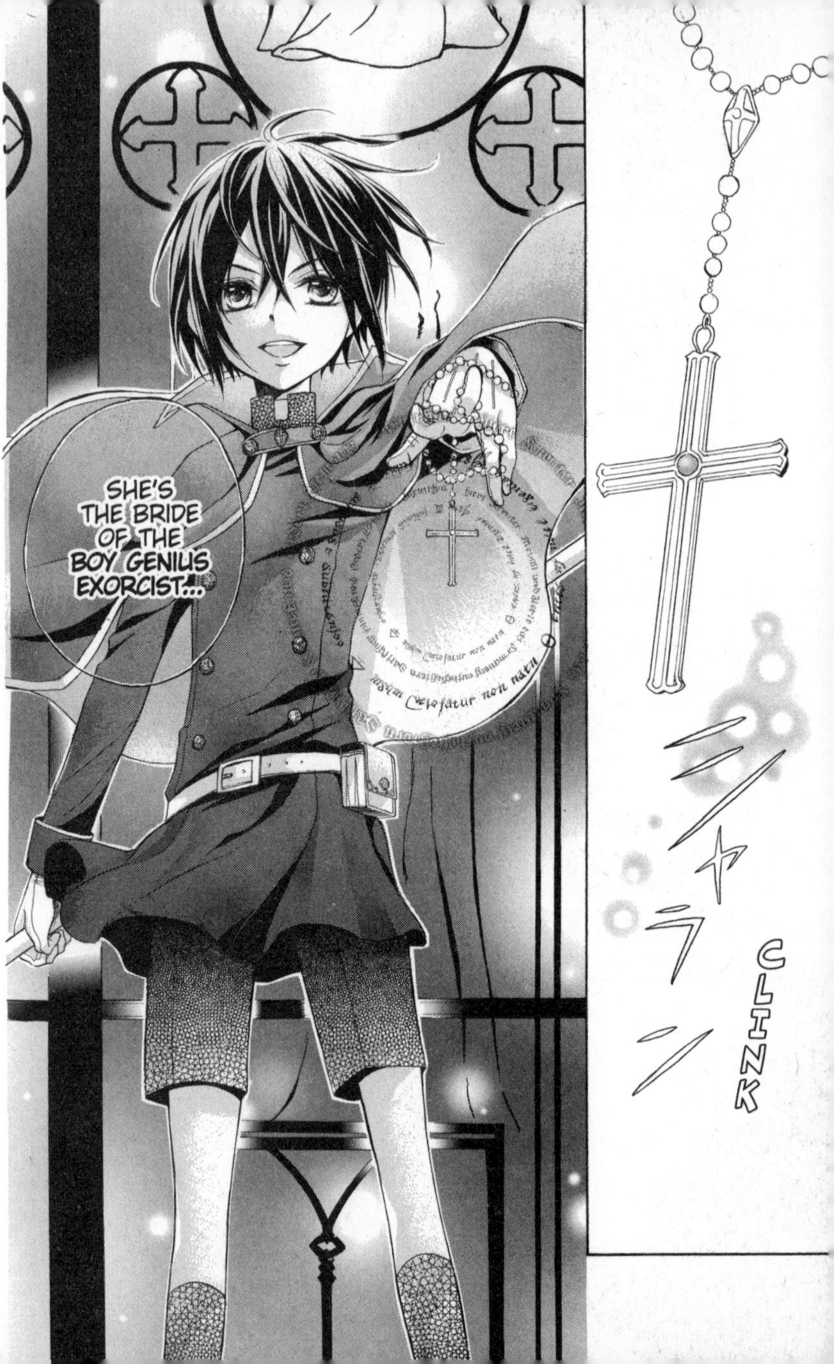
シャラン
CLINK
SHE'S THE BRIDE OF THE BOY GENIUS EXORCIST...

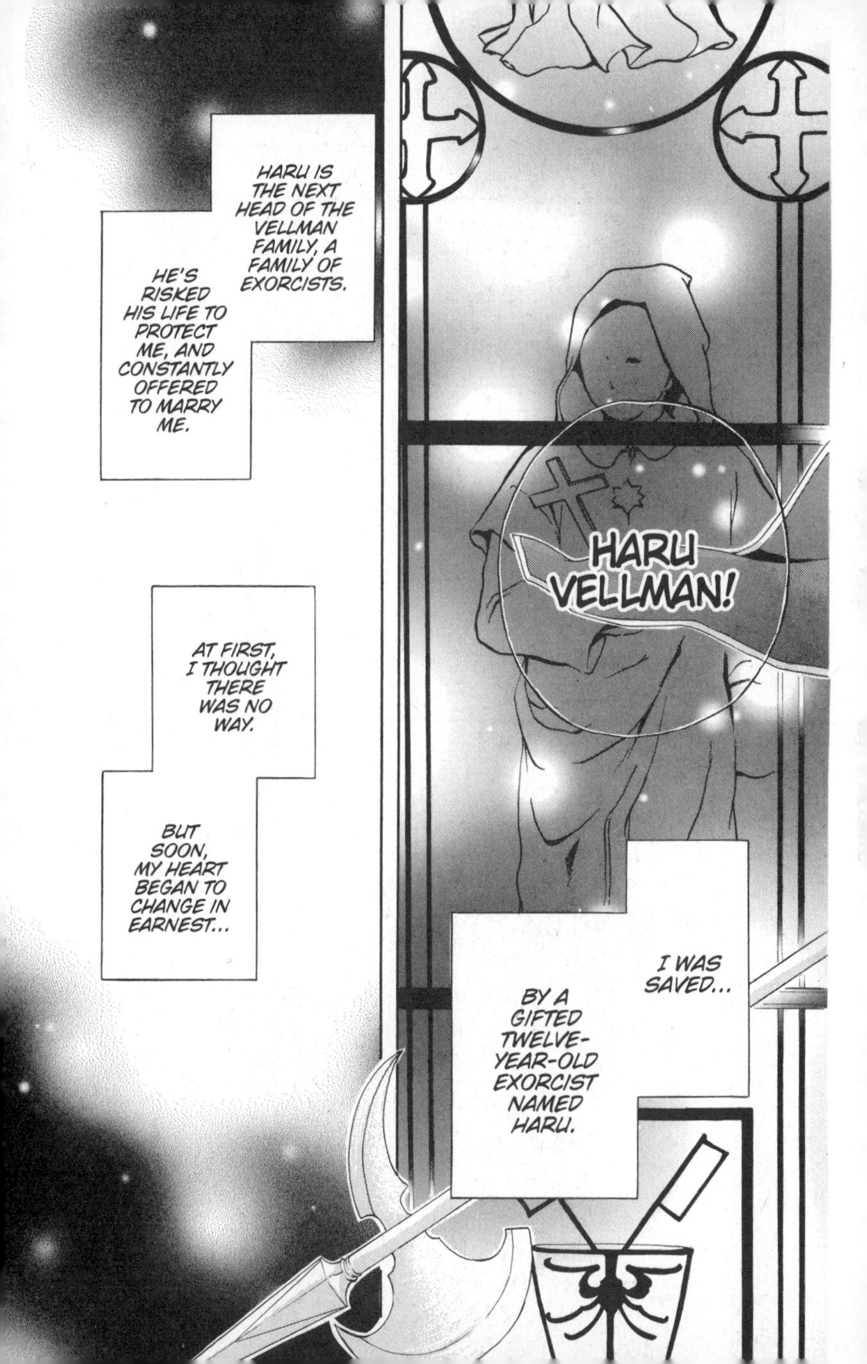
HARU VELLMAN!
I WAS SAVED...
BY A GIFTED TWELVE-YEAR-OLD EXORCIST NAMED HARU.
HARU IS THE NEXT HEAD OF THE VELLMAN FAMILY, A FAMILY OF EXORCISTS.
HE'S RISKED HIS LIFE TO PROTECT ME, AND CONSTANTLY OFFERED TO MARRY ME.
AT FIRST, I THOUGHT THERE WAS NO WAY.
BUT SOON, MY HEART BEGAN TO CHANGE IN EARNEST...

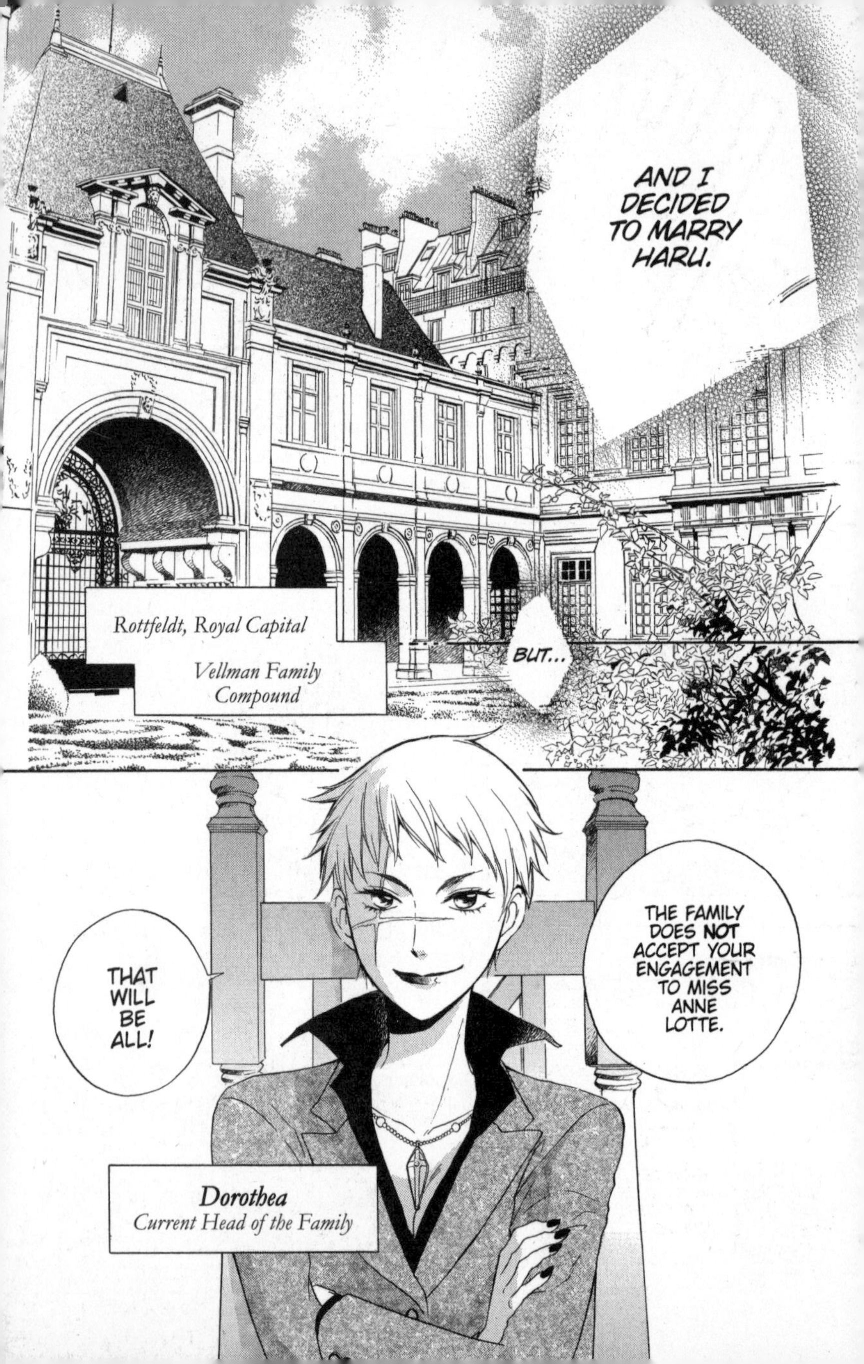
AND I DECIDED TO MARRY HARU.
BUT...
Rottfeldt, Royal Capital
Vellman Family Compound
THE FAMILY DOES **NOT** ACCEPT YOUR ENGAGEMENT TO MISS ANNE LOTTE.
THAT WILL BE ALL!
Dorothea
Current Head of the Family

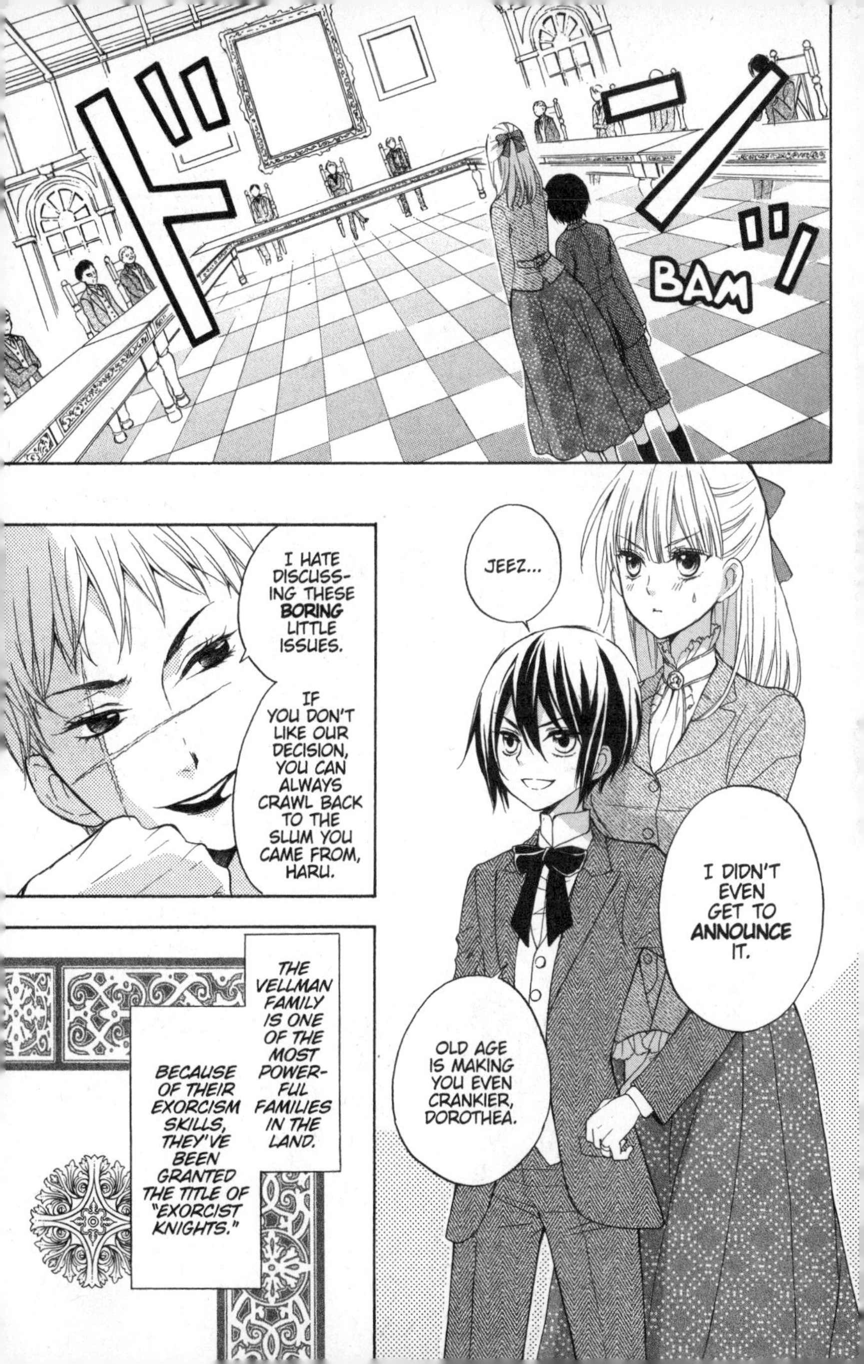
BAM
JEEZ...
I DIDN'T EVEN GET TO ANNOUNCE IT.
OLD AGE IS MAKING YOU EVEN CRANKIER, DOROTHEA.
I HATE DISCUSSING THESE BORING LITTLE ISSUES.
IF YOU DON'T LIKE OUR DECISION, YOU CAN ALWAYS CRAWL BACK TO THE SLUM YOU CAME FROM, HARU.
THE VELLMAN FAMILY IS ONE OF THE MOST POWERFUL FAMILIES IN THE LAND.
BECAUSE OF THEIR EXORCISM SKILLS, THEY'VE BEEN GRANTED THE TITLE OF "EXORCIST KNIGHTS."

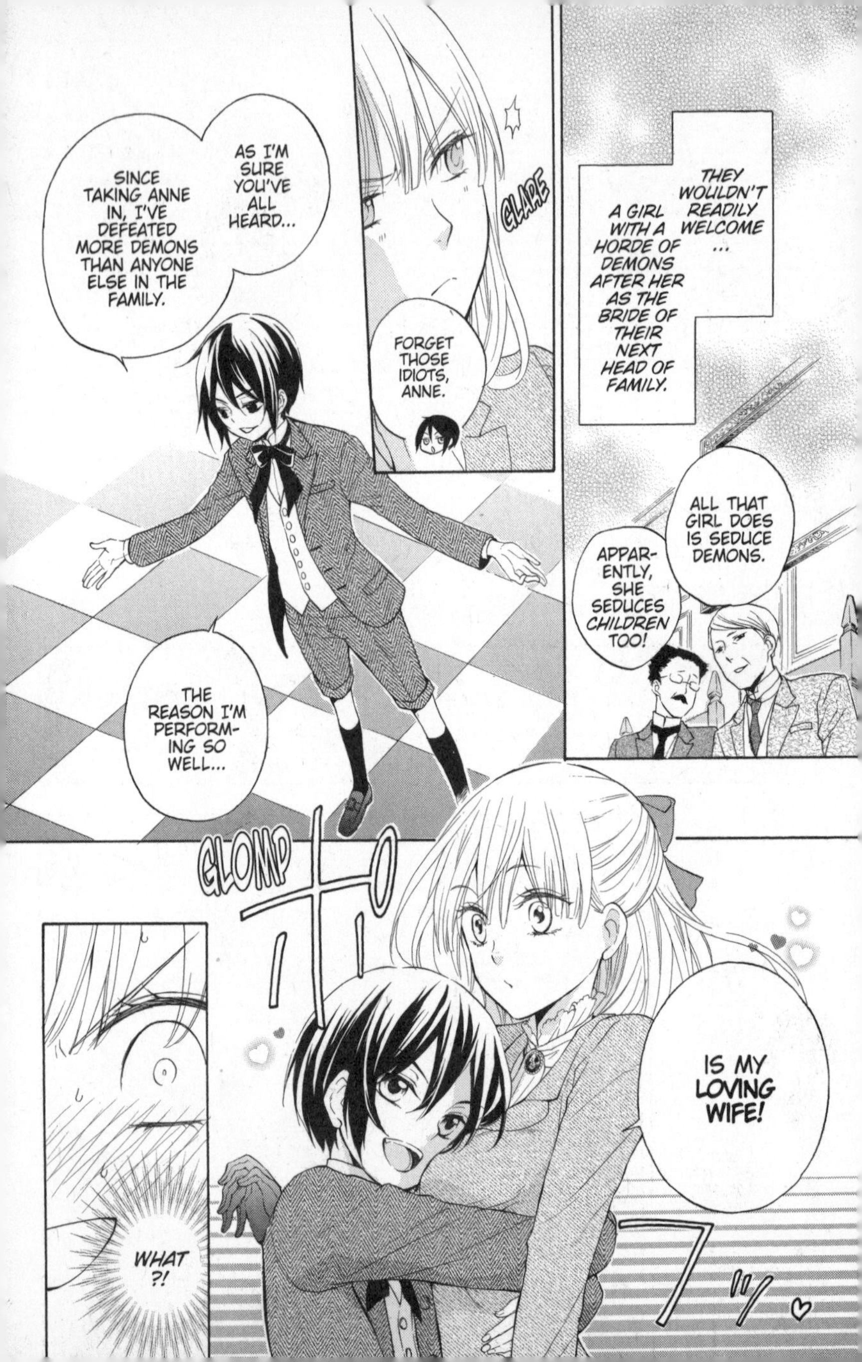

THEY WOULDN'T READILY WELCOME ...
A GIRL WITH A HORDE OF DEMONS AFTER HER AS THE BRIDE OF THEIR NEXT HEAD OF FAMILY.
ALL THAT GIRL DOES IS SEDUCE DEMONS.
APPARENTLY, SHE SEDUCES CHILDREN TOO!
GLARE
FORGET THOSE IDIOTS, ANNE.
AS I'M SURE YOU'VE ALL HEARD...
SINCE TAKING ANNE IN, I'VE DEFEATED MORE DEMONS THAN ANYONE ELSE IN THE FAMILY.
THE REASON I'M PERFORMING SO WELL...
GLOMP
IS MY LOVING WIFE!
WHAT ?!

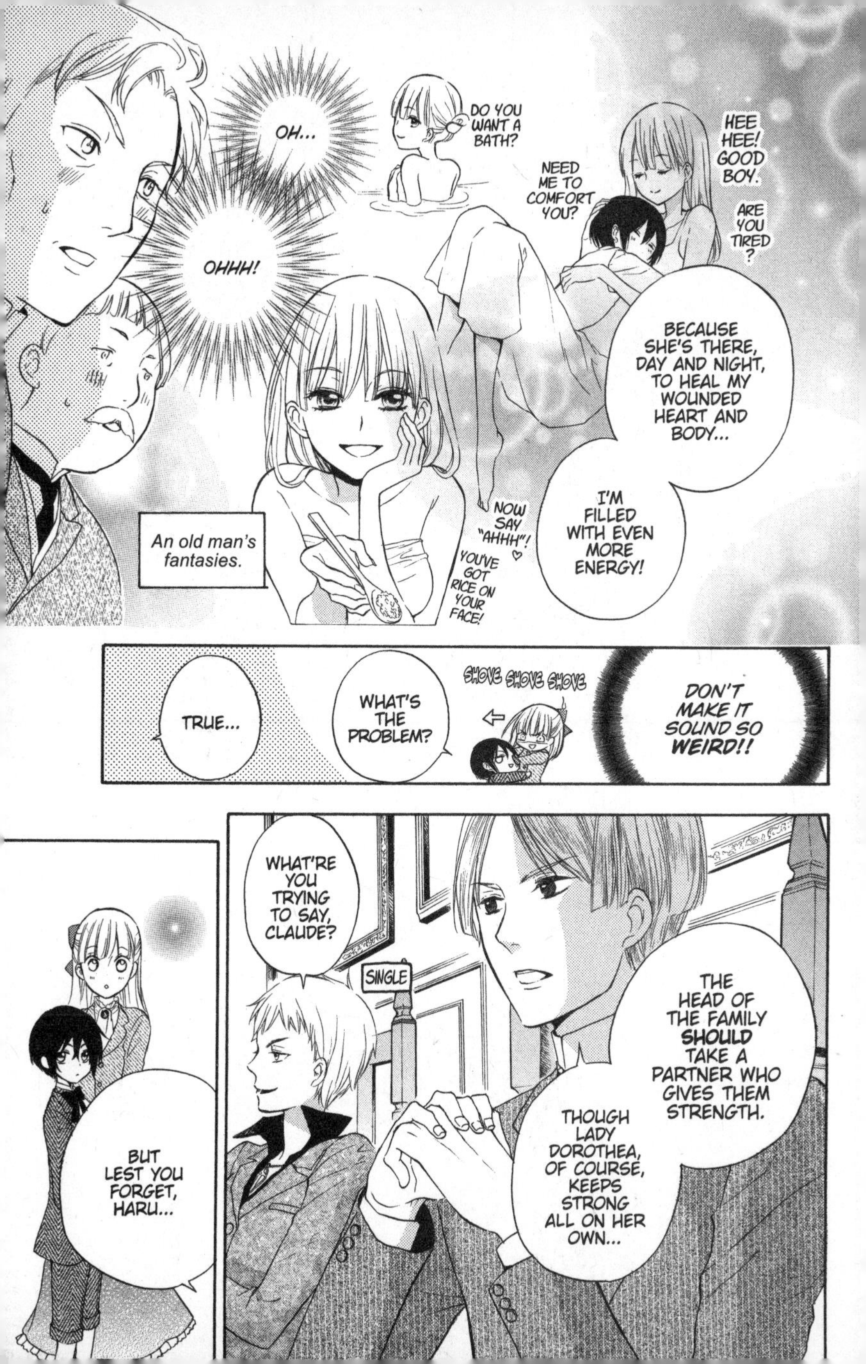
HEE HEE! GOOD BOY.
ARE YOU TIRED?
NEED ME TO COMFORT YOU?
DO YOU WANT A BATH?
OH...
OHHH!
BECAUSE SHE'S THERE, DAY AND NIGHT, TO HEAL MY WOUNDED HEART AND BODY...
I'M FILLED WITH EVEN MORE ENERGY!
NOW SAY "AHHH"! ♡
YOU'VE GOT RICE ON YOUR FACE!
An old man's fantasies.
DON'T MAKE IT SOUND SO WEIRD!!
SHOVE SHOVE SHOVE
WHAT'S THE PROBLEM?
TRUE...
WHAT'RE YOU TRYING TO SAY, CLAUDE?
THE HEAD OF THE FAMILY SHOULD TAKE A PARTNER WHO GIVES THEM STRENGTH.
THOUGH LADY DOROTHEA, OF COURSE, KEEPS STRONG ALL ON HER OWN...
SINGLE
BUT LEST YOU FORGET, HARU...

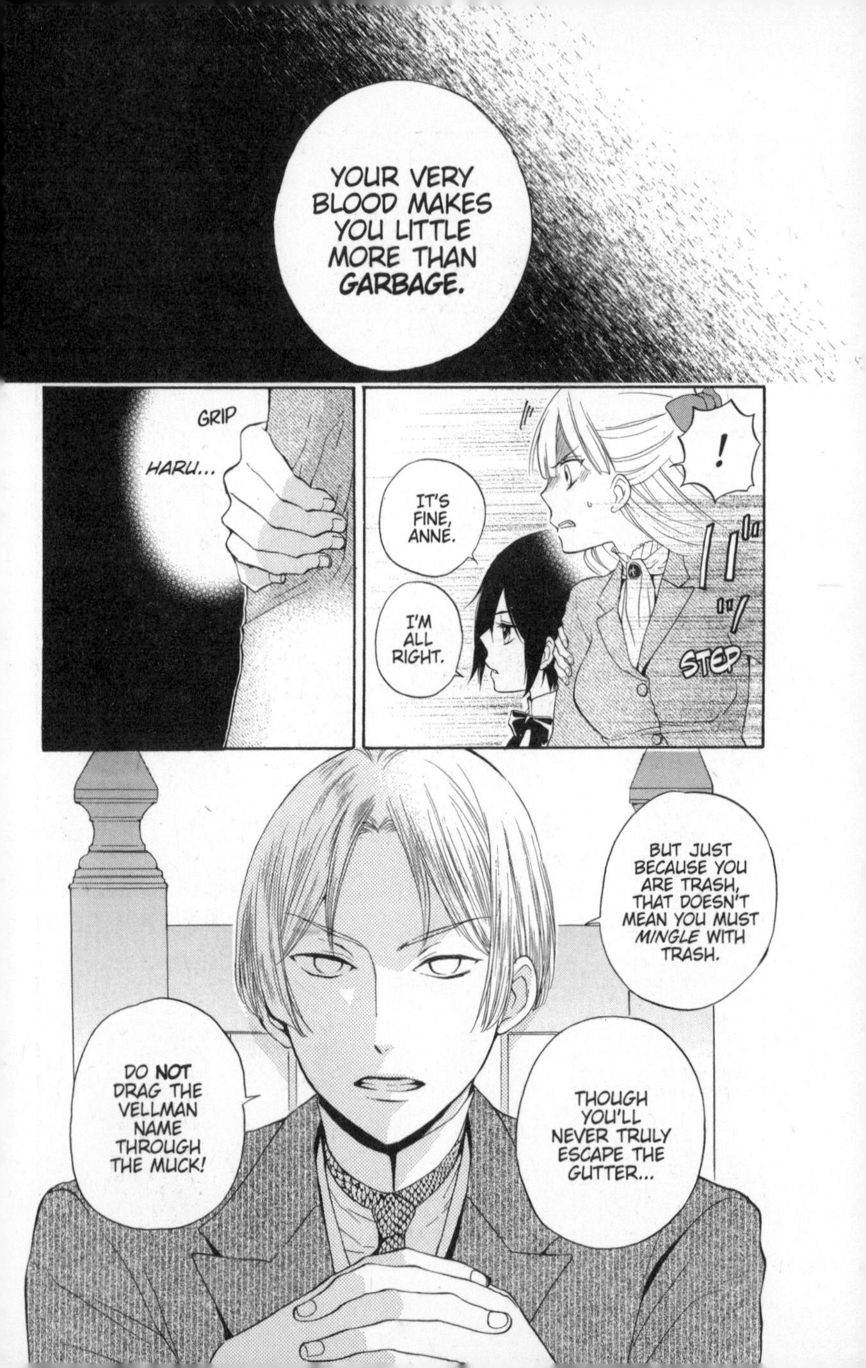
YOUR VERY BLOOD MAKES YOU LITTLE MORE THAN GARBAGE.
!
IT'S FINE, ANNE.
I'M ALL RIGHT.
STEP
GRIP
HARU...
BUT JUST BECAUSE YOU ARE TRASH, THAT DOESN'T MEAN YOU MUST *MINGLE* WITH TRASH.
THOUGH YOU'LL NEVER TRULY ESCAPE THE GUTTER...
DO **NOT** DRAG THE VELLMAN NAME THROUGH THE MUCK!

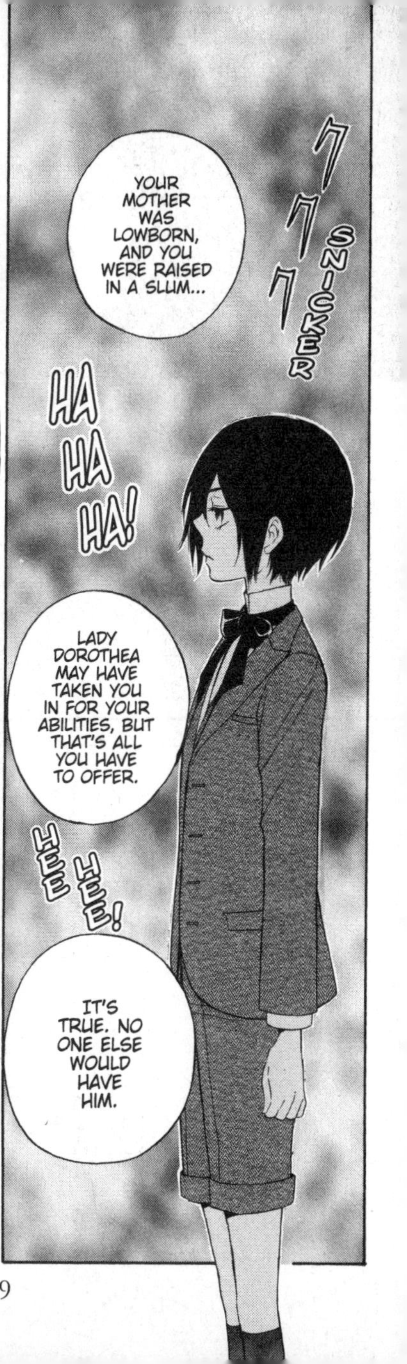
クククク
SNICKER
YOUR MOTHER WAS LOWBORN, AND YOU WERE RAISED IN A SLUM...
HA HA HA!
LADY DOROTHEA MAY HAVE TAKEN YOU IN FOR YOUR ABILITIES, BUT THAT'S ALL YOU HAVE TO OFFER.
HEE HEE!
IT'S TRUE. NO ONE ELSE WOULD HAVE HIM.

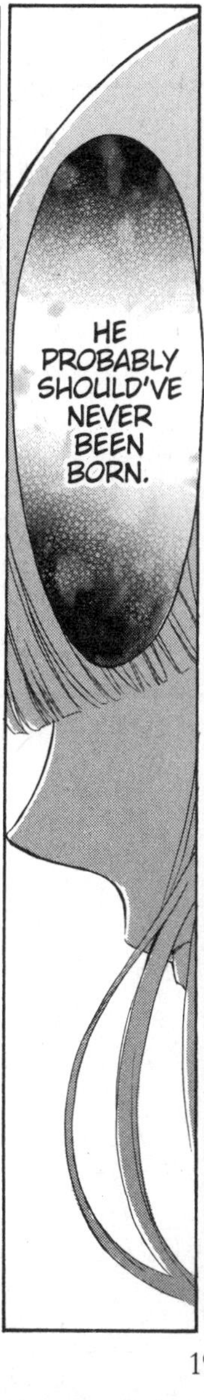
HE PROBABLY SHOULD'VE NEVER BEEN BORN.

Thank you for buying Volume 3 of *The Bride & the Exorcist Knight.*

The series was moved from LaLa to LaLaDX at the start of this volume, so this whole volume is the Convent Arc.

I was really worried at first, since the move would have lots of different effects on the series. For example, the magazine came out every other month, and the paper size got smaller. But thanks to the new bi-monthly schedule, I was able to use many more pages to write a story, which worked really well for me. Now, I'm really hitting a good stride with this series.

Thank you to everyone who followed this work to DX, everyone who picked this up from DX, and everyone reading it for the first time in volumes!

I hope you'll continue to support me!

石原ケイコ
Keiko Ishihara

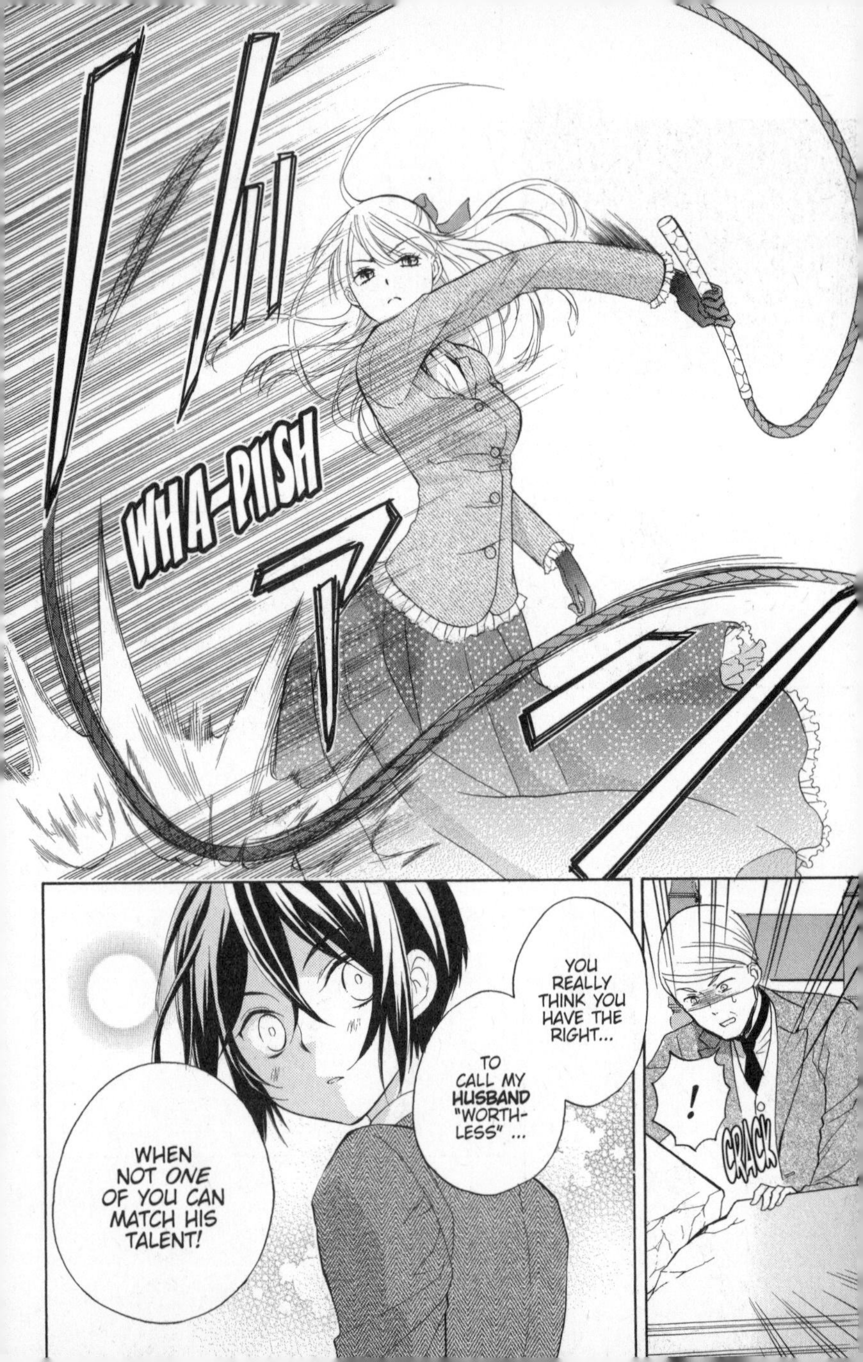
WHA-PIISH
CRACK
!
YOU REALLY THINK YOU HAVE THE RIGHT...
TO CALL MY **HUSBAND** "WORTH-LESS" ...
WHEN NOT *ONE* OF YOU CAN MATCH HIS TALENT!

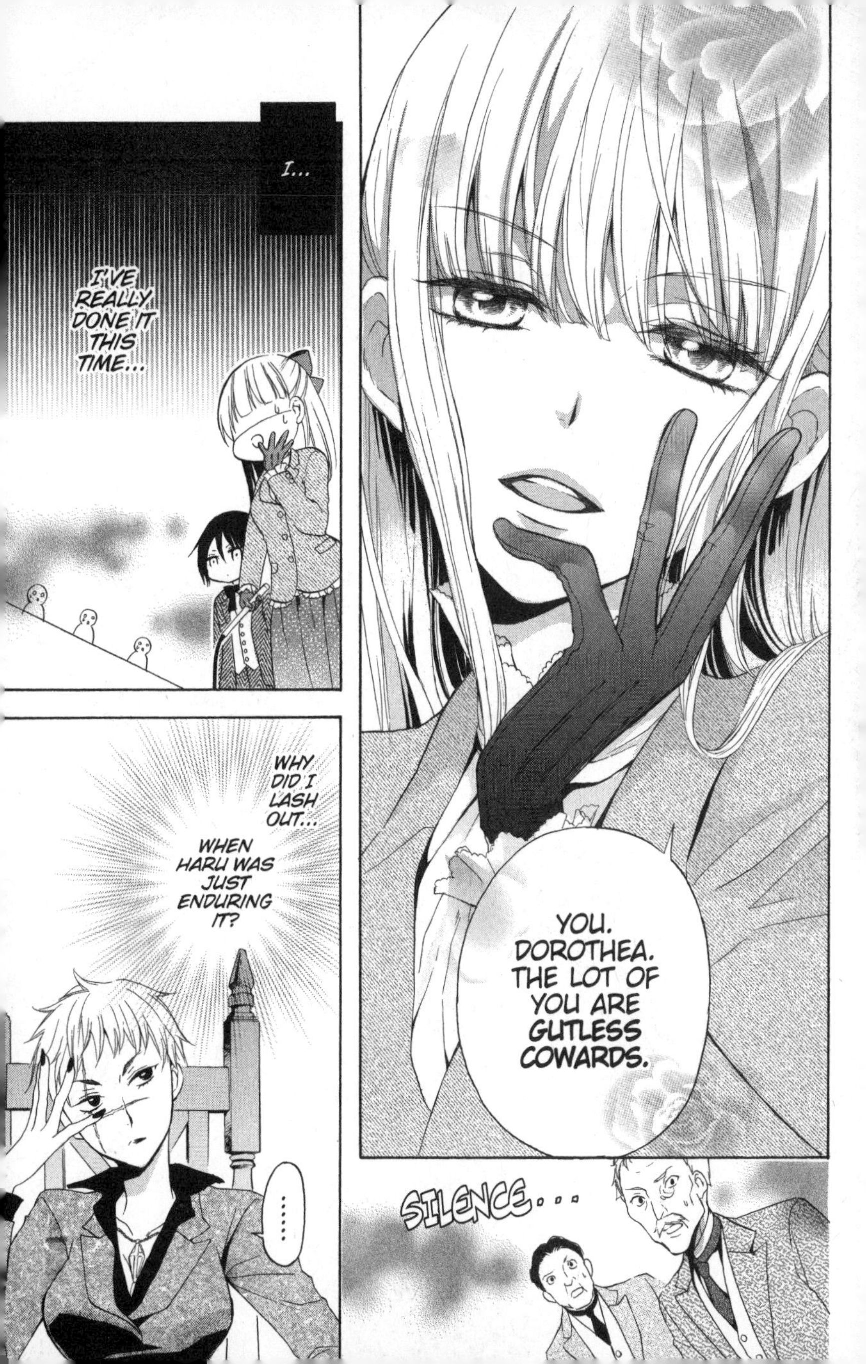
YOU. DOROTHEA. THE LOT OF YOU ARE GUTLESS COWARDS.
SILENCE...
I...
I'VE REALLY DONE IT THIS TIME...
WHY DID I LASH OUT...
WHEN HARU WAS JUST ENDURING IT?
......

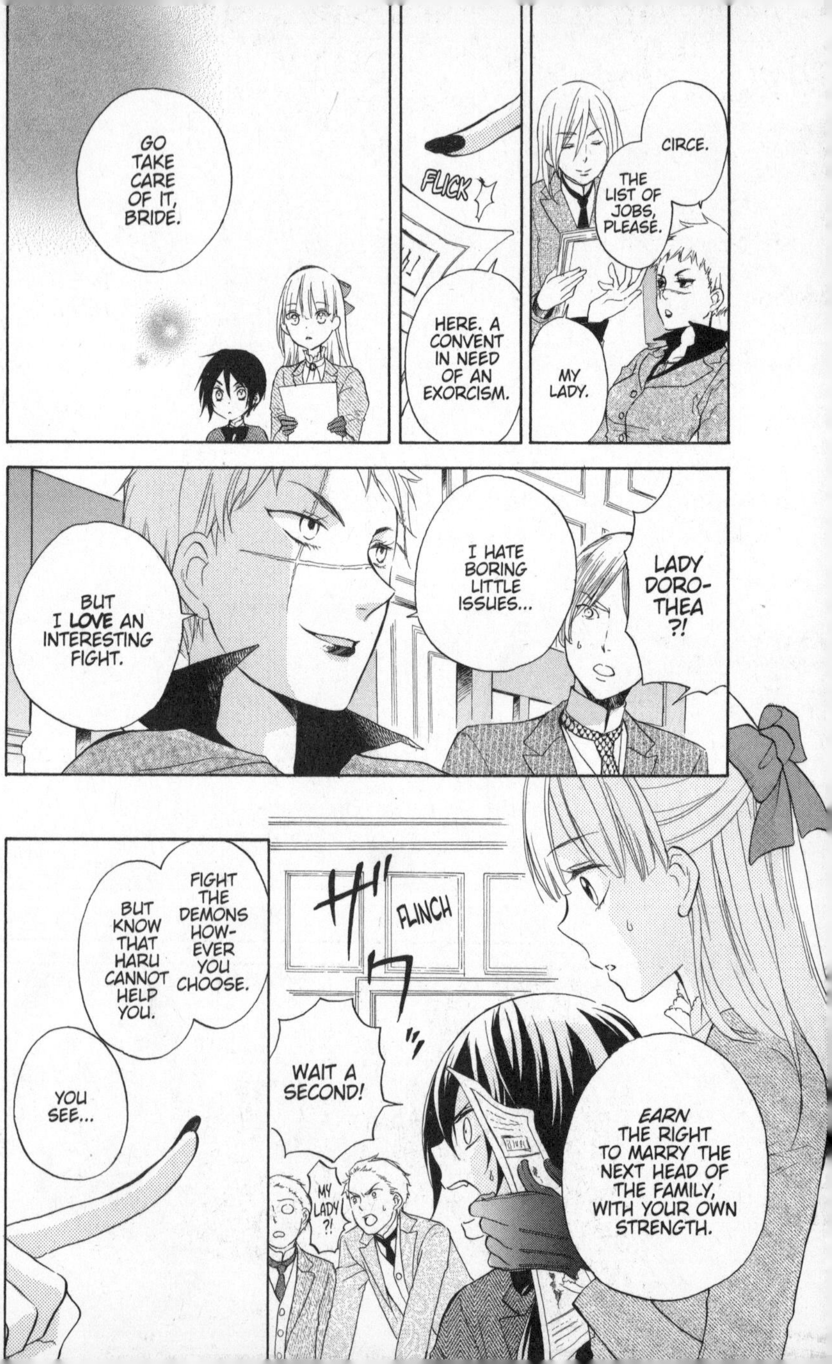
CIRCE.
THE LIST OF JOBS, PLEASE.
MY LADY.
FLICK
HERE. A CONVENT IN NEED OF AN EXORCISM.
GO TAKE CARE OF IT, BRIDE.
LADY DORO-THEA?!
I HATE BORING LITTLE ISSUES...
BUT I LOVE AN INTERESTING FIGHT.
FLINCH
EARN THE RIGHT TO MARRY THE NEXT HEAD OF THE FAMILY, WITH YOUR OWN STRENGTH.
WAIT A SECOND!
MY LADY?!
FIGHT THE DEMONS HOW-EVER YOU CHOOSE.
BUT KNOW THAT HARU CANNOT HELP YOU.
YOU SEE...

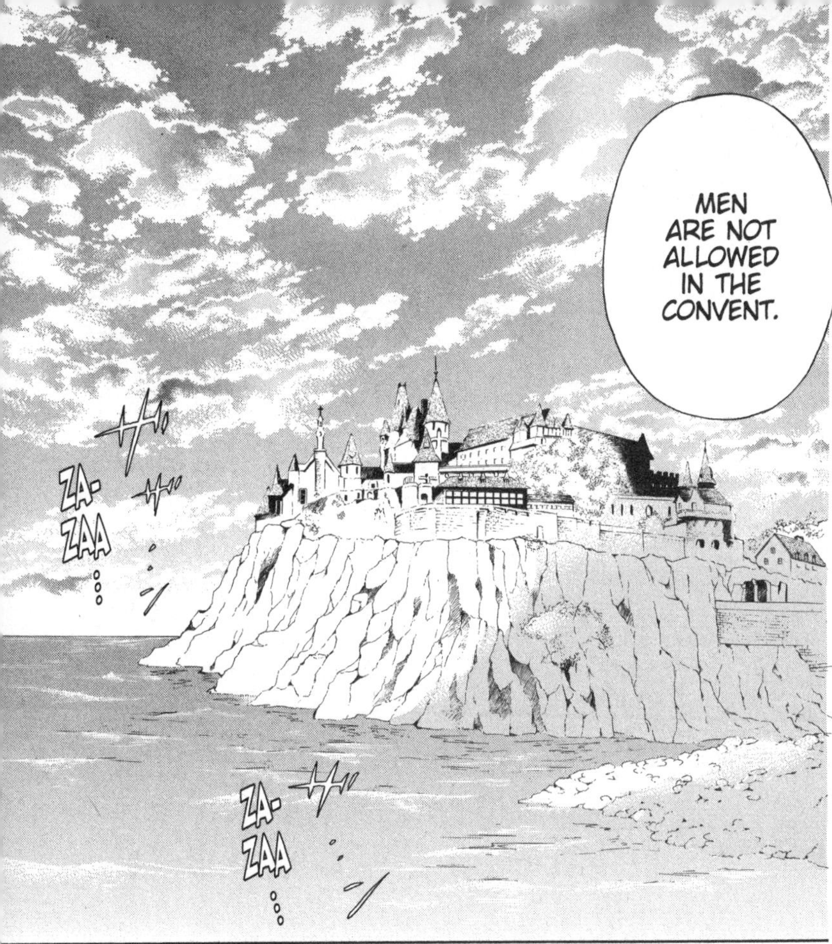
MEN ARE NOT ALLOWED IN THE CONVENT.
ZA-ZAA...
ZA-ZAA...

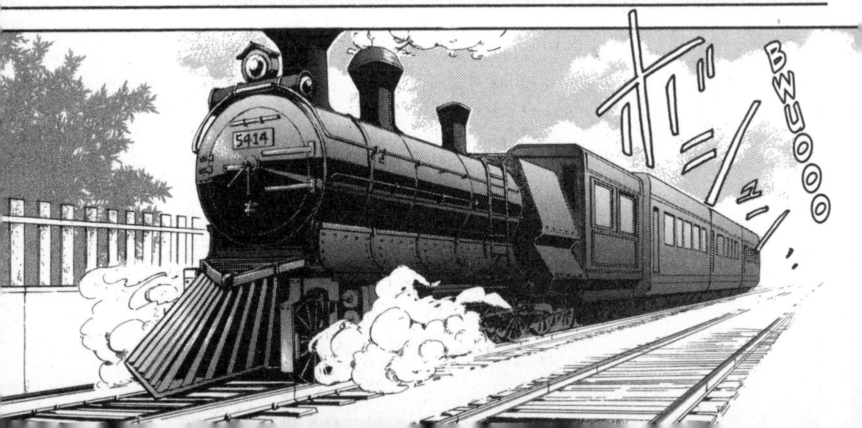
BWUOOOO

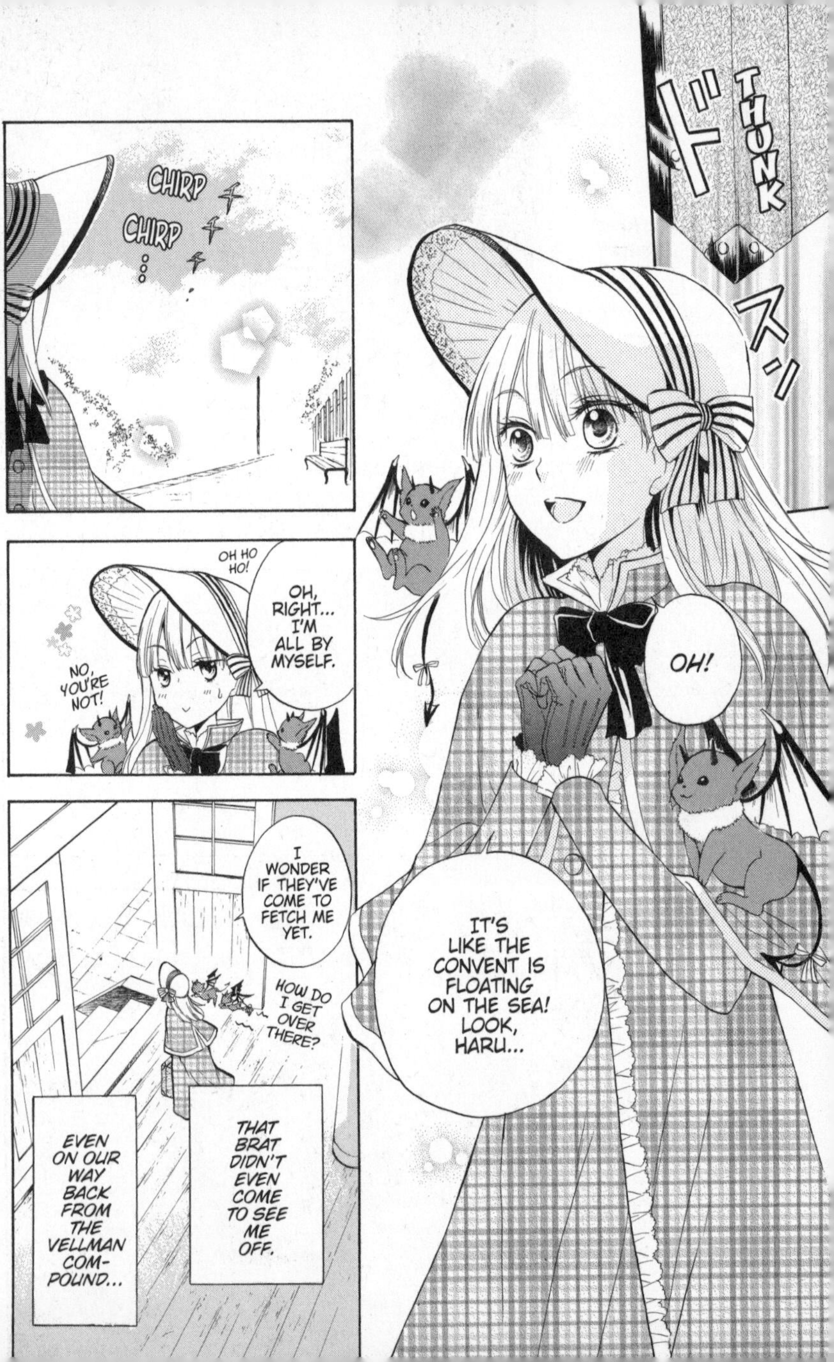
THUNK
OH!
IT'S LIKE THE CONVENT IS FLOATING ON THE SEA! LOOK, HARU...
CHIRP
CHIRP
OH, RIGHT... I'M ALL BY MYSELF.
OH HO HO!
NO, YOU'RE NOT!
I WONDER IF THEY'VE COME TO FETCH ME YET.
HOW DO I GET OVER THERE?
THAT BRAT DIDN'T EVEN COME TO SEE ME OFF.
EVEN ON OUR WAY BACK FROM THE VELLMAN COM-POUND...

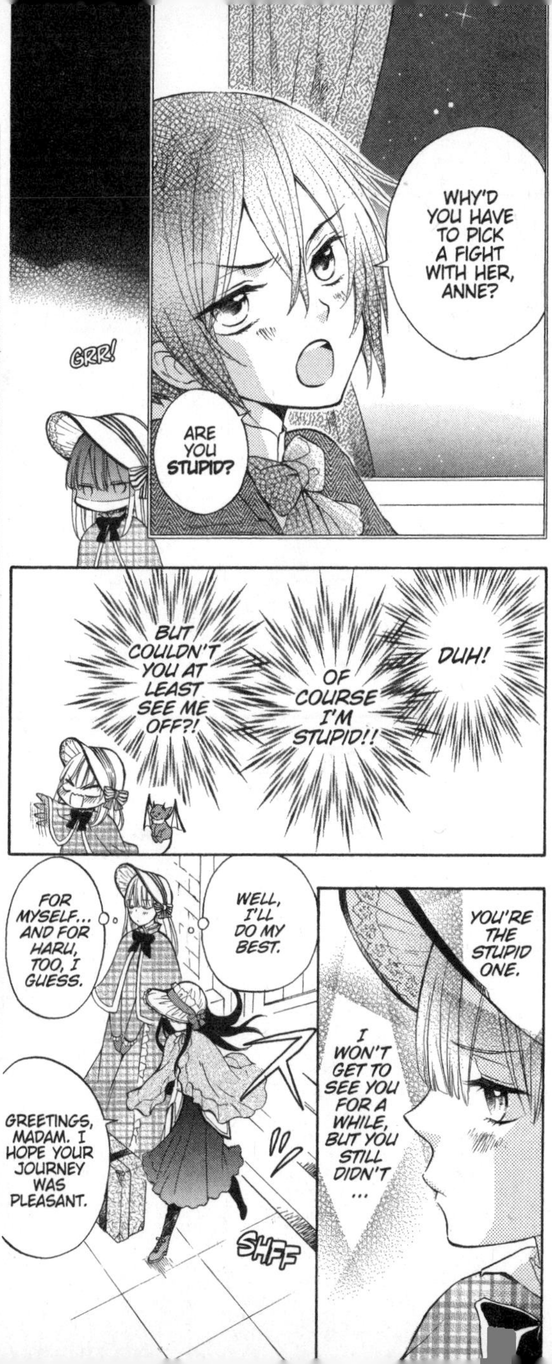
WHY'D YOU HAVE TO PICK A FIGHT WITH HER, ANNE?
ARE YOU STUPID?
GRR!
DUH!
OF COURSE I'M STUPID!!
BUT COULDN'T YOU AT LEAST SEE ME OFF?!
YOU'RE THE STUPID ONE.
I WON'T GET TO SEE YOU FOR A WHILE, BUT YOU STILL DIDN'T ...
WELL, I'LL DO MY BEST.
FOR MYSELF... AND FOR HARU, TOO, I GUESS.
SHFF
GREETINGS, MADAM. I HOPE YOUR JOURNEY WAS PLEASANT.
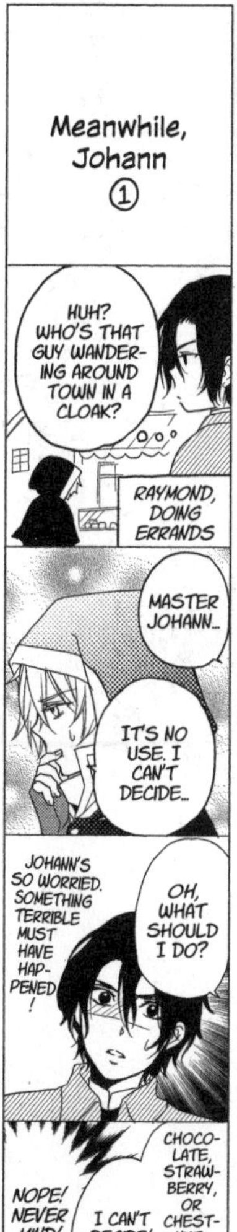
Meanwhile, Johann ①
HUH? WHO'S THAT GUY WANDERING AROUND TOWN IN A CLOAK?
RAYMOND, DOING ERRANDS
MASTER JOHANN...
IT'S NO USE. I CAN'T DECIDE...
OH, WHAT SHOULD I DO?
JOHANN'S SO WORRIED. SOMETHING TERRIBLE MUST HAVE HAPPENED!
CHOCOLATE, STRAWBERRY, OR CHESTNUT...
I CAN'T DECIDE!
NOPE! NEVER MIND!

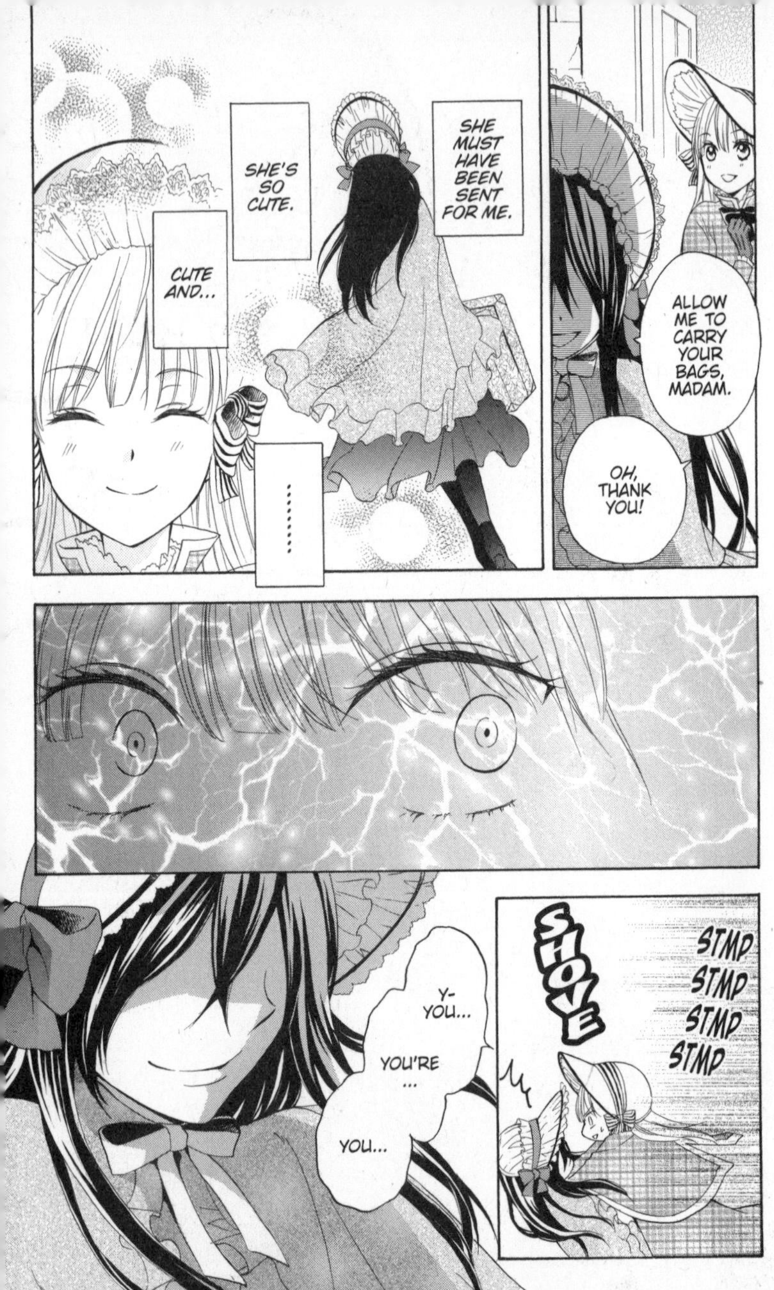
ALLOW ME TO CARRY YOUR BAGS, MADAM.
OH, THANK YOU!
SHE MUST HAVE BEEN SENT FOR ME.
SHE'S SO CUTE.
CUTE AND...
......
SHOVE
STMP STMP STMP STMP
Y- YOU...
YOU'RE ...
YOU...

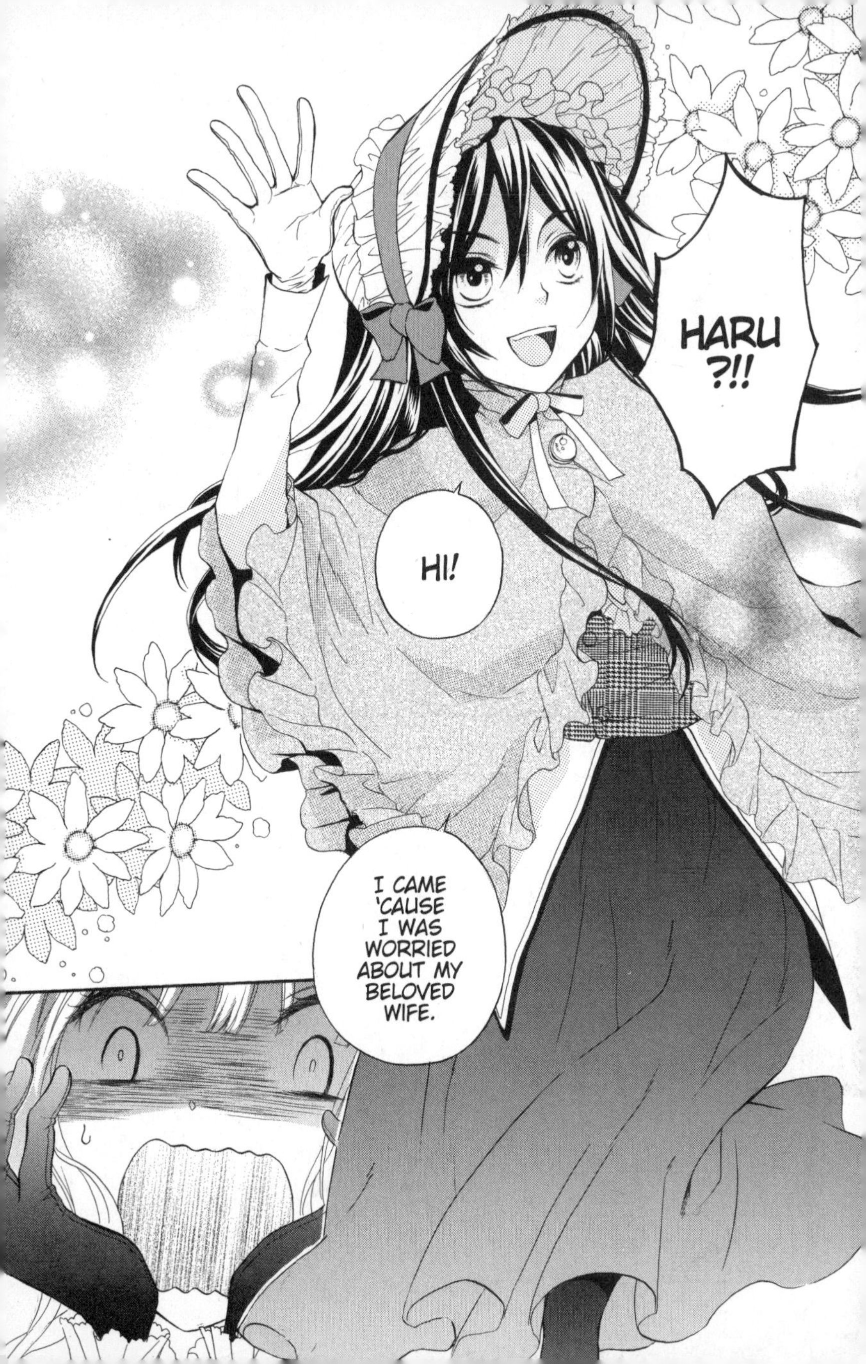
HARU ?!!
HI!
I CAME 'CAUSE I WAS WORRIED ABOUT MY BELOVED WIFE.

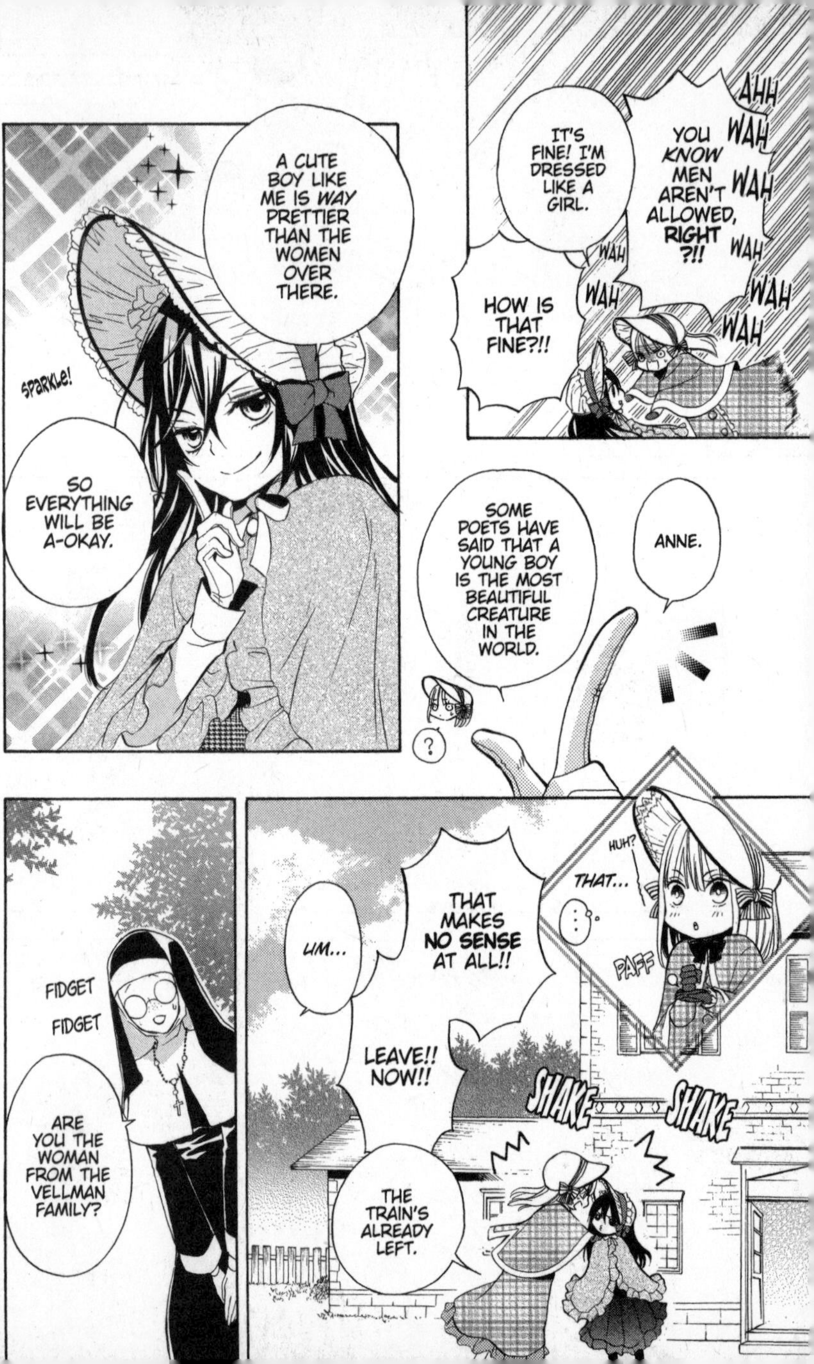
AHH
WAH
WAH
YOU KNOW MEN AREN'T ALLOWED, RIGHT?!!
WAH
WAH
IT'S FINE! I'M DRESSED LIKE A GIRL.
WAH
WAH
WAH
HOW IS THAT FINE?!!
A CUTE BOY LIKE ME IS WAY PRETTIER THAN THE WOMEN OVER THERE.
SPARKLE!
SO EVERYTHING WILL BE A-OKAY.
ANNE.
SOME POETS HAVE SAID THAT A YOUNG BOY IS THE MOST BEAUTIFUL CREATURE IN THE WORLD.
?
HUH?
THAT...
...
PAFF
THAT MAKES NO SENSE AT ALL!!
UM...
LEAVE!! NOW!!
SHAKE
SHAKE
THE TRAIN'S ALREADY LEFT.
FIDGET
FIDGET
ARE YOU THE WOMAN FROM THE VELLMAN FAMILY?

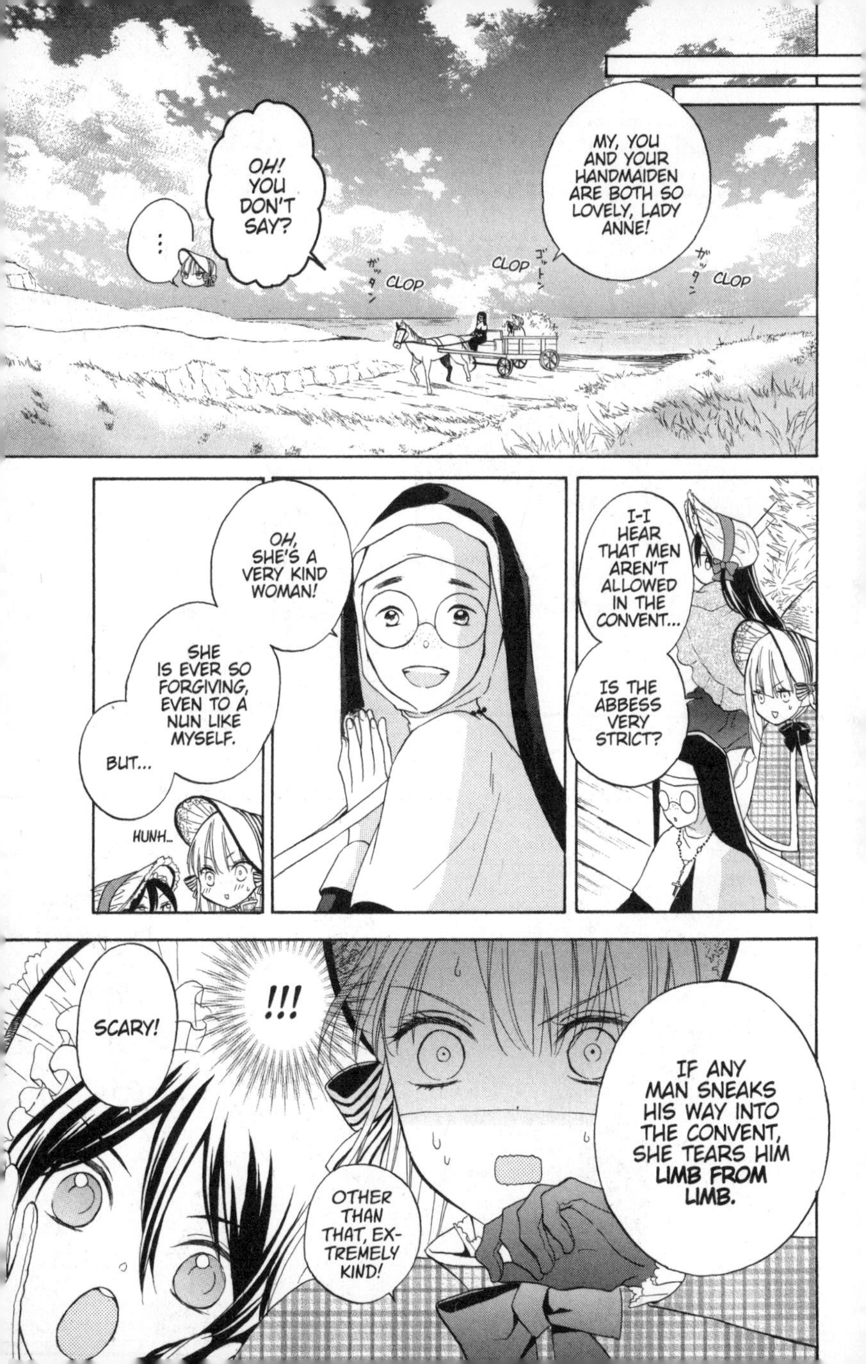
MY, YOU AND YOUR HANDMAIDEN ARE BOTH SO LOVELY, LADY ANNE!
CLOP
CLOP
CLOP
OH! YOU DON'T SAY?
...
I-I HEAR THAT MEN AREN'T ALLOWED IN THE CONVENT...
IS THE ABBESS VERY STRICT?
OH, SHE'S A VERY KIND WOMAN!
SHE IS EVER SO FORGIVING, EVEN TO A NUN LIKE MYSELF.
BUT...
HUNH...
IF ANY MAN SNEAKS HIS WAY INTO THE CONVENT, SHE TEARS HIM **LIMB FROM LIMB.**
OTHER THAN THAT, EX-TREMELY KIND!
!!!
SCARY!

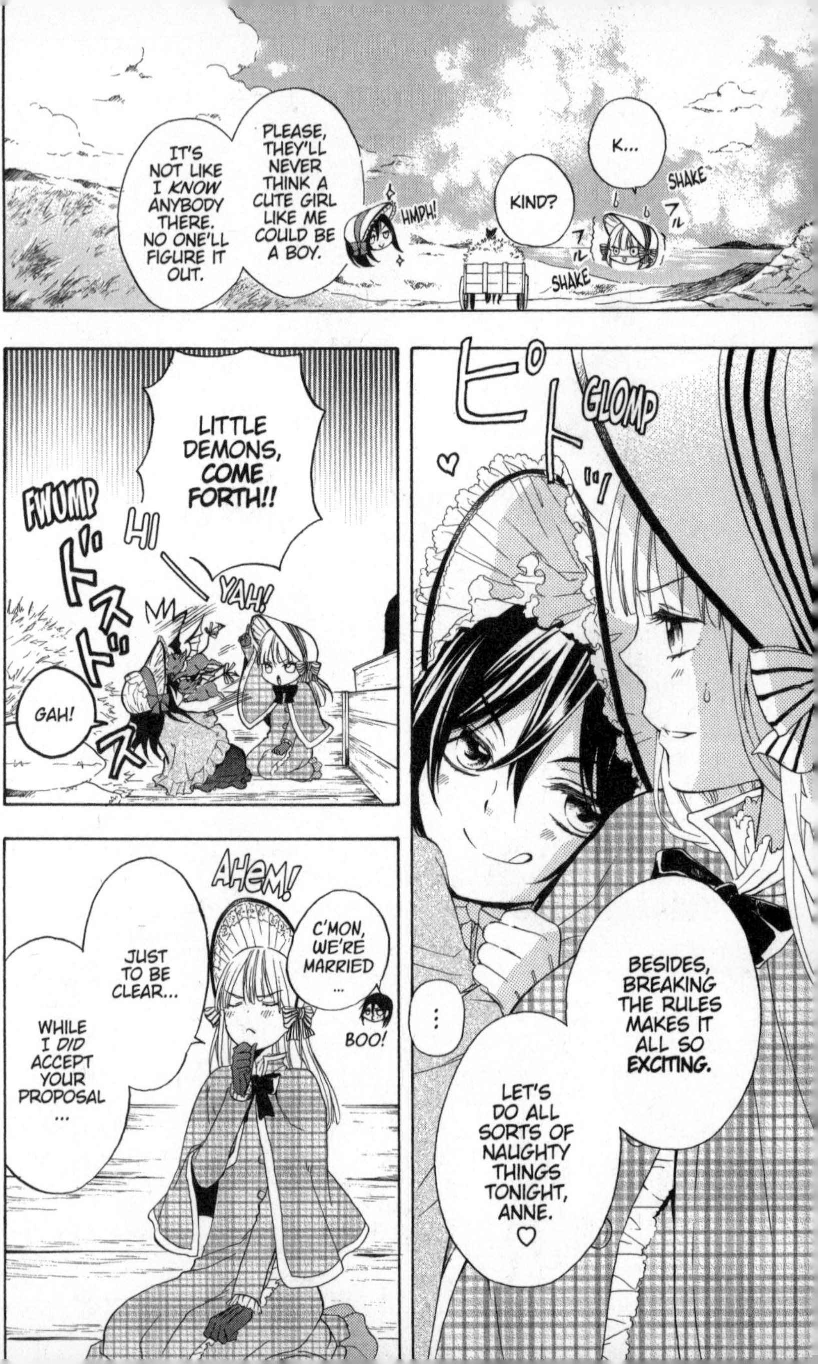
K...
SHAKE
KIND?
SHAKE
HMPH!
PLEASE, THEY'LL NEVER THINK A CUTE GIRL LIKE ME COULD BE A BOY.
IT'S NOT LIKE I *KNOW* ANYBODY THERE. NO ONE'LL FIGURE IT OUT.
GLOMP
...
BESIDES, BREAKING THE RULES MAKES IT ALL SO **EXCITING.**
LET'S DO ALL SORTS OF NAUGHTY THINGS TONIGHT, ANNE. ♡
LITTLE DEMONS, COME FORTH!!
FWUMP
HI-YAH!
GAH!
AHEM!
C'MON, WE'RE MARRIED ...
BOO!
JUST TO BE CLEAR...
WHILE I *DID* ACCEPT YOUR PROPOSAL ...

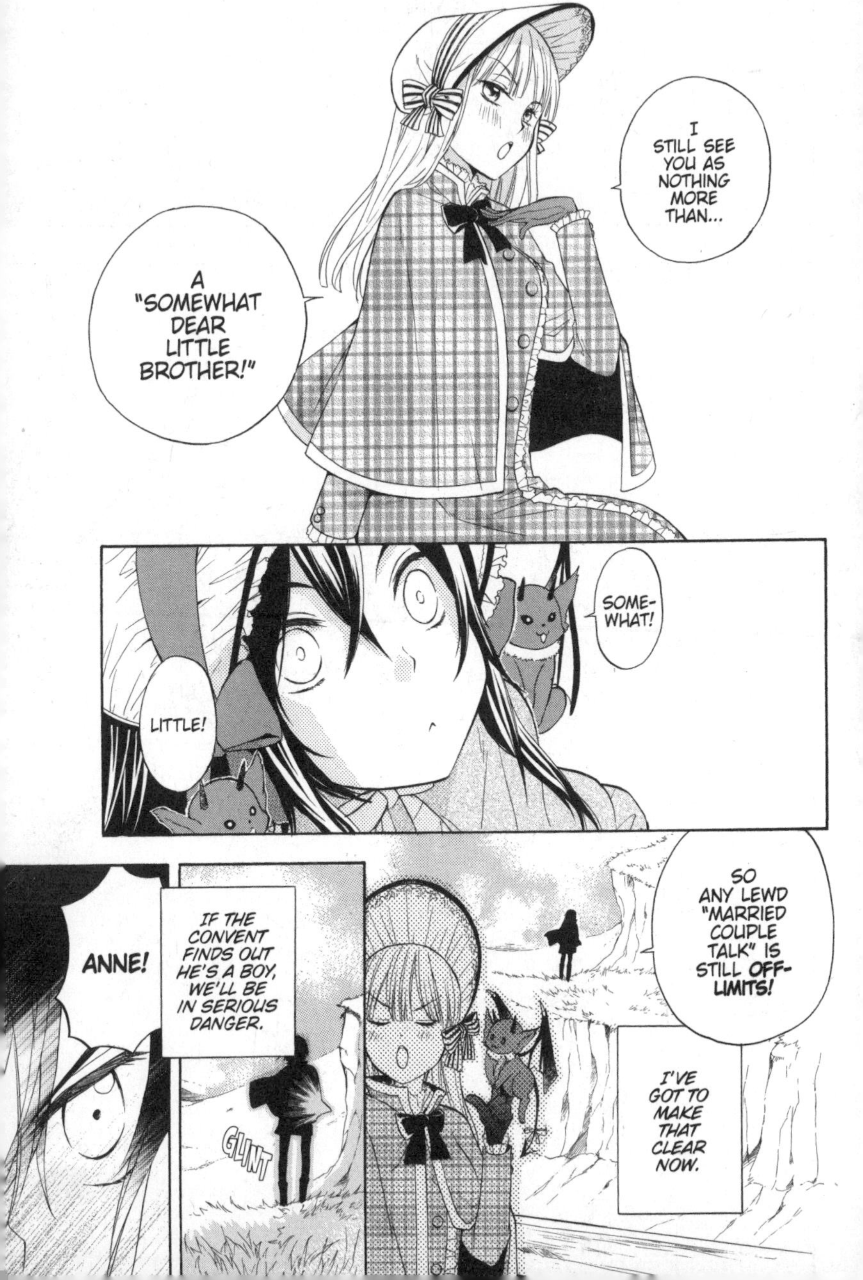
I STILL SEE YOU AS NOTHING MORE THAN...
A "SOMEWHAT DEAR LITTLE BROTHER!"
SOME-WHAT!
LITTLE!
SO ANY LEWD "MARRIED COUPLE TALK" IS STILL OFF-LIMITS!
I'VE GOT TO MAKE THAT CLEAR NOW.
IF THE CONVENT FINDS OUT HE'S A BOY, WE'LL BE IN SERIOUS DANGER.
GLINT
ANNE!

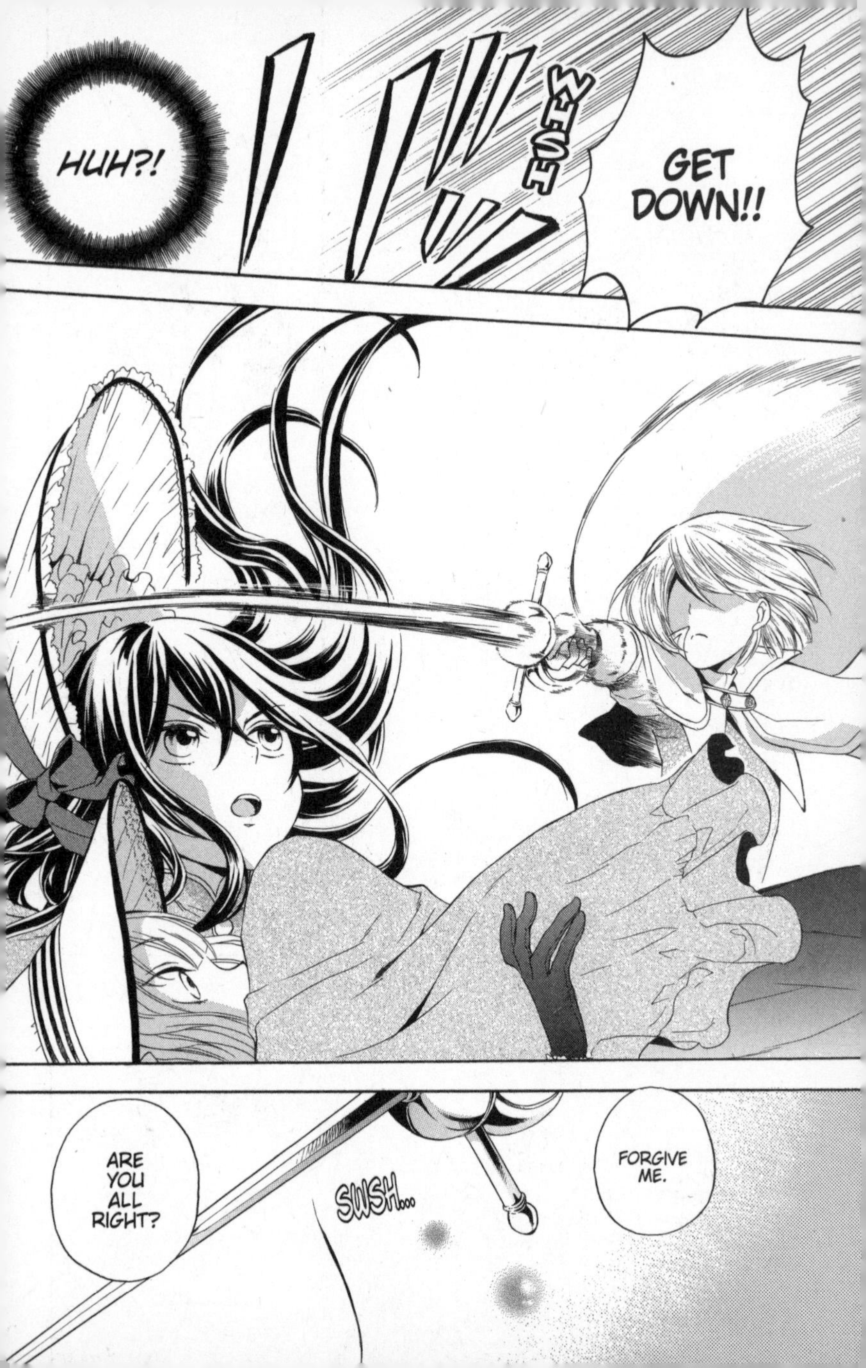
GET DOWN!!
WHISH
HUH?!
FORGIVE ME.
SWSH...
ARE YOU ALL RIGHT?

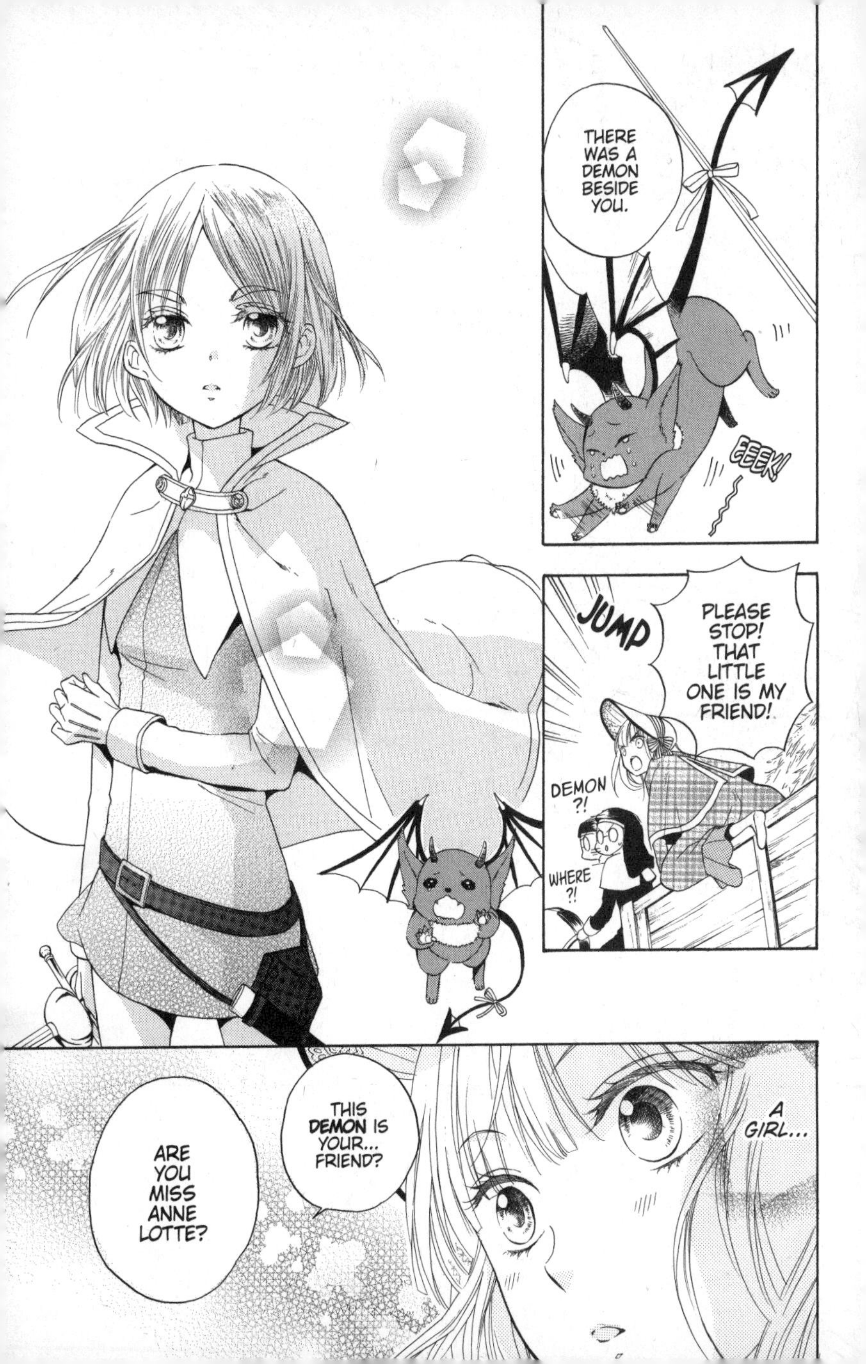
THERE WAS A DEMON BESIDE YOU.
EEEK!
JUMP
PLEASE STOP! THAT LITTLE ONE IS MY FRIEND!
DEMON ?!
WHERE ?!
A GIRL...
THIS DEMON IS YOUR... FRIEND?
ARE YOU MISS ANNE LOTTE?

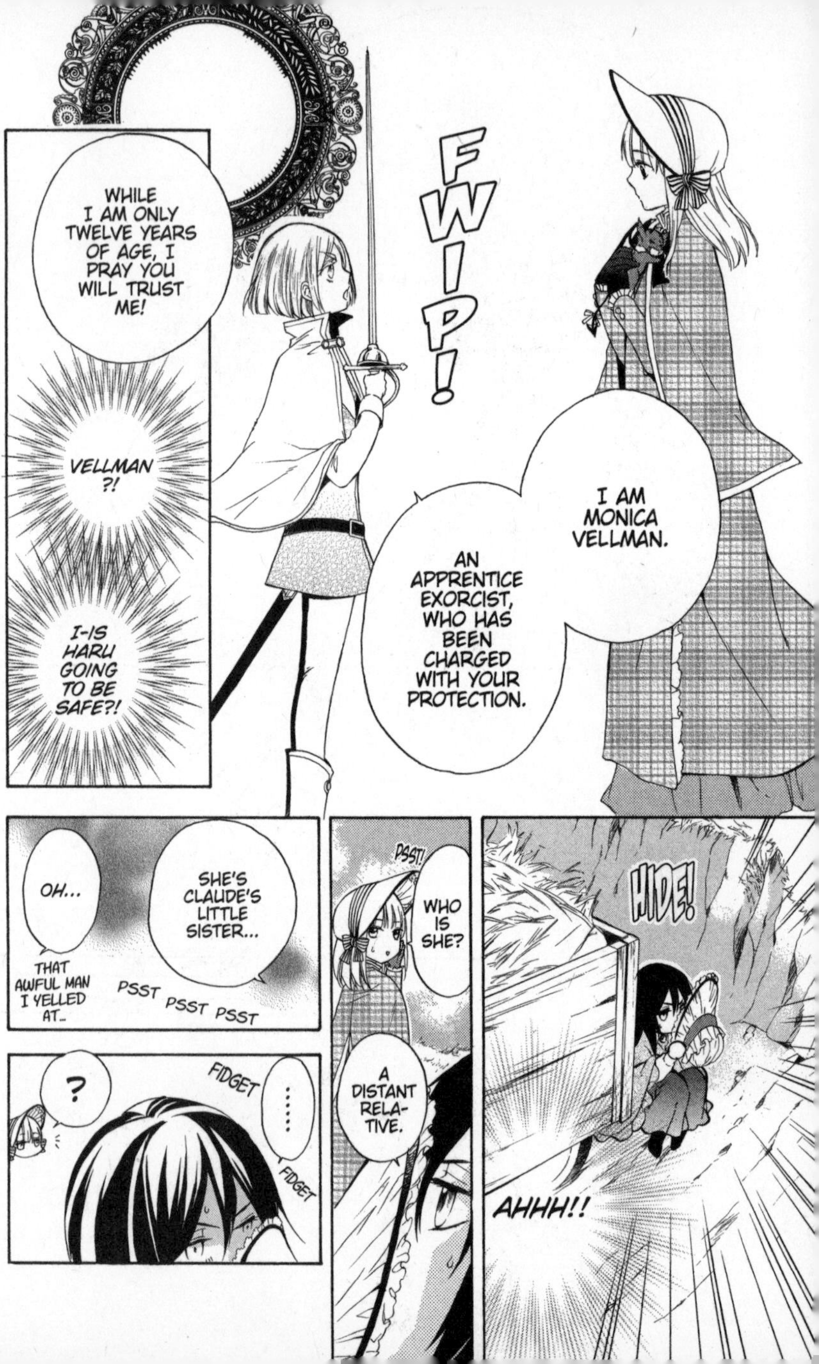
FWIP!
I AM MONICA VELLMAN.
AN APPRENTICE EXORCIST, WHO HAS BEEN CHARGED WITH YOUR PROTECTION.
WHILE I AM ONLY TWELVE YEARS OF AGE, I PRAY YOU WILL TRUST ME!
VELLMAN ?!
I-IS HARU GOING TO BE SAFE?!
HIDE!
AHHH!!
PSST!
WHO IS SHE?
A DISTANT RELA-TIVE.
SHE'S CLAUDE'S LITTLE SISTER...
OH...
THAT AWFUL MAN I YELLED AT..
PSST PSST PSST
FIDGET
......
?
FIDGET

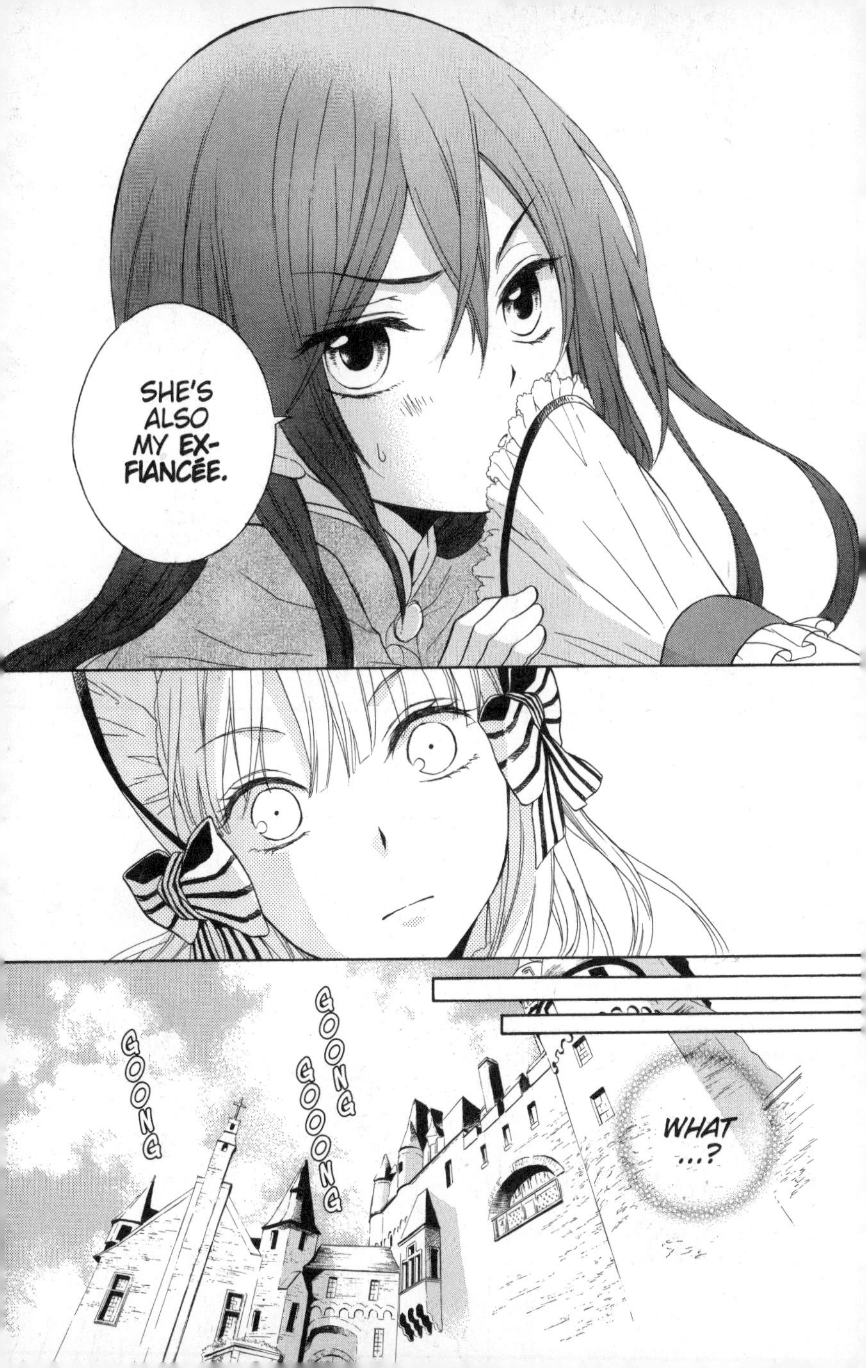
SHE'S ALSO MY EX-FIANCÉE.
WHAT ...?
GOONG
GOOONG
GOONG

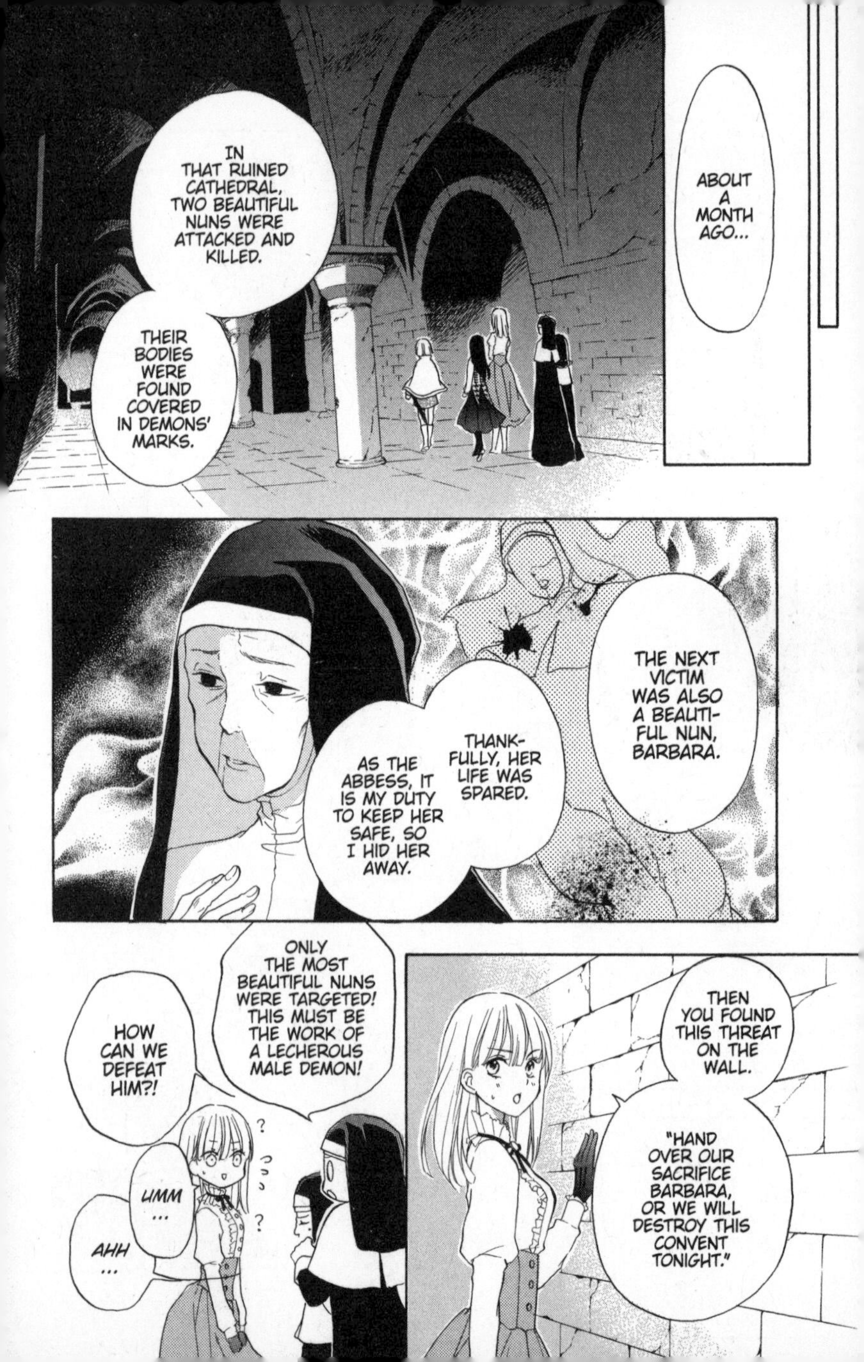
ABOUT A MONTH AGO...
IN THAT RUINED CATHEDRAL, TWO BEAUTIFUL NUNS WERE ATTACKED AND KILLED.
THEIR BODIES WERE FOUND COVERED IN DEMONS' MARKS.
THE NEXT VICTIM WAS ALSO A BEAUTI-FUL NUN, BARBARA.
THANK-FULLY, HER LIFE WAS SPARED.
AS THE ABBESS, IT IS MY DUTY TO KEEP HER SAFE, SO I HID HER AWAY.
THEN YOU FOUND THIS THREAT ON THE WALL.
"HAND OVER OUR SACRIFICE BARBARA, OR WE WILL DESTROY THIS CONVENT TONIGHT."
ONLY THE MOST BEAUTIFUL NUNS WERE TARGETED! THIS MUST BE THE WORK OF A LECHEROUS MALE DEMON!
HOW CAN WE DEFEAT HIM?!
UMM ...
AHH ...

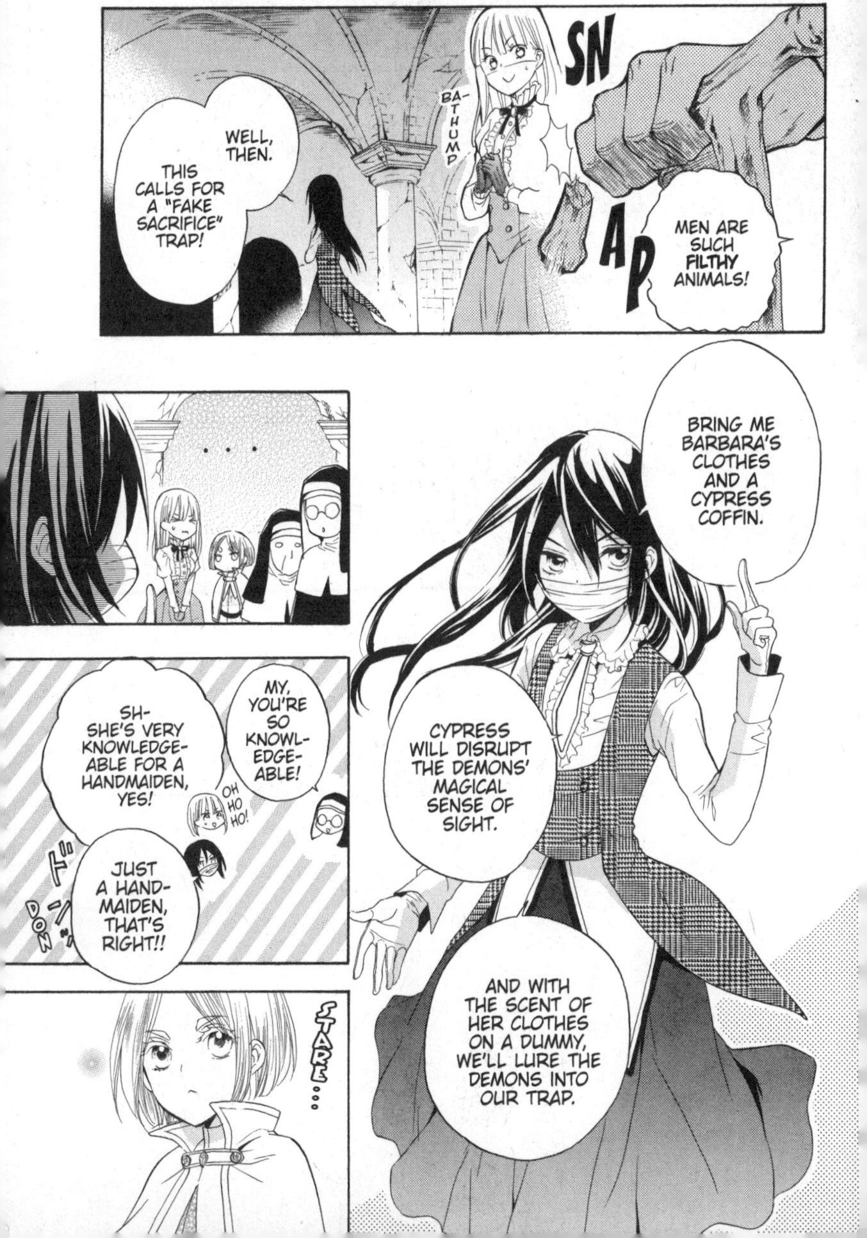
SNAP
MEN ARE SUCH FILTHY ANIMALS!
BA-THUMP
WELL, THEN.
THIS CALLS FOR A "FAKE SACRIFICE" TRAP!
BRING ME BARBARA'S CLOTHES AND A CYPRESS COFFIN.
CYPRESS WILL DISRUPT THE DEMONS' MAGICAL SENSE OF SIGHT.
AND WITH THE SCENT OF HER CLOTHES ON A DUMMY, WE'LL LURE THE DEMONS INTO OUR TRAP.
. . .
MY, YOU'RE SO KNOWL-EDGE-ABLE!
SH-SHE'S VERY KNOWLEDGE-ABLE FOR A HANDMAIDEN, YES!
OH HO HO!
JUST A HAND-MAIDEN, THAT'S RIGHT!!
DON
STARE...

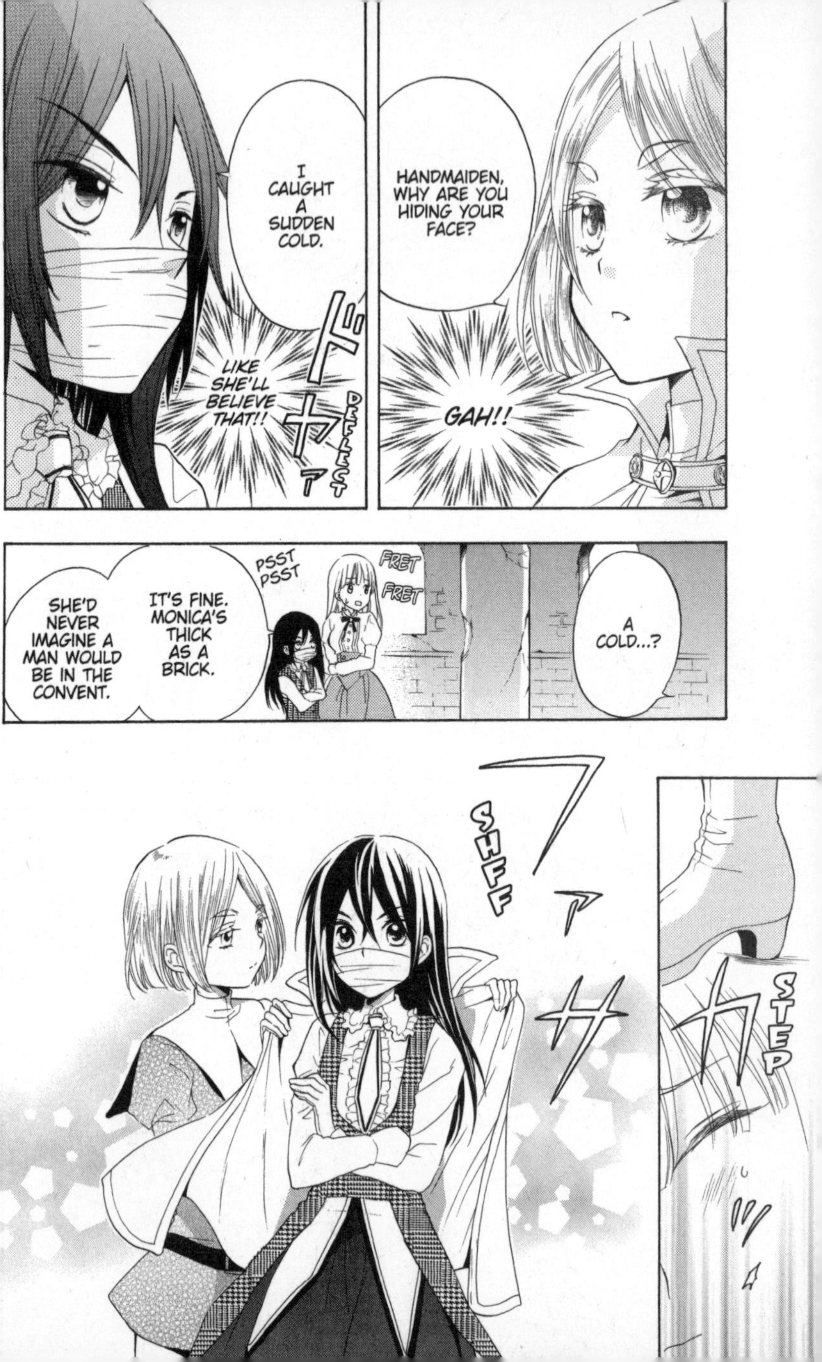
HANDMAIDEN, WHY ARE YOU HIDING YOUR FACE?
GAH!!
I CAUGHT A SUDDEN COLD.
LIKE SHE'LL BELIEVE THAT!!
DEFLECT
A COLD...?
FRET
FRET
PSST PSST
IT'S FINE. MONICA'S THICK AS A BRICK.
SHE'D NEVER IMAGINE A MAN WOULD BE IN THE CONVENT.
STEP
SHFF

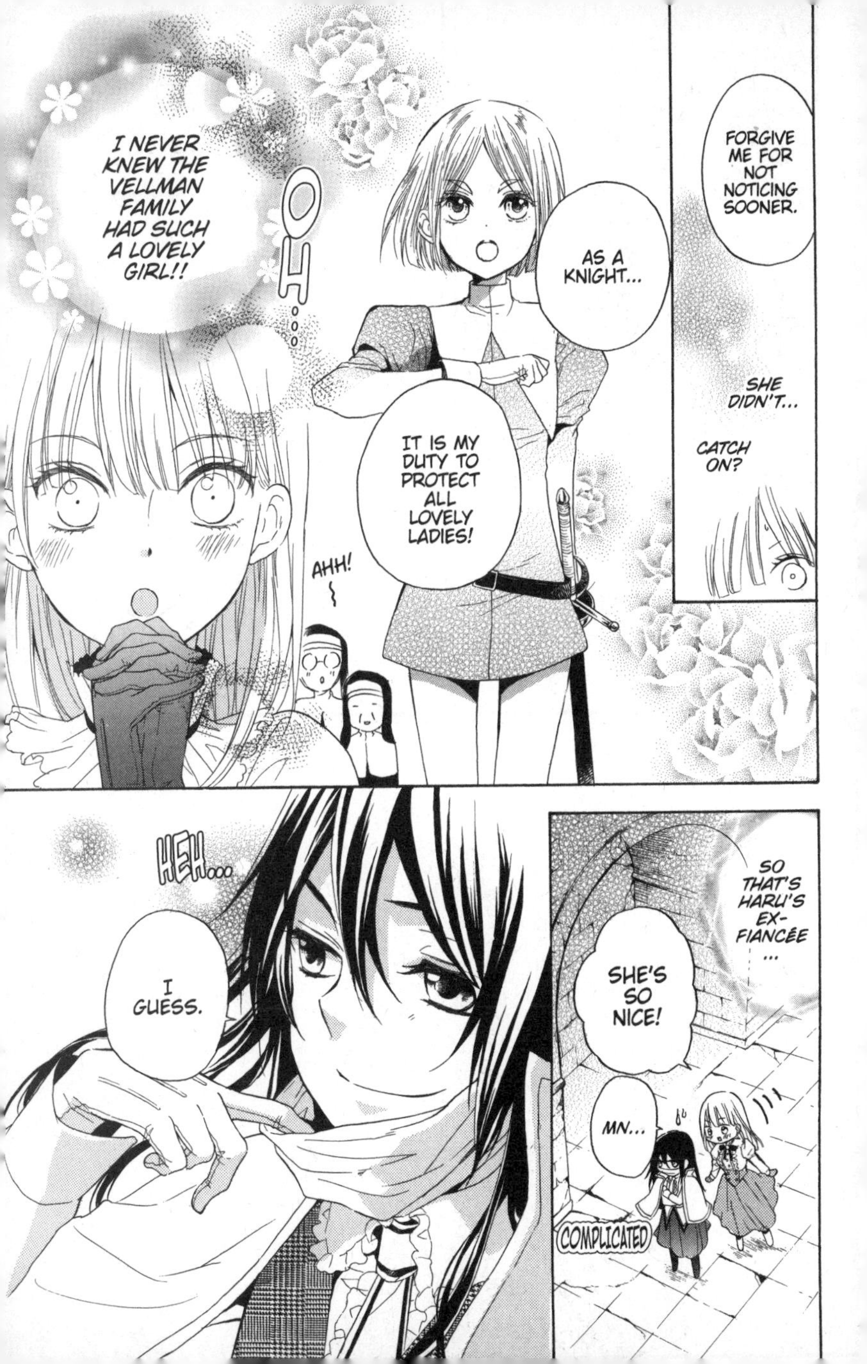
FORGIVE ME FOR NOT NOTICING SOONER.
SHE DIDN'T...
CATCH ON?
AS A KNIGHT...
IT IS MY DUTY TO PROTECT ALL LOVELY LADIES!
OH...
I NEVER KNEW THE VELLMAN FAMILY HAD SUCH A LOVELY GIRL!!
AHH!
SO THAT'S HARU'S EX-FIANCÉE...
SHE'S SO NICE!
MN...
COMPLICATED
HEH...
I GUESS.

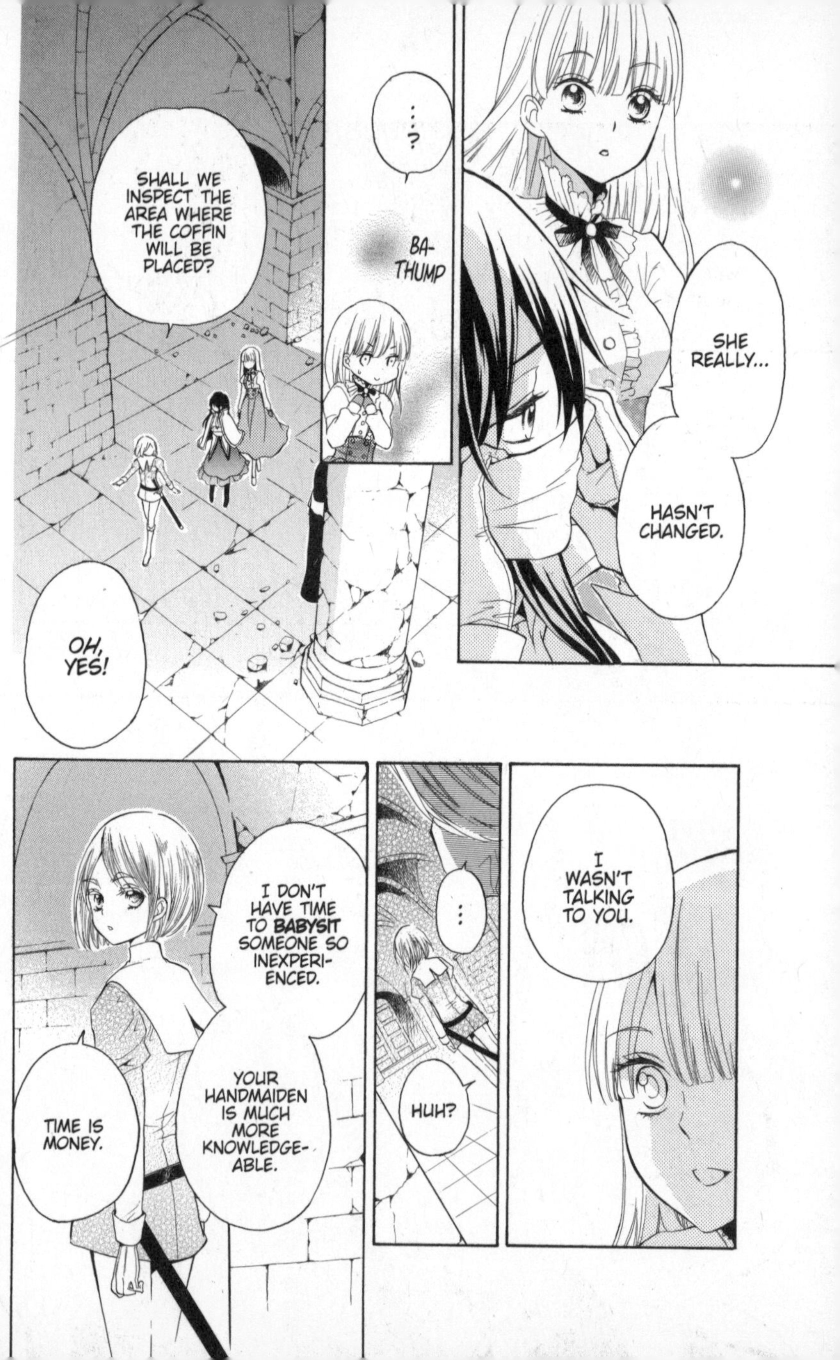
SHE REALLY...
HASN'T CHANGED.
...?
BA-THUMP
SHALL WE INSPECT THE AREA WHERE THE COFFIN WILL BE PLACED?
OH, YES!
I WASN'T TALKING TO YOU.
...
HUH?
I DON'T HAVE TIME TO **BABYSIT** SOMEONE SO INEXPERIENCED.
YOUR HANDMAIDEN IS MUCH MORE KNOWLEDGEABLE.
TIME IS MONEY.

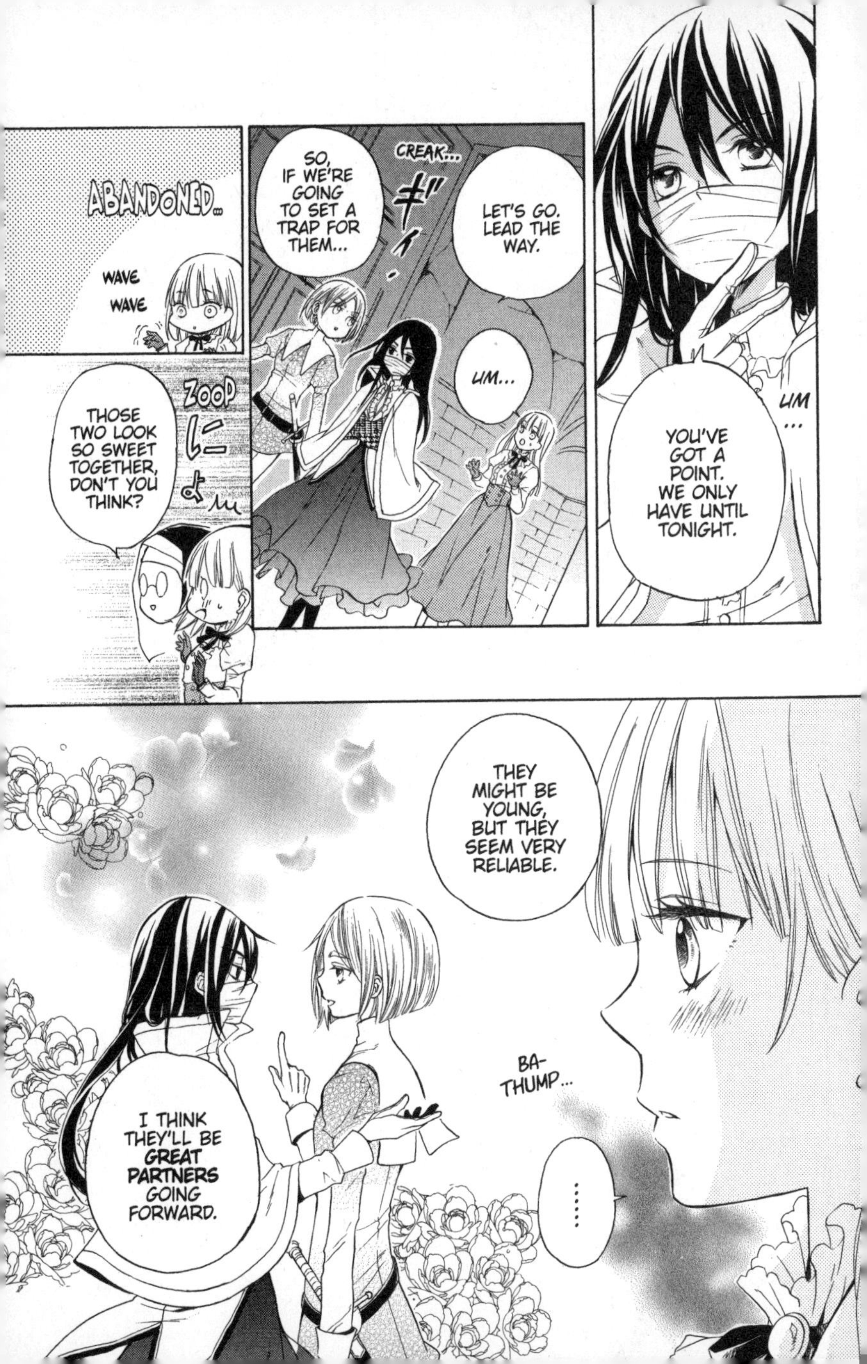
UM ...
YOU'VE GOT A POINT. WE ONLY HAVE UNTIL TONIGHT.
CREAK...
SO, IF WE'RE GOING TO SET A TRAP FOR THEM...
LET'S GO. LEAD THE WAY.
UM...
ABANDONED...
WAVE WAVE
ZOOP
THOSE TWO LOOK SO SWEET TOGETHER, DON'T YOU THINK?
THEY MIGHT BE YOUNG, BUT THEY SEEM VERY RELIABLE.
BA-THUMP...
......
I THINK THEY'LL BE GREAT PARTNERS GOING FORWARD.

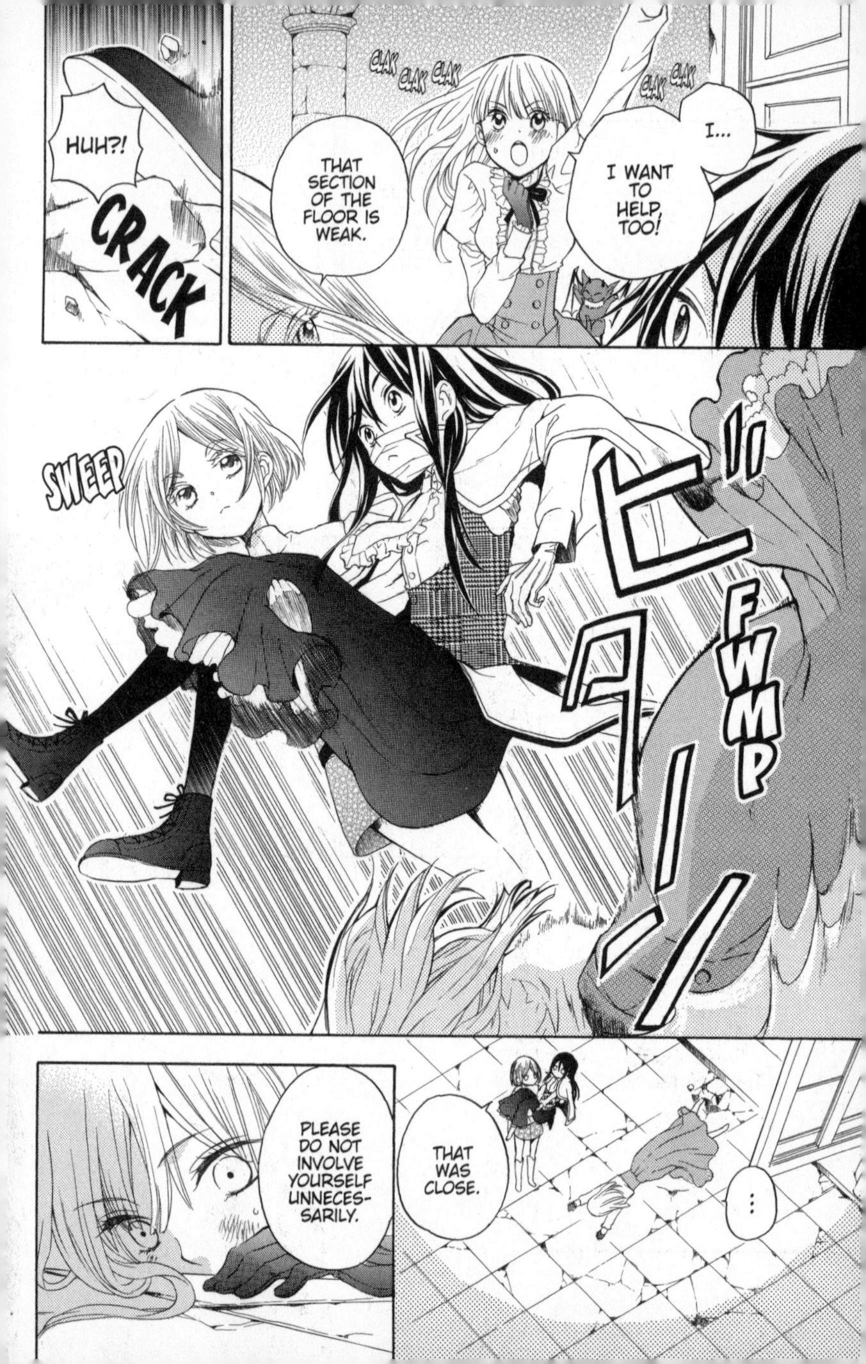
CLAK CLAK CLAK
CLAK CLAK
I... I WANT TO HELP, TOO!
THAT SECTION OF THE FLOOR IS WEAK.
HUH?!
CRACK
ビターン
FWMP
SWEEP
THAT WAS CLOSE.
...
PLEASE DO NOT INVOLVE YOURSELF UNNECES-SARILY.

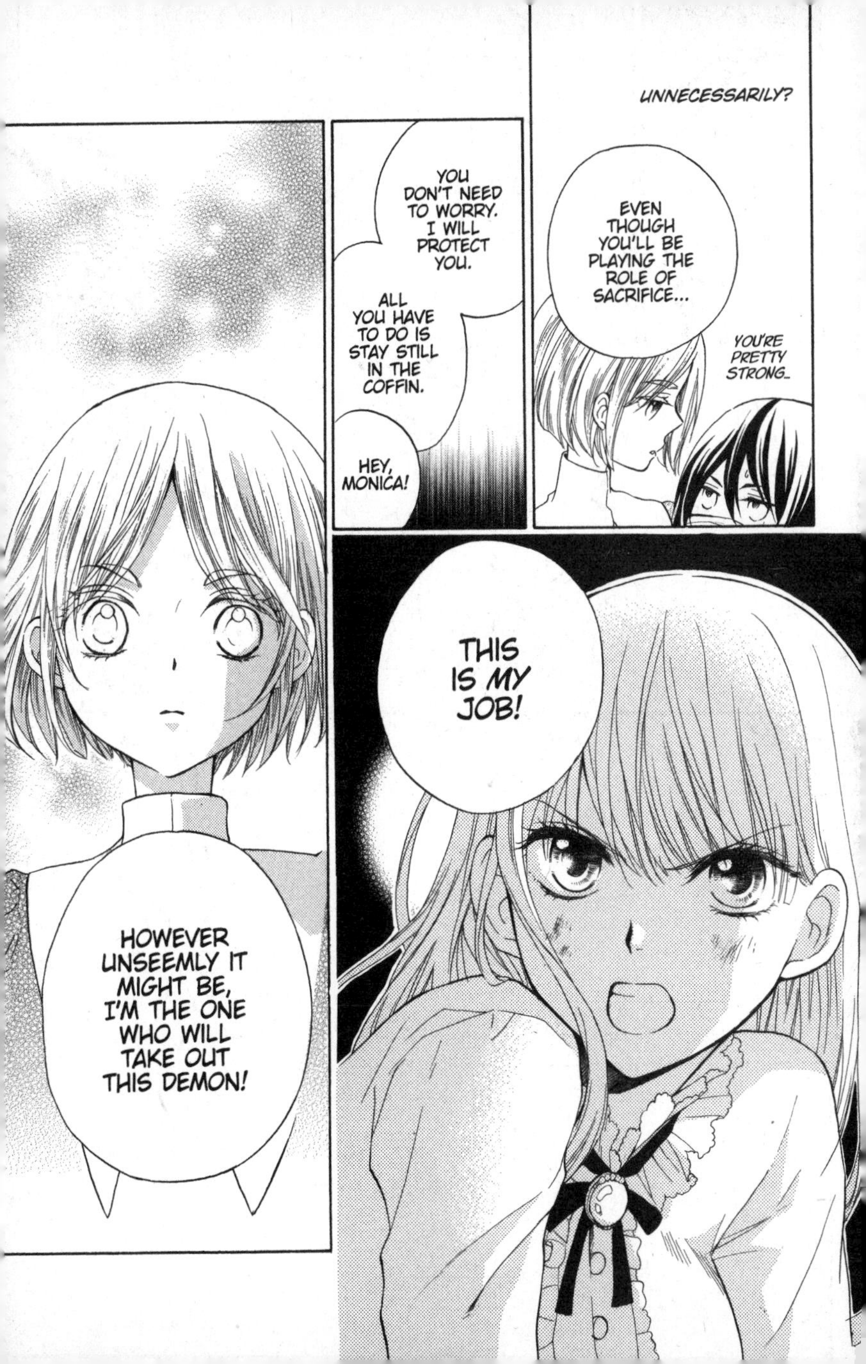
UNNECESSARILY?
EVEN THOUGH YOU'LL BE PLAYING THE ROLE OF SACRIFICE...
YOU'RE PRETTY STRONG..
YOU DON'T NEED TO WORRY. I WILL PROTECT YOU.
ALL YOU HAVE TO DO IS STAY STILL IN THE COFFIN.
HEY, MONICA!
THIS IS *MY* JOB!
HOWEVER UNSEEMLY IT MIGHT BE, I'M THE ONE WHO WILL TAKE OUT THIS DEMON!

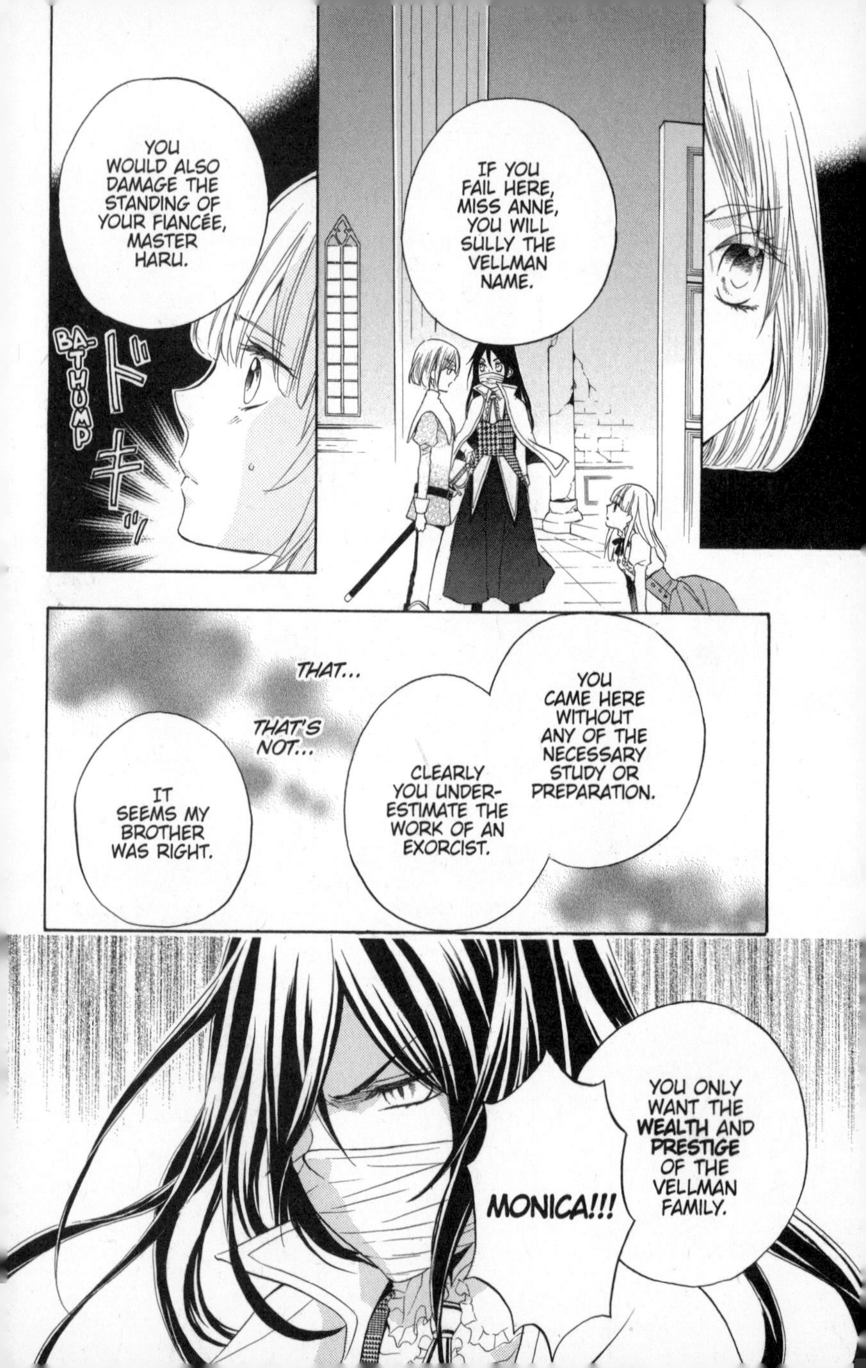
IF YOU FAIL HERE, MISS ANNE, YOU WILL SULLY THE VELLMAN NAME.
YOU WOULD ALSO DAMAGE THE STANDING OF YOUR FIANCÉE, MASTER HARU.
BA-THUMP
YOU CAME HERE WITHOUT ANY OF THE NECESSARY STUDY OR PREPARATION.
CLEARLY YOU UNDER-ESTIMATE THE WORK OF AN EXORCIST.
THAT...
THAT'S NOT...
IT SEEMS MY BROTHER WAS RIGHT.
YOU ONLY WANT THE WEALTH AND PRESTIGE OF THE VELLMAN FAMILY.
MONICA!!!

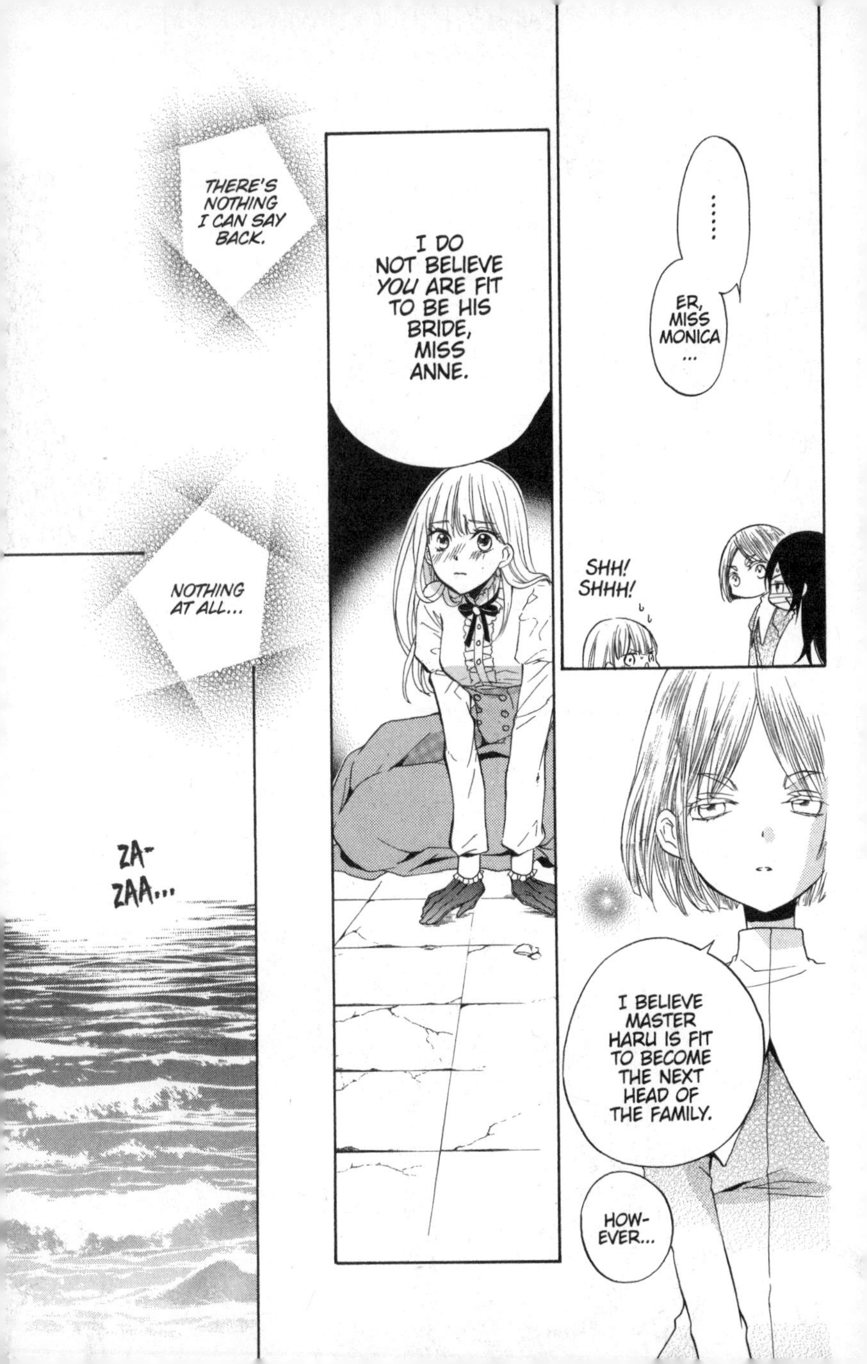
......
ER, MISS MONICA ...
SHH! SHHH!
I BELIEVE MASTER HARU IS FIT TO BECOME THE NEXT HEAD OF THE FAMILY.
HOW-EVER...
I DO NOT BELIEVE YOU ARE FIT TO BE HIS BRIDE, MISS ANNE.
THERE'S NOTHING I CAN SAY BACK.
NOTHING AT ALL...
ZA-ZAA...

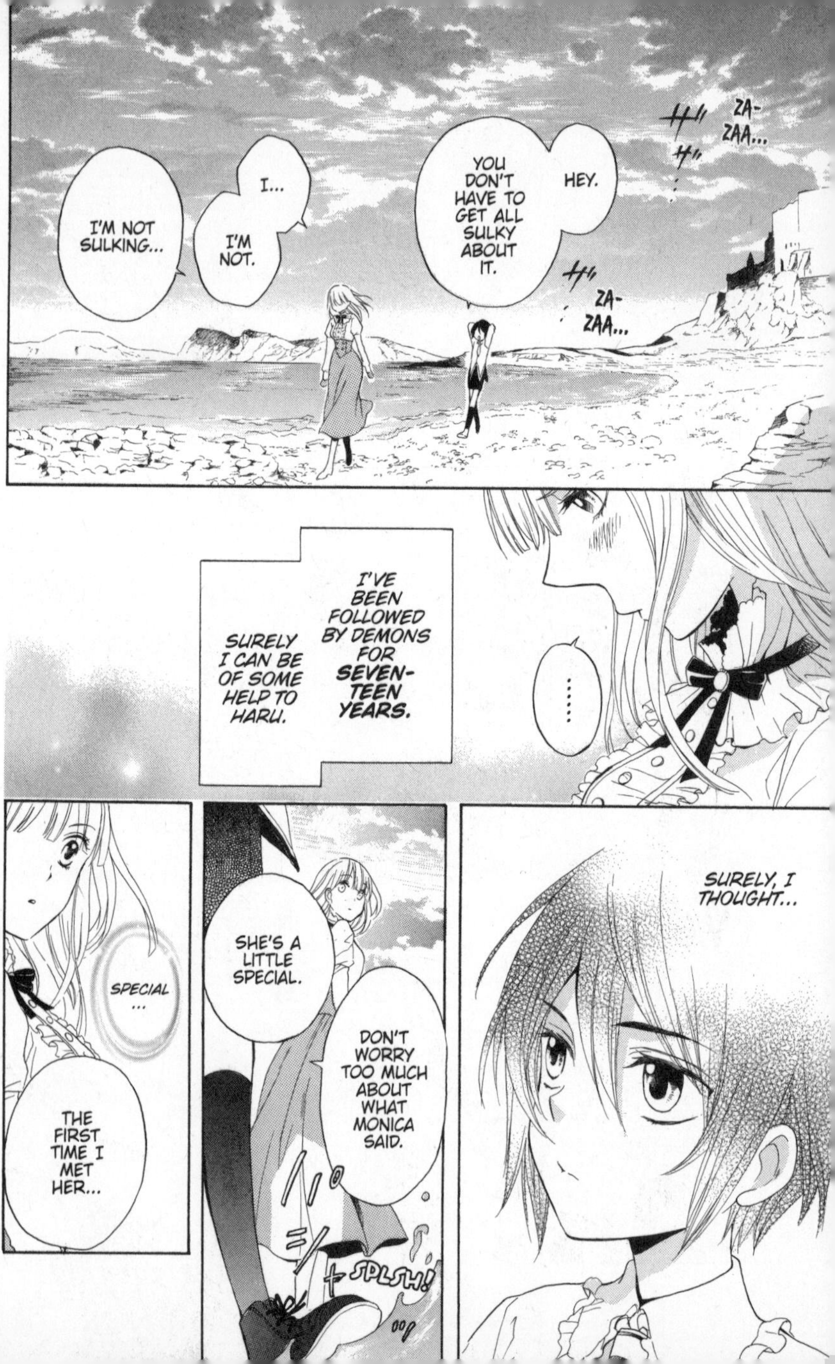
ZA-ZAA...
HEY.
YOU DON'T HAVE TO GET ALL SULKY ABOUT IT.
I...
I'M NOT.
I'M NOT SULKING...
ZA-ZAA...
......
I'VE BEEN FOLLOWED BY DEMONS FOR SEVENTEEN YEARS.
SURELY I CAN BE OF SOME HELP TO HARU.
SURELY, I THOUGHT...
SHE'S A LITTLE SPECIAL.
DON'T WORRY TOO MUCH ABOUT WHAT MONICA SAID.
SPLSH!
SPECIAL...
THE FIRST TIME I MET HER...

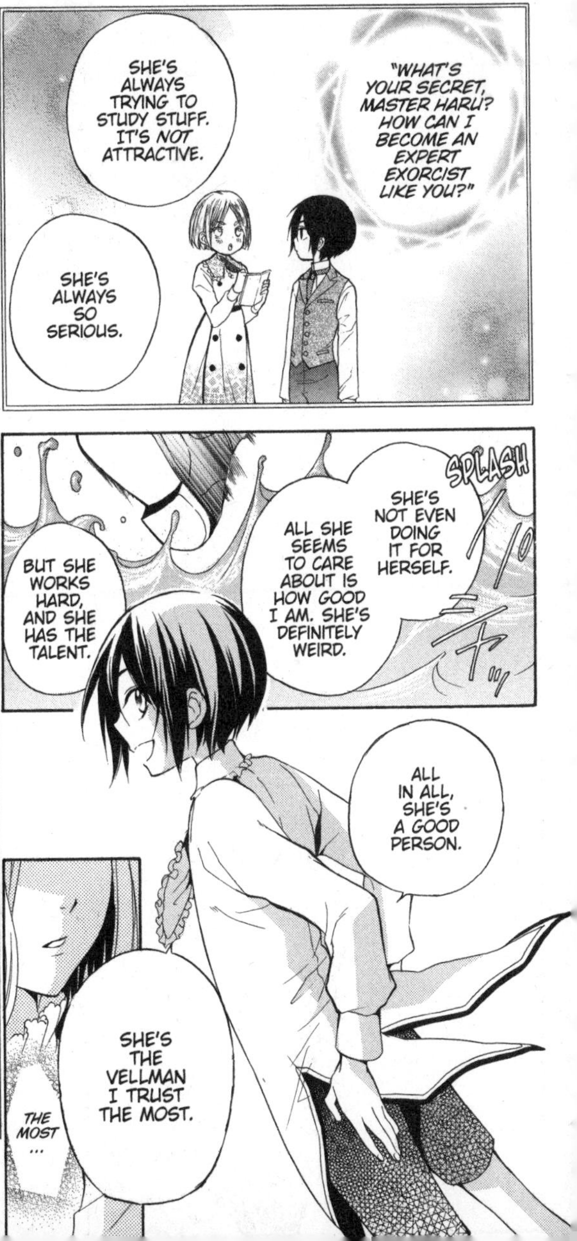
"WHAT'S YOUR SECRET, MASTER HARU? HOW CAN I BECOME AN EXPERT EXORCIST LIKE YOU?"
SHE'S ALWAYS TRYING TO STUDY STUFF. IT'S NOT ATTRACTIVE.
SHE'S ALWAYS SO SERIOUS.
SPLASH
SHE'S NOT EVEN DOING IT FOR HERSELF.
ALL SHE SEEMS TO CARE ABOUT IS HOW GOOD I AM. SHE'S DEFINITELY WEIRD.
BUT SHE WORKS HARD, AND SHE HAS THE TALENT.
ALL IN ALL, SHE'S A GOOD PERSON.
SHE'S THE VELLMAN I TRUST THE MOST.
THE MOST ...

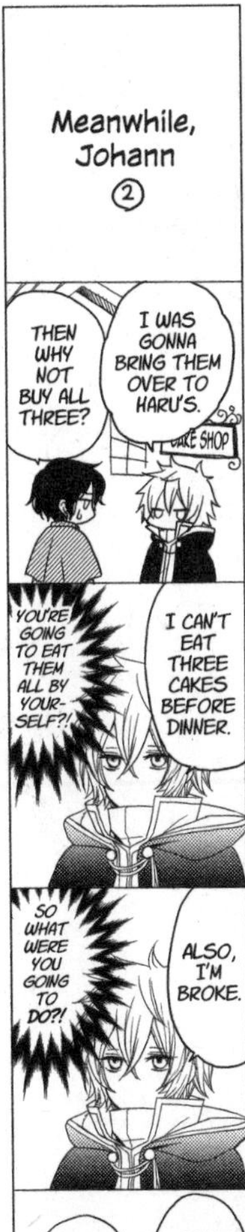
Meanwhile, Johann ②
I WAS GONNA BRING THEM OVER TO HARU'S.
THEN WHY NOT BUY ALL THREE?
CAKE SHOP
I CAN'T EAT THREE CAKES BEFORE DINNER.
YOU'RE GOING TO EAT THEM ALL BY YOURSELF?!
ALSO, I'M BROKE.
SO WHAT WERE YOU GOING TO DO?!
FINE, I'LL BUY THEM!
YOU SURE? THANKS.

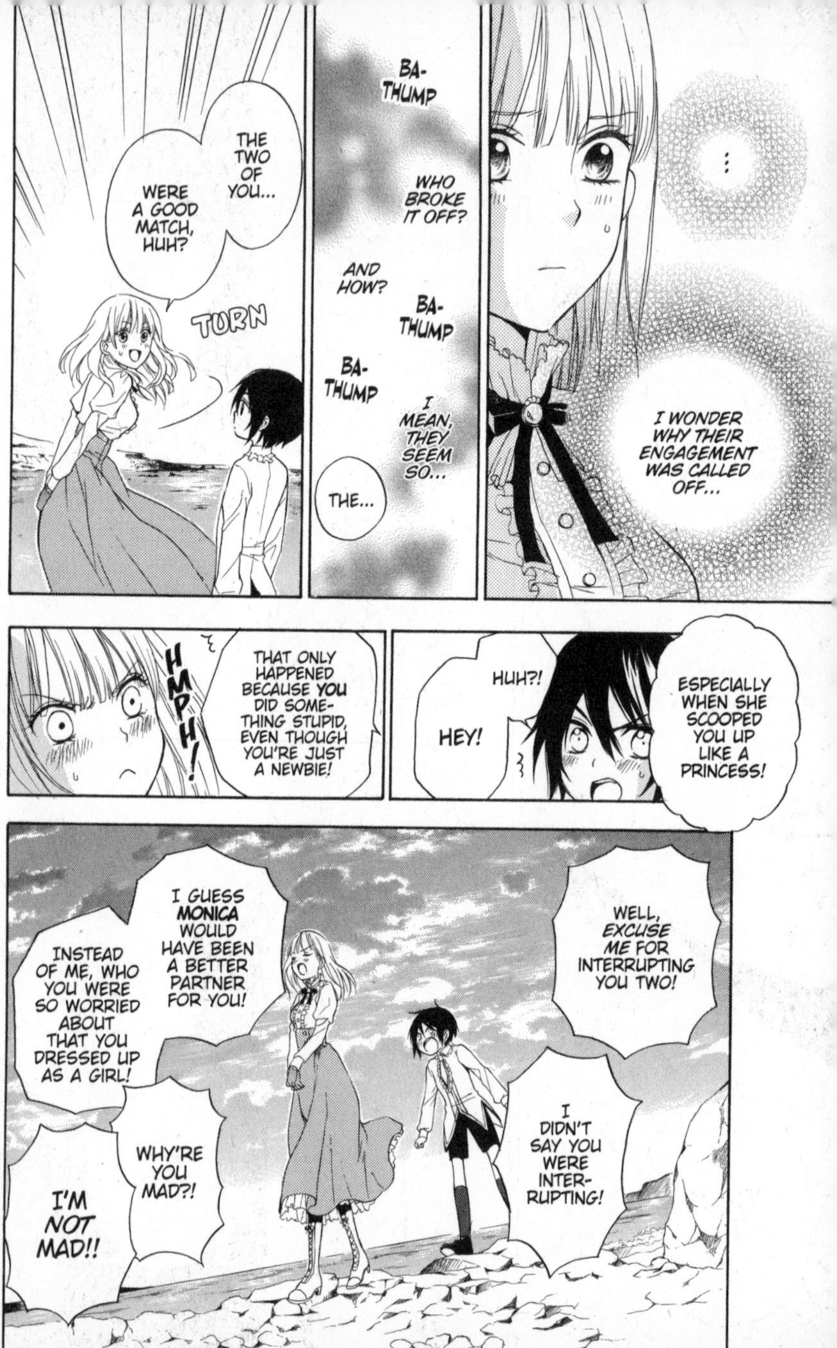
...
I WONDER WHY THEIR ENGAGEMENT WAS CALLED OFF...
BA-THUMP
WHO BROKE IT OFF?
AND HOW?
BA-THUMP
I MEAN, THEY SEEM SO...
BA-THUMP
THE...
THE TWO OF YOU... WERE A GOOD MATCH, HUH?
TURN
ESPECIALLY WHEN SHE SCOOPED YOU UP LIKE A PRINCESS!
HUH?!
HEY!
HMPH!
THAT ONLY HAPPENED BECAUSE **YOU** DID SOME-THING STUPID, EVEN THOUGH YOU'RE JUST A NEWBIE!
WELL, *EXCUSE* ME FOR INTERRUPTING YOU TWO!
I GUESS **MONICA** WOULD HAVE BEEN A BETTER PARTNER FOR YOU!
INSTEAD OF ME, WHO YOU WERE SO WORRIED ABOUT THAT YOU DRESSED UP AS A GIRL!
I DIDN'T SAY YOU WERE INTER-RUPTING!
WHY'RE YOU MAD?!
I'M *NOT* MAD!!

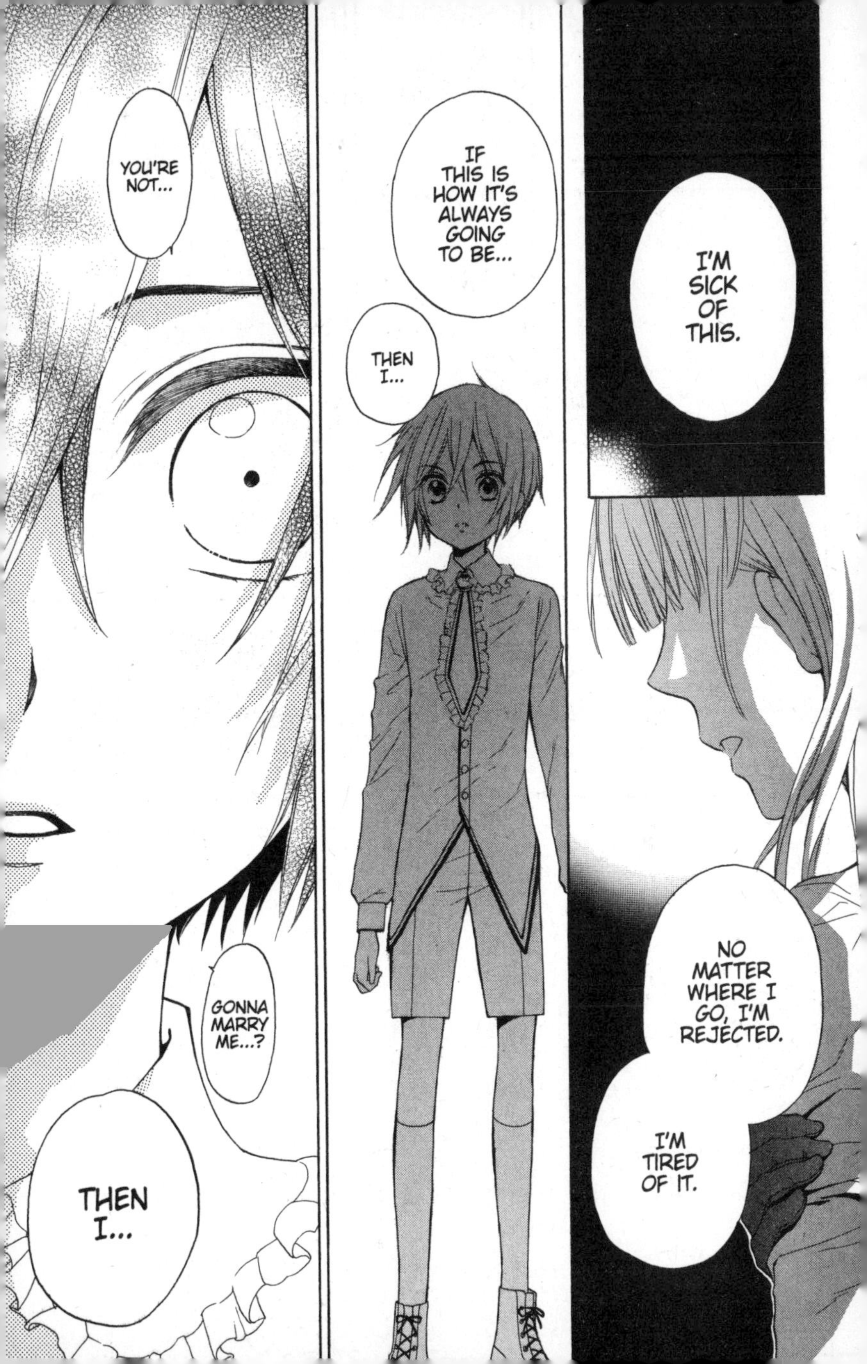
I'M SICK OF THIS.
NO MATTER WHERE I GO, I'M REJECTED.
I'M TIRED OF IT.
IF THIS IS HOW IT'S ALWAYS GOING TO BE...
THEN I...
YOU'RE NOT...
GONNA MARRY ME...?
THEN I...

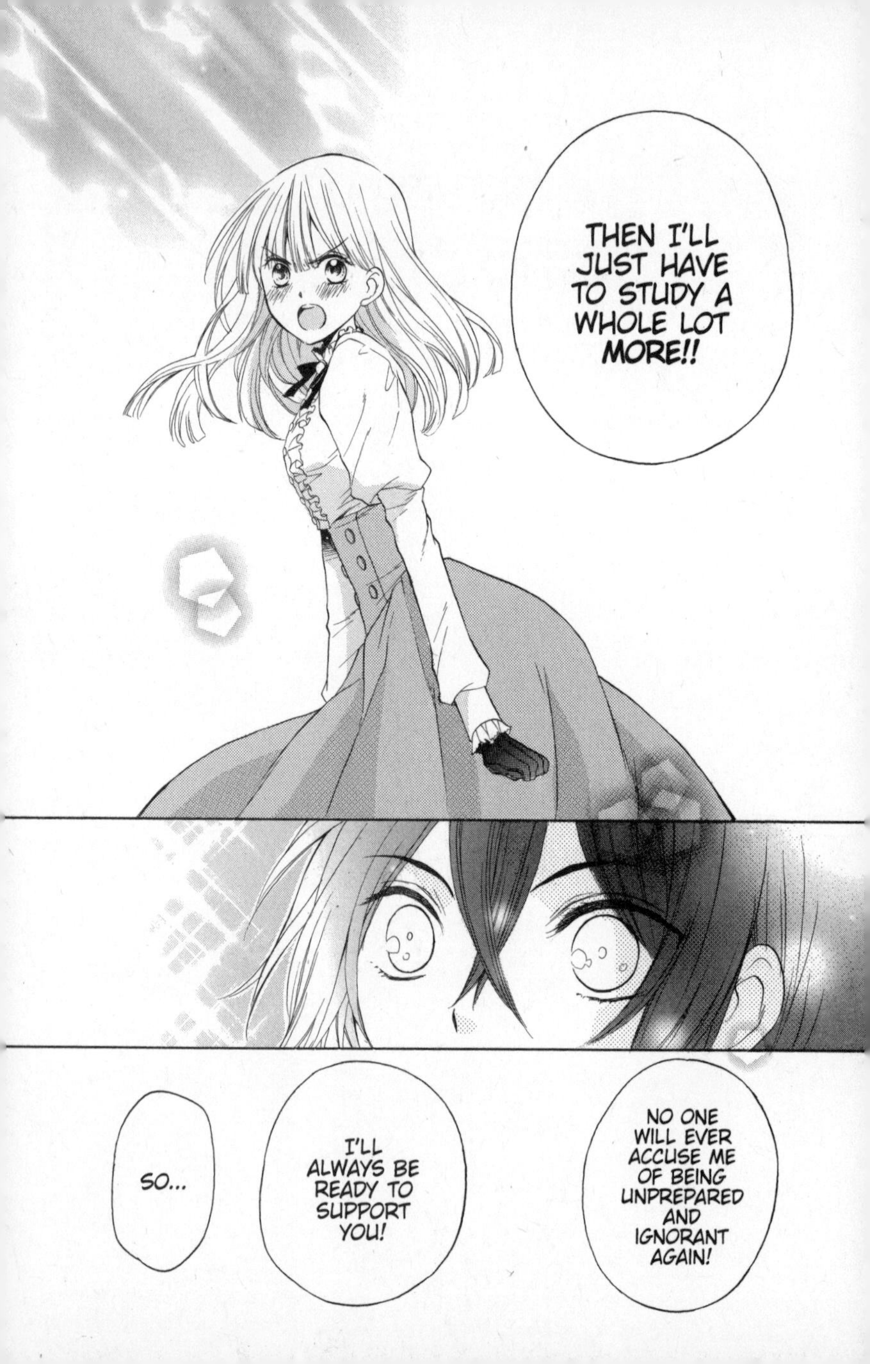
THEN I'LL JUST HAVE TO STUDY A WHOLE LOT MORE!!
NO ONE WILL EVER ACCUSE ME OF BEING UNPREPARED AND IGNORANT AGAIN!
I'LL ALWAYS BE READY TO SUPPORT YOU!
SO...

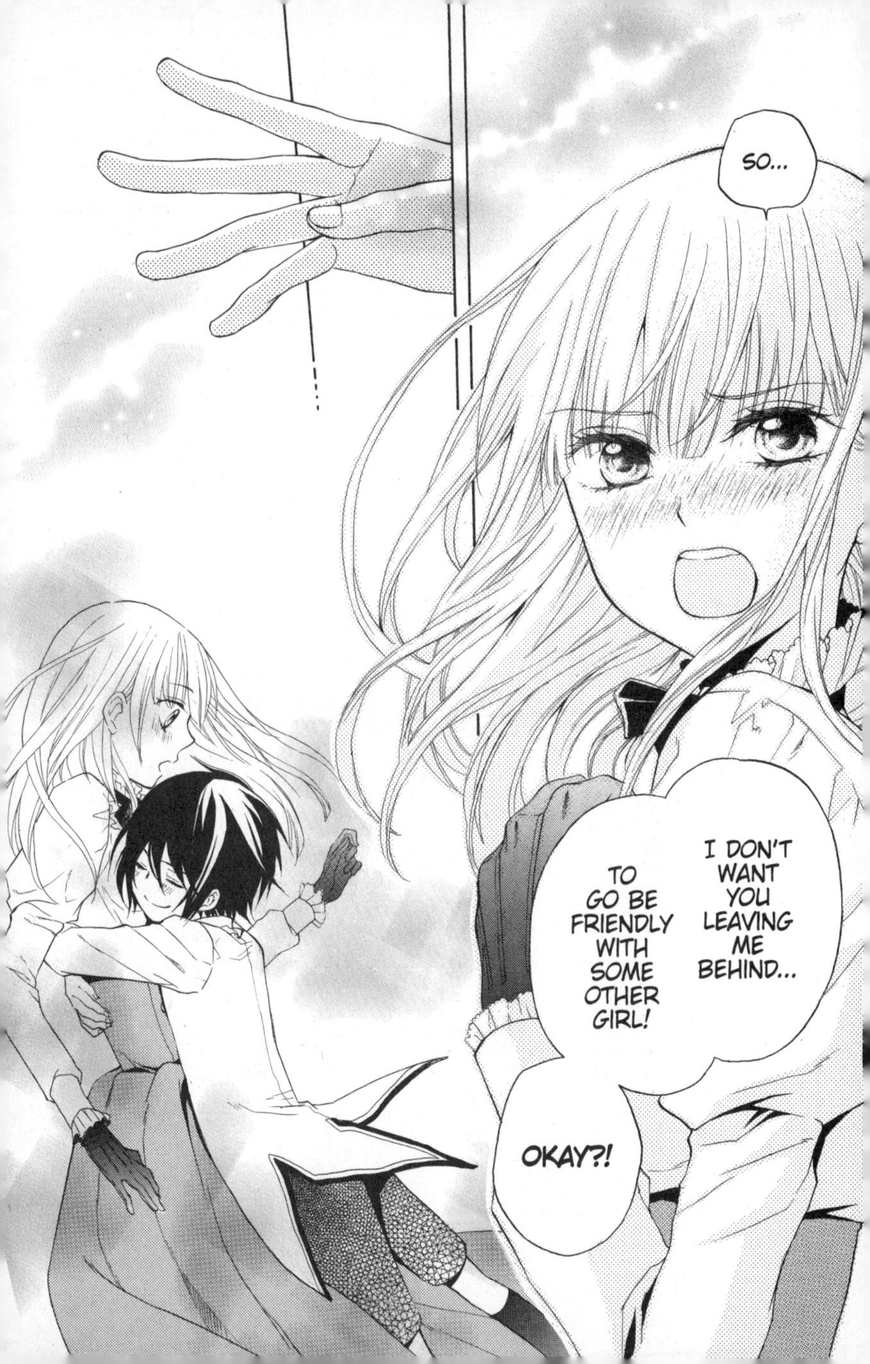
SO...
I DON'T WANT YOU LEAVING ME BEHIND... TO GO BE FRIENDLY WITH SOME OTHER GIRL!
OKAY?!

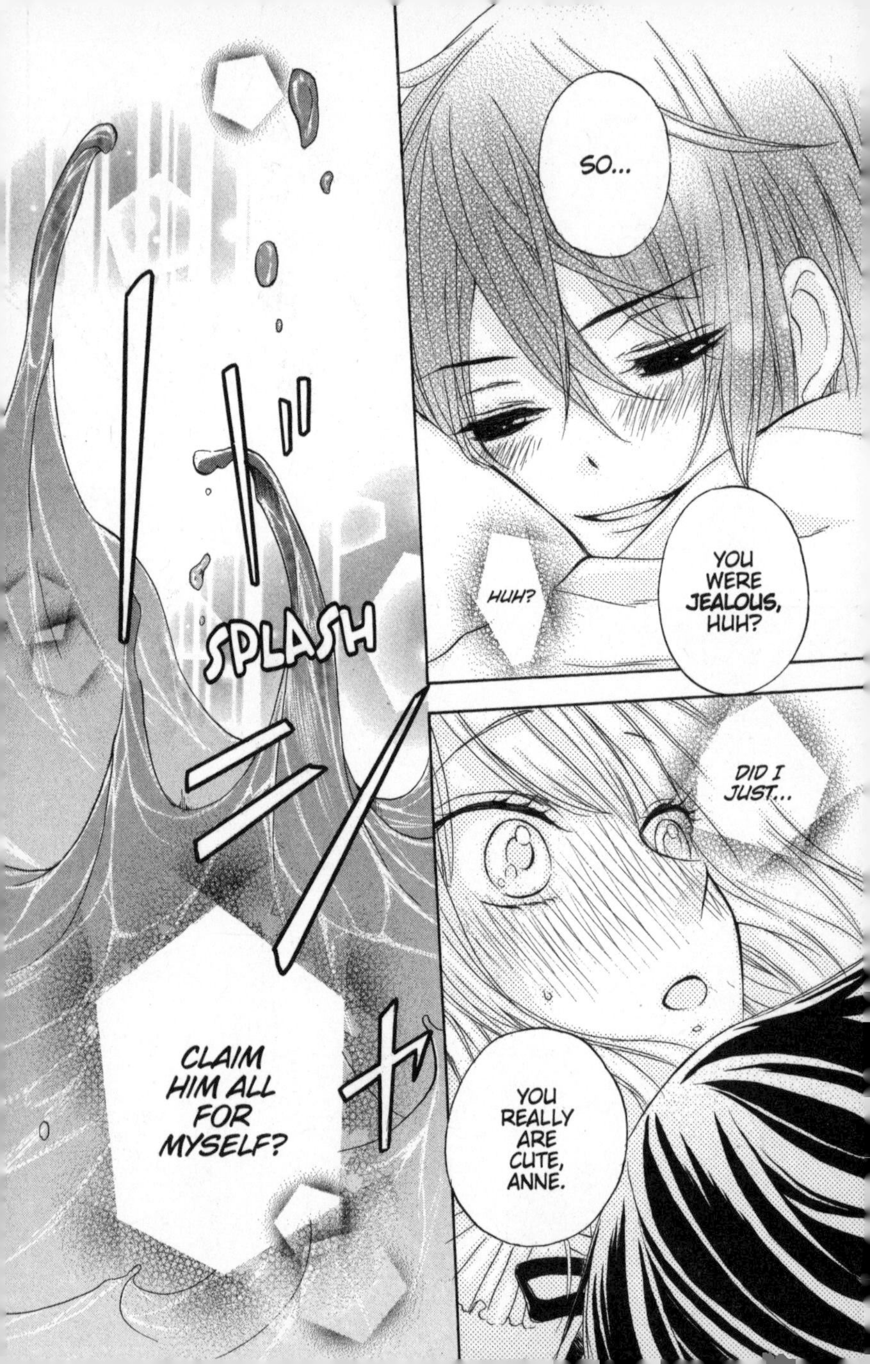
SO...
YOU WERE JEALOUS, HUH?
HUH?
DID I JUST...
YOU REALLY ARE CUTE, ANNE.
SPLASH
CLAIM HIM ALL FOR MYSELF?

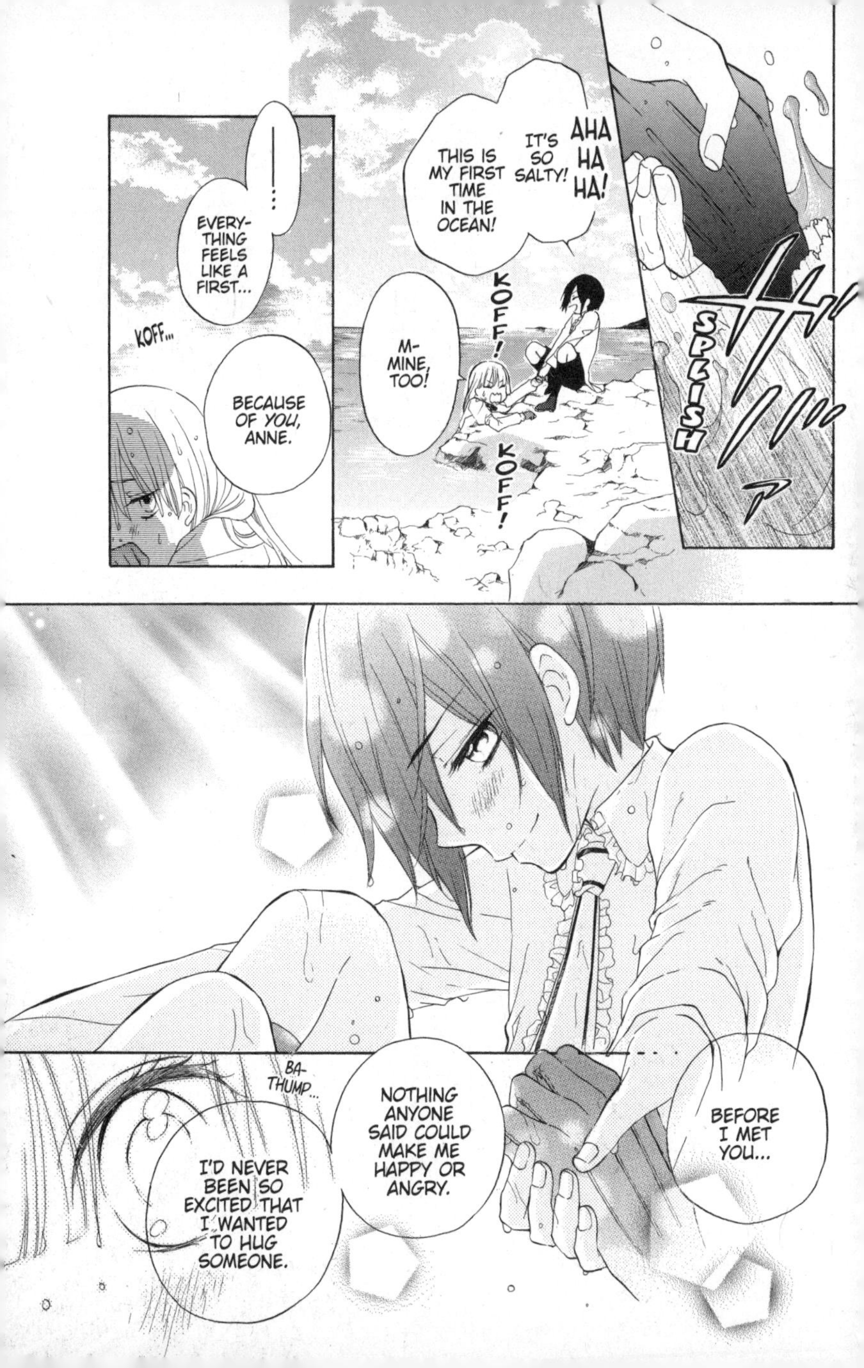
SPLISH
ア
AHA HA HA!
IT'S SO SALTY!
THIS IS MY FIRST TIME IN THE OCEAN!
KOFF!
M-MINE, TOO!
KOFF!
......!
EVERY-THING FEELS LIKE A FIRST...
KOFF...
BECAUSE OF YOU, ANNE.
...
BEFORE I MET YOU...
NOTHING ANYONE SAID COULD MAKE ME HAPPY OR ANGRY.
BA-THUMP...
I'D NEVER BEEN SO EXCITED THAT I WANTED TO HUG SOMEONE.

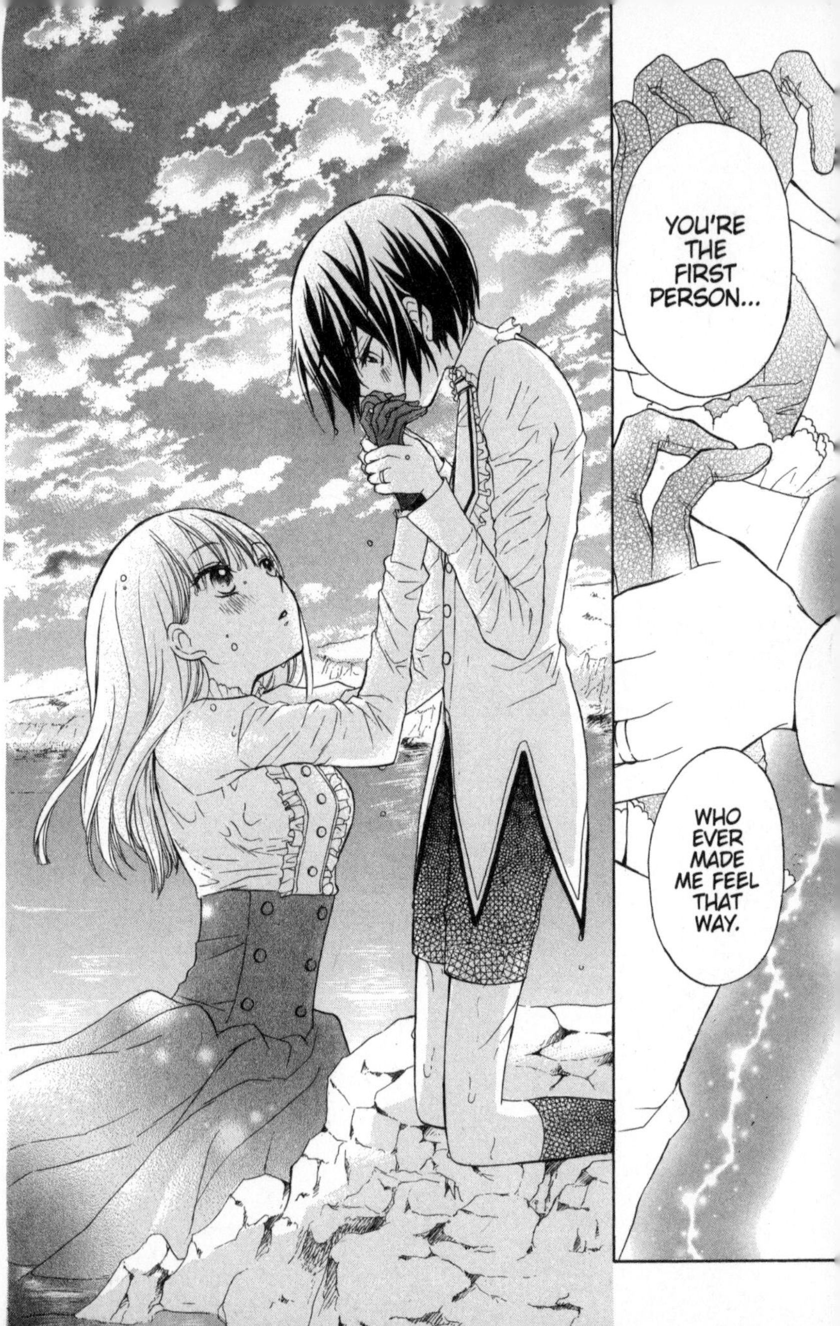
YOU'RE THE FIRST PERSON...
WHO EVER MADE ME FEEL THAT WAY.

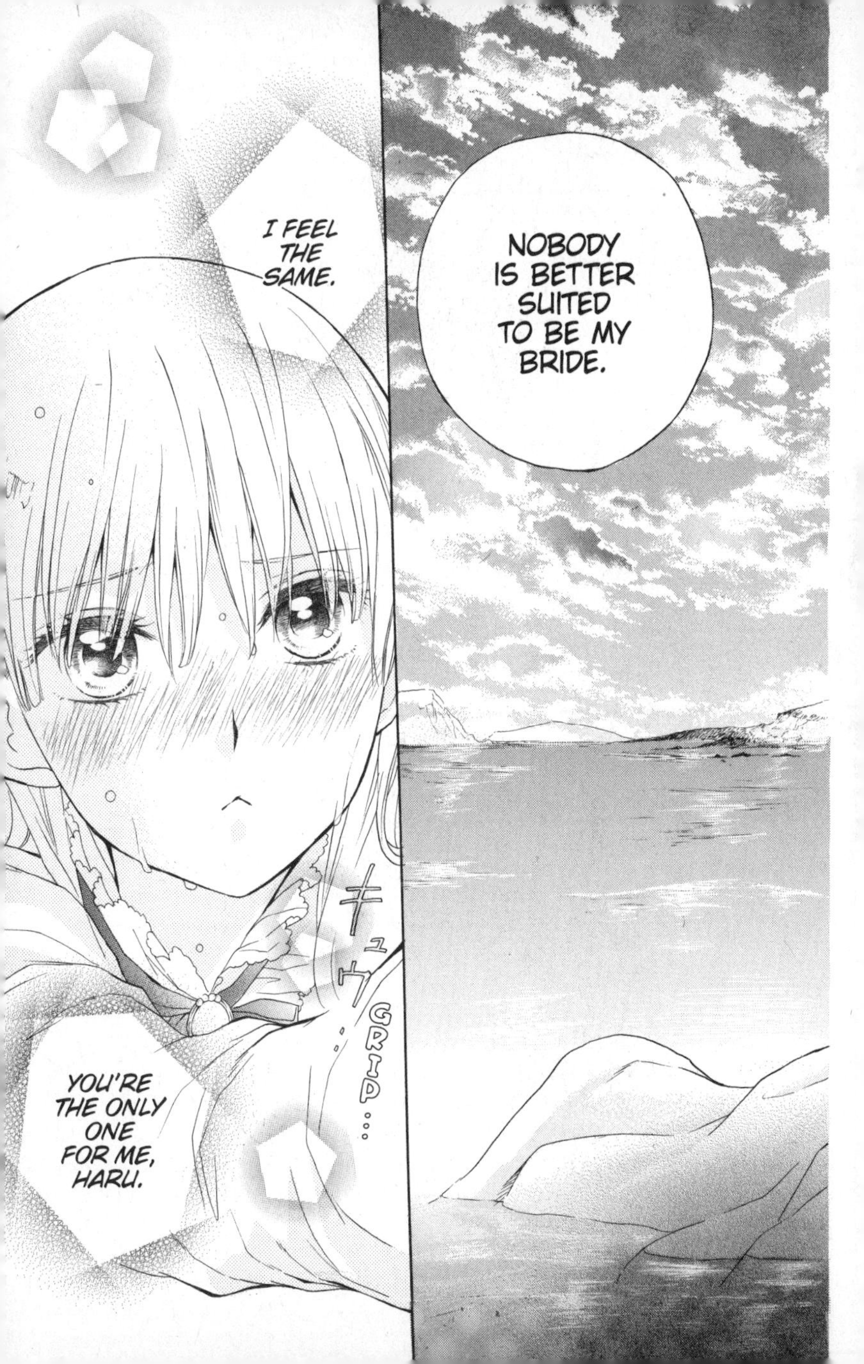
NOBODY IS BETTER SUITED TO BE MY BRIDE.
I FEEL THE SAME.
キュウ…
GRIP...
YOU'RE THE ONLY ONE FOR ME, HARU.

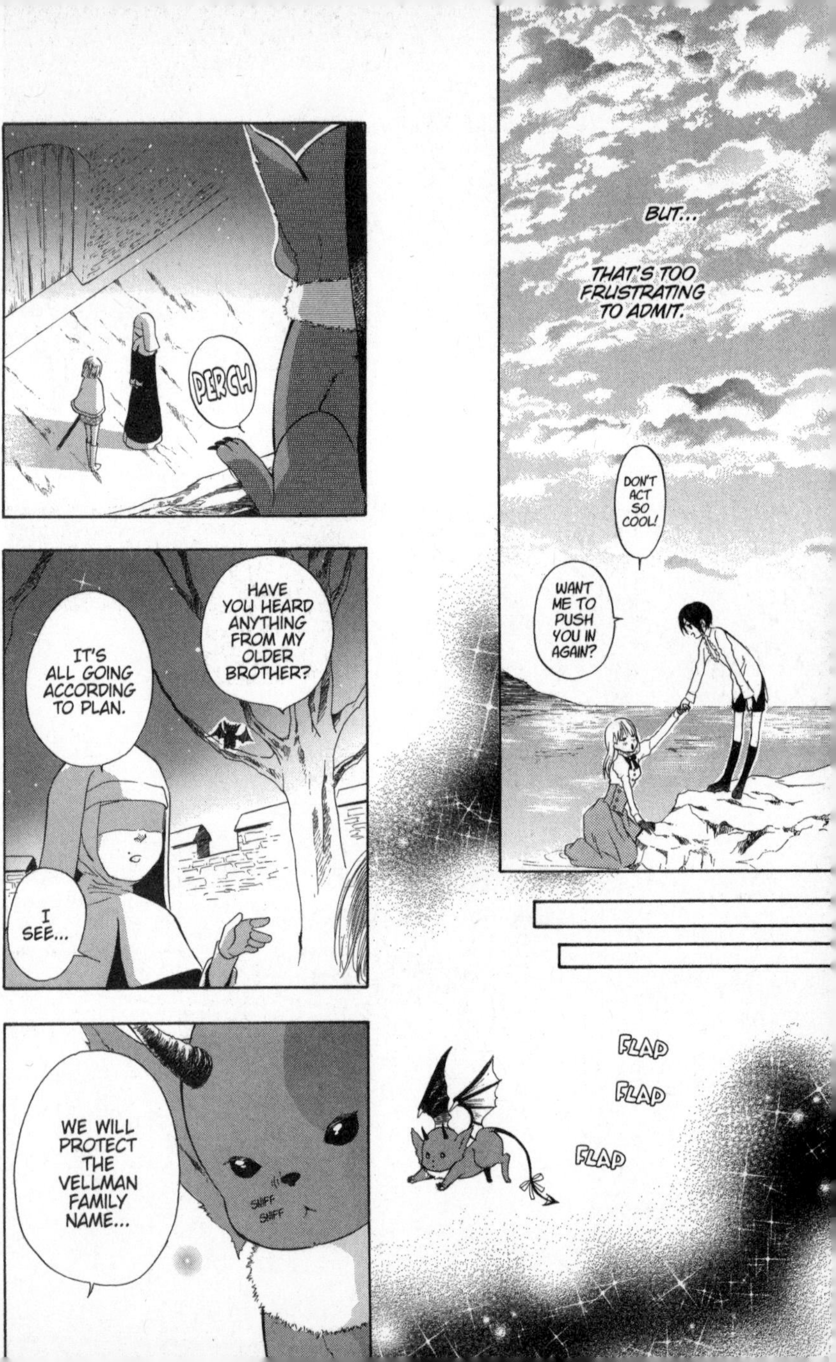
BUT...
THAT'S TOO FRUSTRATING TO ADMIT.
DON'T ACT SO COOL!
WANT ME TO PUSH YOU IN AGAIN?
FLAP
FLAP
FLAP
PERCH
HAVE YOU HEARD ANYTHING FROM MY OLDER BROTHER?
IT'S ALL GOING ACCORDING TO PLAN.
I SEE...
WE WILL PROTECT THE VELLMAN FAMILY NAME...
SNIFF SNIFF

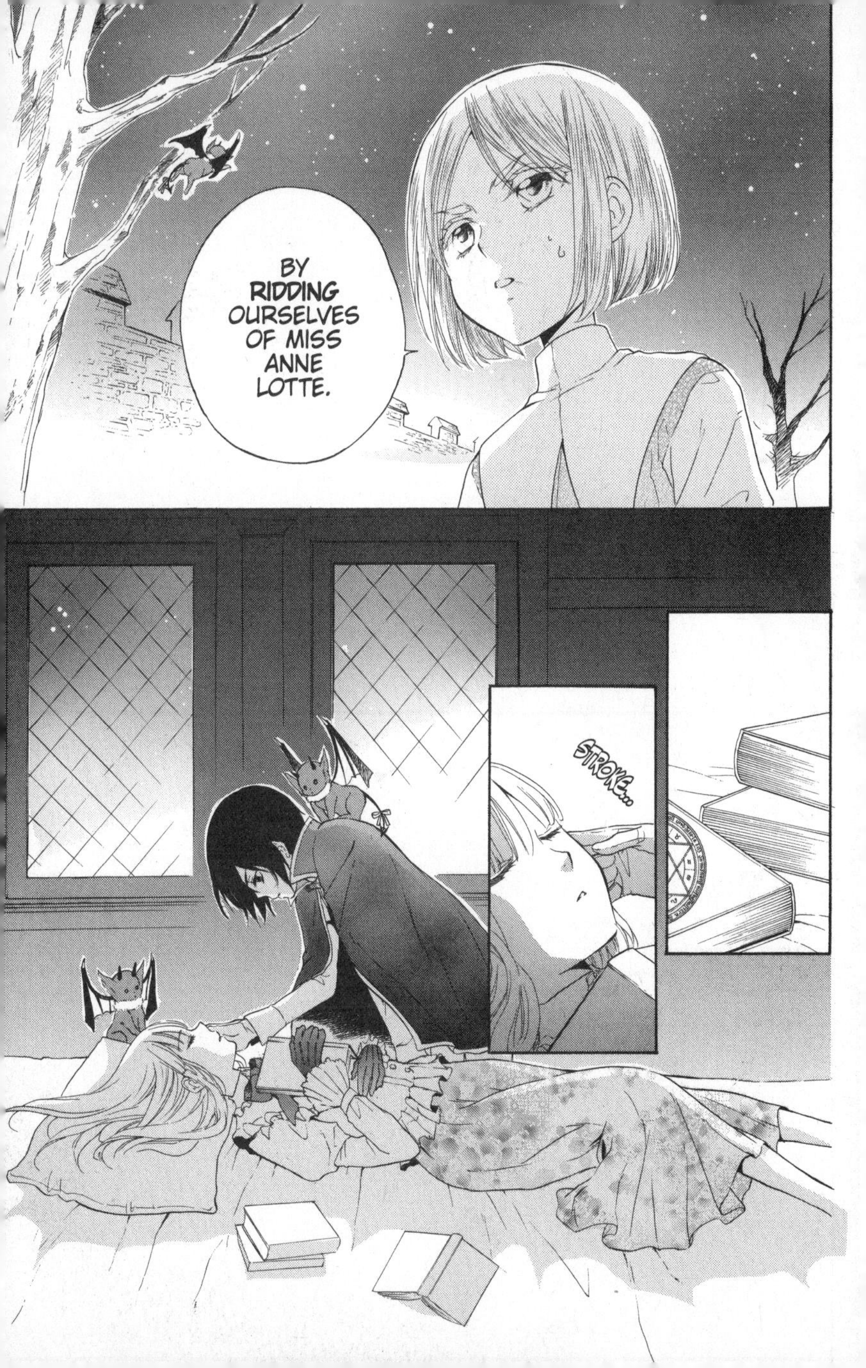
BY RIDDING OURSELVES OF MISS ANNE LOTTE.
STROKE...

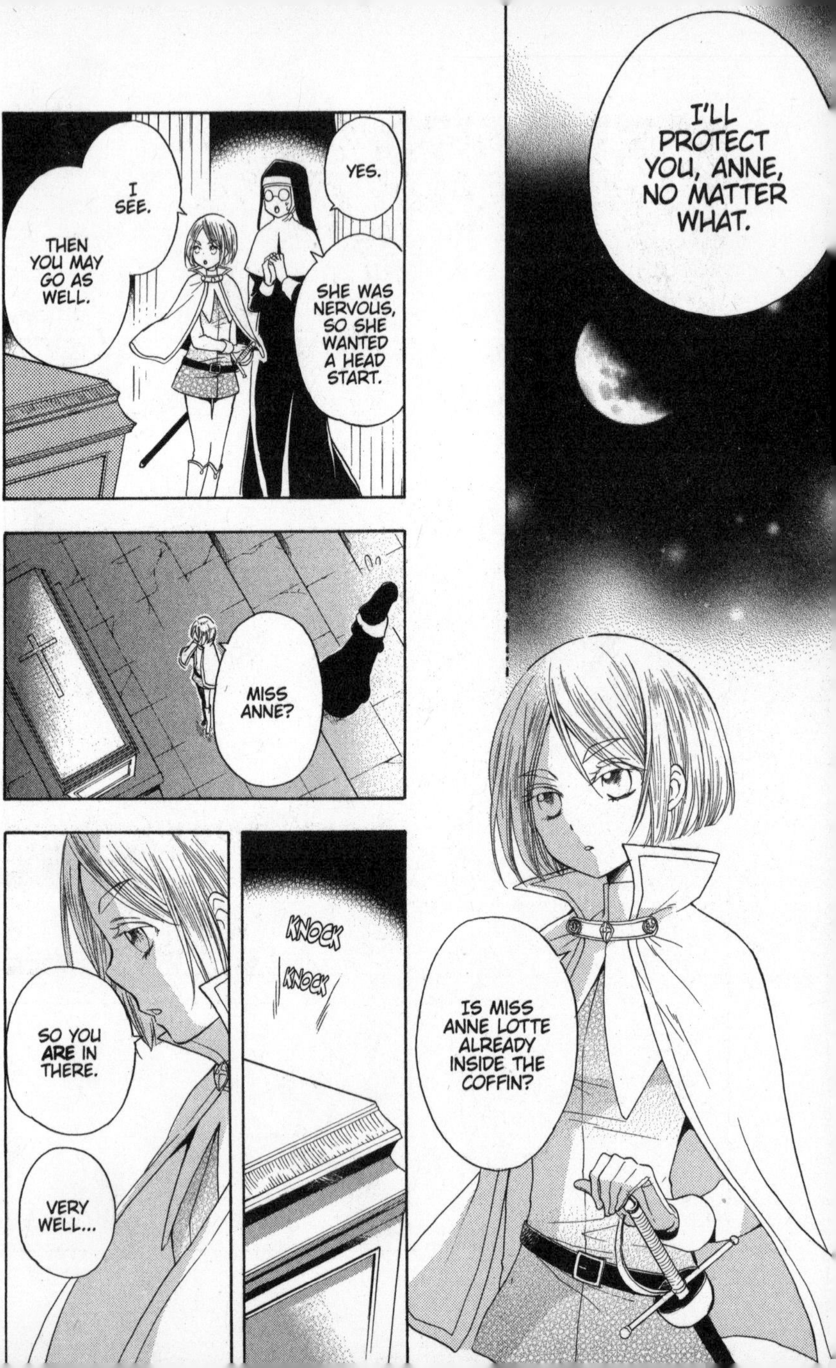
I'LL PROTECT YOU, ANNE, NO MATTER WHAT.
IS MISS ANNE LOTTE ALREADY INSIDE THE COFFIN?
YES.
SHE WAS NERVOUS, SO SHE WANTED A HEAD START.
I SEE.
THEN YOU MAY GO AS WELL.
MISS ANNE?
KNOCK
KNOCK
SO YOU ARE IN THERE.
VERY WELL...

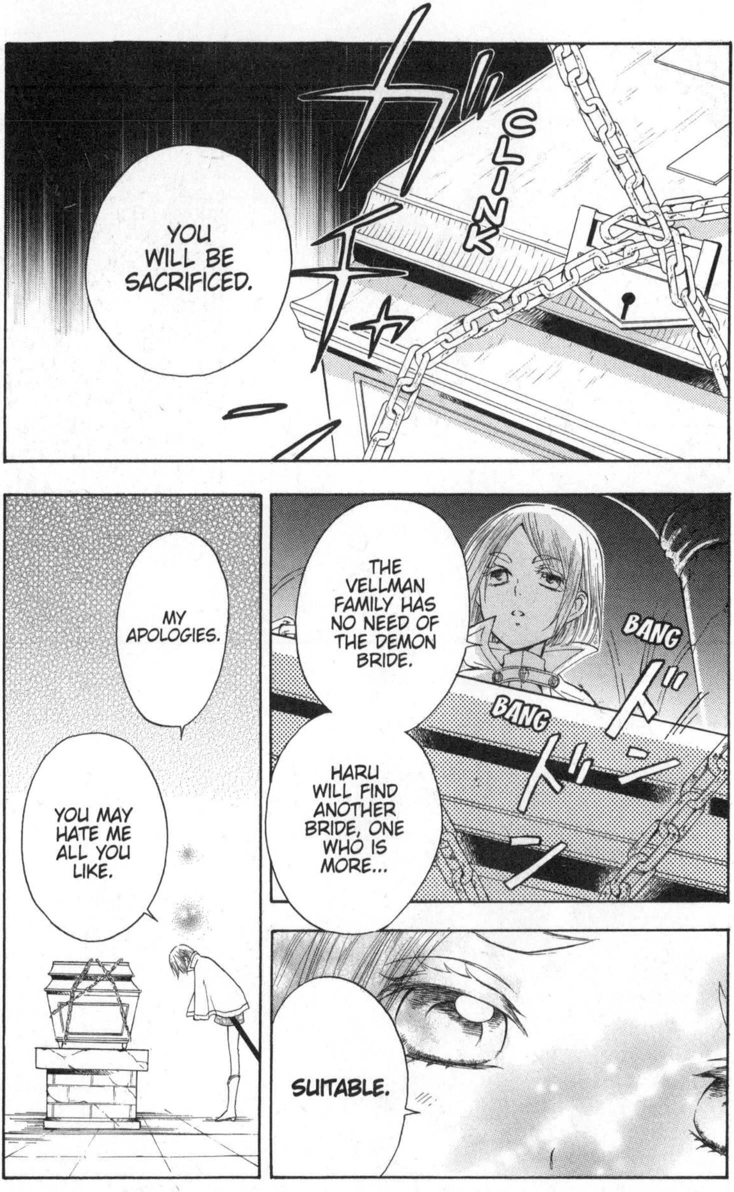
CLINK
YOU WILL BE SACRIFICED.
THE VELLMAN FAMILY HAS NO NEED OF THE DEMON BRIDE.
BANG
BANG
HARU WILL FIND ANOTHER BRIDE, ONE WHO IS MORE...
SUITABLE.
MY APOLOGIES.
YOU MAY HATE ME ALL YOU LIKE.

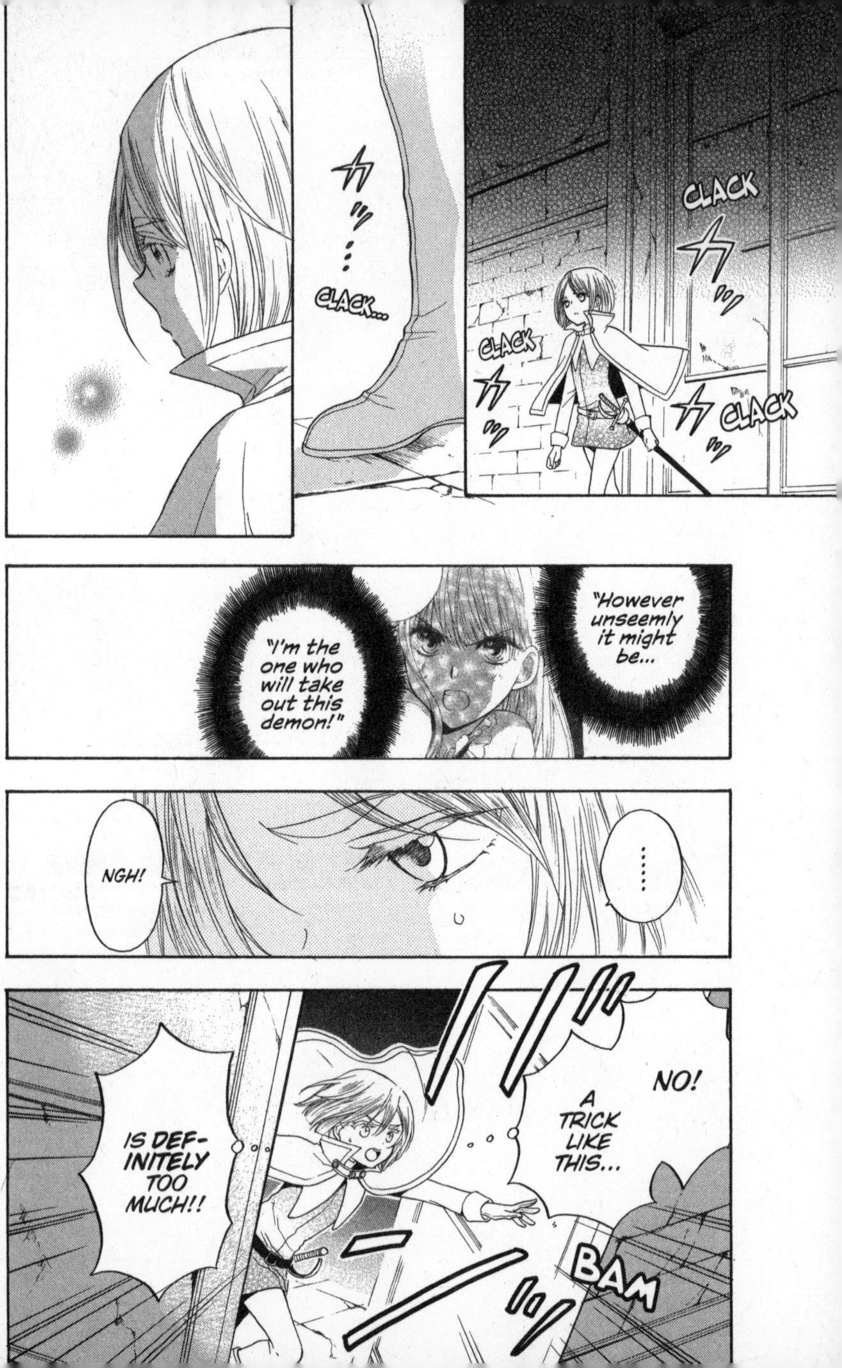
CLACK
CLACK
CLACK
CLACK...
"However unseemly it might be...
"I'm the one who will take out this demon!"
......
NGH!
NO!
A TRICK LIKE THIS...
IS DEF-INITELY TOO MUCH!!
BAM

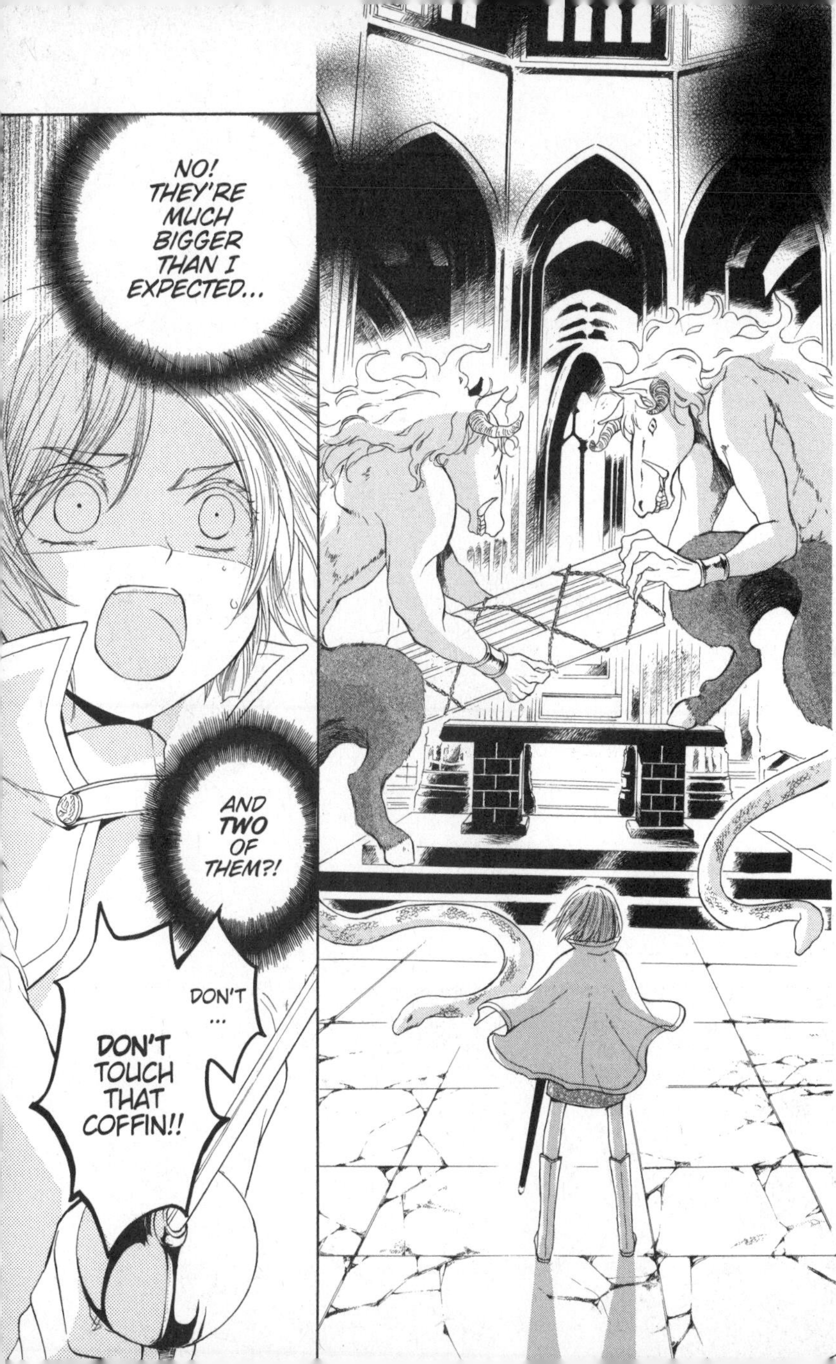
NO! THEY'RE MUCH BIGGER THAN I EXPECTED...
AND TWO OF THEM?!
DON'T ...
DON'T TOUCH THAT COFFIN!!

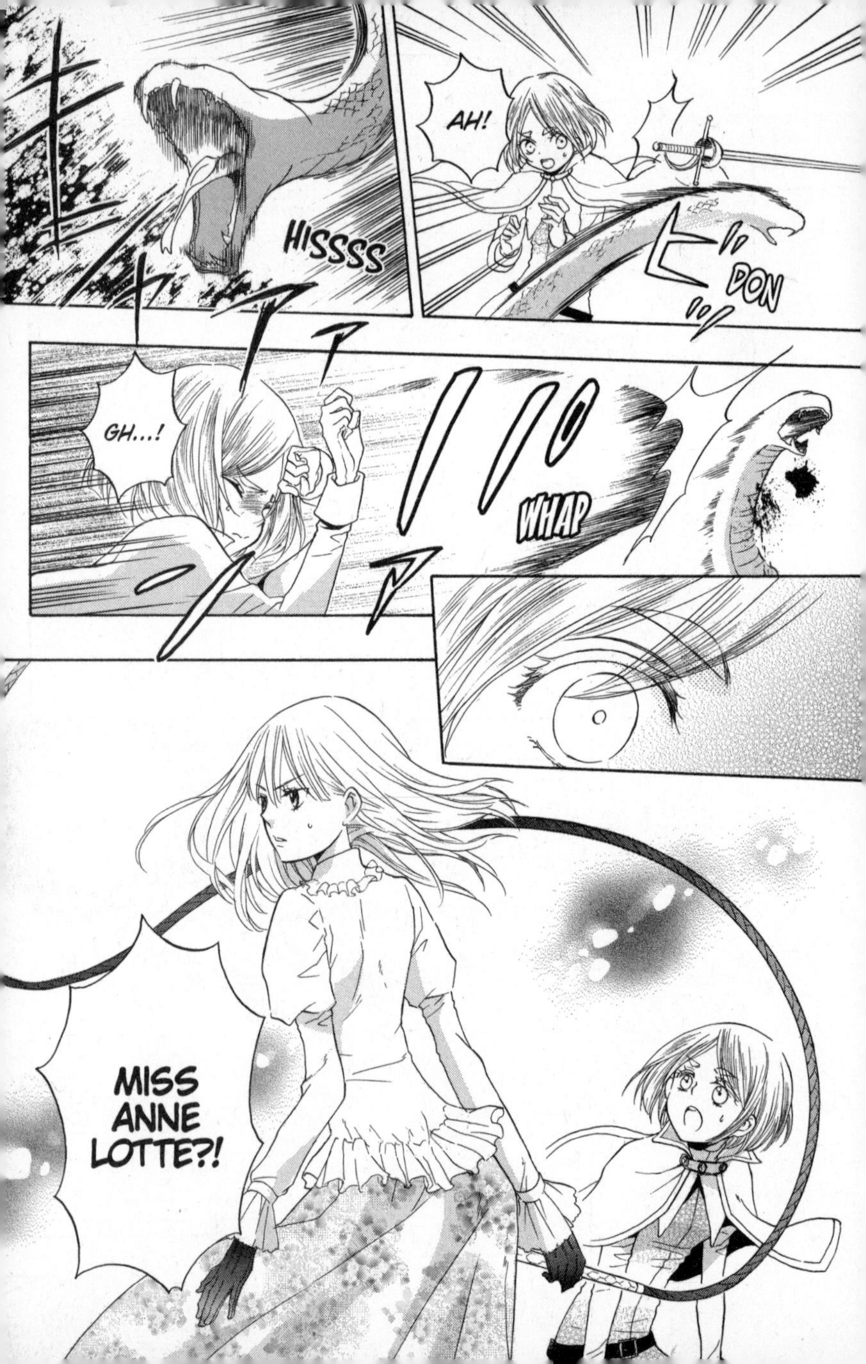
AH!
DON
HISSSS
GH...!
WHAP
MISS ANNE LOTTE?!

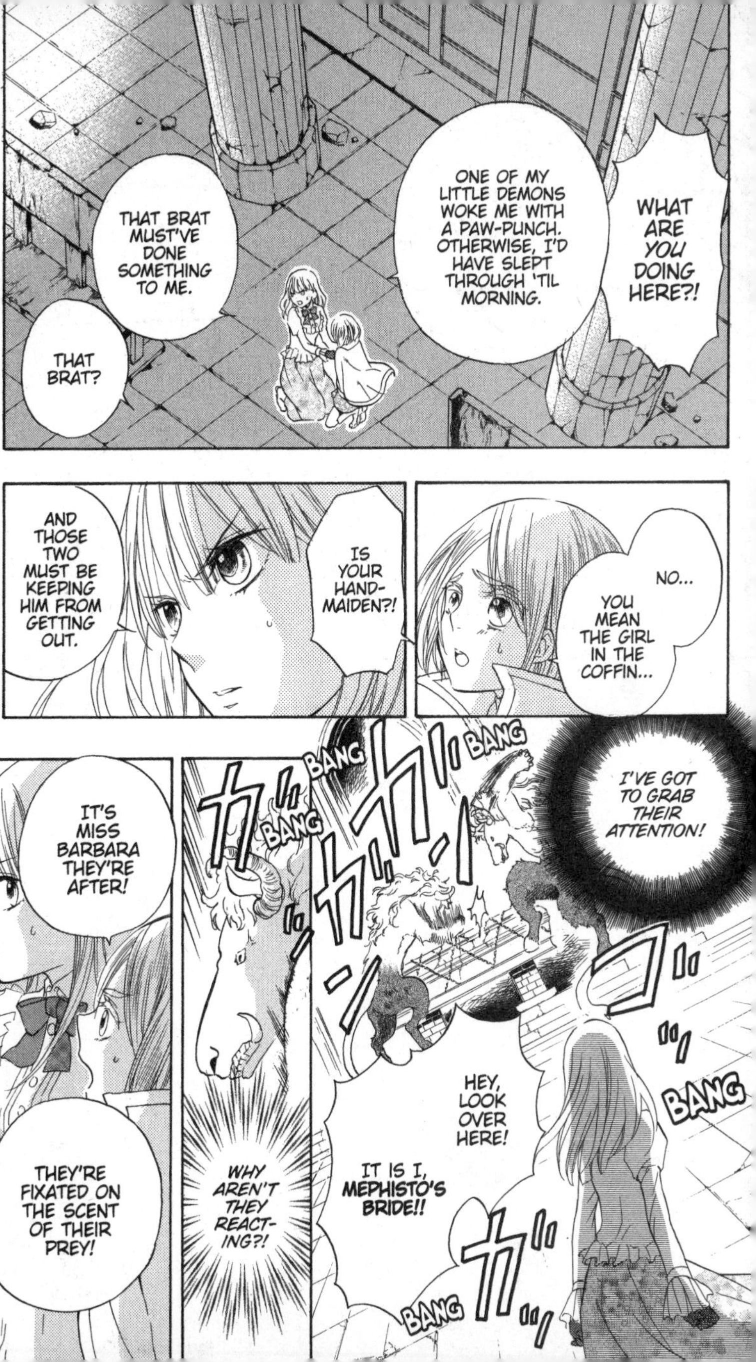
WHAT ARE YOU DOING HERE?!
ONE OF MY LITTLE DEMONS WOKE ME WITH A PAW-PUNCH. OTHERWISE, I'D HAVE SLEPT THROUGH 'TIL MORNING.
THAT BRAT MUST'VE DONE SOMETHING TO ME.
THAT BRAT?
NO...
YOU MEAN THE GIRL IN THE COFFIN...
IS YOUR HAND-MAIDEN?!
AND THOSE TWO MUST BE KEEPING HIM FROM GETTING OUT.
BANG
BANG
BANG
I'VE GOT TO GRAB THEIR ATTENTION!
BANG
HEY, LOOK OVER HERE!
IT IS I, MEPHISTO'S BRIDE!!
WHY AREN'T THEY REACT-ING?!
BANG
IT'S MISS BARBARA THEY'RE AFTER!
THEY'RE FIXATED ON THE SCENT OF THEIR PREY!

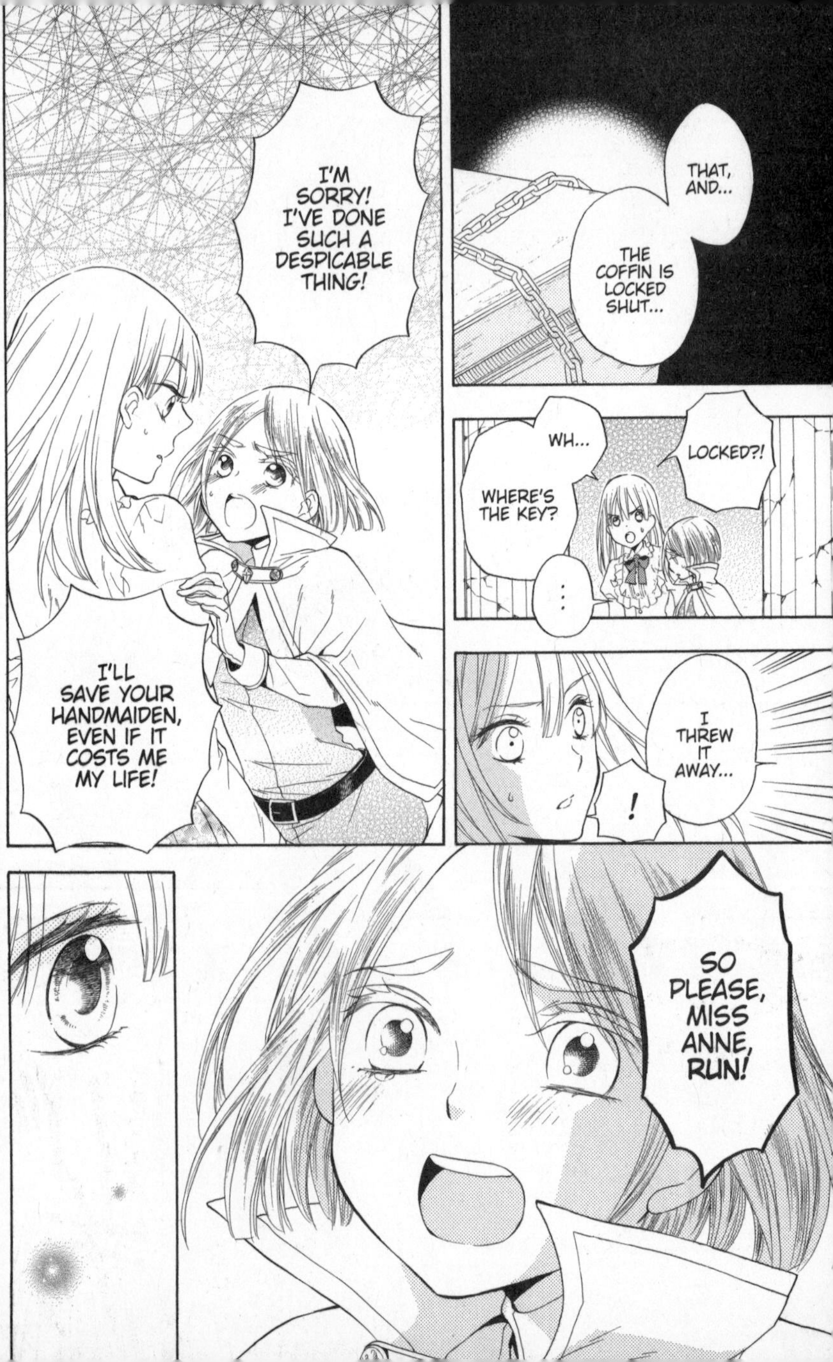
THAT, AND...
THE COFFIN IS LOCKED SHUT...
LOCKED?!
WH... WHERE'S THE KEY?
...
I THREW IT AWAY...
!
I'M SORRY! I'VE DONE SUCH A DESPICABLE THING!
I'LL SAVE YOUR HANDMAIDEN, EVEN IF IT COSTS ME MY LIFE!
SO PLEASE, MISS ANNE, RUN!

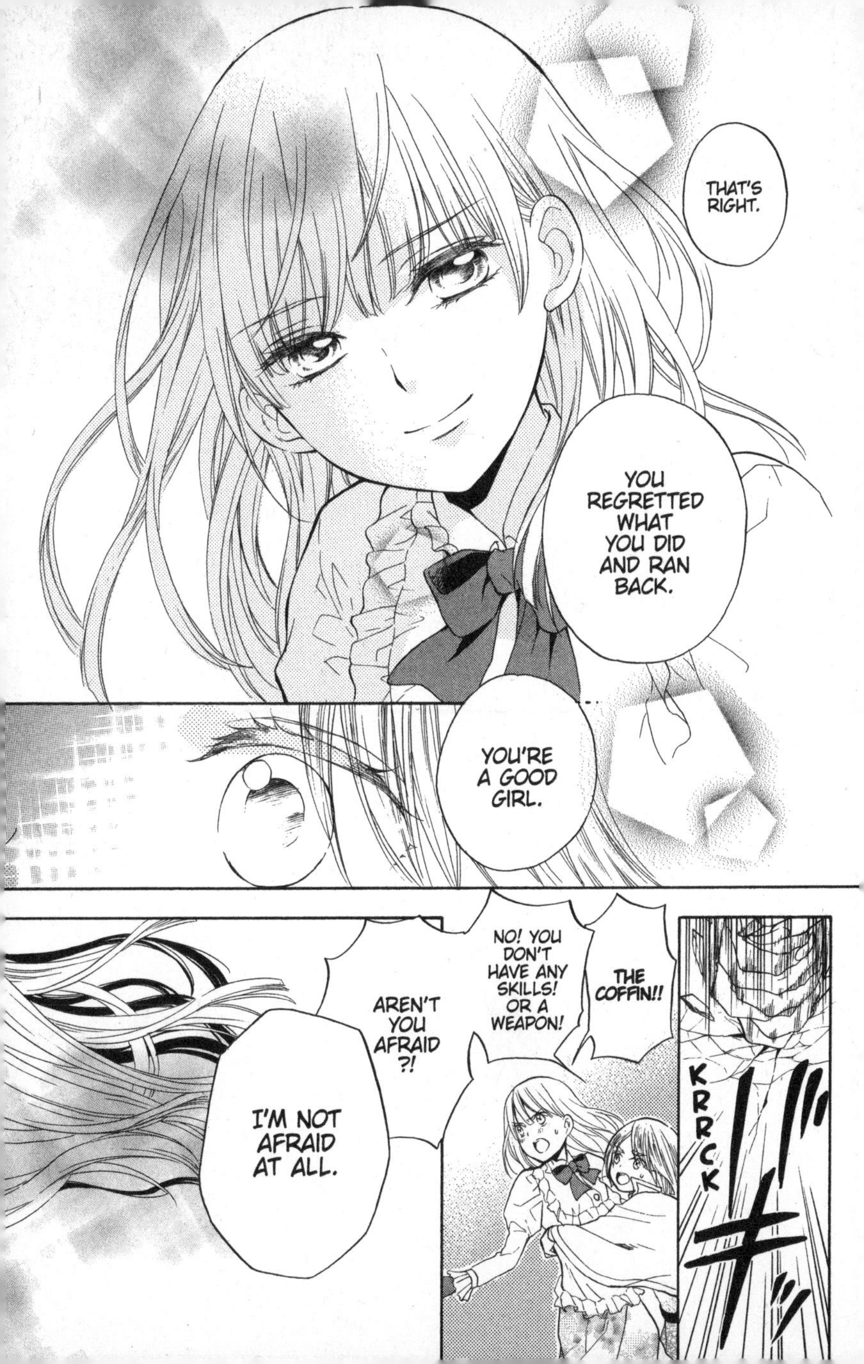
THAT'S RIGHT.
YOU REGRETTED WHAT YOU DID AND RAN BACK.
YOU'RE A GOOD GIRL.
KRRCK
THE COFFIN!!
NO! YOU DON'T HAVE ANY SKILLS! OR A WEAPON!
AREN'T YOU AFRAID?!
I'M NOT AFRAID AT ALL.

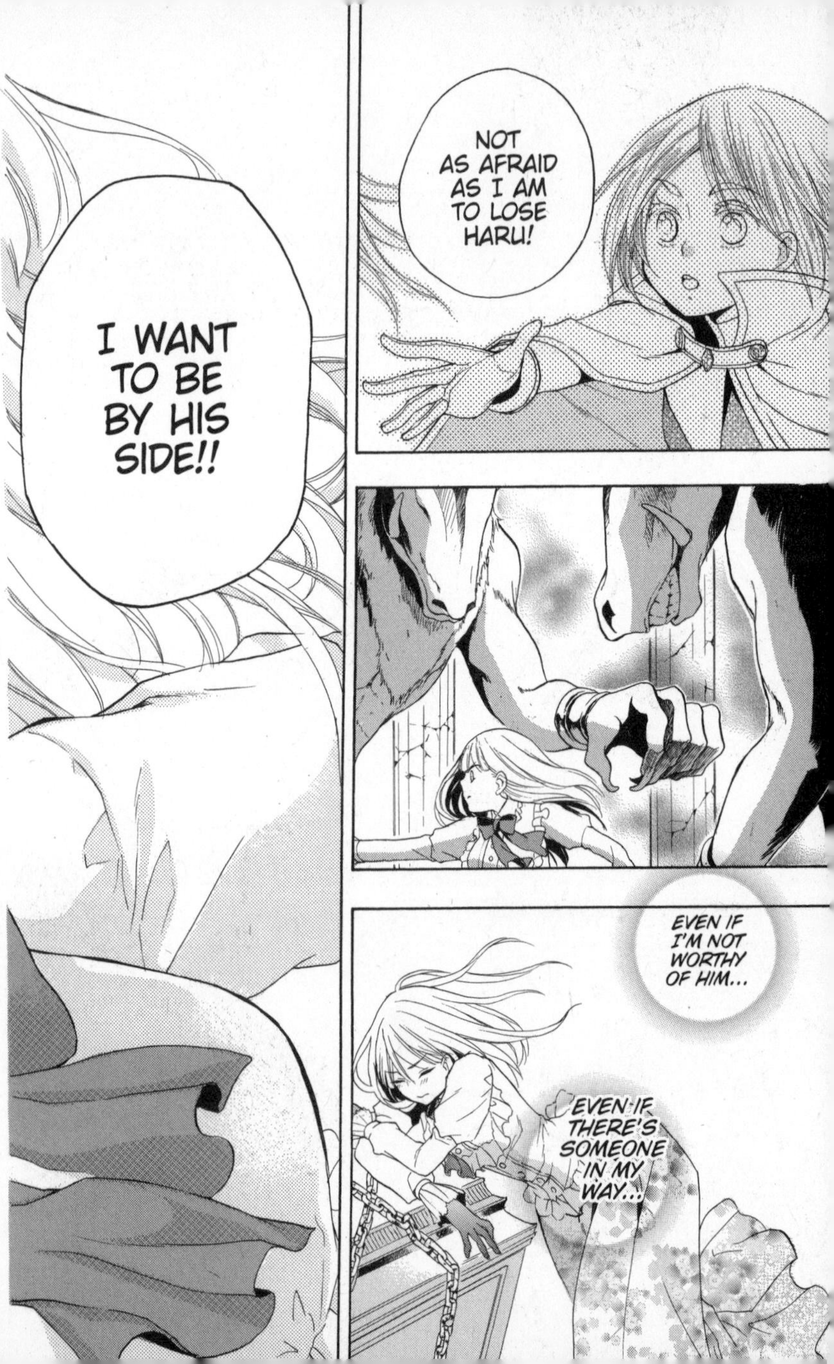
NOT AS AFRAID AS I AM TO LOSE HARU!
EVEN IF I'M NOT WORTHY OF HIM...
EVEN IF THERE'S SOMEONE IN MY WAY...
I WANT TO BE BY HIS SIDE!!

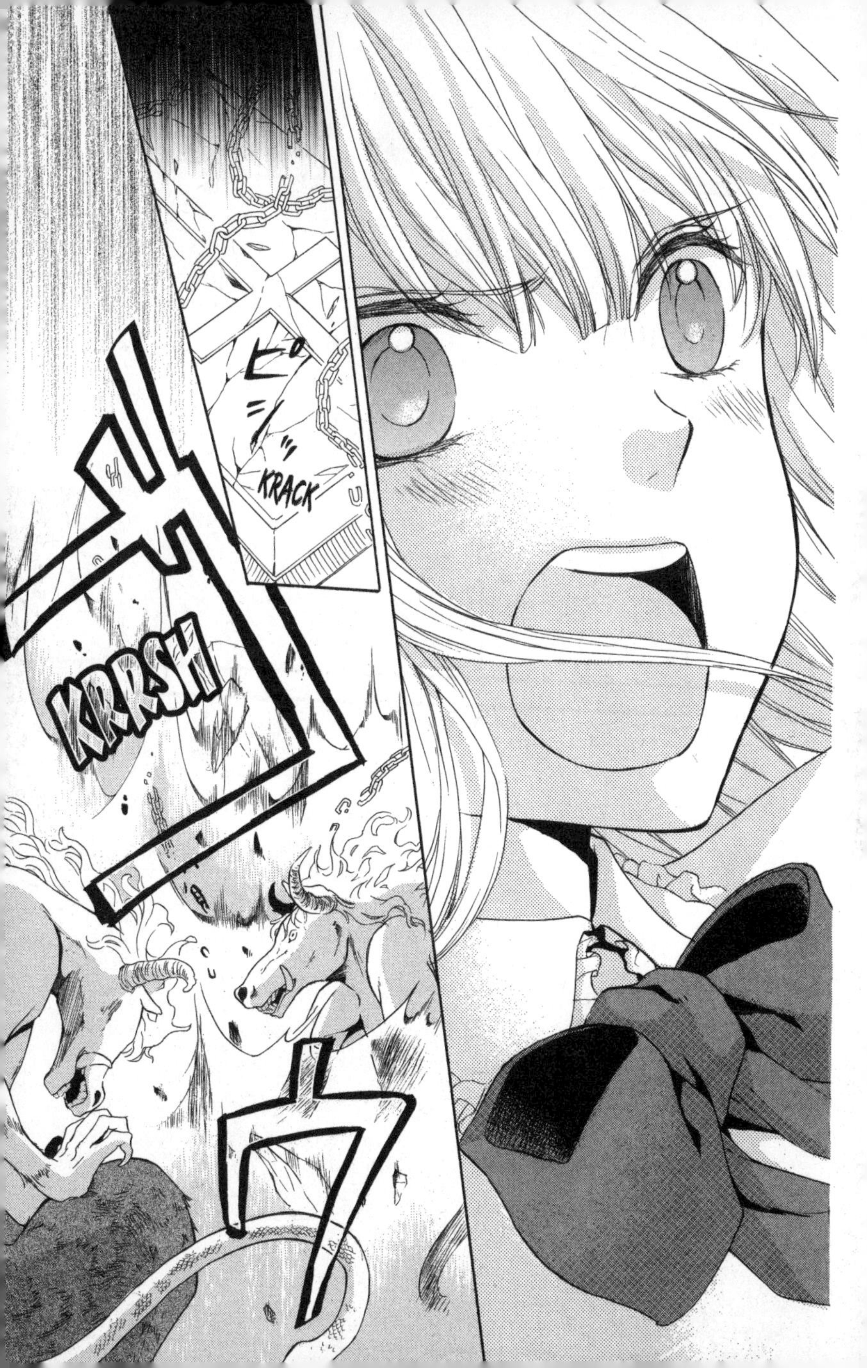
KRACK
KRRSH

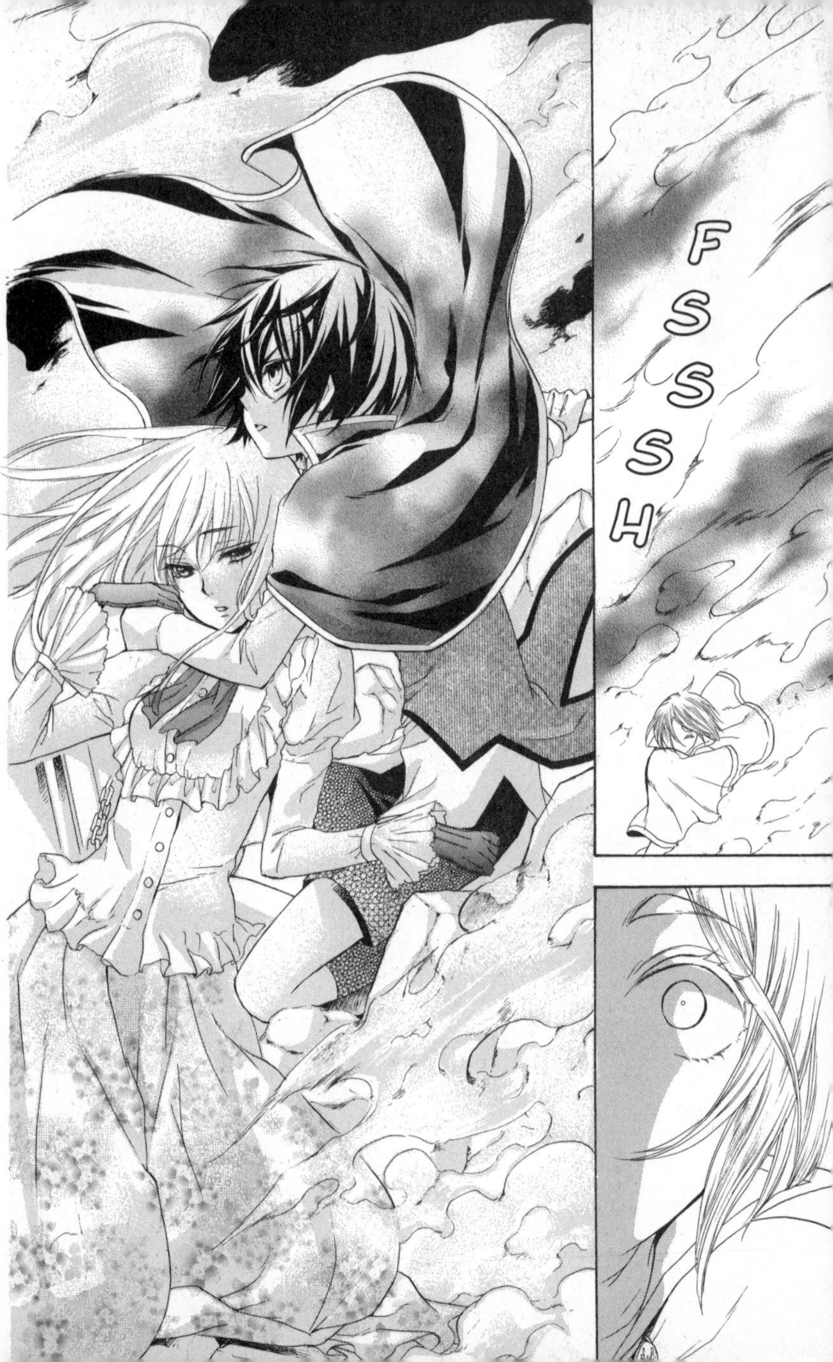
FSSSH

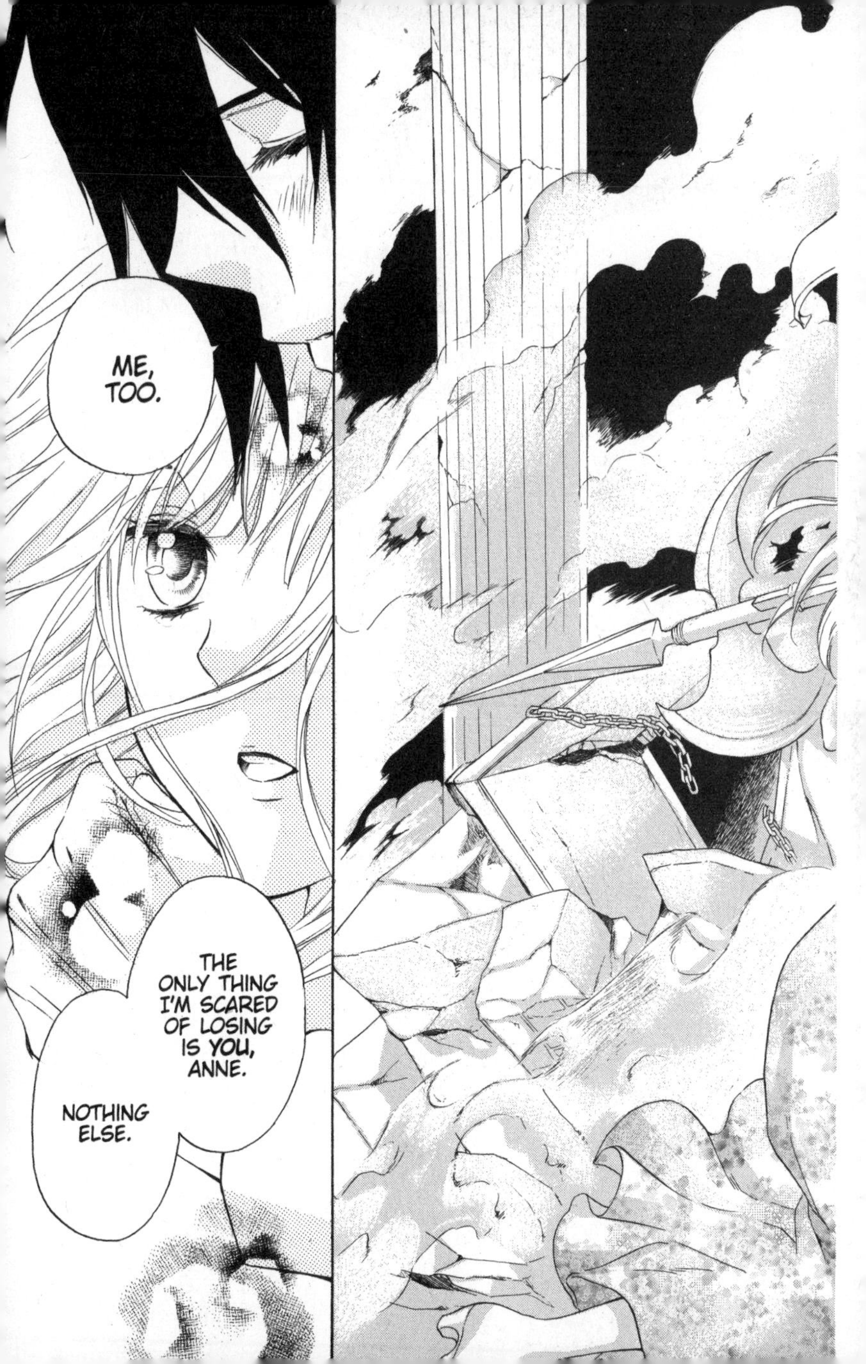
ME, TOO.
THE ONLY THING I'M SCARED OF LOSING IS YOU, ANNE.
NOTHING ELSE.

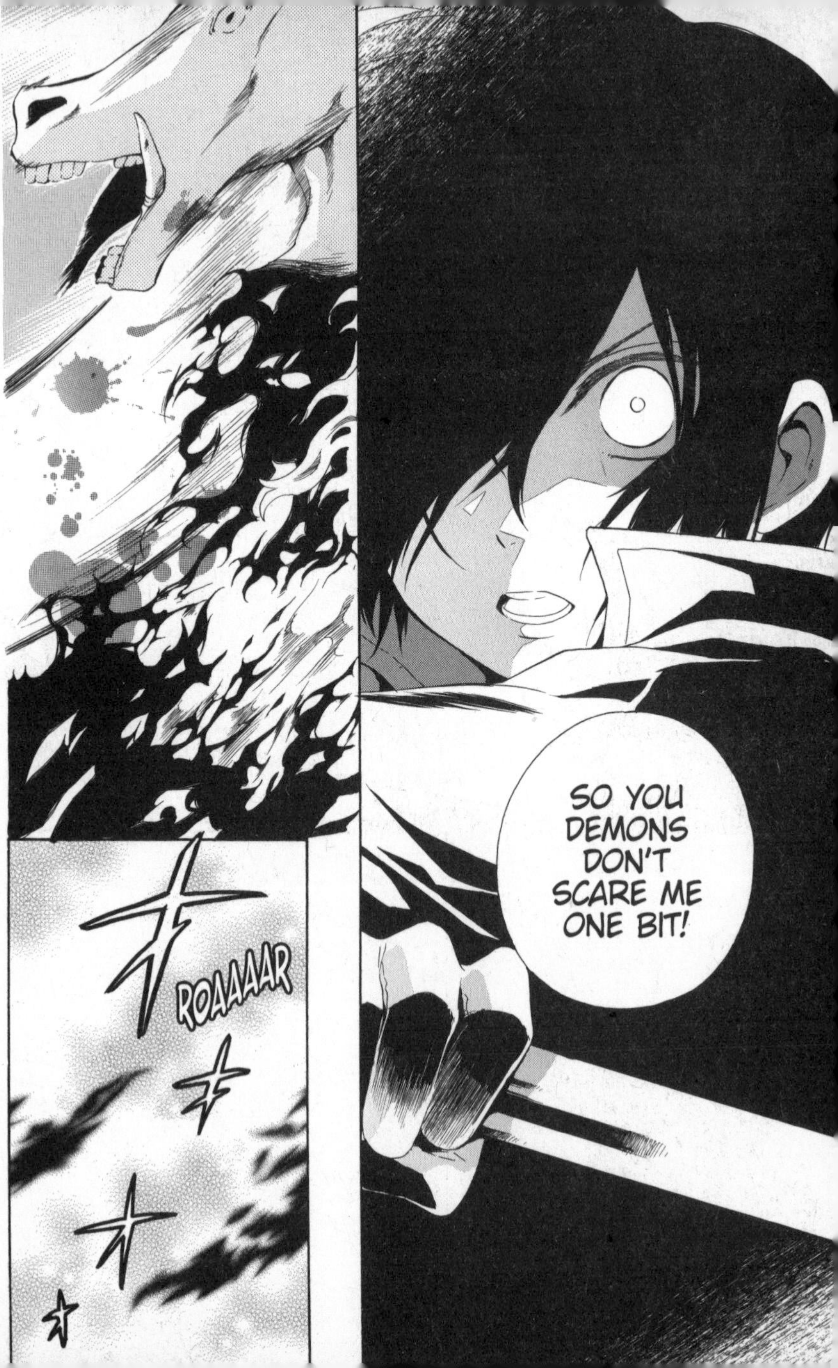
SO YOU DEMONS DON'T SCARE ME ONE BIT!
ROAAAAR

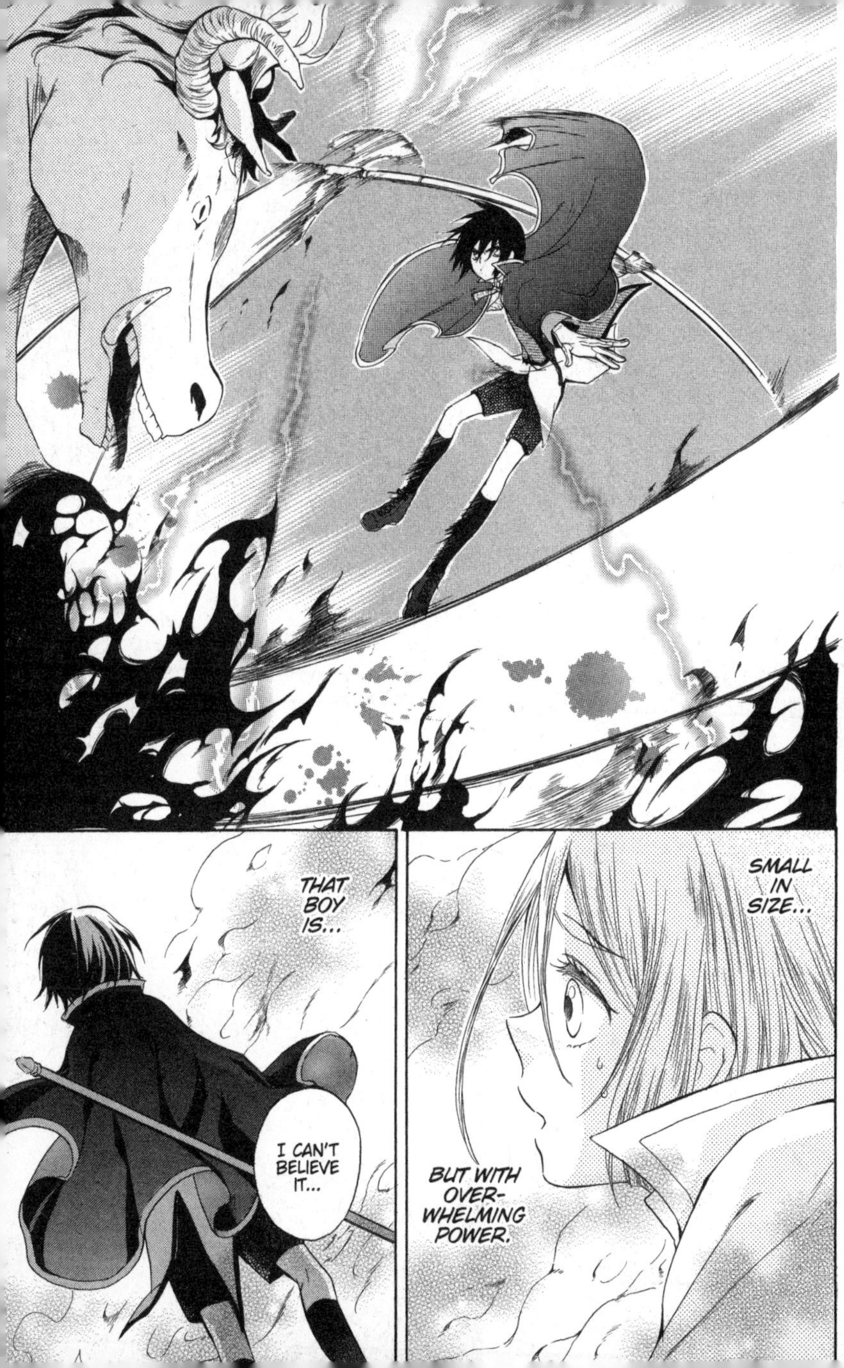
SMALL IN SIZE...
BUT WITH OVER-WHELMING POWER.
THAT BOY IS...
I CAN'T BELIEVE IT...

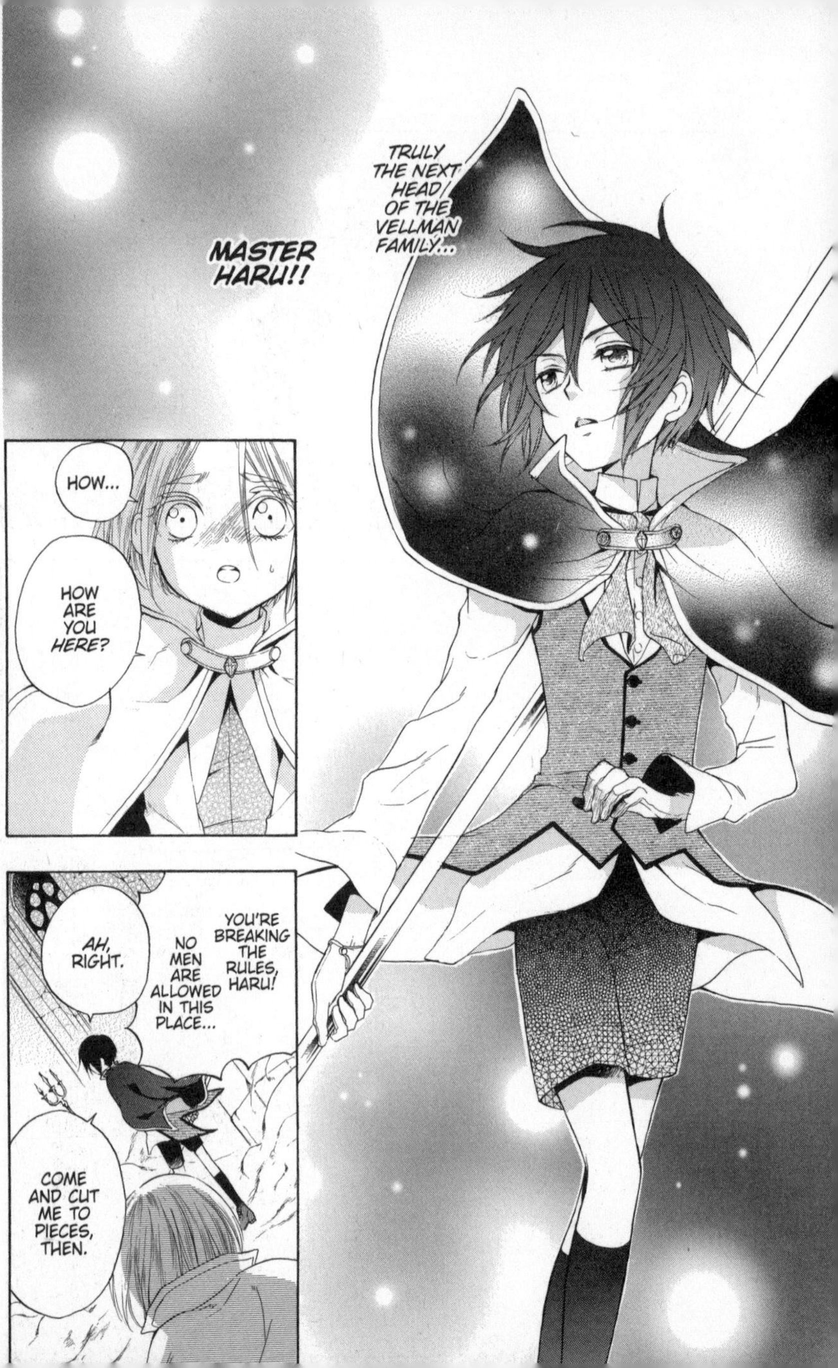
TRULY THE NEXT HEAD OF THE VELLMAN FAMILY...
MASTER HARU!!
HOW...
HOW ARE YOU HERE?
YOU'RE BREAKING THE RULES, HARU!
NO MEN ARE ALLOWED IN THIS PLACE...
AH, RIGHT.
COME AND CUT ME TO PIECES, THEN.

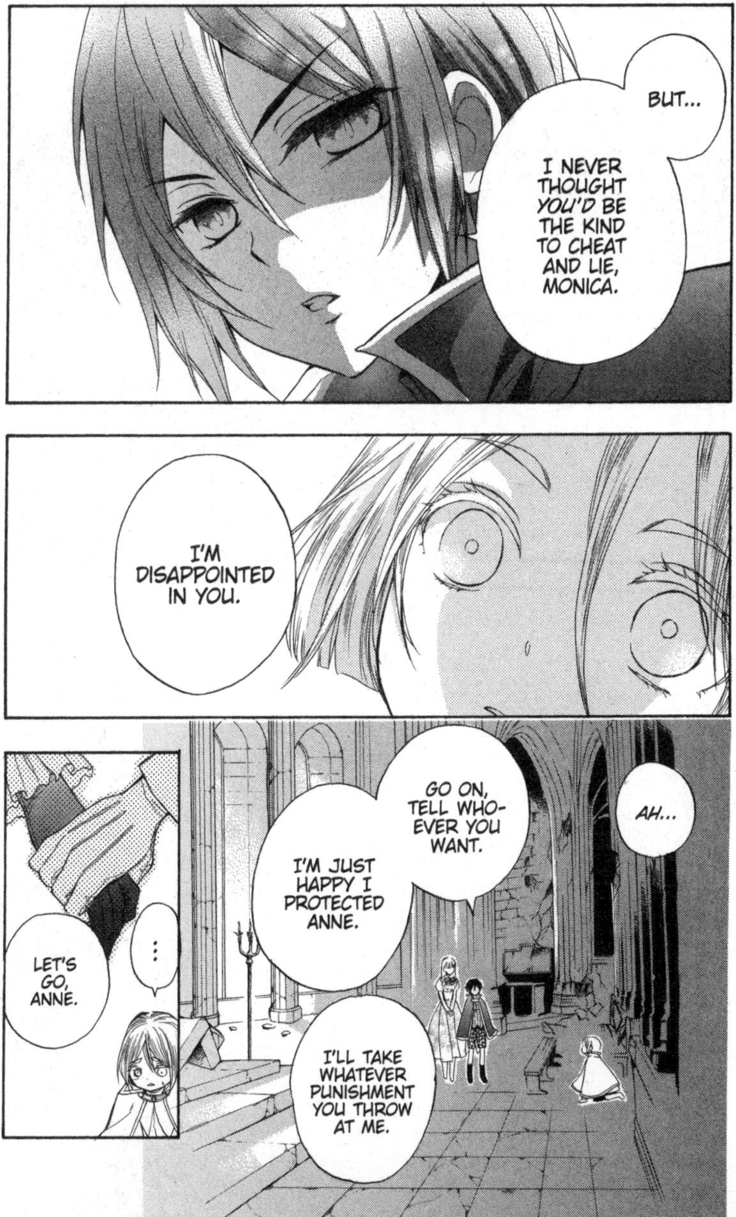

BUT...
I NEVER THOUGHT YOU'D BE THE KIND TO CHEAT AND LIE, MONICA.
I'M DISAPPOINTED IN YOU.
AH...
GO ON, TELL WHO-EVER YOU WANT.
I'M JUST HAPPY I PROTECTED ANNE.
I'LL TAKE WHATEVER PUNISHMENT YOU THROW AT ME.
...
LET'S GO, ANNE.

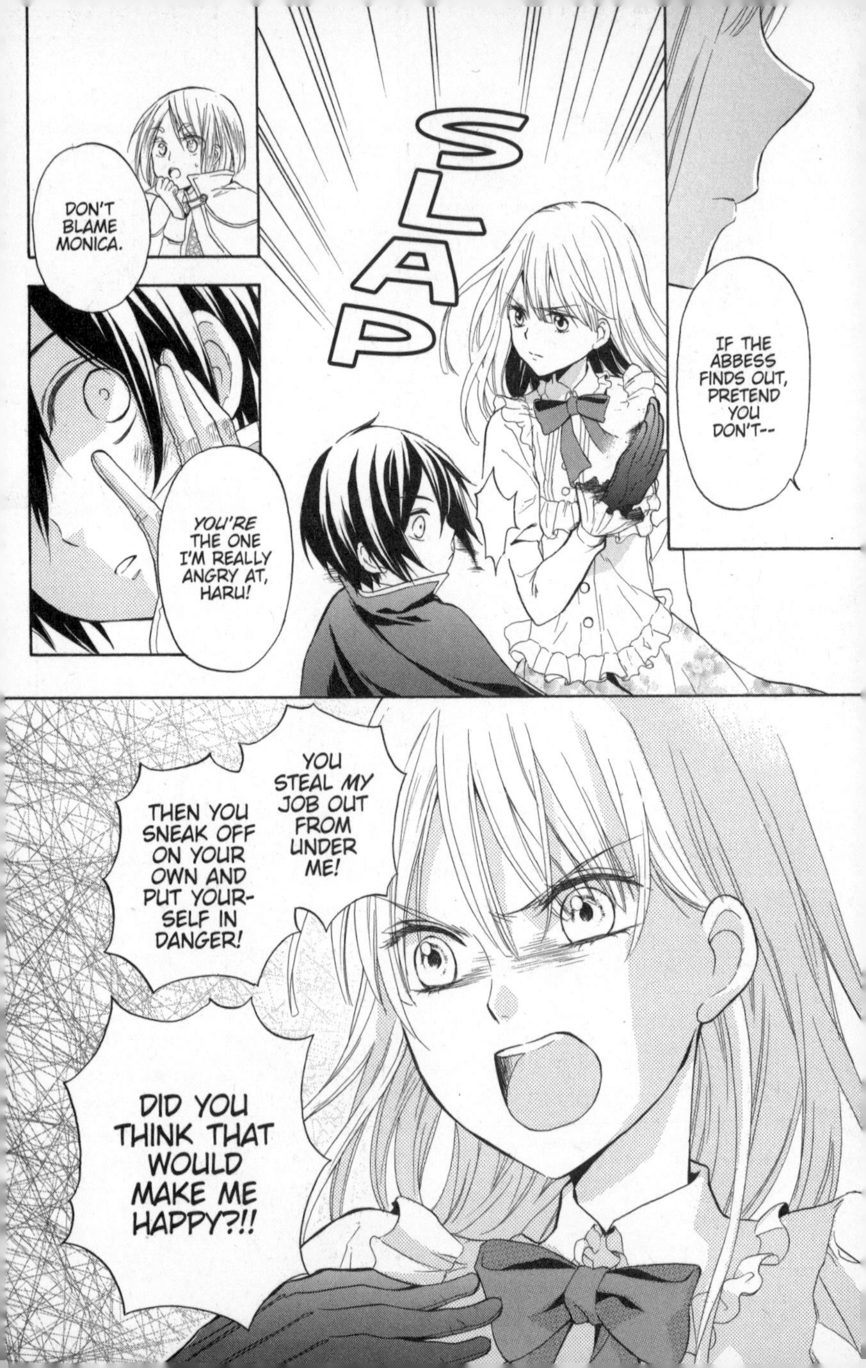
IF THE ABBESS FINDS OUT, PRETEND YOU DON'T--
DON'T BLAME MONICA.
SLAP
YOU'RE THE ONE I'M REALLY ANGRY AT, HARU!
YOU STEAL *MY* JOB OUT FROM UNDER ME!
THEN YOU SNEAK OFF ON YOUR OWN AND PUT YOUR-SELF IN DANGER!
DID YOU THINK THAT WOULD MAKE ME HAPPY?!!

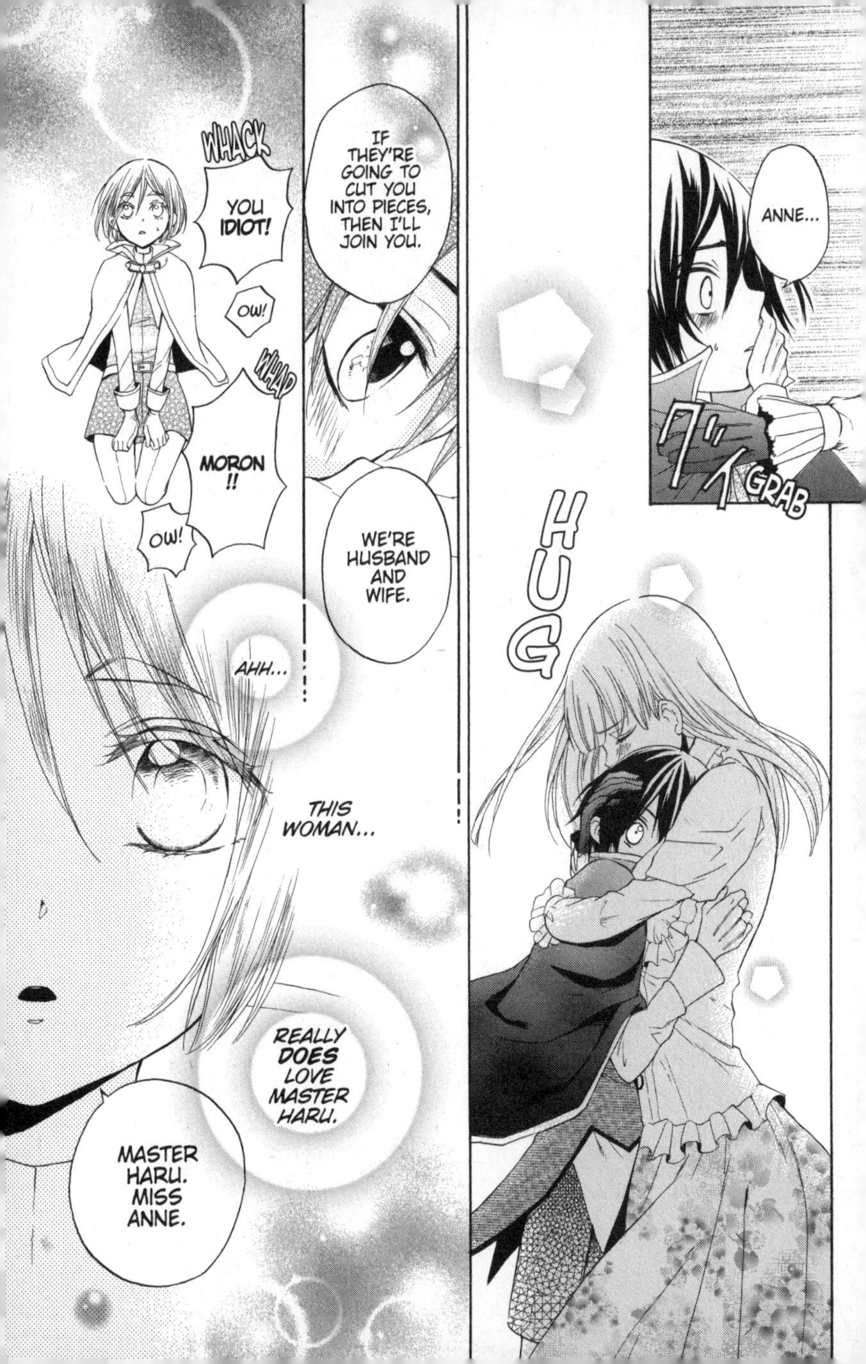
ANNE...
グイ
GRAB
HUG
IF THEY'RE GOING TO CUT YOU INTO PIECES, THEN I'LL JOIN YOU.
WE'RE HUSBAND AND WIFE.
WHACK
YOU IDIOT!
OW!
WHAP
MORON !!
OW!
AHH...
THIS WOMAN...
REALLY DOES LOVE MASTER HARU.
MASTER HARU. MISS ANNE.

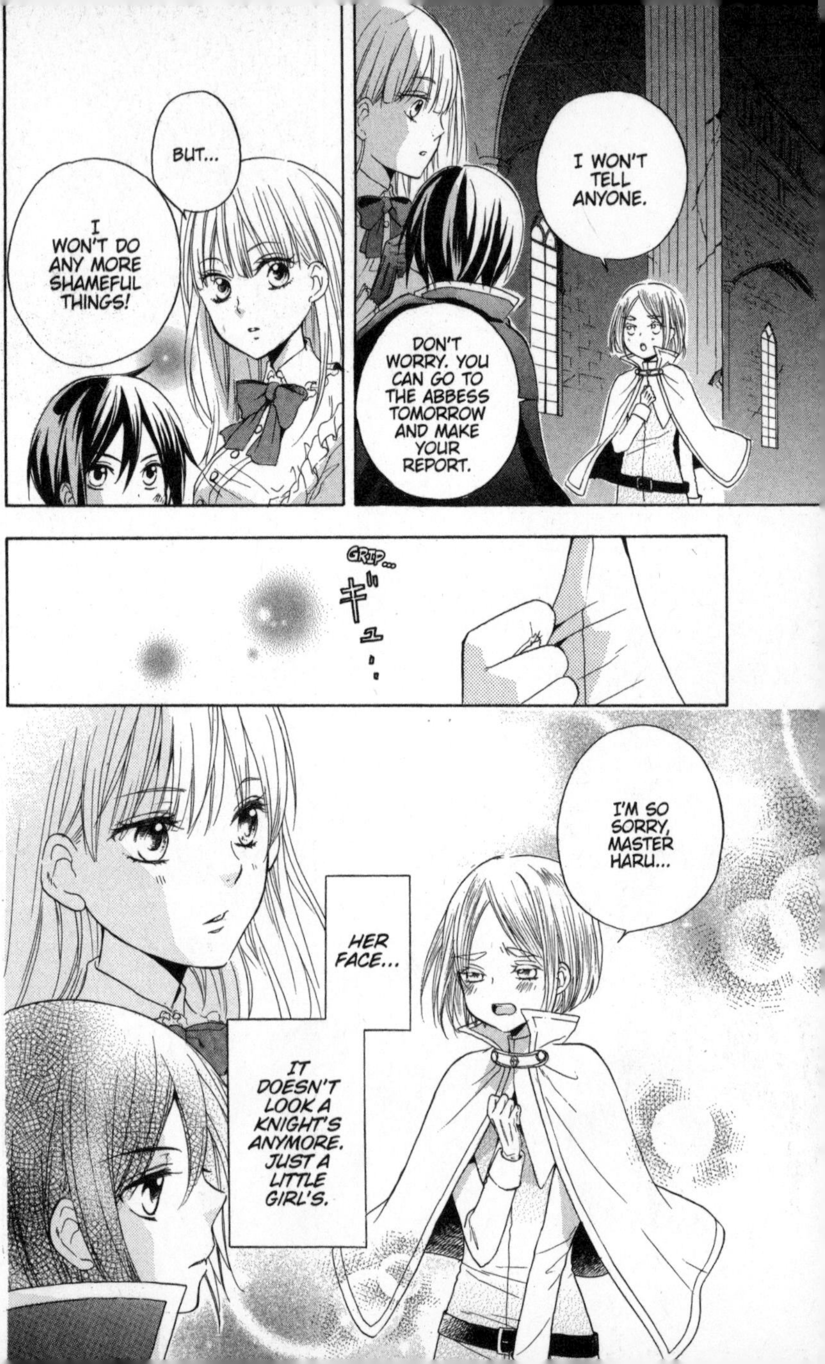
I WON'T TELL ANYONE.
DON'T WORRY. YOU CAN GO TO THE ABBESS TOMORROW AND MAKE YOUR REPORT.
BUT...
I WON'T DO ANY MORE SHAMEFUL THINGS!
GRIP...
ギュ...
I'M SO SORRY, MASTER HARU...
HER FACE...
IT DOESN'T LOOK A KNIGHT'S ANYMORE. JUST A LITTLE GIRL'S.

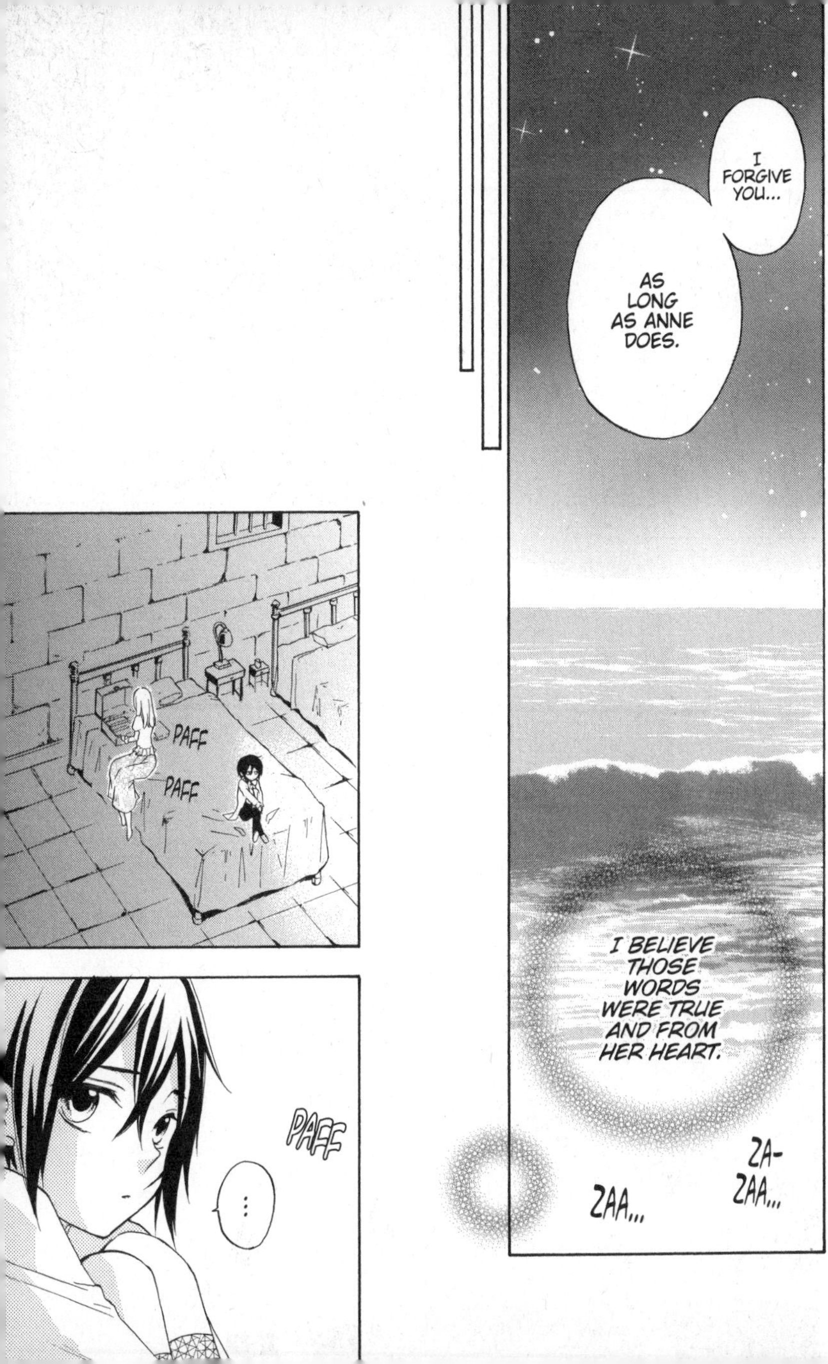
I FORGIVE YOU...
AS LONG AS ANNE DOES.
I BELIEVE THOSE WORDS WERE TRUE AND FROM HER HEART.
ZA-ZAA...
ZAA...
PAFF
PAFF
PAFF
...

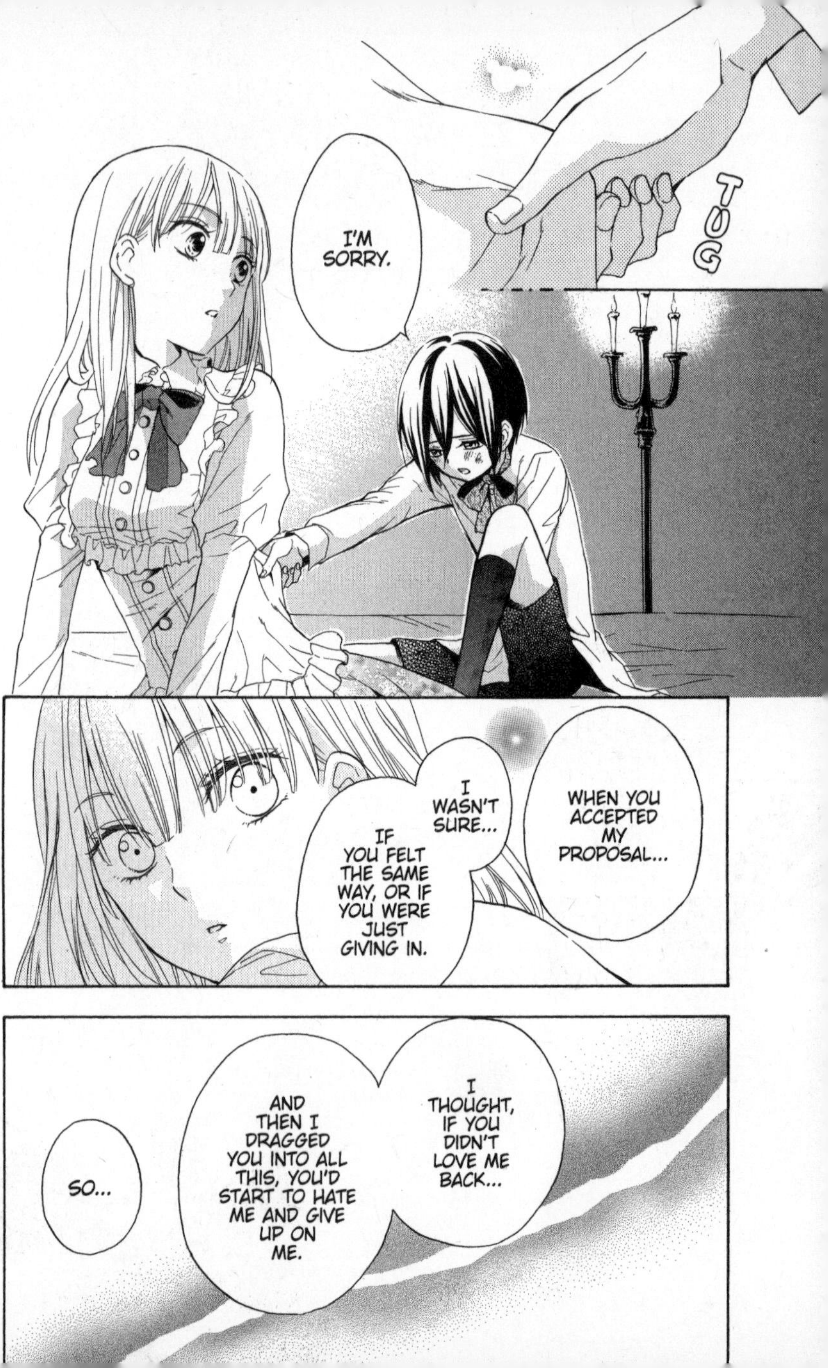
TUG
I'M SORRY.
WHEN YOU ACCEPTED MY PROPOSAL...
I WASN'T SURE...
IF YOU FELT THE SAME WAY, OR IF YOU WERE JUST GIVING IN.
I THOUGHT, IF YOU DIDN'T LOVE ME BACK...
AND THEN I DRAGGED YOU INTO ALL THIS, YOU'D START TO HATE ME AND GIVE UP ON ME.
SO...

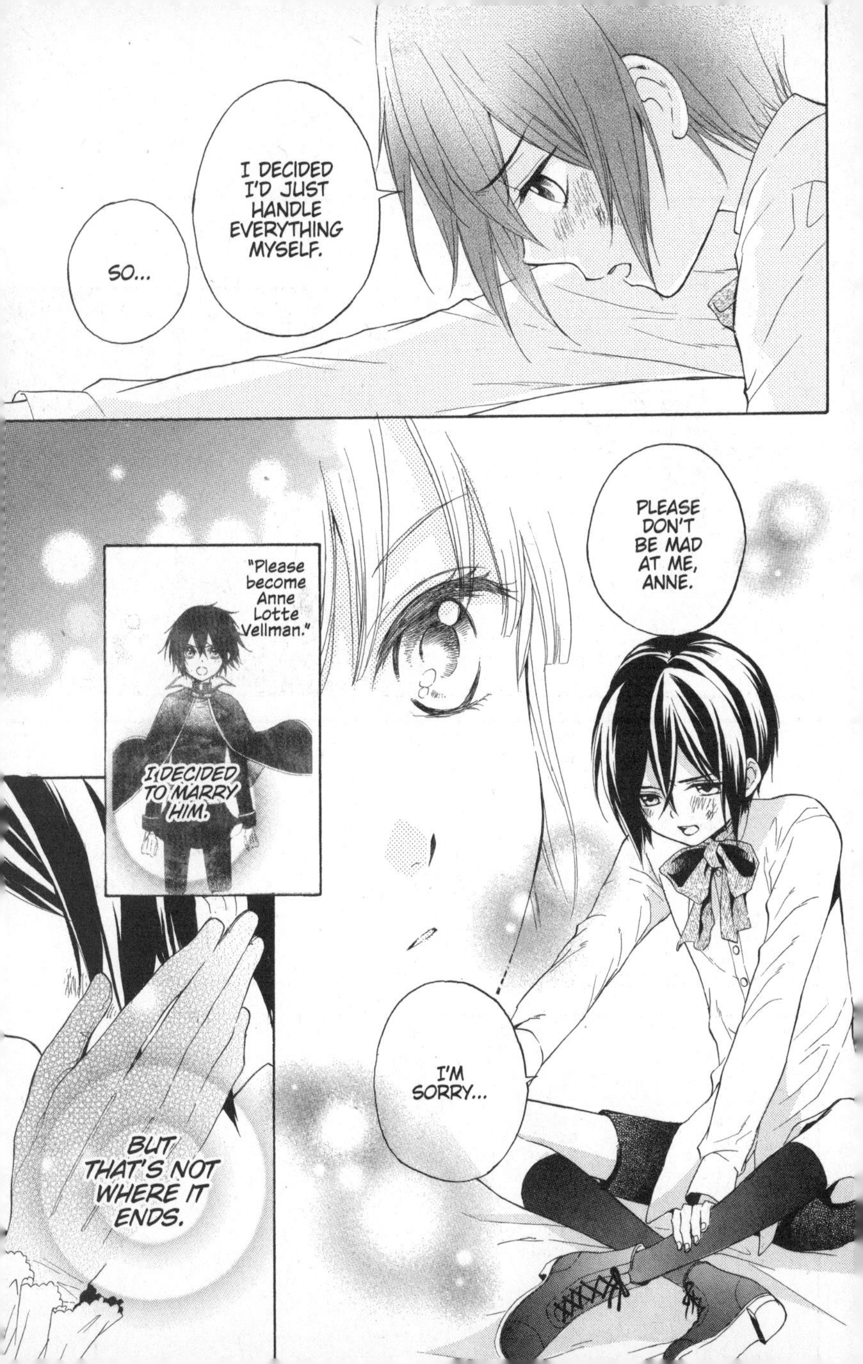
I DECIDED I'D JUST HANDLE EVERYTHING MYSELF.
SO...
PLEASE DON'T BE MAD AT ME, ANNE.
"Please become Anne Lotte Vellman."
I DECIDED TO MARRY HIM.
I'M SORRY...
BUT THAT'S NOT WHERE IT ENDS.

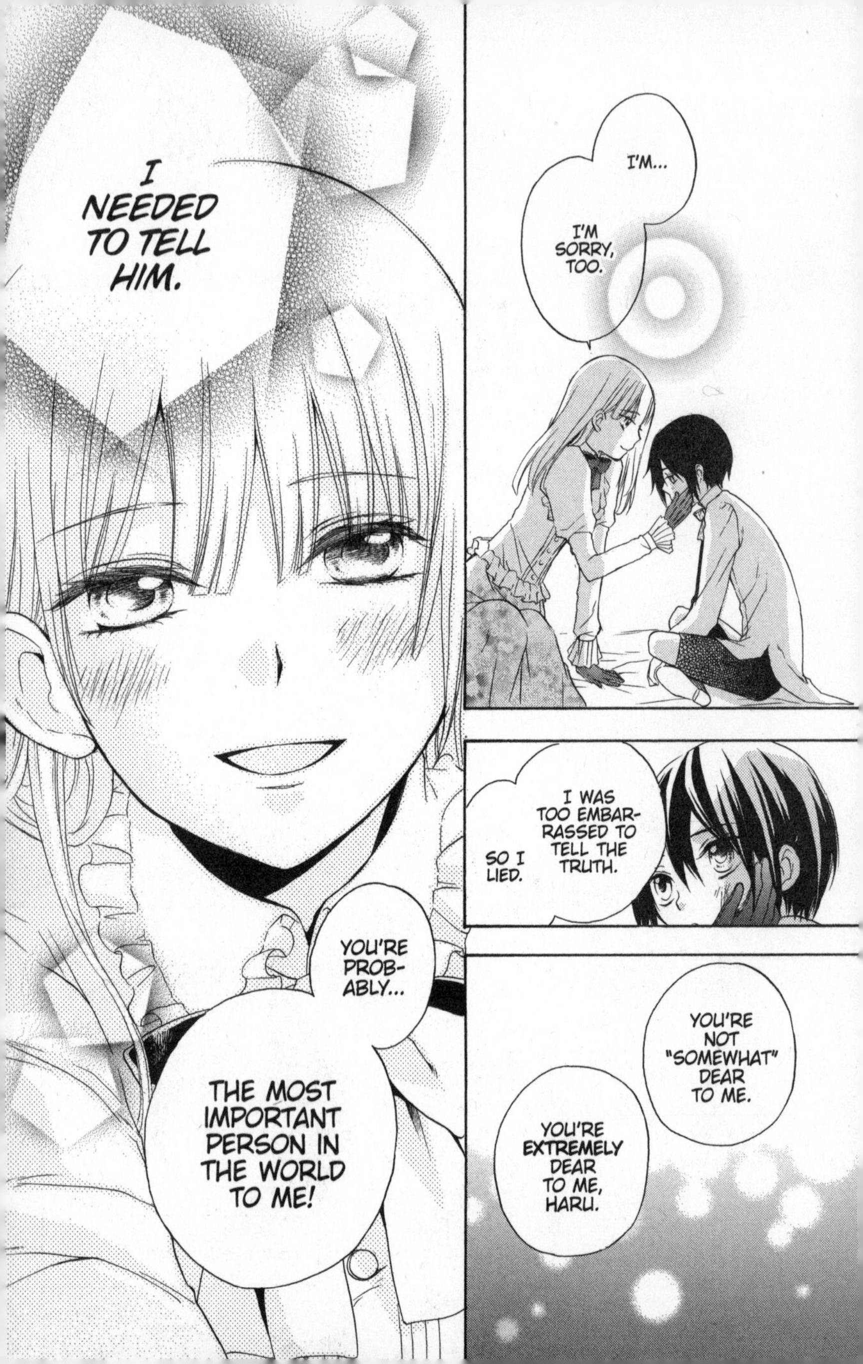
I'M...
I'M SORRY, TOO.
I WAS TOO EMBARRASSED TO TELL THE TRUTH.
SO I LIED.
YOU'RE NOT "SOMEWHAT" DEAR TO ME.
YOU'RE EXTREMELY DEAR TO ME, HARU.
I NEEDED TO TELL HIM.
YOU'RE PROBABLY...
THE MOST IMPORTANT PERSON IN THE WORLD TO ME!

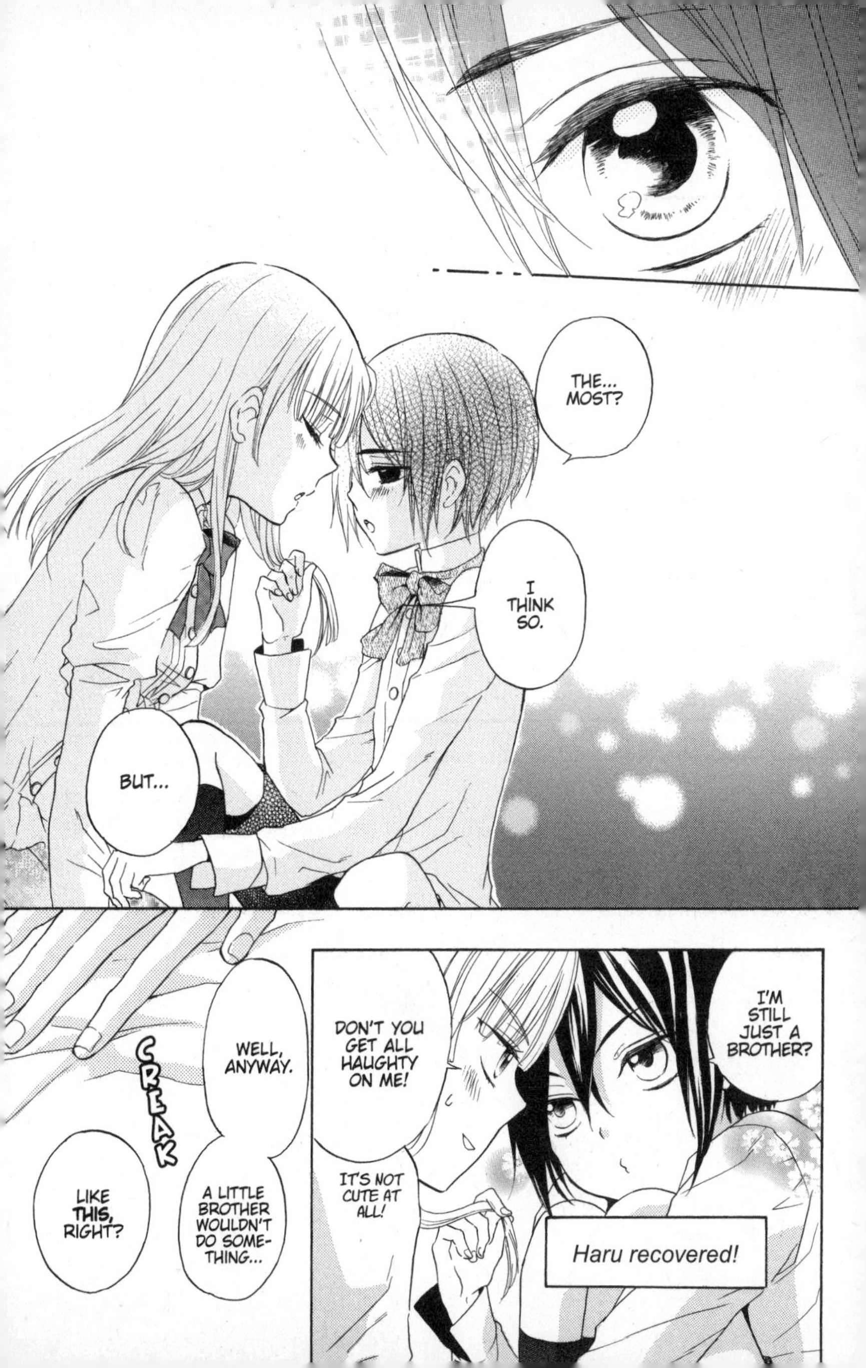
THE... MOST?
I THINK SO.
BUT...
I'M STILL JUST A BROTHER?
DON'T YOU GET ALL HAUGHTY ON ME!
IT'S NOT CUTE AT ALL!
Haru recovered!
WELL, ANYWAY.
CREAK
A LITTLE BROTHER WOULDN'T DO SOME-THING...
LIKE **THIS**, RIGHT?

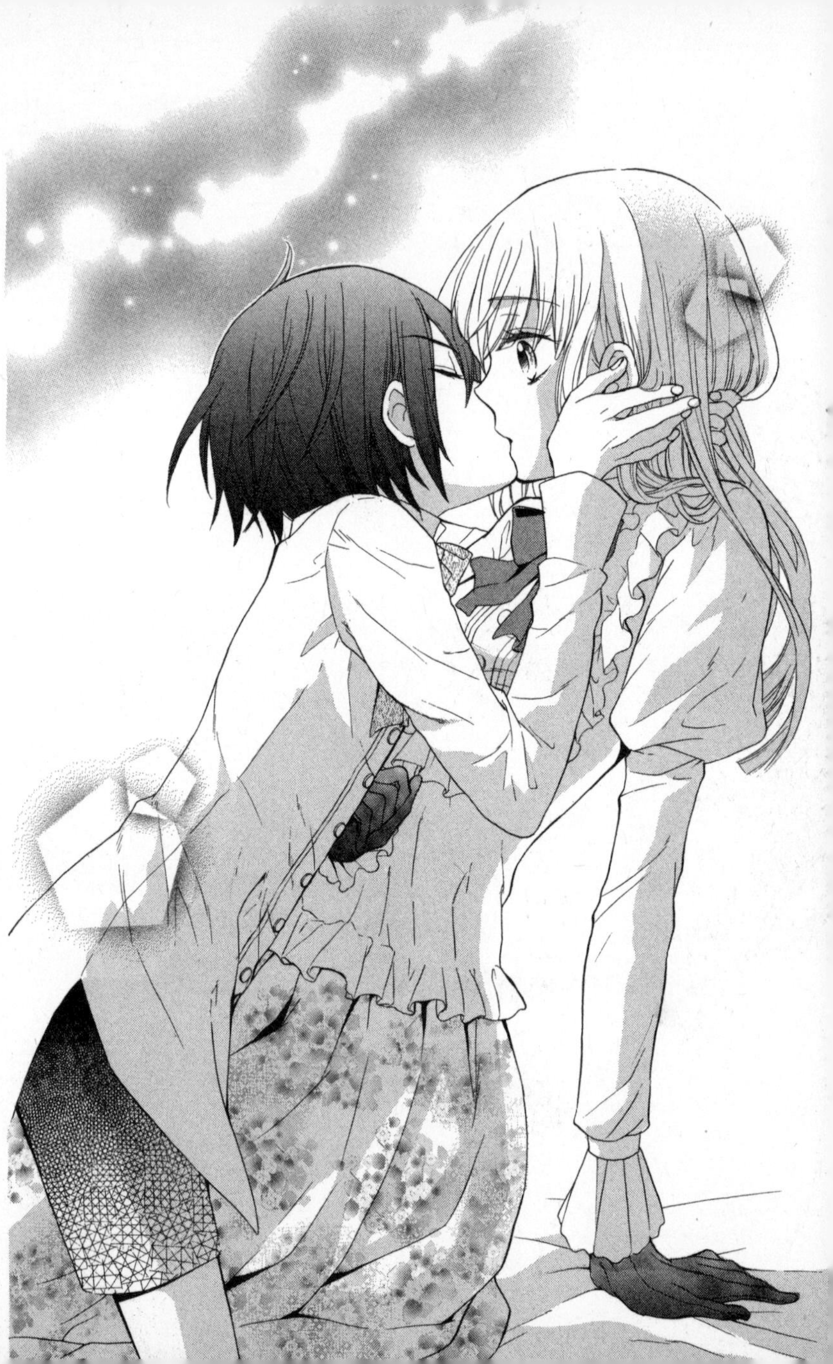

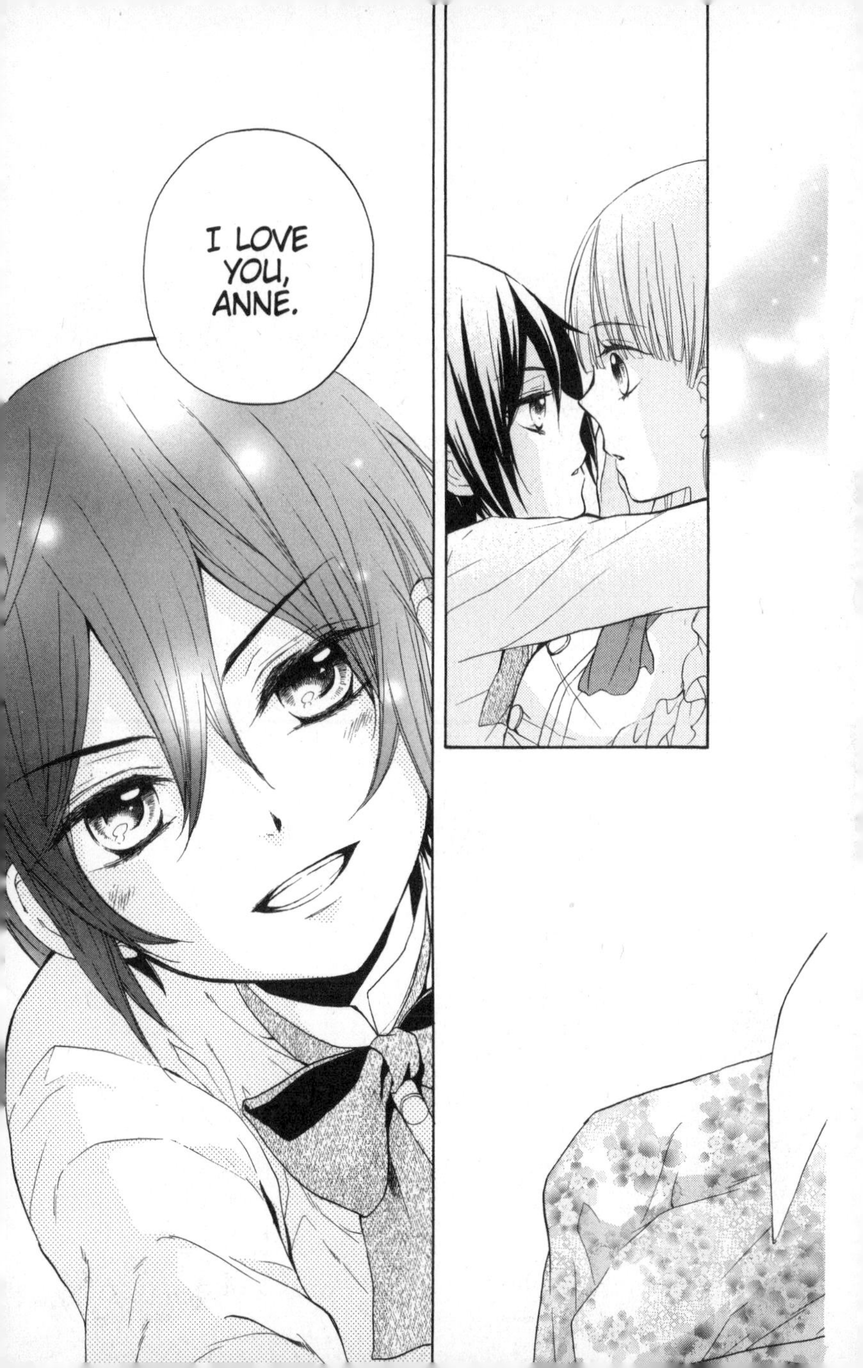
I LOVE YOU, ANNE.

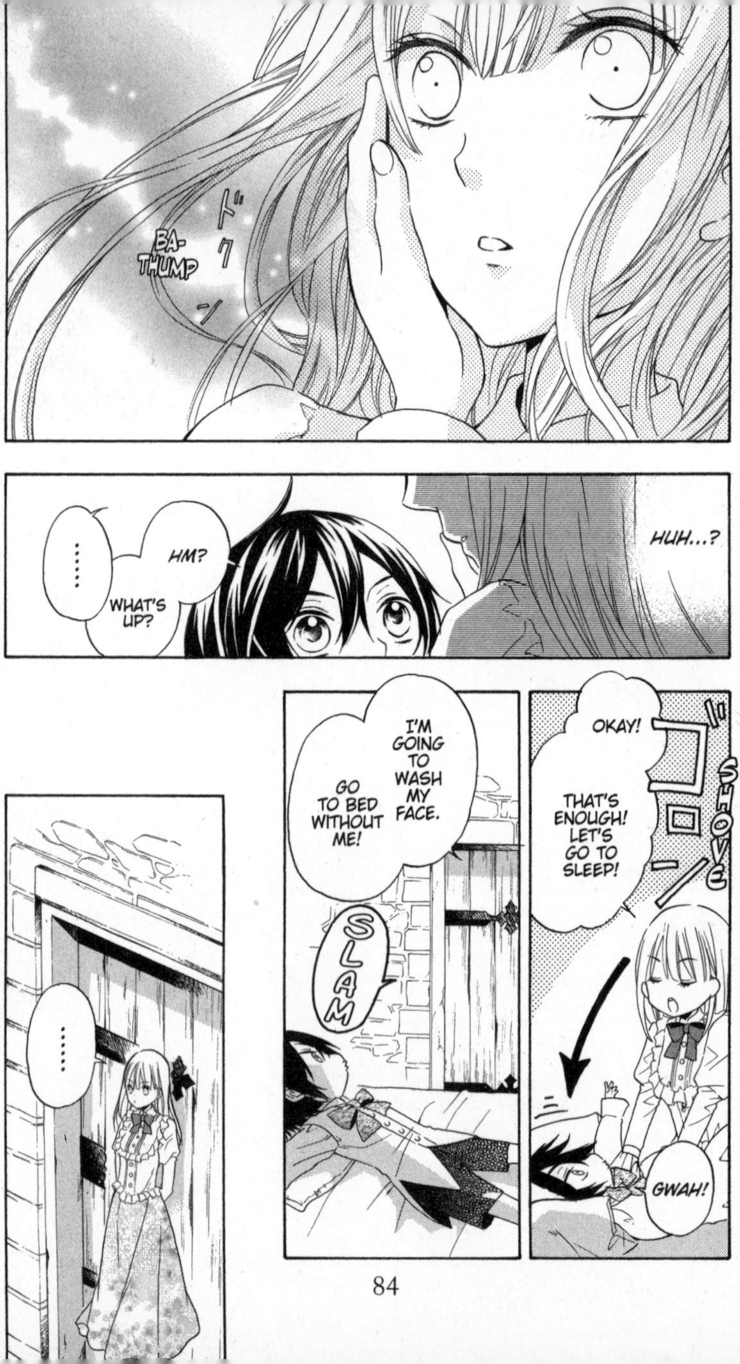
BA-THUMP
ドクン
HUH...?
HM? WHAT'S UP?
......
OKAY! THAT'S ENOUGH! LET'S GO TO SLEEP!
ゴローン
SHOVE
GWAH!
I'M GOING TO WASH MY FACE.
GO TO BED WITHOUT ME!
SLAM
......

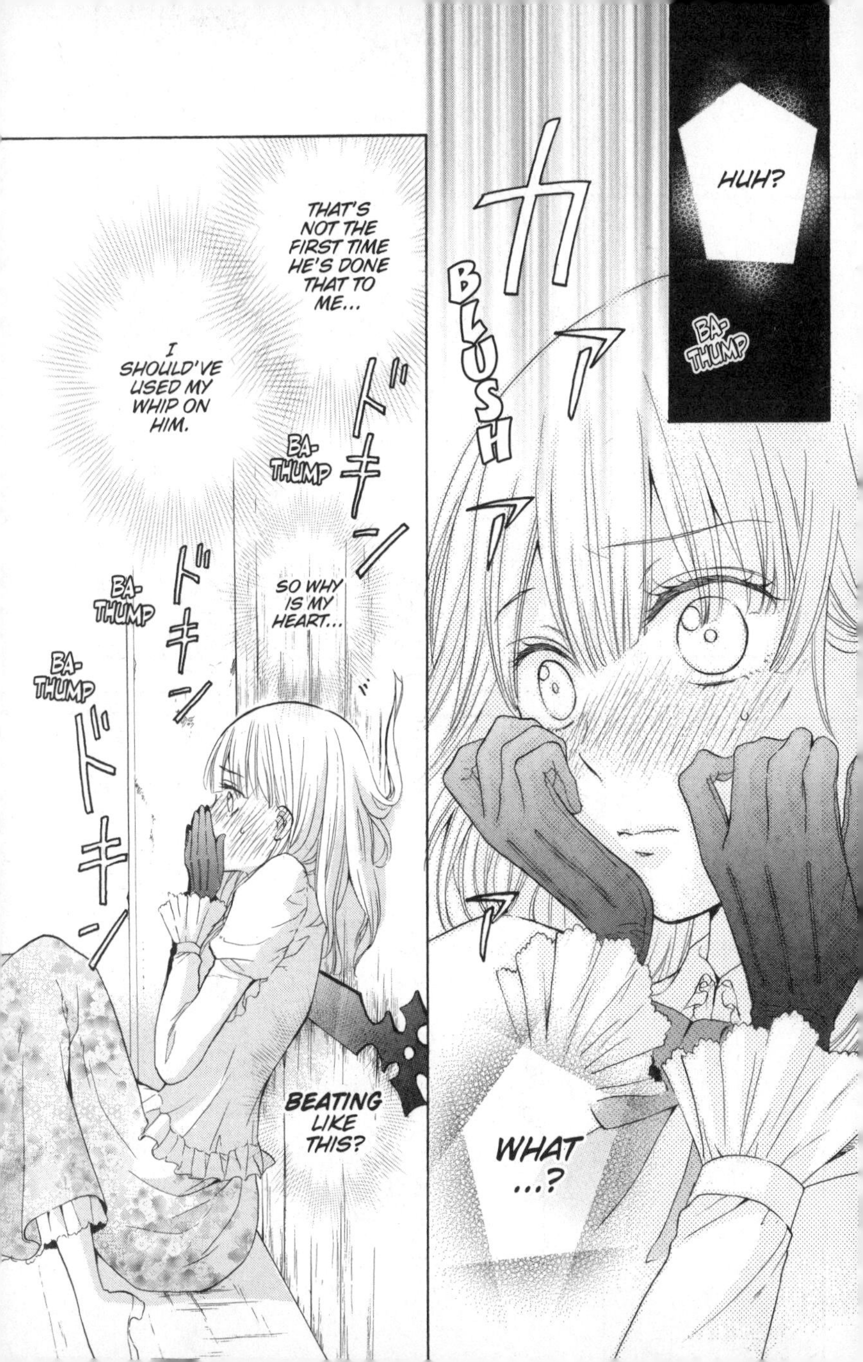
HUH?
BA-THUMP
カアアア
BLUSH
WHAT ...?
THAT'S NOT THE FIRST TIME HE'S DONE THAT TO ME...
I SHOULD'VE USED MY WHIP ON HIM.
ドキーン
BA-THUMP
ドキーン
BA-THUMP
SO WHY IS MY HEART...
ドキーン
BA-THUMP
BEATING LIKE THIS?

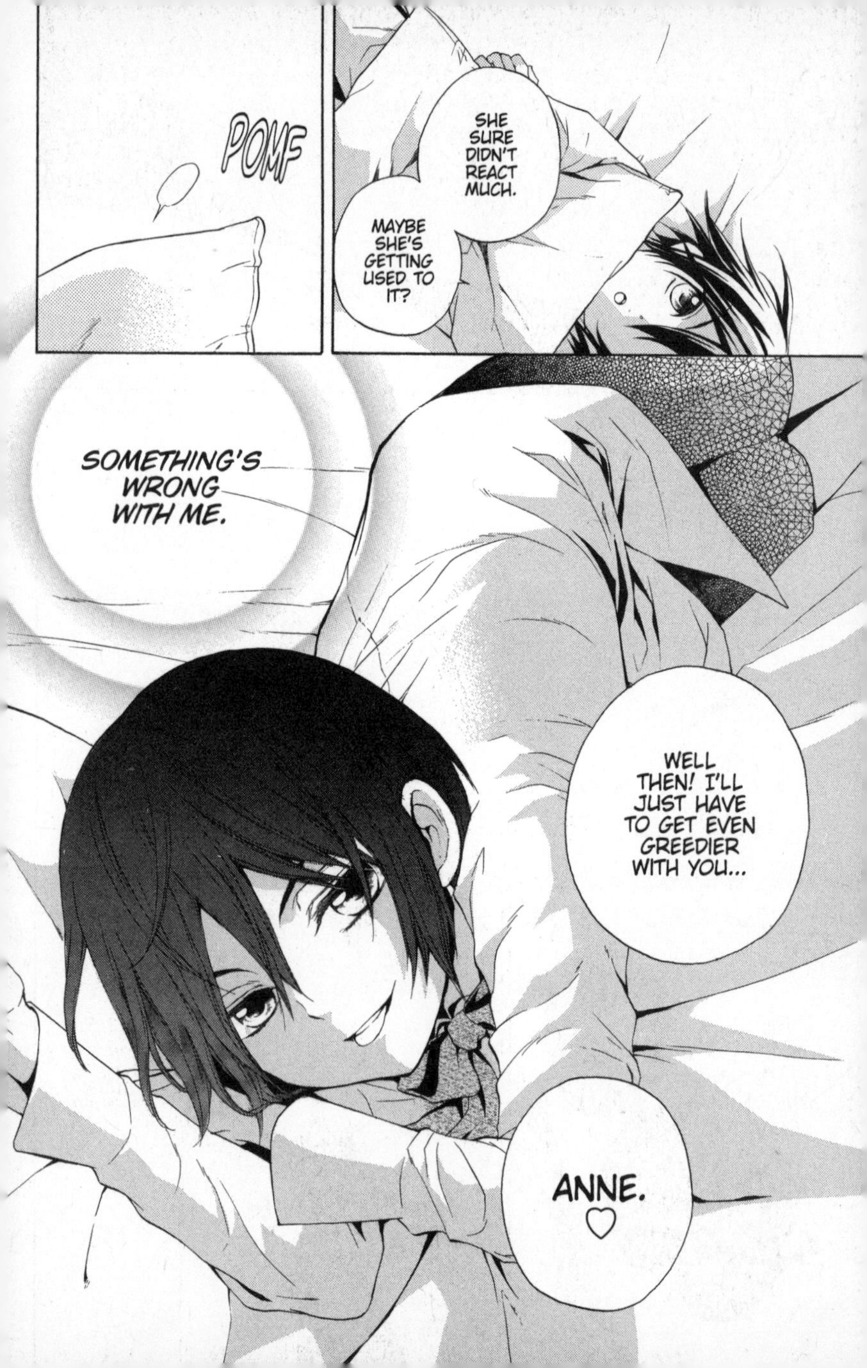
SHE SURE DIDN'T REACT MUCH.
MAYBE SHE'S GETTING USED TO IT?
POMF
SOMETHING'S WRONG WITH ME.
WELL THEN! I'LL JUST HAVE TO GET EVEN GREEDIER WITH YOU...
ANNE. ♡

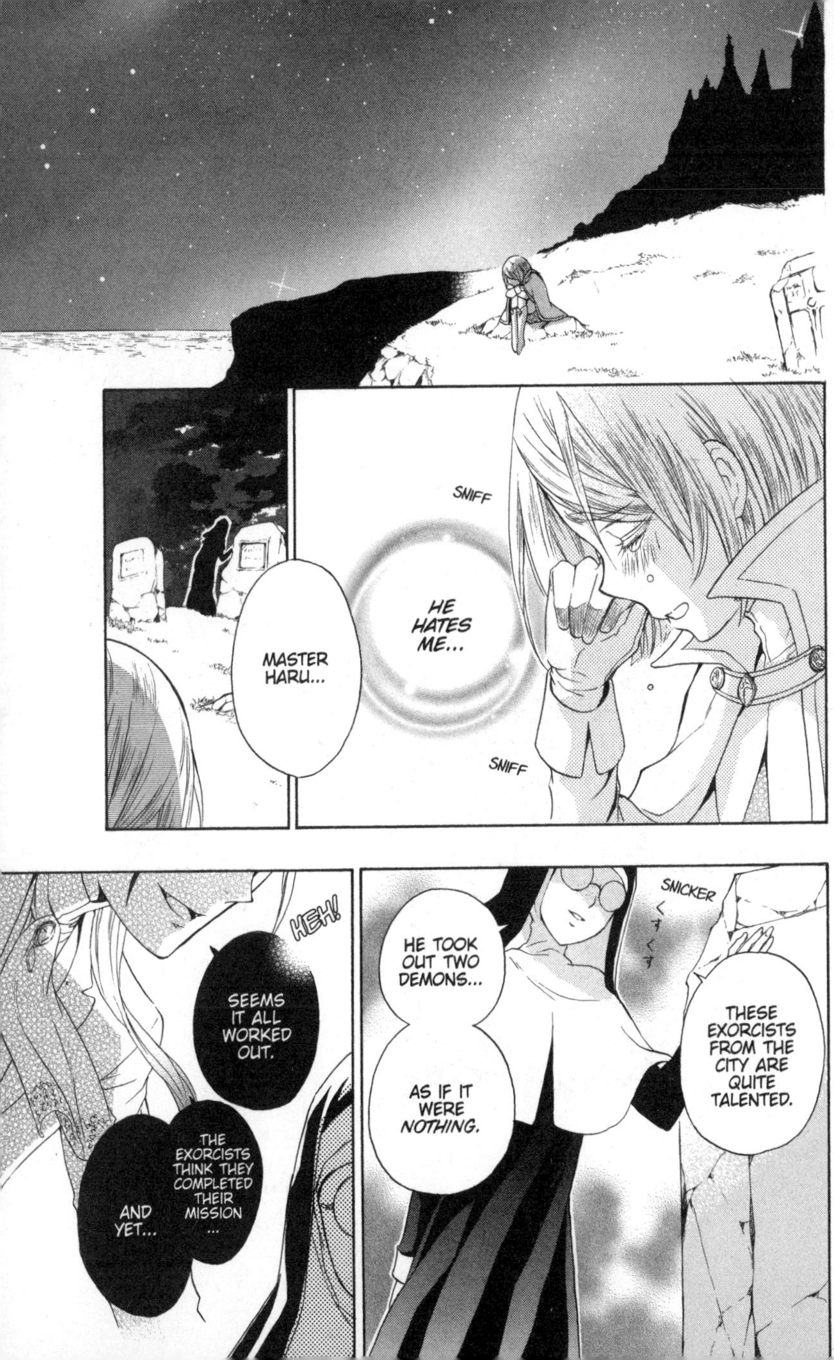
SNIFF
HE HATES ME...
SNIFF
MASTER HARU...
SNICKER
くすくす
THESE EXORCISTS FROM THE CITY ARE QUITE TALENTED.
HE TOOK OUT TWO DEMONS...
AS IF IT WERE NOTHING.
HEH!
SEEMS IT ALL WORKED OUT.
THE EXORCISTS THINK THEY COMPLETED THEIR MISSION...
AND YET...

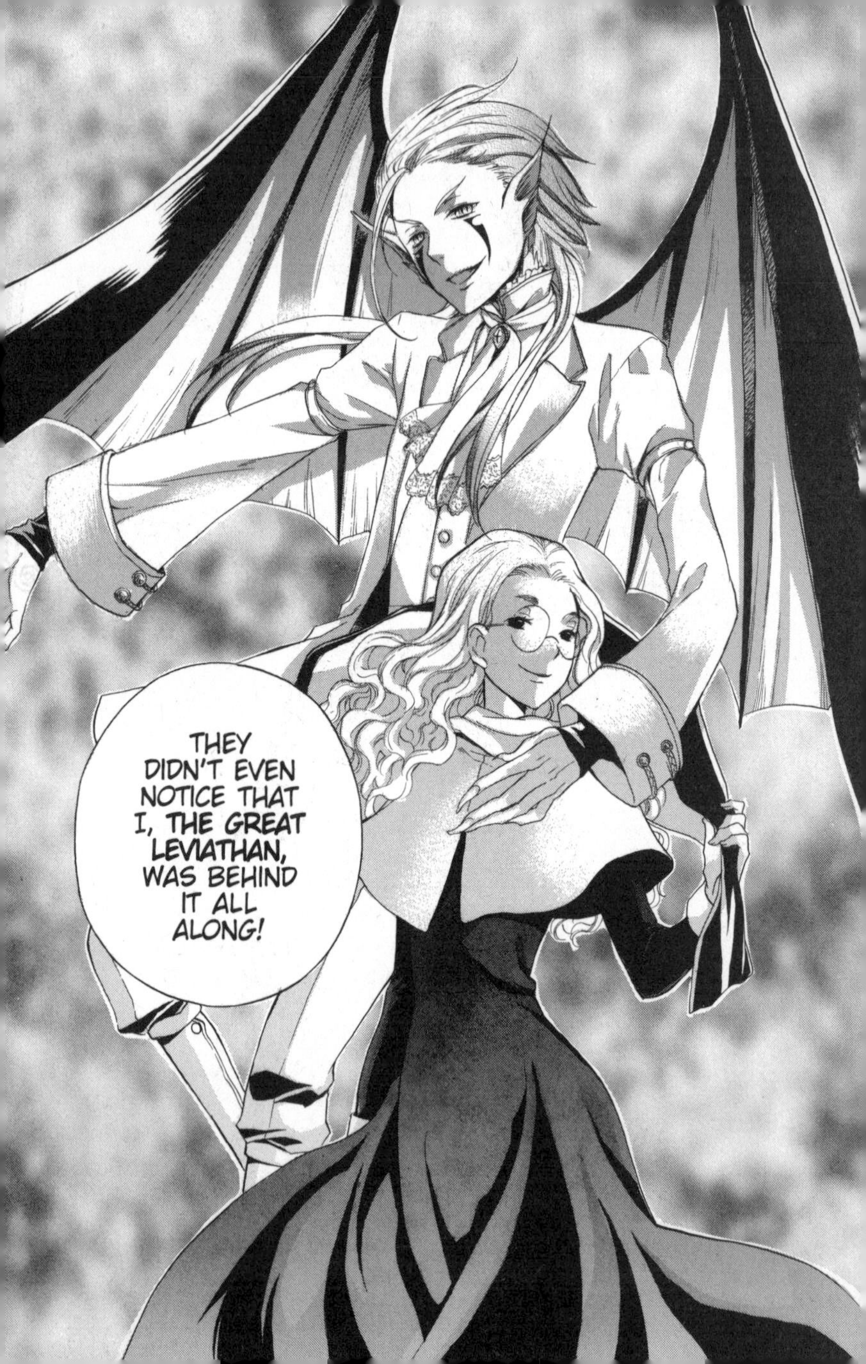
THEY DIDN'T EVEN NOTICE THAT I, THE GREAT LEVIATHAN, WAS BEHIND IT ALL ALONG!

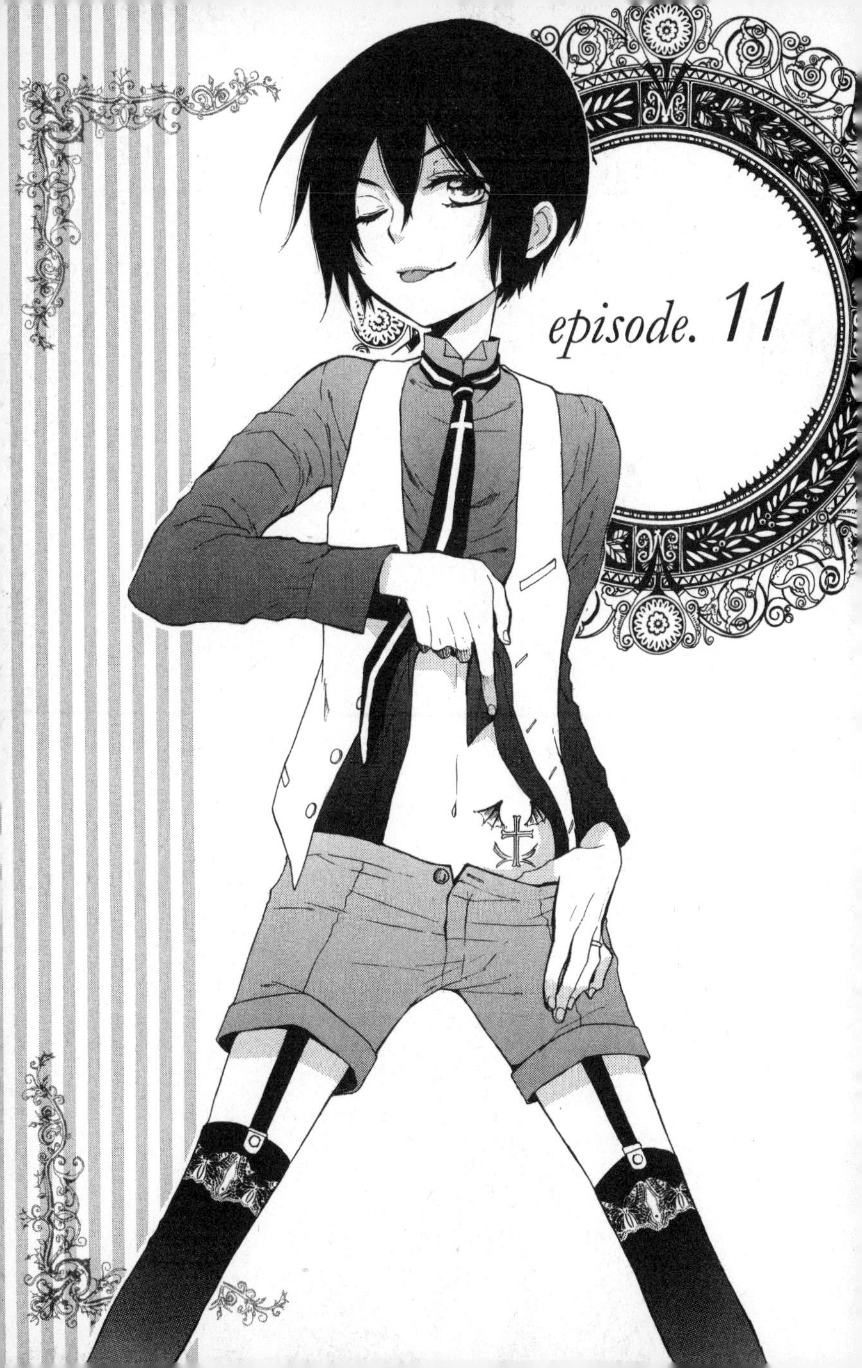
episode. 11

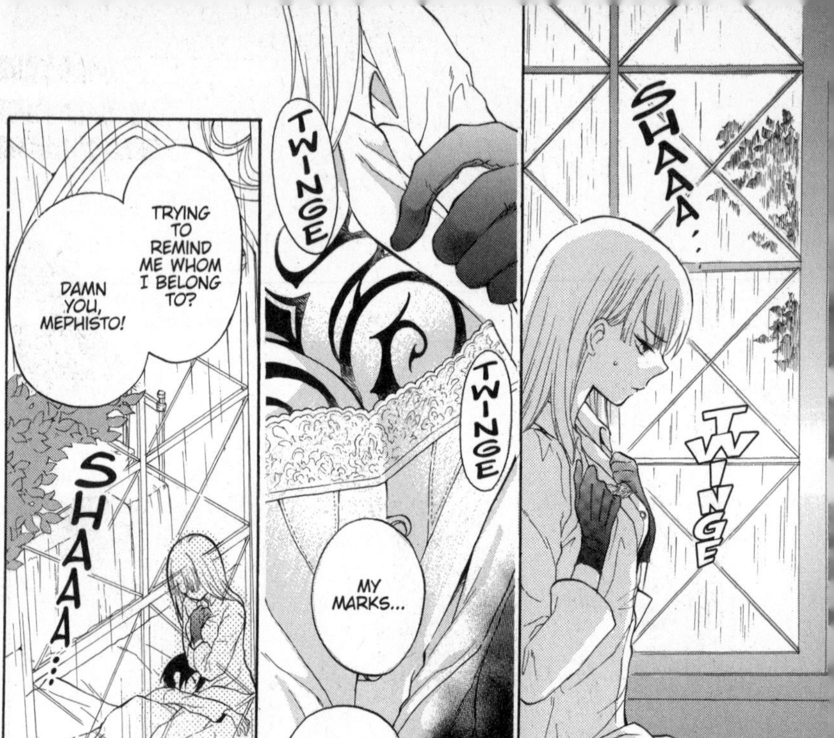
SHAAA..
TWINGE
TWINGE
TWINGE
MY MARKS...
THEY'RE GROWING AGAIN.
TRYING TO REMIND ME WHOM I BELONG TO?
DAMN YOU, MEPHISTO!
SHAAA...

Monica Vellman (12)

Weapon: Exorcist's rapier
Armor: Exorcist's cape (white)

A young exorcist who's very serious about her work. Her thick eyebrows give her a charming appearance. At first, I thought about making her character an older girl around Anne's age, but I decided it would be cute if Anne's rival was a devoted, young girl. She's clumsy and has low self-esteem, but she has the most common sense of anyone in the series.

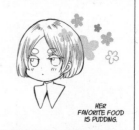

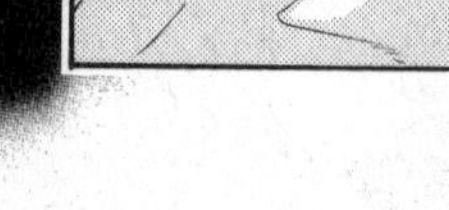
HER FAVORITE FOOD IS PUDDING.

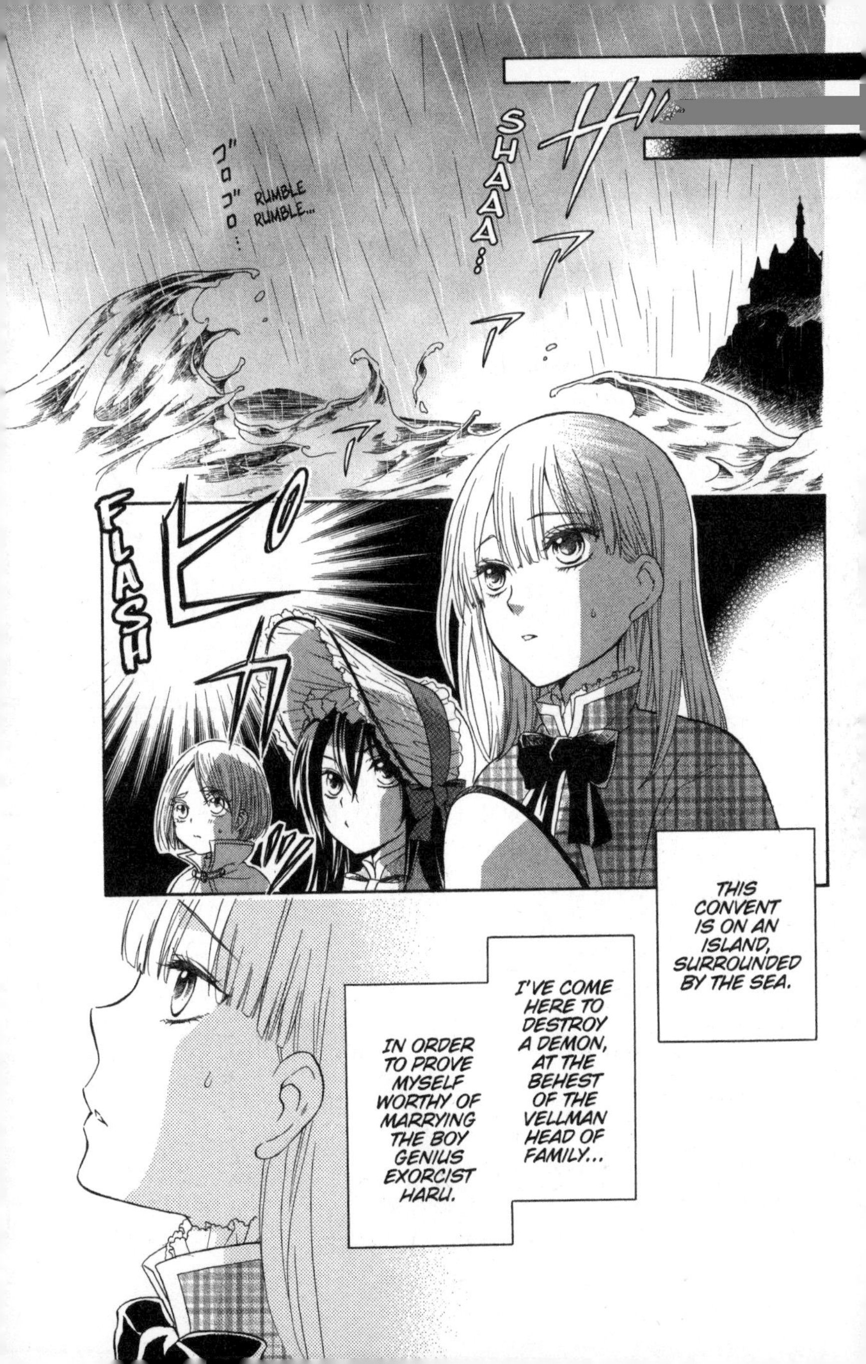
SHAAAA...
RUMBLE RUMBLE...
FLASH
THIS CONVENT IS ON AN ISLAND, SURROUNDED BY THE SEA.
I'VE COME HERE TO DESTROY A DEMON, AT THE BEHEST OF THE VELLMAN HEAD OF FAMILY...
IN ORDER TO PROVE MYSELF WORTHY OF MARRYING THE BOY GENIUS EXORCIST HARU.

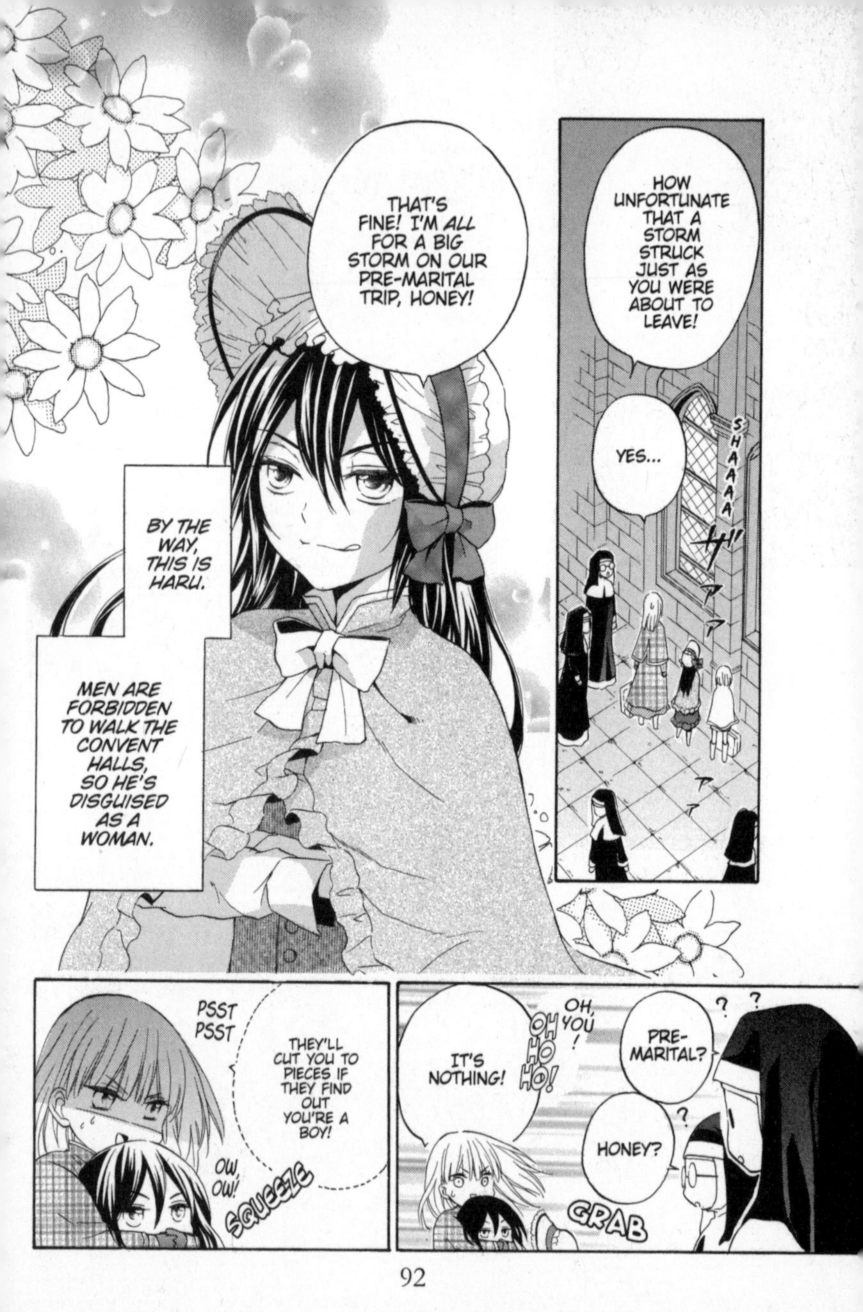

HOW UNFORTUNATE THAT A STORM STRUCK JUST AS YOU WERE ABOUT TO LEAVE!
YES...
SHAAAAA
THAT'S FINE! I'M *ALL* FOR A BIG STORM ON OUR PRE-MARITAL TRIP, HONEY!
BY THE WAY, THIS IS HARU.
MEN ARE FORBIDDEN TO WALK THE CONVENT HALLS, SO HE'S DISGUISED AS A WOMAN.
PRE-MARITAL?
HONEY?
OH, YOU!
OH HO HO!
IT'S NOTHING!
GRAB
THEY'LL CUT YOU TO PIECES IF THEY FIND OUT YOU'RE A BOY!
PSST PSST
OW, OW!
SQUEEZE

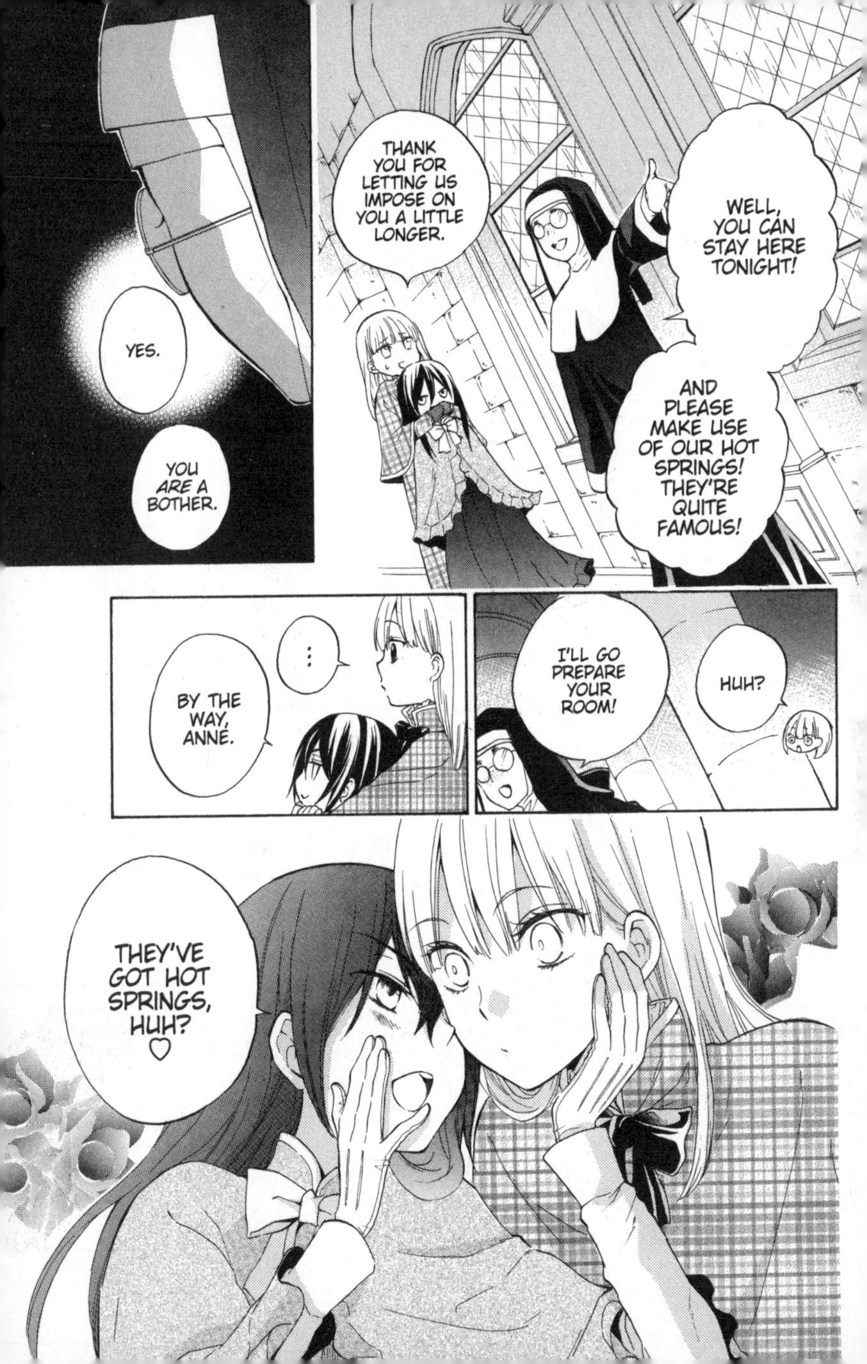
WELL, YOU CAN STAY HERE TONIGHT!
THANK YOU FOR LETTING US IMPOSE ON YOU A LITTLE LONGER.
AND PLEASE MAKE USE OF OUR HOT SPRINGS! THEY'RE QUITE FAMOUS!
YES.
YOU *ARE* A BOTHER.
HUH?
I'LL GO PREPARE YOUR ROOM!
...
BY THE WAY, ANNE.
THEY'VE GOT HOT SPRINGS, HUH? ♡

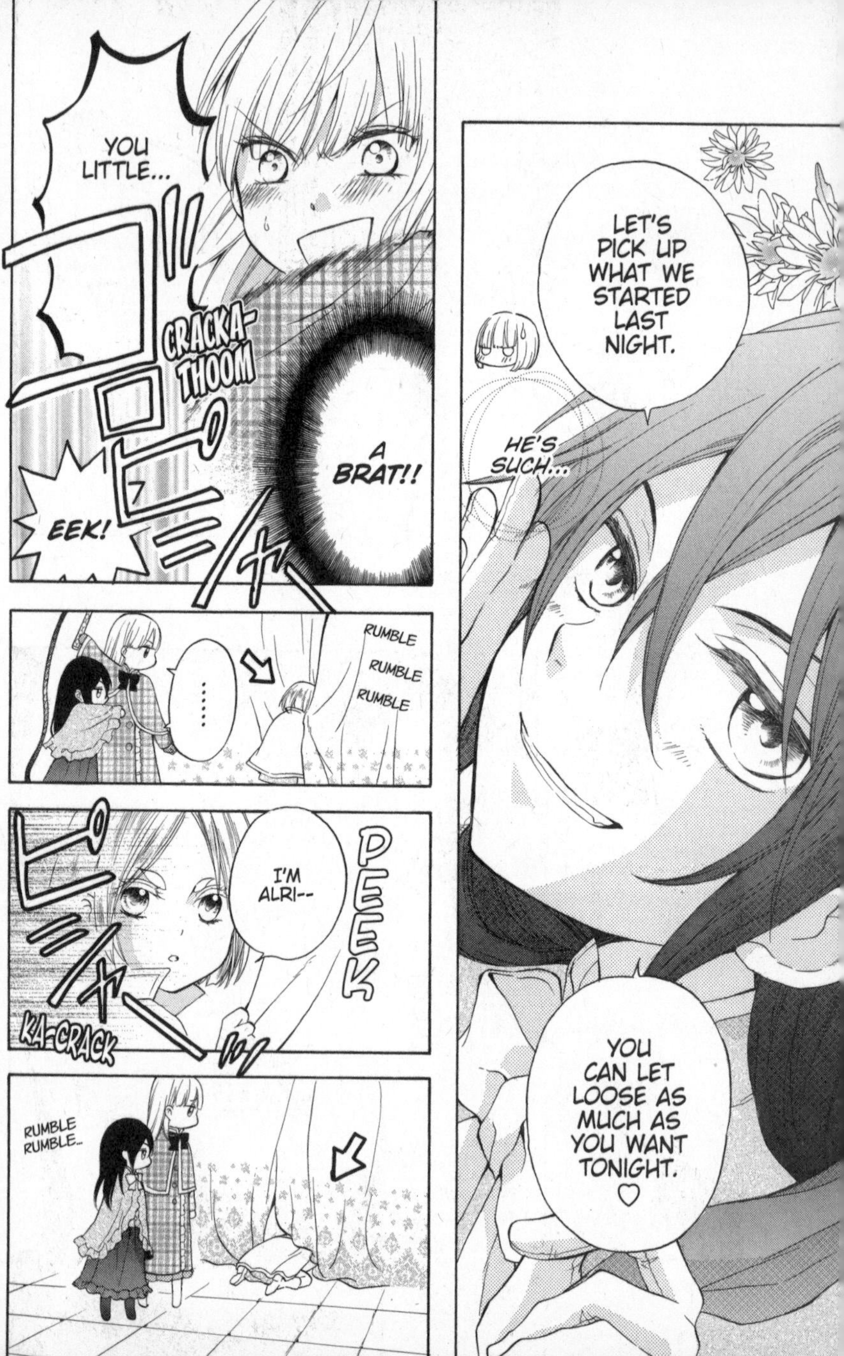
LET'S PICK UP WHAT WE STARTED LAST NIGHT.
HE'S SUCH...
YOU CAN LET LOOSE AS MUCH AS YOU WANT TONIGHT. ♡
YOU LITTLE...
CRACKA-THOOM
A BRAT!!
EEK!
......
RUMBLE RUMBLE RUMBLE
PEEK
I'M ALRI--
KA-CRACK
RUMBLE RUMBLE...

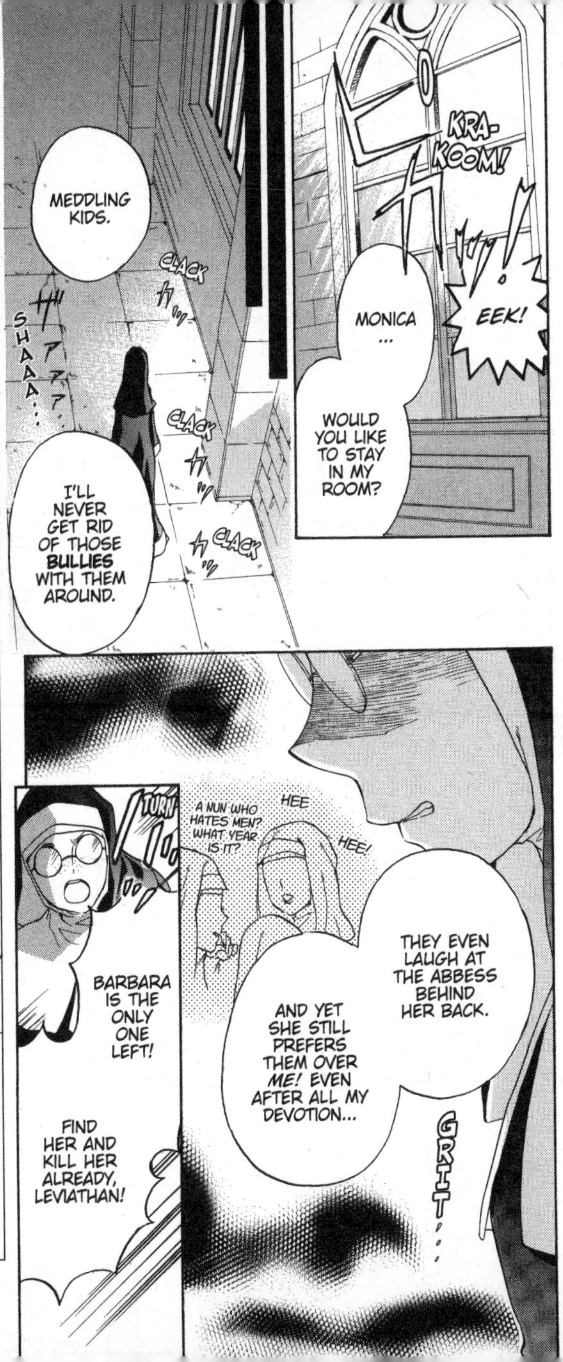
KRA-KOOM!
EEK!
MONICA...
WOULD YOU LIKE TO STAY IN MY ROOM?
MEDDLING KIDS.
CLACK
SHAAA...
CLACK
I'LL NEVER GET RID OF THOSE **BULLIES** WITH THEM AROUND.
CLACK
THEY EVEN LAUGH AT THE ABBESS BEHIND HER BACK.
AND YET SHE STILL PREFERS THEM OVER *ME!* EVEN AFTER ALL MY DEVOTION...
GRIT...
TURN
A NUN WHO HATES MEN? WHAT YEAR IS IT?
HEE
HEE!
BARBARA IS THE ONLY ONE LEFT!
FIND HER AND KILL HER ALREADY, LEVIATHAN!

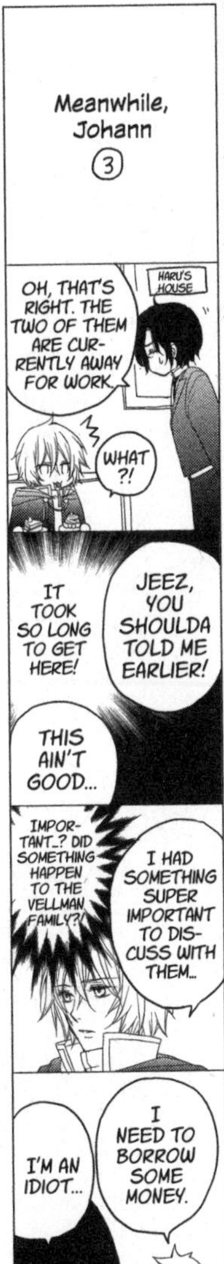
Meanwhile, Johann ③
HARU'S HOUSE
OH, THAT'S RIGHT. THE TWO OF THEM ARE CURRENTLY AWAY FOR WORK.
WHAT?!
JEEZ, YOU SHOULDA TOLD ME EARLIER!
IT TOOK SO LONG TO GET HERE!
THIS AIN'T GOOD...
I HAD SOMETHING SUPER IMPORTANT TO DISCUSS WITH THEM...
IMPORTANT..? DID SOMETHING HAPPEN TO THE VELLMAN FAMILY?!
I NEED TO BORROW SOME MONEY.
I'M AN IDIOT...

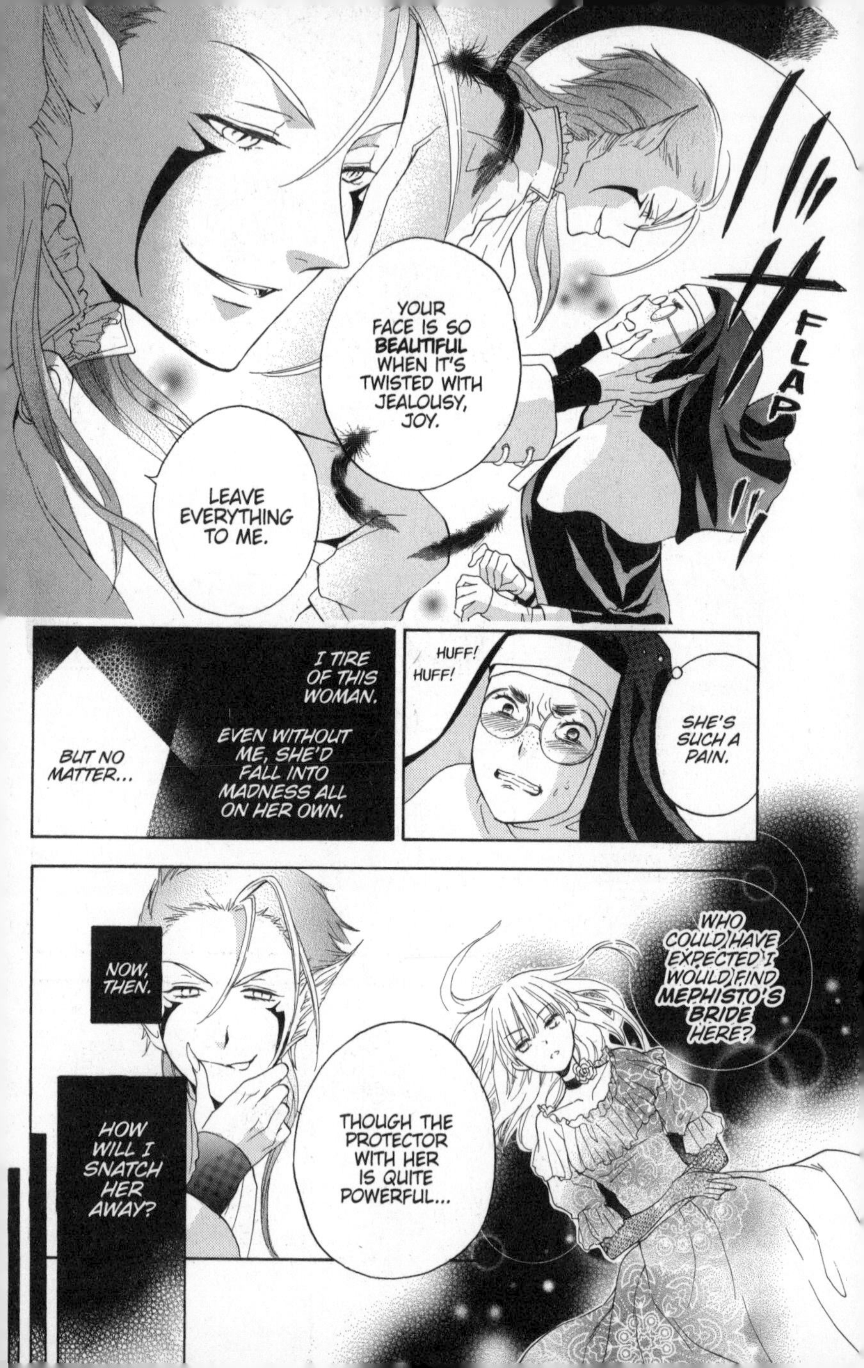
FLAP
YOUR FACE IS SO **BEAUTIFUL** WHEN IT'S TWISTED WITH JEALOUSY, JOY.
LEAVE EVERYTHING TO ME.
HUFF! HUFF!
SHE'S SUCH A PAIN.
I TIRE OF THIS WOMAN.
EVEN WITHOUT ME, SHE'D FALL INTO MADNESS ALL ON HER OWN.
BUT NO MATTER...
WHO COULD HAVE EXPECTED I WOULD FIND MEPHISTO'S BRIDE HERE?
THOUGH THE PROTECTOR WITH HER IS QUITE POWERFUL...
NOW, THEN.
HOW WILL I SNATCH HER AWAY?

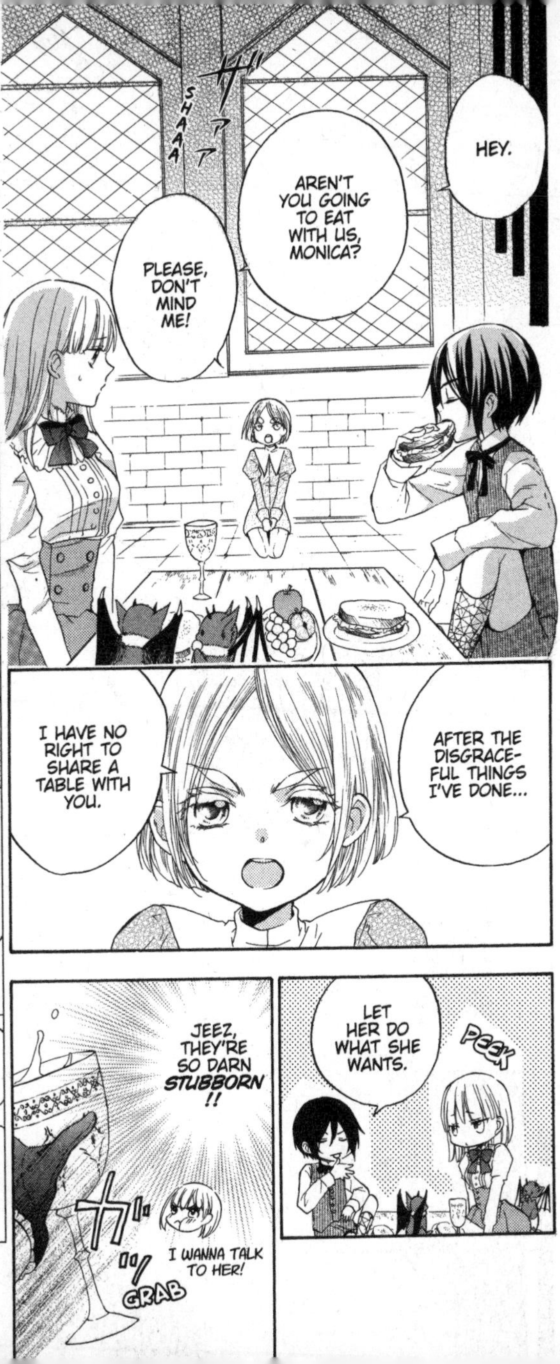
HEY.
SHAAA
AREN'T YOU GOING TO EAT WITH US, MONICA?
PLEASE, DON'T MIND ME!
AFTER THE DISGRACEFUL THINGS I'VE DONE...
I HAVE NO RIGHT TO SHARE A TABLE WITH YOU.
LET HER DO WHAT SHE WANTS.
PEEK
JEEZ, THEY'RE SO DARN STUBBORN!!
I WANNA TALK TO HER!
GRAB

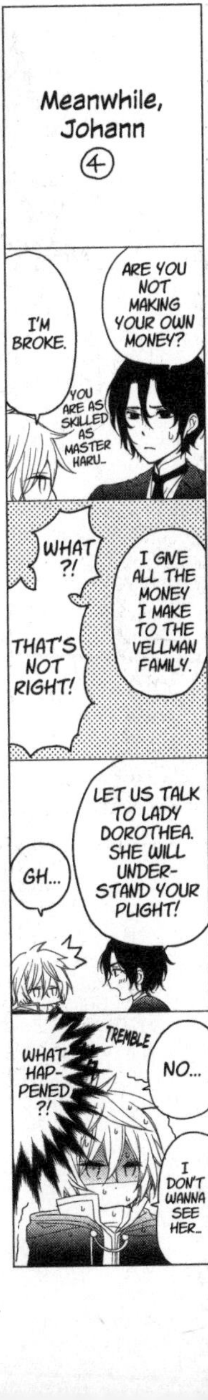
Meanwhile, Johann ④
ARE YOU NOT MAKING YOUR OWN MONEY?
I'M BROKE.
YOU ARE AS SKILLED AS MASTER HARU...
I GIVE ALL THE MONEY I MAKE TO THE VELLMAN FAMILY.
WHAT?!
THAT'S NOT RIGHT!
LET US TALK TO LADY DOROTHEA. SHE WILL UNDERSTAND YOUR PLIGHT!
GH...
NO...
TREMBLE
WHAT HAPPENED?!
I DON'T WANNA SEE HER...

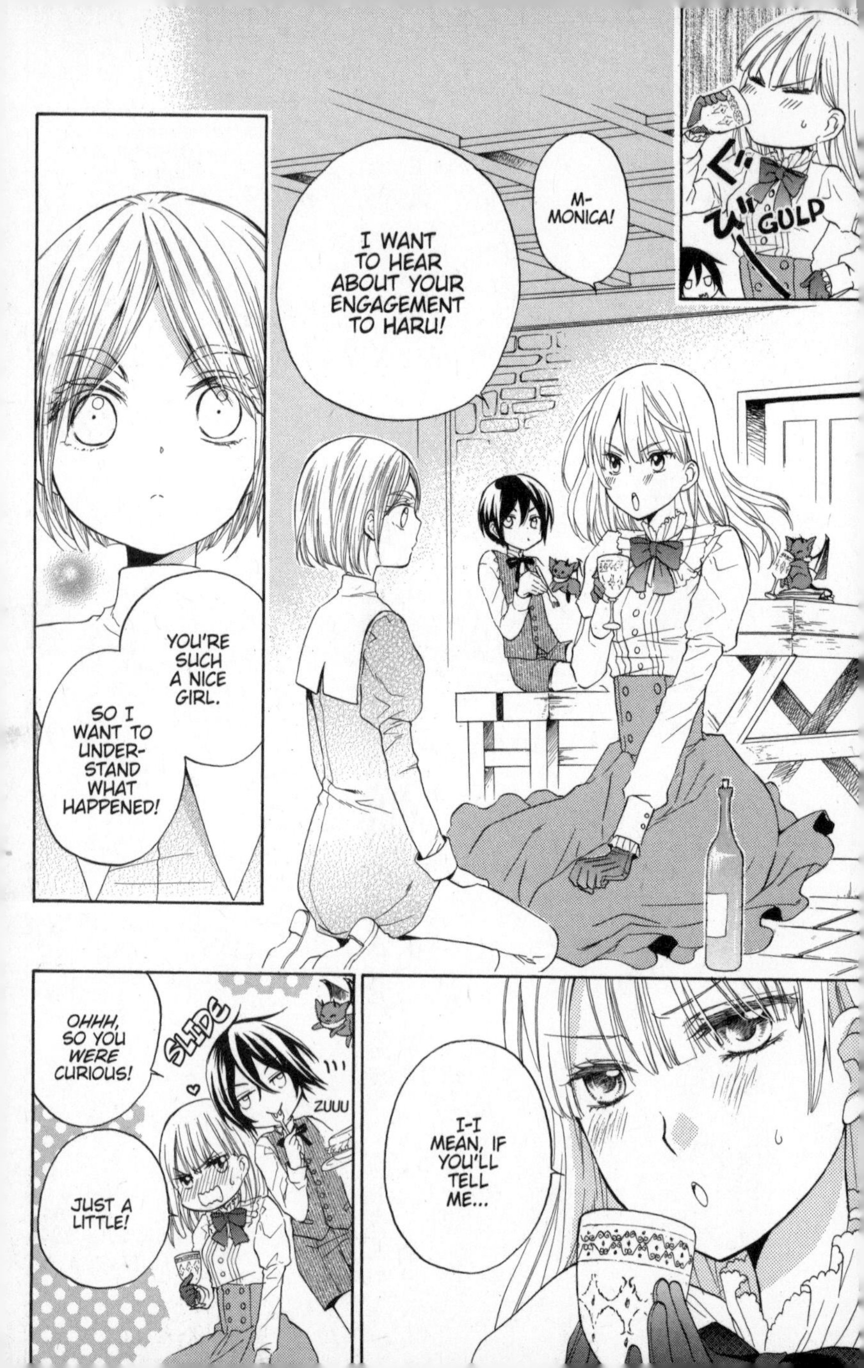
ぐ
び
GULP
M-MONICA!
I WANT TO HEAR ABOUT YOUR ENGAGEMENT TO HARU!
YOU'RE SUCH A NICE GIRL.
SO I WANT TO UNDERSTAND WHAT HAPPENED!
I-I MEAN, IF YOU'LL TELL ME...
SLIDE
OHHH, SO YOU WERE CURIOUS!
ZUUU
JUST A LITTLE!

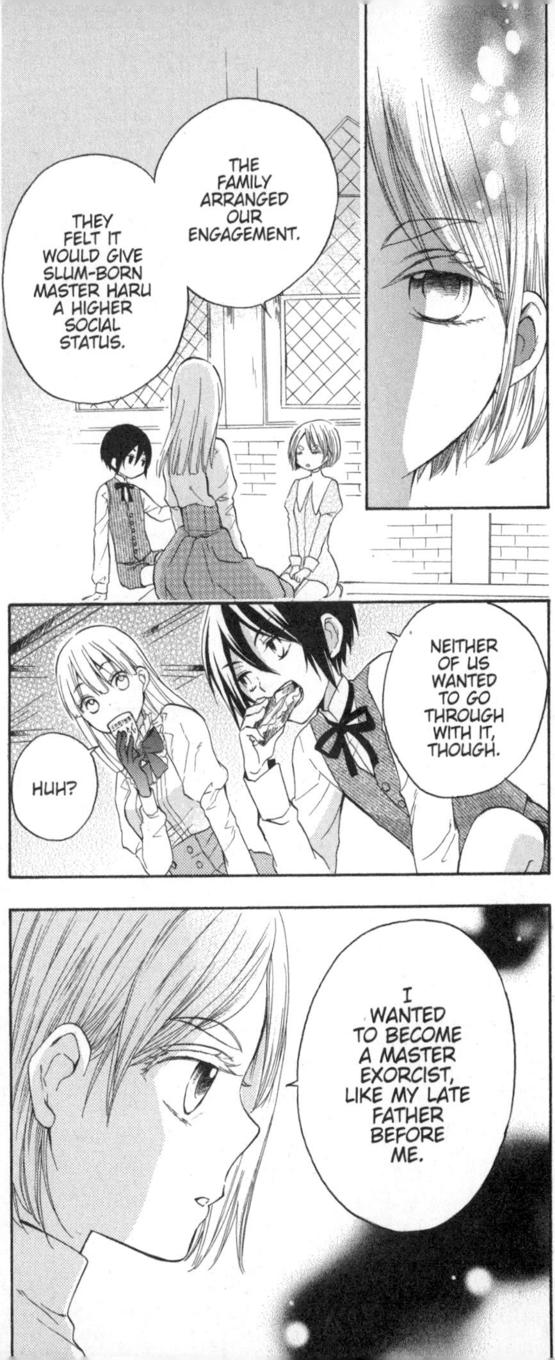
THE FAMILY ARRANGED OUR ENGAGEMENT.
THEY FELT IT WOULD GIVE SLUM-BORN MASTER HARU A HIGHER SOCIAL STATUS.
NEITHER OF US WANTED TO GO THROUGH WITH IT, THOUGH.
HUH?
I WANTED TO BECOME A MASTER EXORCIST, LIKE MY LATE FATHER BEFORE ME.
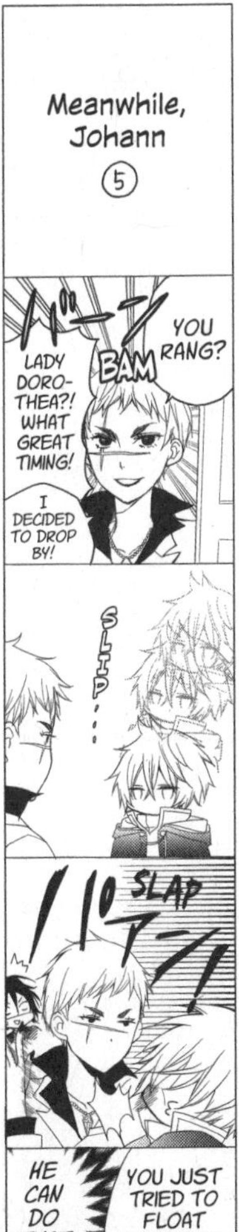
Meanwhile, Johann
⑤
バーン
BAM
YOU RANG?
LADY DOROTHEA?! WHAT GREAT TIMING!
I DECIDED TO DROP BY!
SLIP...
パァーン
SLAP
YOU JUST TRIED TO FLOAT YOUR SOUL AWAY, DIDN'T YOU?
HE CAN DO THAT?!

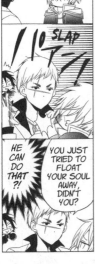

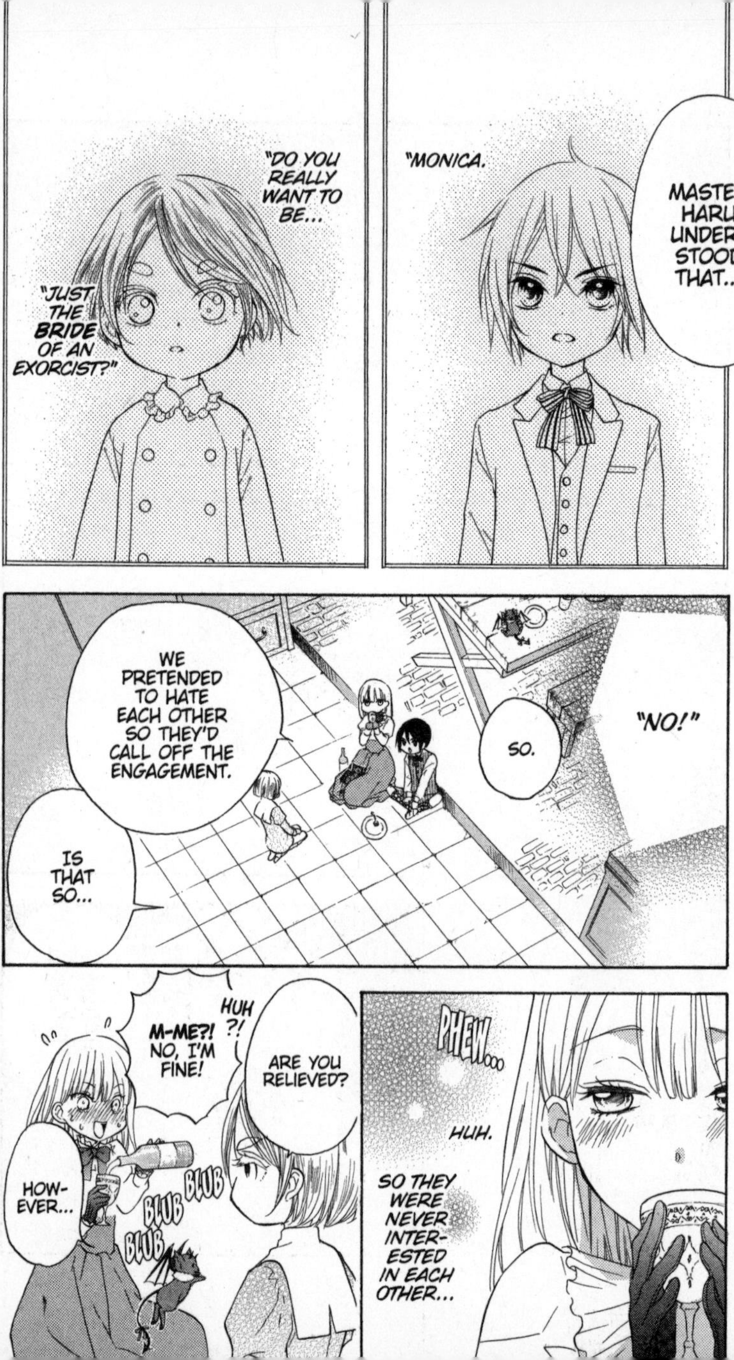
MASTER HARU UNDERSTOOD THAT...
"MONICA.
"DO YOU REALLY WANT TO BE...
"JUST THE BRIDE OF AN EXORCIST?"
"NO!"
SO.
WE PRETENDED TO HATE EACH OTHER SO THEY'D CALL OFF THE ENGAGEMENT.
IS THAT SO...
PHEW...
HUH.
SO THEY WERE NEVER INTERESTED IN EACH OTHER...
ARE YOU RELIEVED?
HUH ?!
M-ME?! NO, I'M FINE!
HOW-EVER...
BLUB
BLUB
BLUB

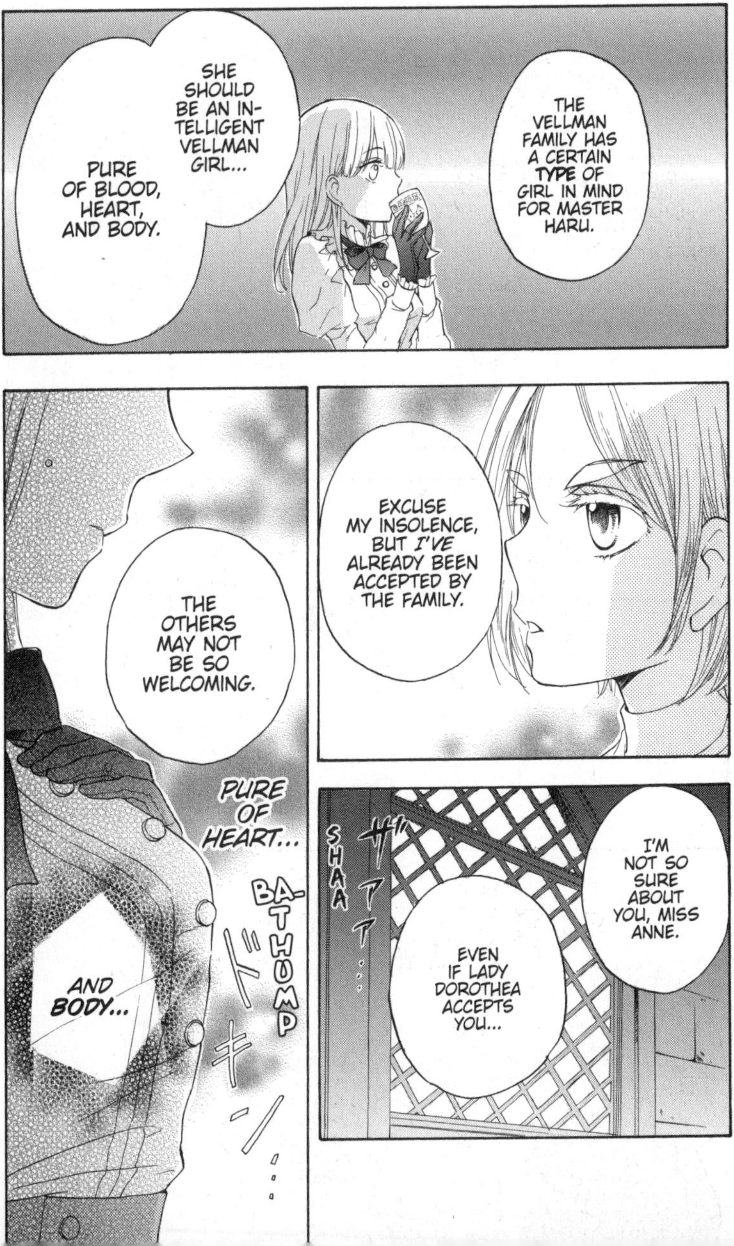
THE VELLMAN FAMILY HAS A CERTAIN **TYPE** OF GIRL IN MIND FOR MASTER HARU.
SHE SHOULD BE AN IN-TELLIGENT VELLMAN GIRL...
PURE OF BLOOD, HEART, AND BODY.
EXCUSE MY INSOLENCE, BUT *I'VE* ALREADY BEEN ACCEPTED BY THE FAMILY.
I'M NOT SO SURE ABOUT YOU, MISS ANNE.
EVEN IF LADY DOROTHEA ACCEPTS YOU...
SHAA
THE OTHERS MAY NOT BE SO WELCOMING.
PURE OF HEART...
BA-THUMP
AND BODY...

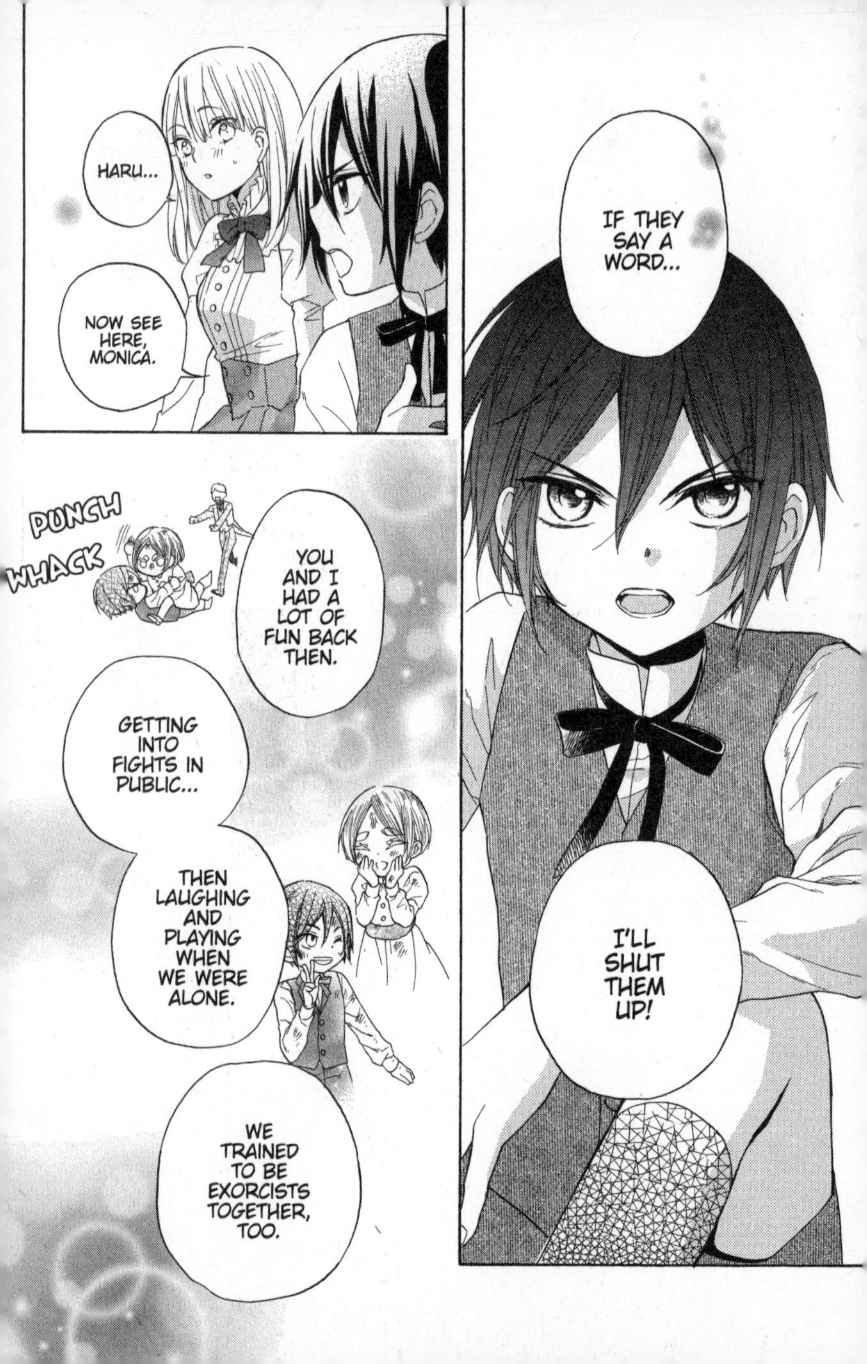
IF THEY SAY A WORD...
I'LL SHUT THEM UP!
HARU...
NOW SEE HERE, MONICA.
PUNCH
WHACK
YOU AND I HAD A LOT OF FUN BACK THEN.
GETTING INTO FIGHTS IN PUBLIC...
THEN LAUGHING AND PLAYING WHEN WE WERE ALONE.
WE TRAINED TO BE EXORCISTS TOGETHER, TOO.

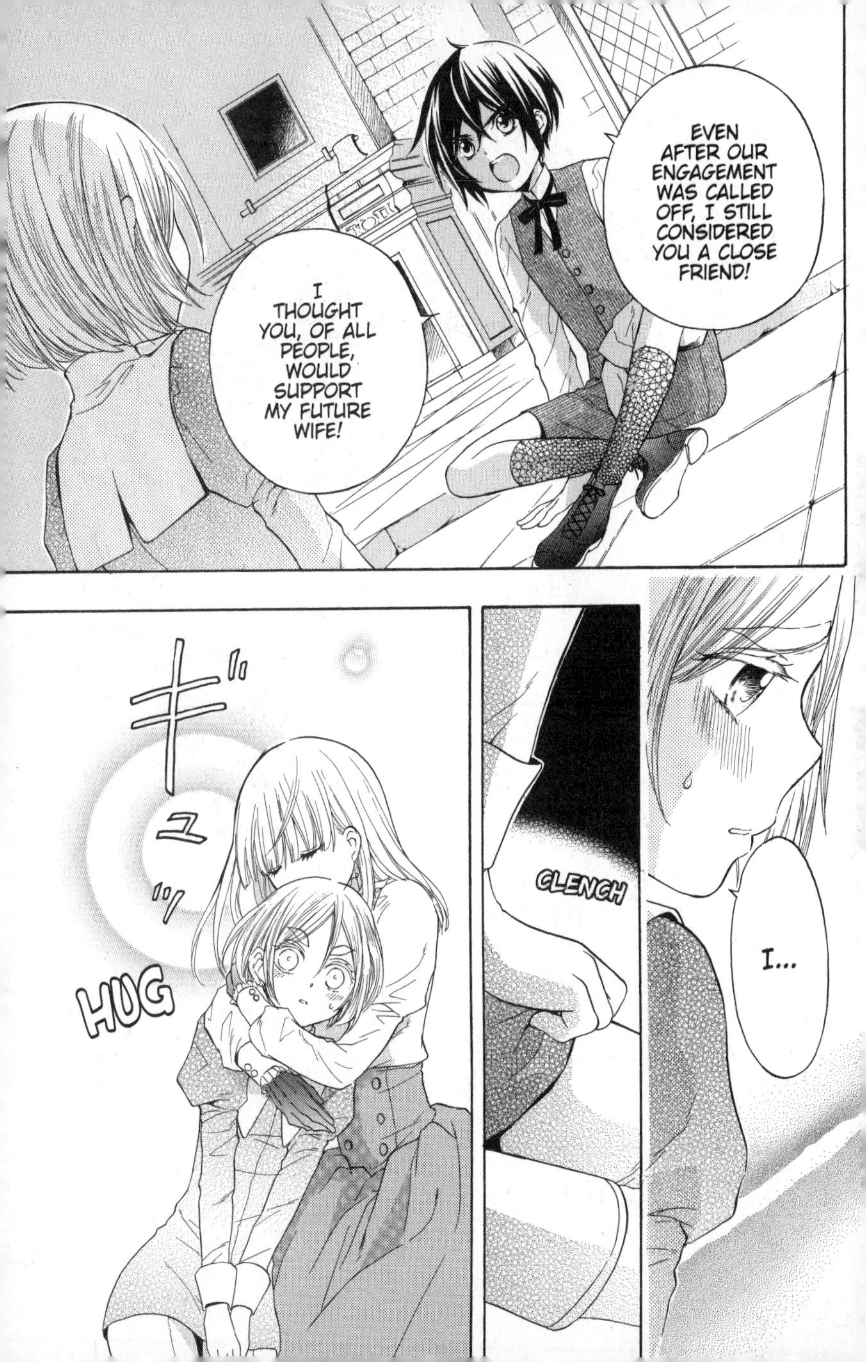
EVEN AFTER OUR ENGAGEMENT WAS CALLED OFF, I STILL CONSIDERED YOU A CLOSE FRIEND!
I THOUGHT YOU, OF ALL PEOPLE, WOULD SUPPORT MY FUTURE WIFE!
I...
CLENCH
ギュッ
HUG

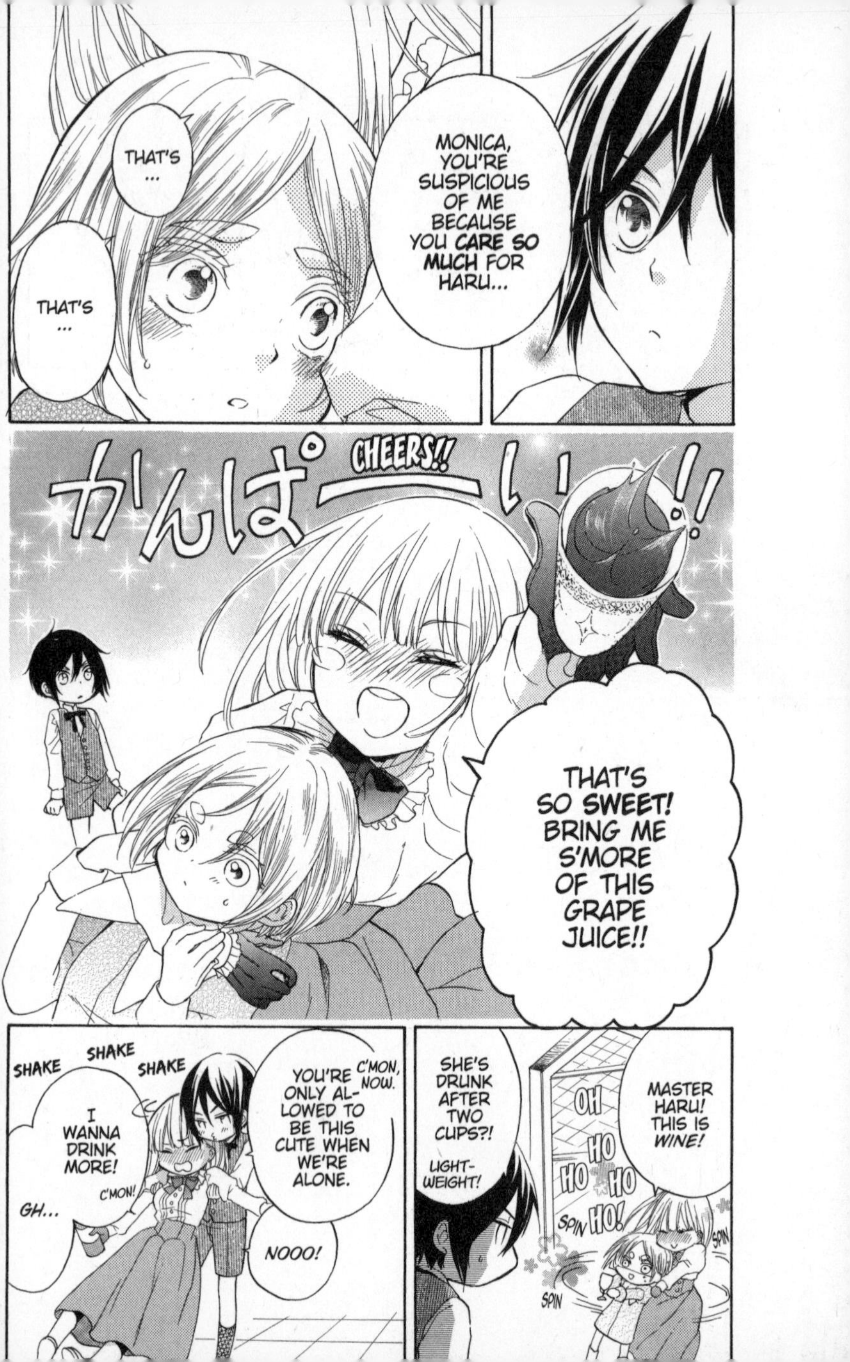
MONICA, YOU'RE SUSPICIOUS OF ME BECAUSE YOU CARE SO MUCH FOR HARU...
THAT'S ...
THAT'S ...
かんぱーい!!
CHEERS!!
THAT'S SO SWEET! BRING ME S'MORE OF THIS GRAPE JUICE!!
MASTER HARU! THIS IS WINE!
OH HO HO HO HO HO!
SPIN
SPIN
SPIN
SHE'S DRUNK AFTER TWO CUPS?!
LIGHT-WEIGHT!
C'MON, NOW.
YOU'RE ONLY AL-LOWED TO BE THIS CUTE WHEN WE'RE ALONE.
SHAKE
SHAKE
SHAKE
I WANNA DRINK MORE!
C'MON!
GH...
NOOO!

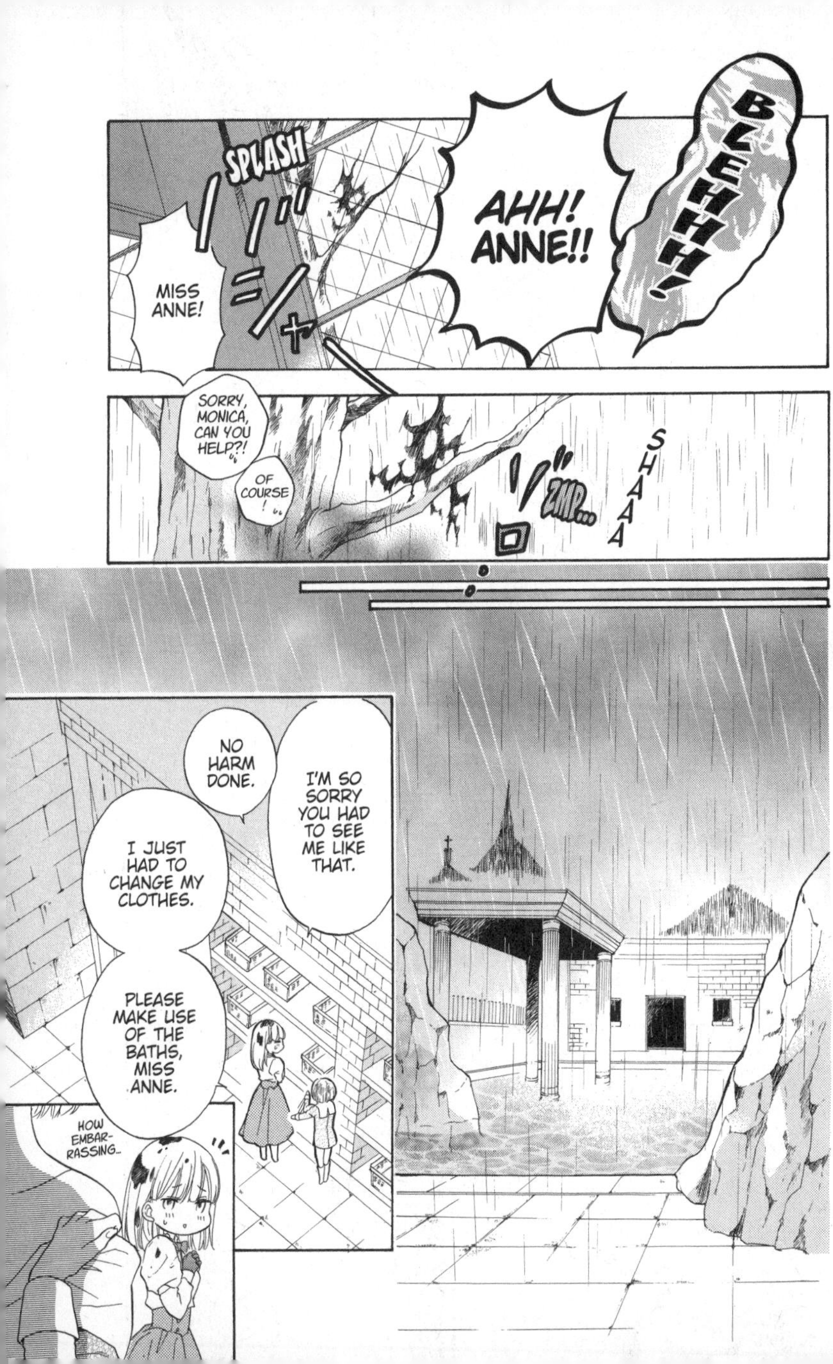
BLEHHH!
AHH! ANNE!!
SPLASH
MISS ANNE!
SORRY, MONICA, CAN YOU HELP?!
OF COURSE!
ZMP...
SHAAA
I'M SO SORRY YOU HAD TO SEE ME LIKE THAT.
NO HARM DONE.
I JUST HAD TO CHANGE MY CLOTHES.
PLEASE MAKE USE OF THE BATHS, MISS ANNE.
HOW EMBARRASSING...

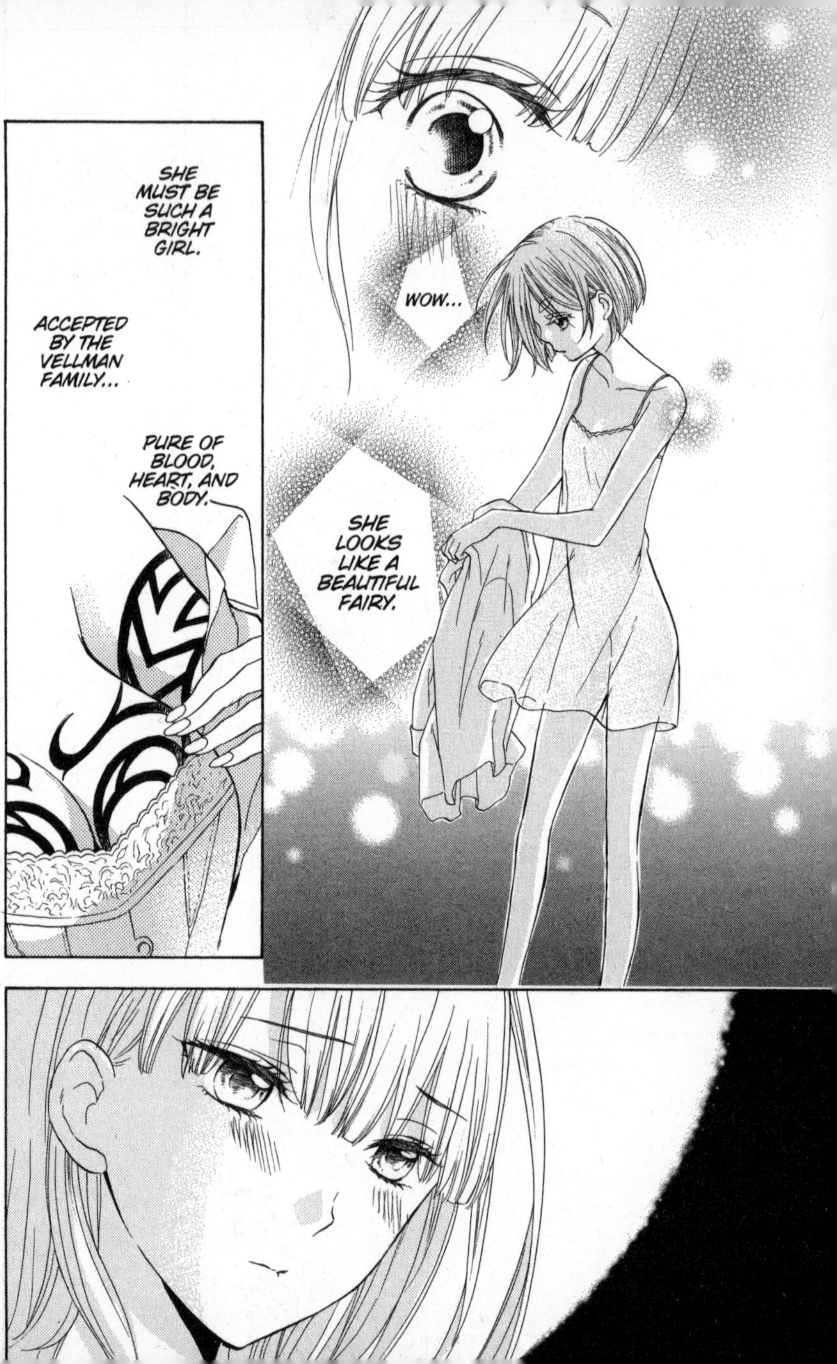
WOW...
SHE LOOKS LIKE A BEAUTIFUL FAIRY.
SHE MUST BE SUCH A BRIGHT GIRL.
ACCEPTED BY THE VELLMAN FAMILY...
PURE OF BLOOD, HEART, AND BODY.

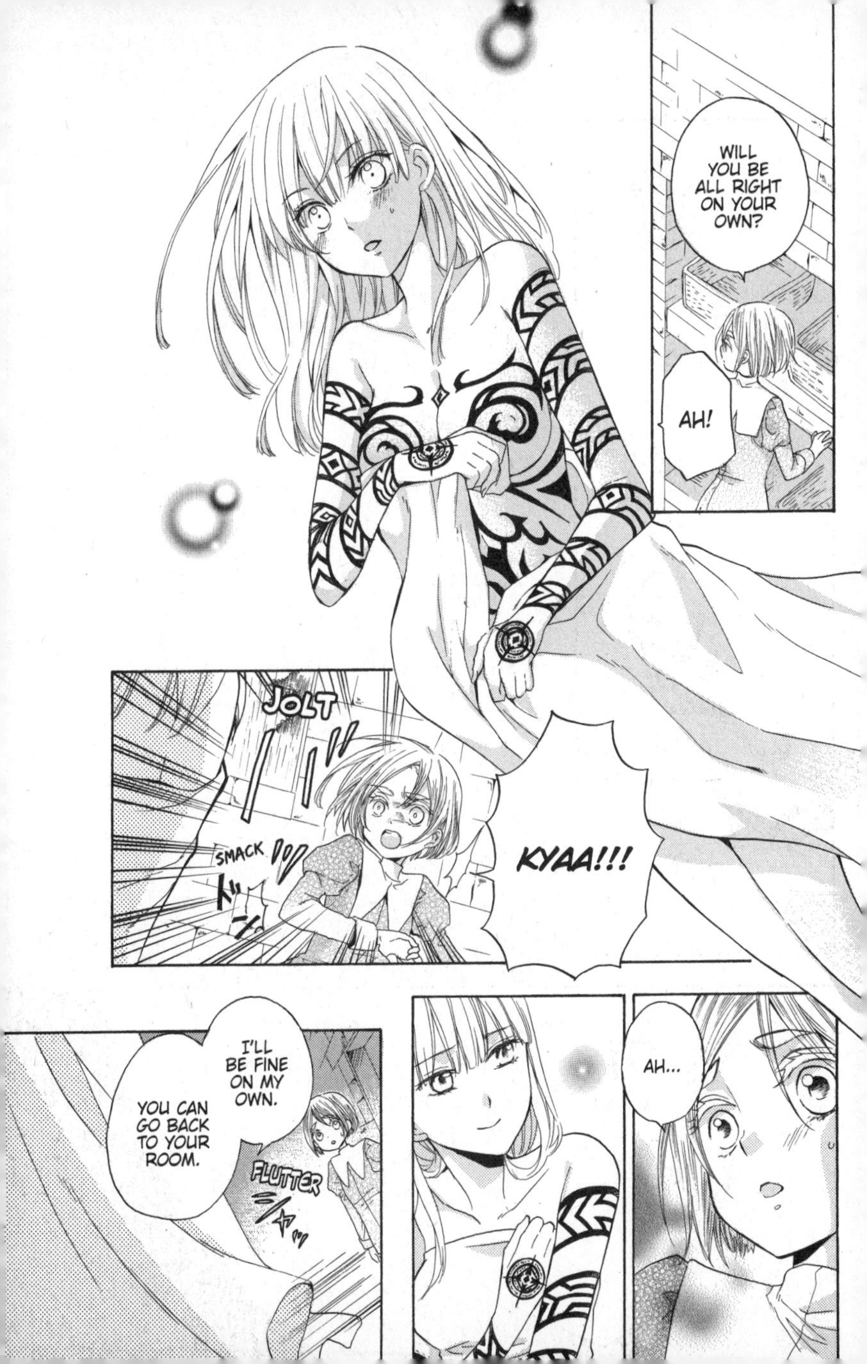
WILL YOU BE ALL RIGHT ON YOUR OWN?
AH!
KYAA!!!
JOLT
SMACK
AH...
I'LL BE FINE ON MY OWN.
YOU CAN GO BACK TO YOUR ROOM.
FLUTTER

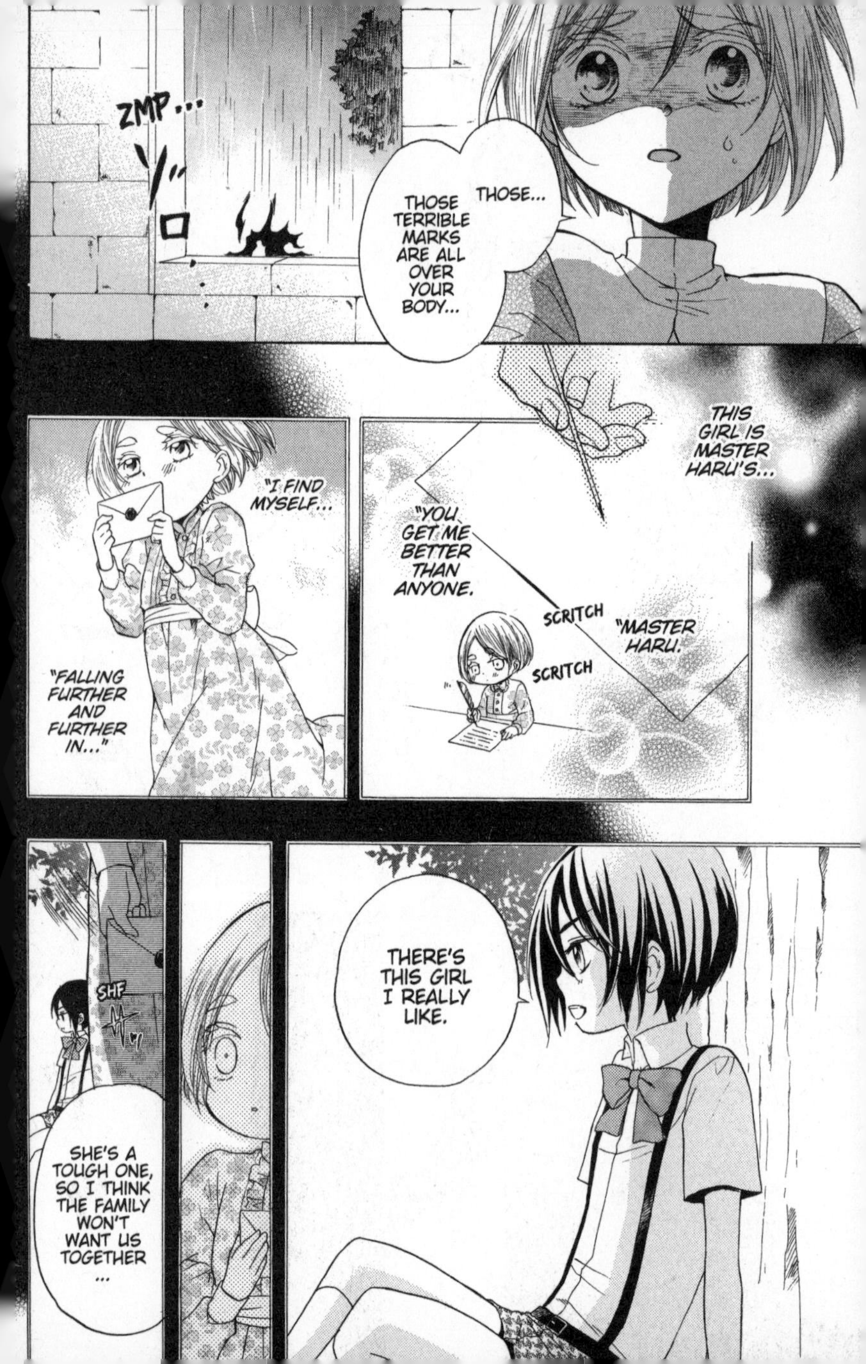
ZMP...
THOSE...
THOSE TERRIBLE MARKS ARE ALL OVER YOUR BODY...
THIS GIRL IS MASTER HARU'S...
"MASTER HARU.
"YOU GET ME BETTER THAN ANYONE.
SCRITCH
SCRITCH
"I FIND MYSELF...
"FALLING FURTHER AND FURTHER IN..."
THERE'S THIS GIRL I REALLY LIKE.
SHF
SHE'S A TOUGH ONE, SO I THINK THE FAMILY WON'T WANT US TOGETHER ...

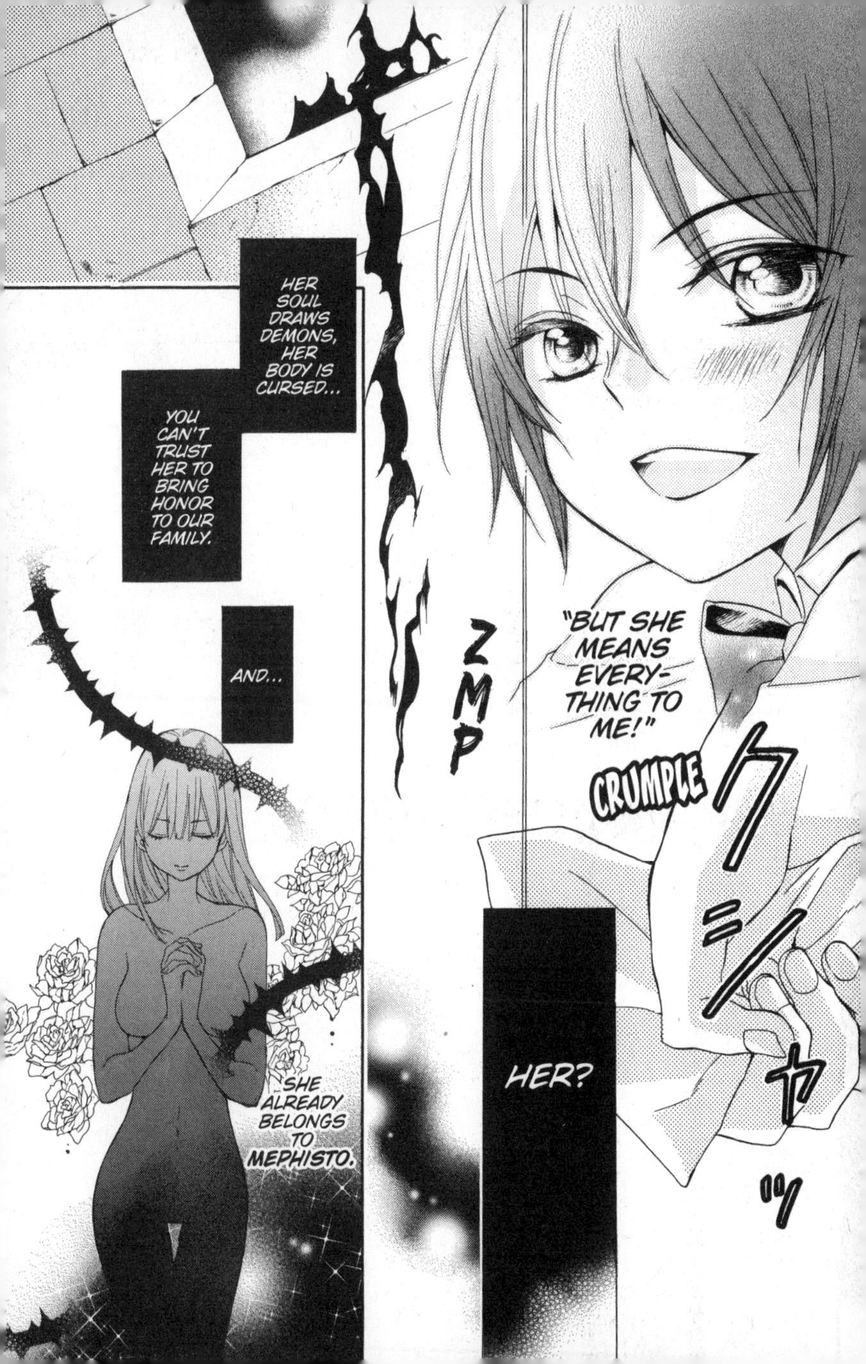
"BUT SHE MEANS EVERY-THING TO ME!"
CRUMPLE
HER?
ZMP
HER SOUL DRAWS DEMONS, HER BODY IS CURSED...
YOU CAN'T TRUST HER TO BRING HONOR TO OUR FAMILY.
AND...
SHE ALREADY BELONGS TO MEPHISTO.

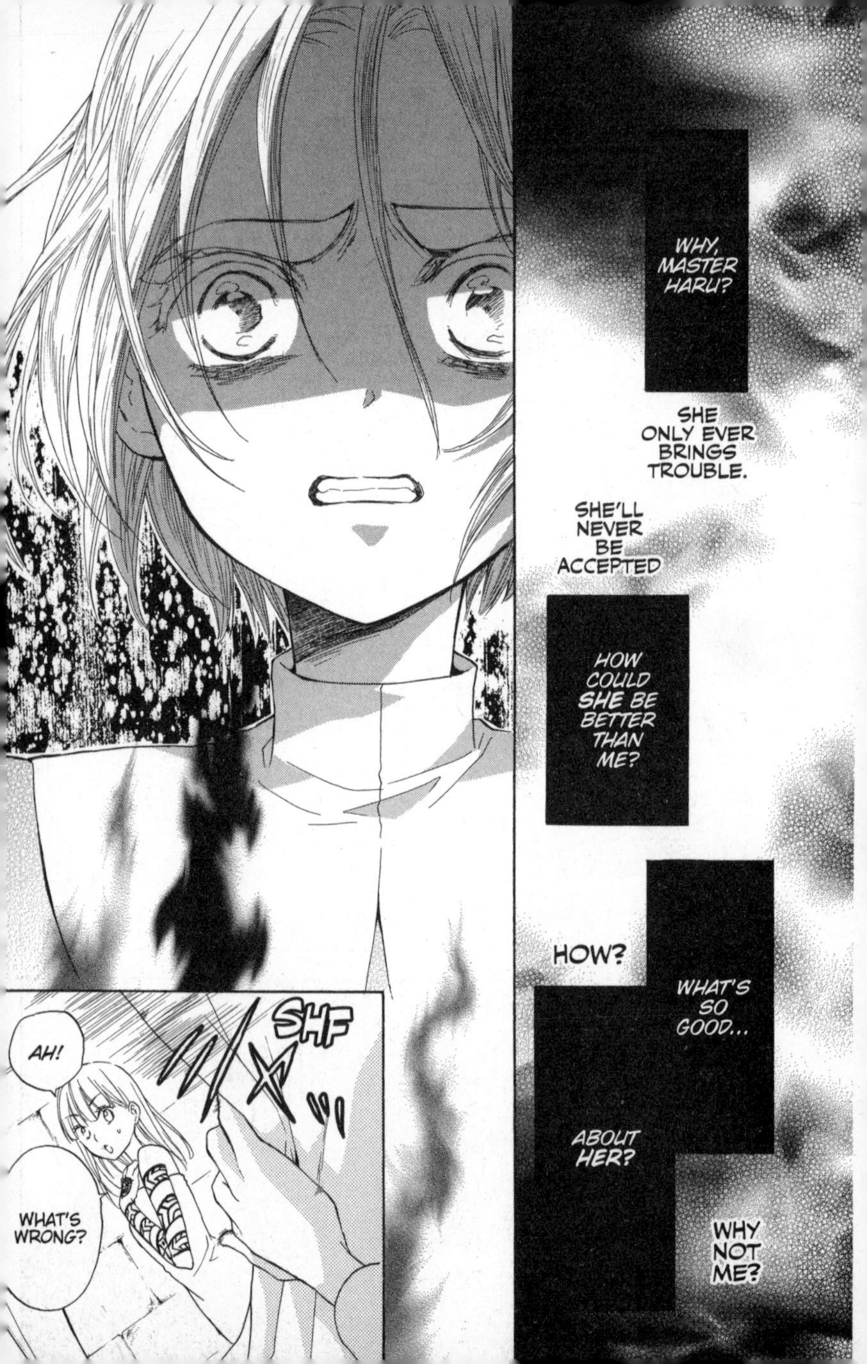
WHY, MASTER HARU?
SHE ONLY EVER BRINGS TROUBLE.
SHE'LL NEVER BE ACCEPTED
HOW COULD SHE BE BETTER THAN ME?
HOW?
WHAT'S SO GOOD...
ABOUT HER?
WHY NOT ME?
SHF
AH!
WHAT'S WRONG?

SLAM

DO YOU *REALLY* THINK YOU CAN MARRY HARU?

YOU?

WITH THAT **REPULSIVE** BODY OF YOURS?!

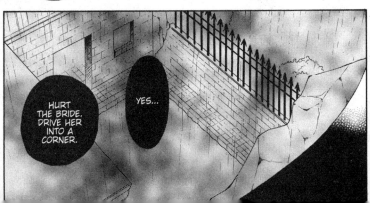

HURT THE BRIDE. DRIVE HER INTO A CORNER.

YES...

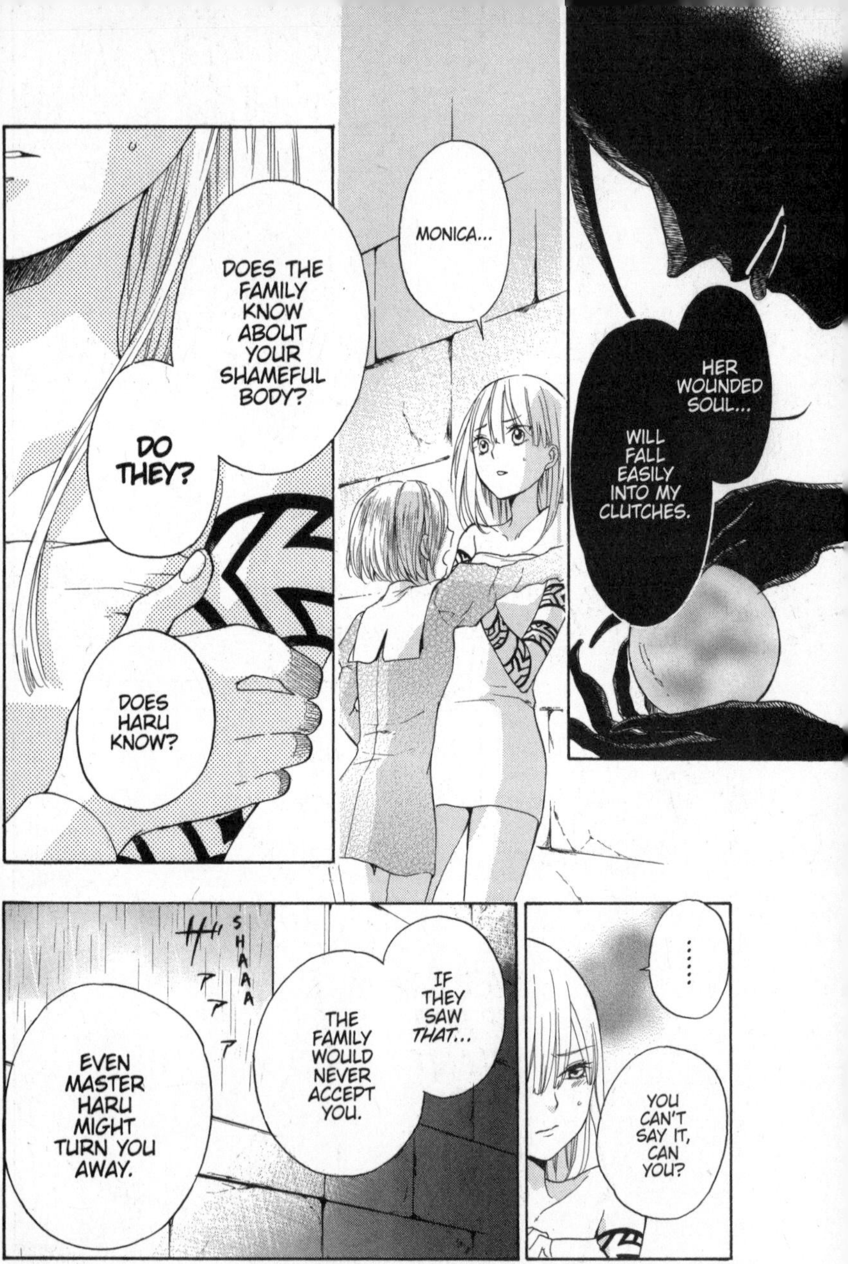
HER WOUNDED SOUL...
WILL FALL EASILY INTO MY CLUTCHES.
MONICA...
DOES THE FAMILY KNOW ABOUT YOUR SHAMEFUL BODY?
DO THEY?
DOES HARU KNOW?
......
YOU CAN'T SAY IT, CAN YOU?
SHAAA
IF THEY SAW *THAT*...
THE FAMILY WOULD NEVER ACCEPT YOU.
EVEN MASTER HARU MIGHT TURN YOU AWAY.

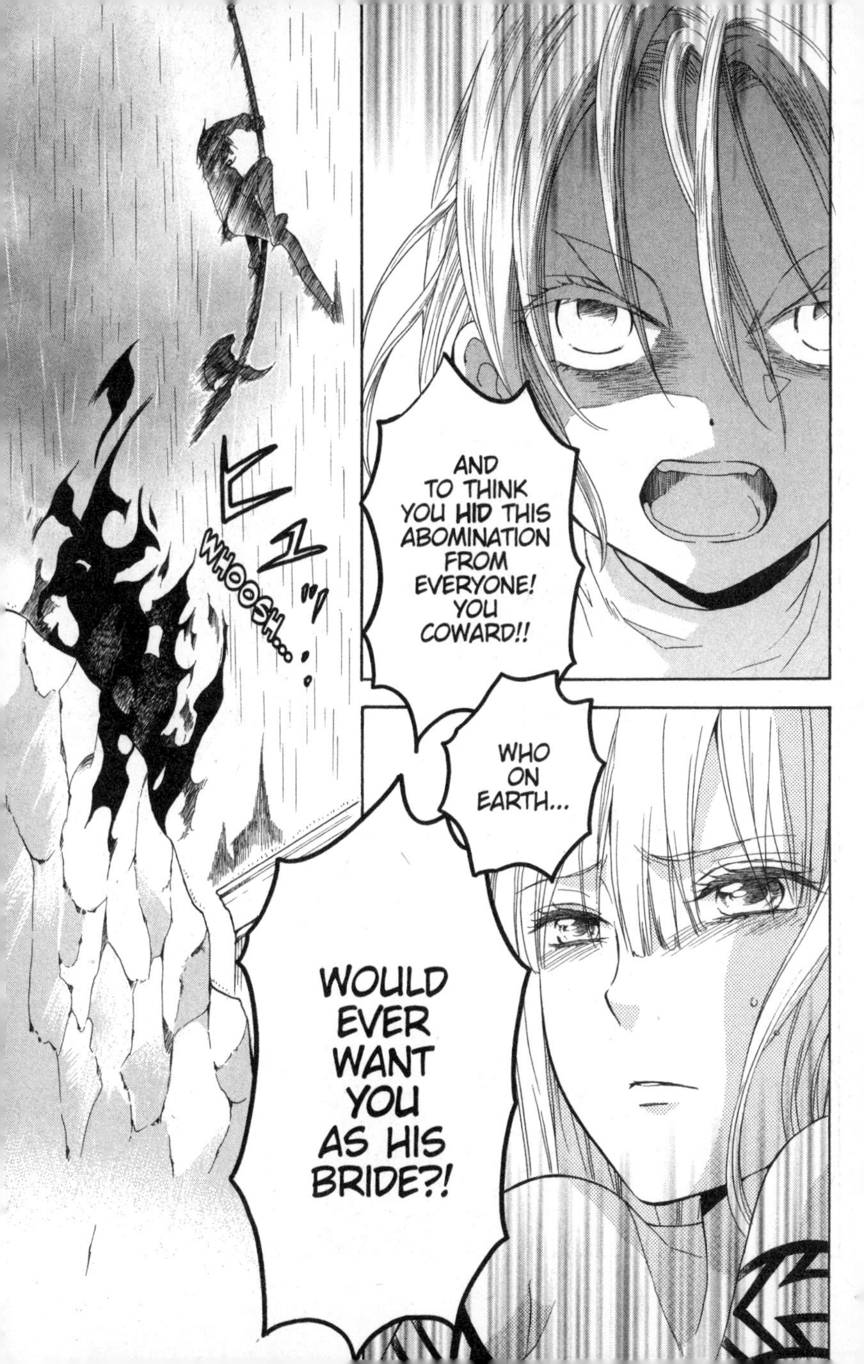
AND TO THINK YOU HID THIS ABOMINATION FROM EVERYONE! YOU COWARD!!
WHO ON EARTH...
WOULD EVER WANT YOU AS HIS BRIDE?!
WHOOSH...

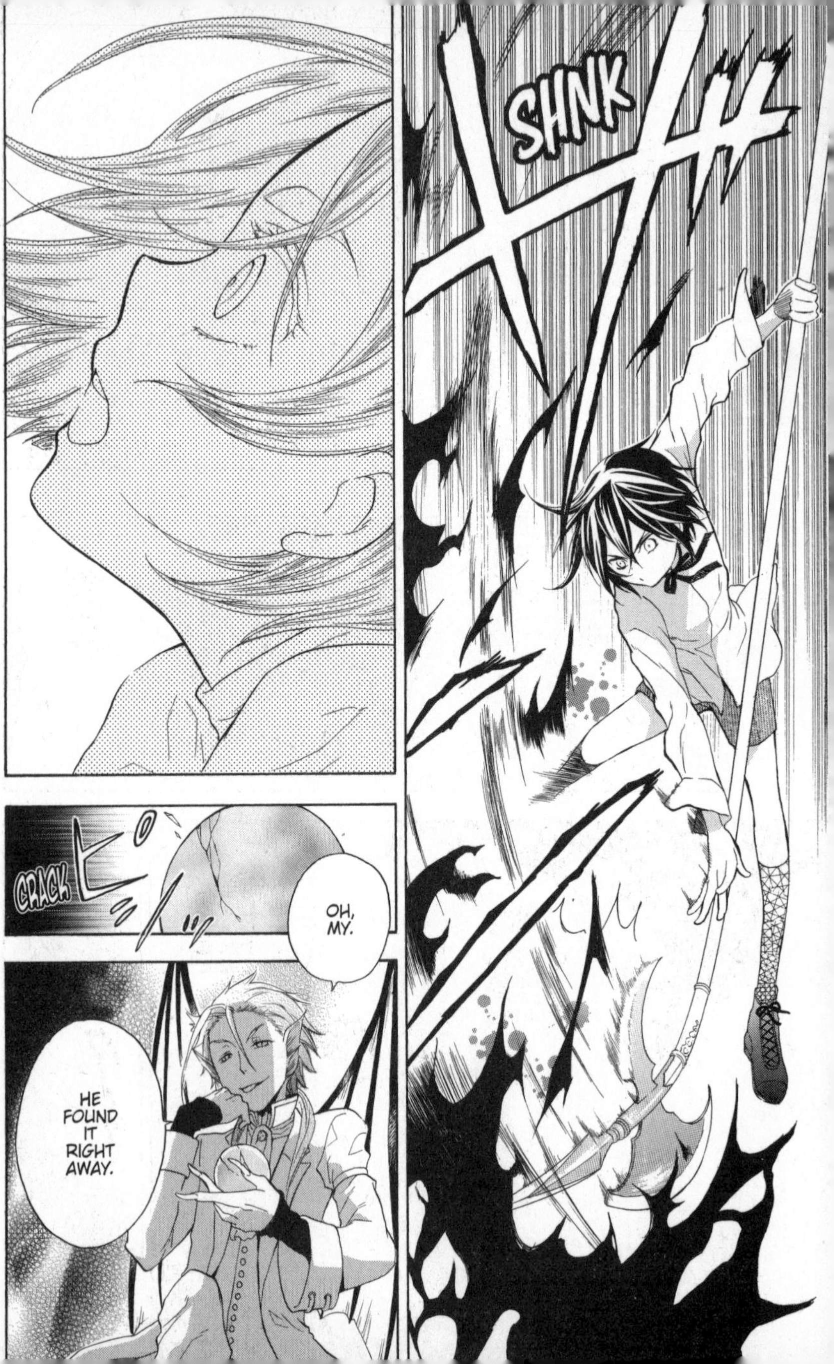
SHNK
CRACK
OH, MY.
HE FOUND IT RIGHT AWAY.

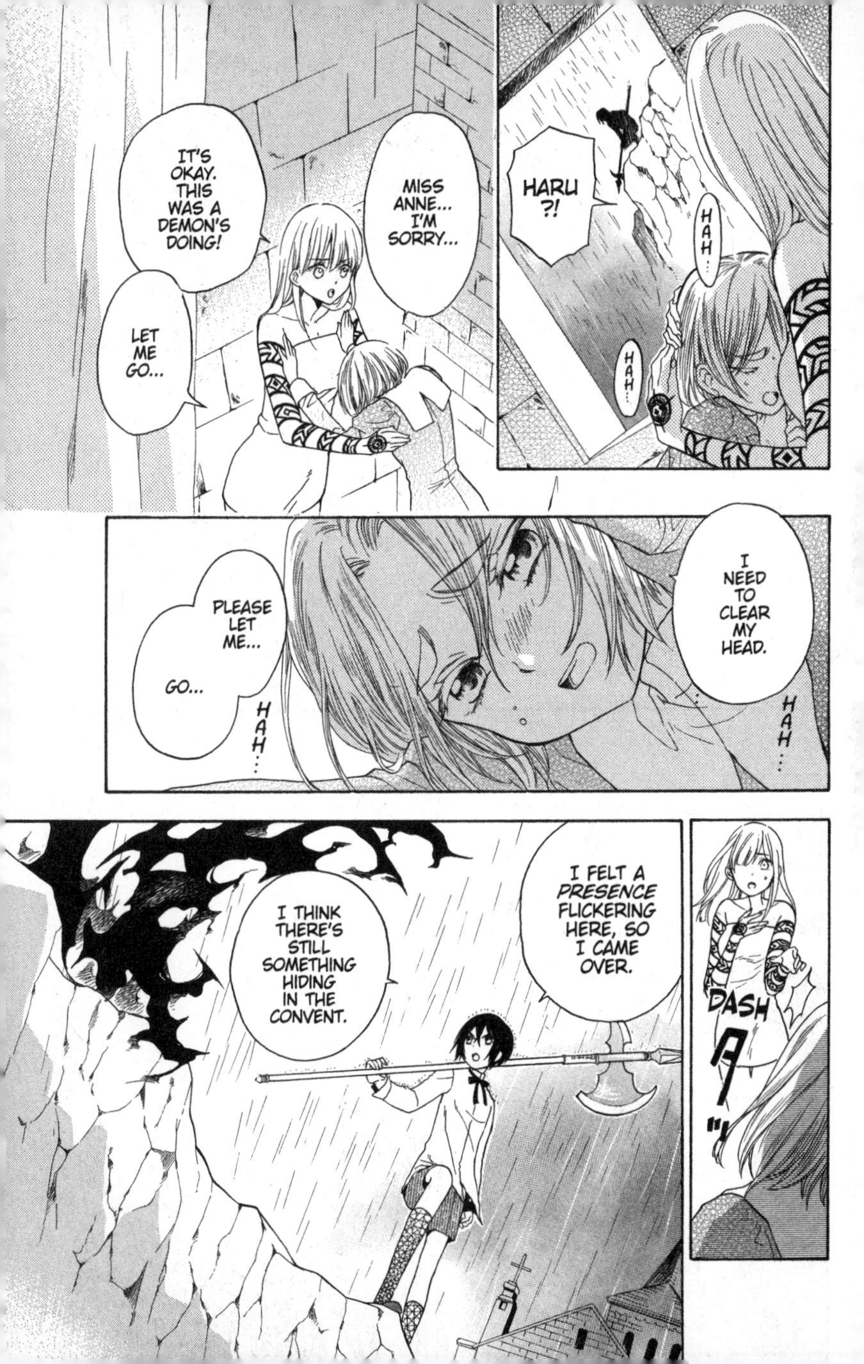
HARU ?!
HAH...
HAH...
MISS ANNE... I'M SORRY...
IT'S OKAY. THIS WAS A DEMON'S DOING!
LET ME GO...
I NEED TO CLEAR MY HEAD.
HAH...
PLEASE LET ME...
GO...
HAH...
DASH
I FELT A *PRESENCE* FLICKERING HERE, SO I CAME OVER.
I THINK THERE'S STILL SOMETHING HIDING IN THE CONVENT.

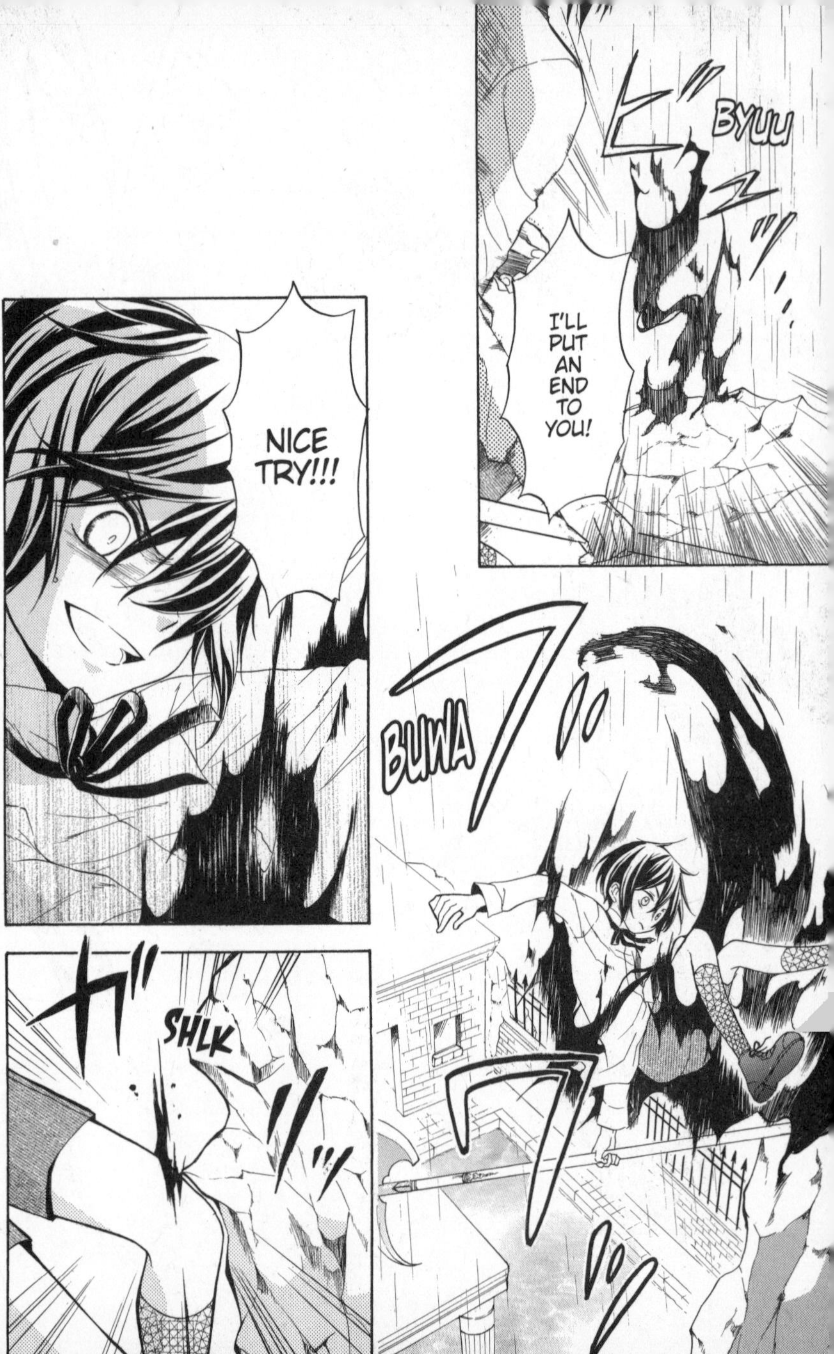
BYUU
I'LL PUT AN END TO YOU!
NICE TRY!!!
BUWA
SHLK

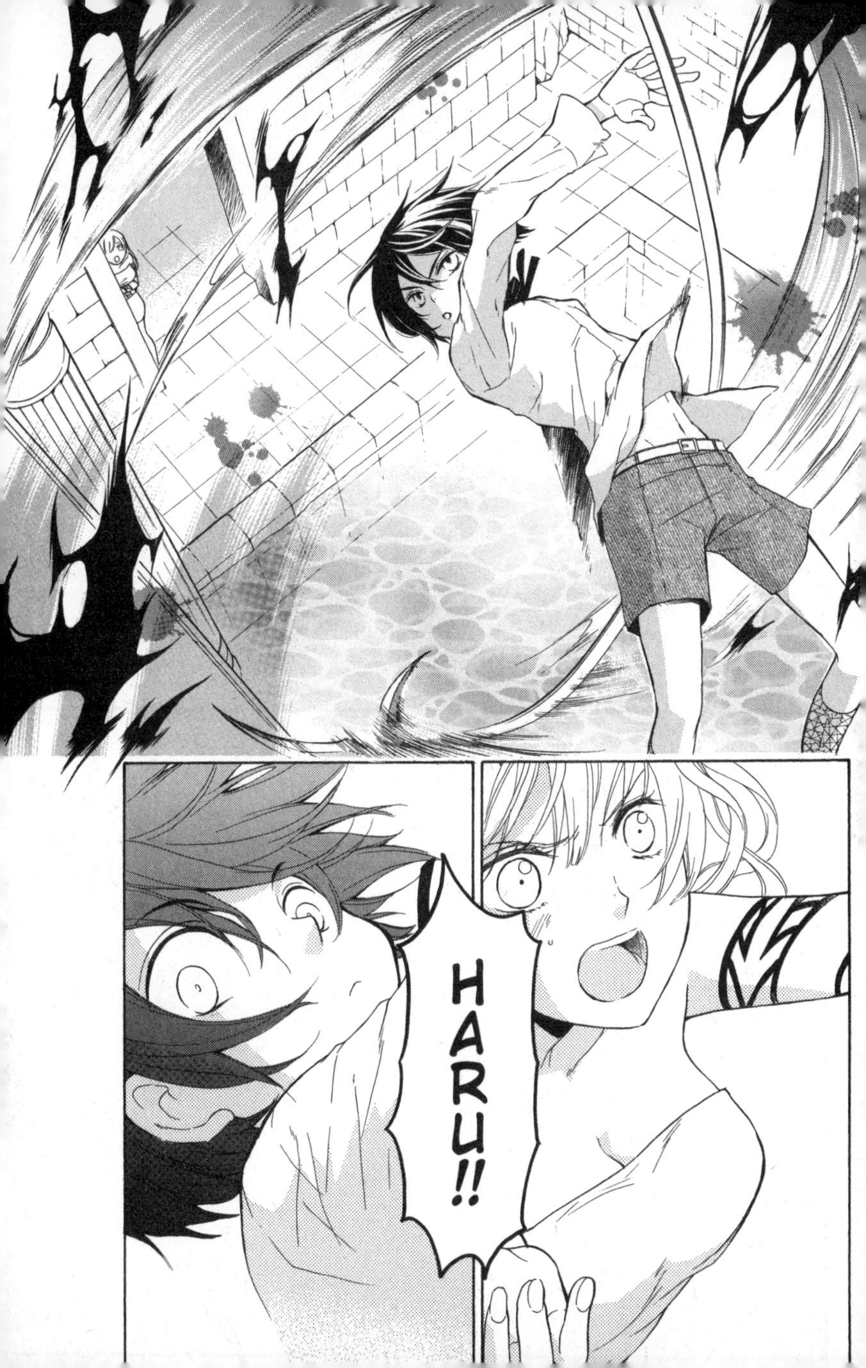
HARU!!

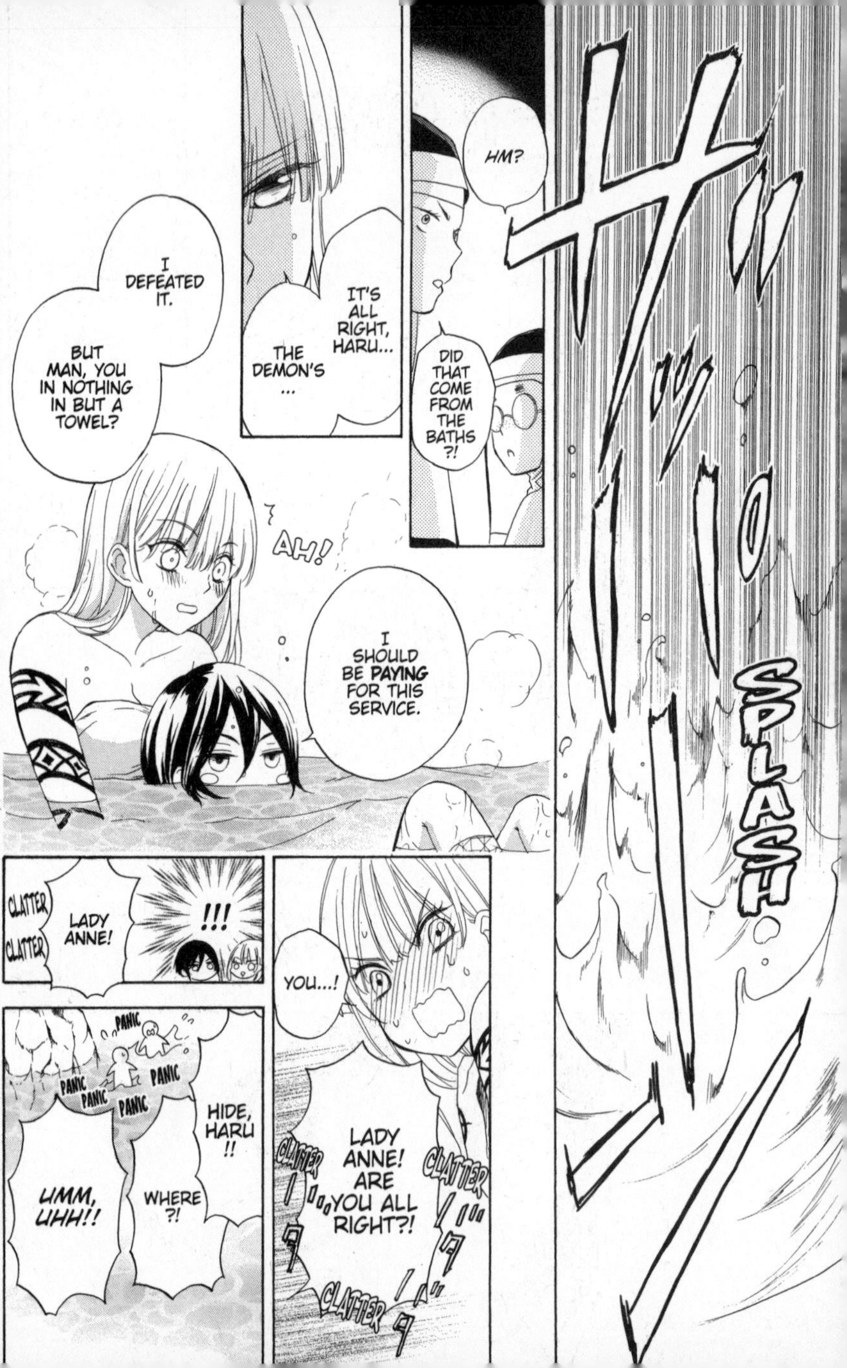
SPLASH
HM?
DID THAT COME FROM THE BATHS?!
IT'S ALL RIGHT, HARU...
THE DEMON'S ...
I DEFEATED IT.
BUT MAN, YOU IN NOTHING IN BUT A TOWEL?
AH!
I SHOULD BE PAYING FOR THIS SERVICE.
YOU...!
CLATTER
LADY ANNE! ARE YOU ALL RIGHT?!
CLATTER
CLATTER
!!!
LADY ANNE!
CLATTER
CLATTER
PANIC
PANIC
PANIC
PANIC
PANIC
HIDE, HARU!!
WHERE?!
UMM, UHH!!

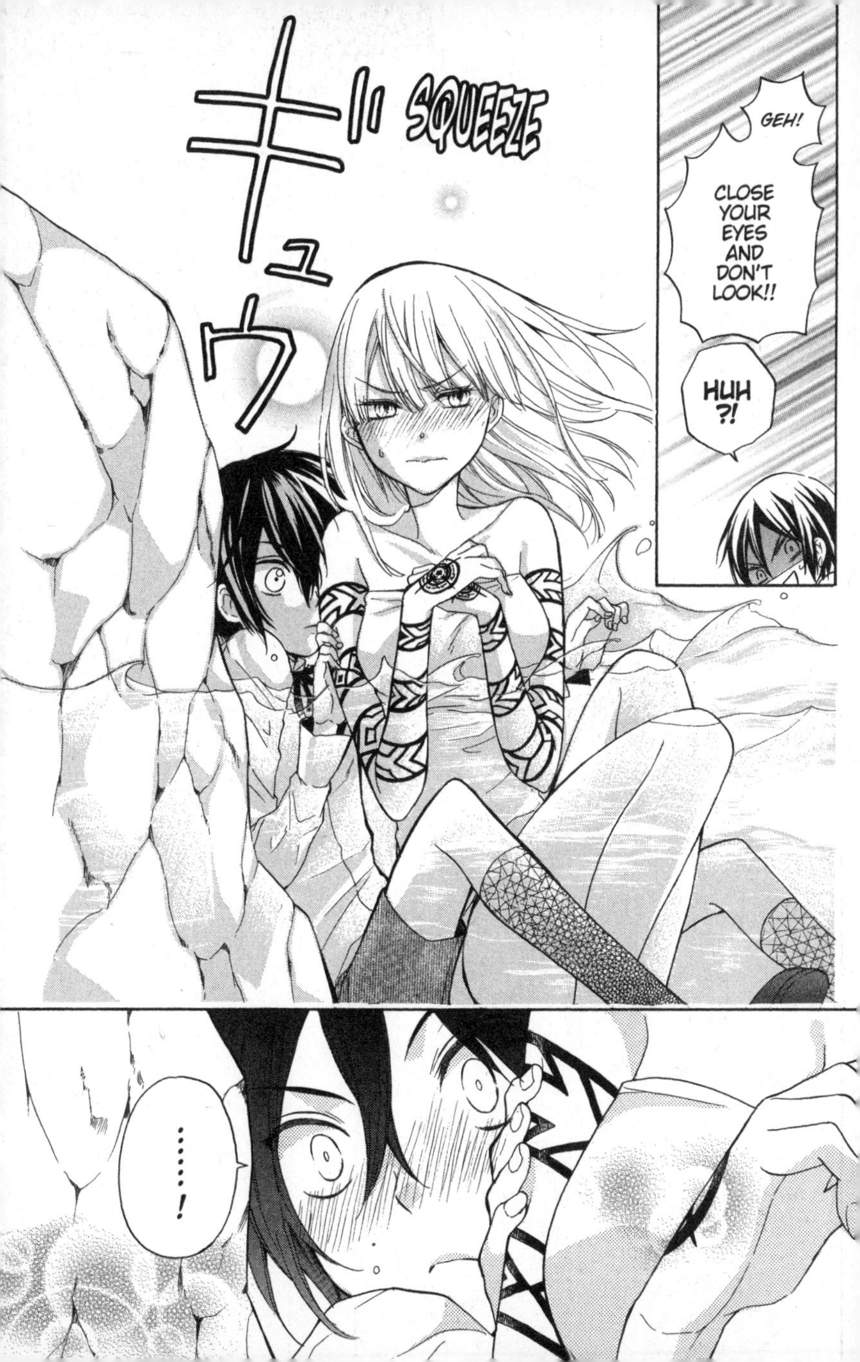
GEH!
CLOSE YOUR EYES AND DON'T LOOK!!
HUH?!
キュッ
SQUEEZE
......!

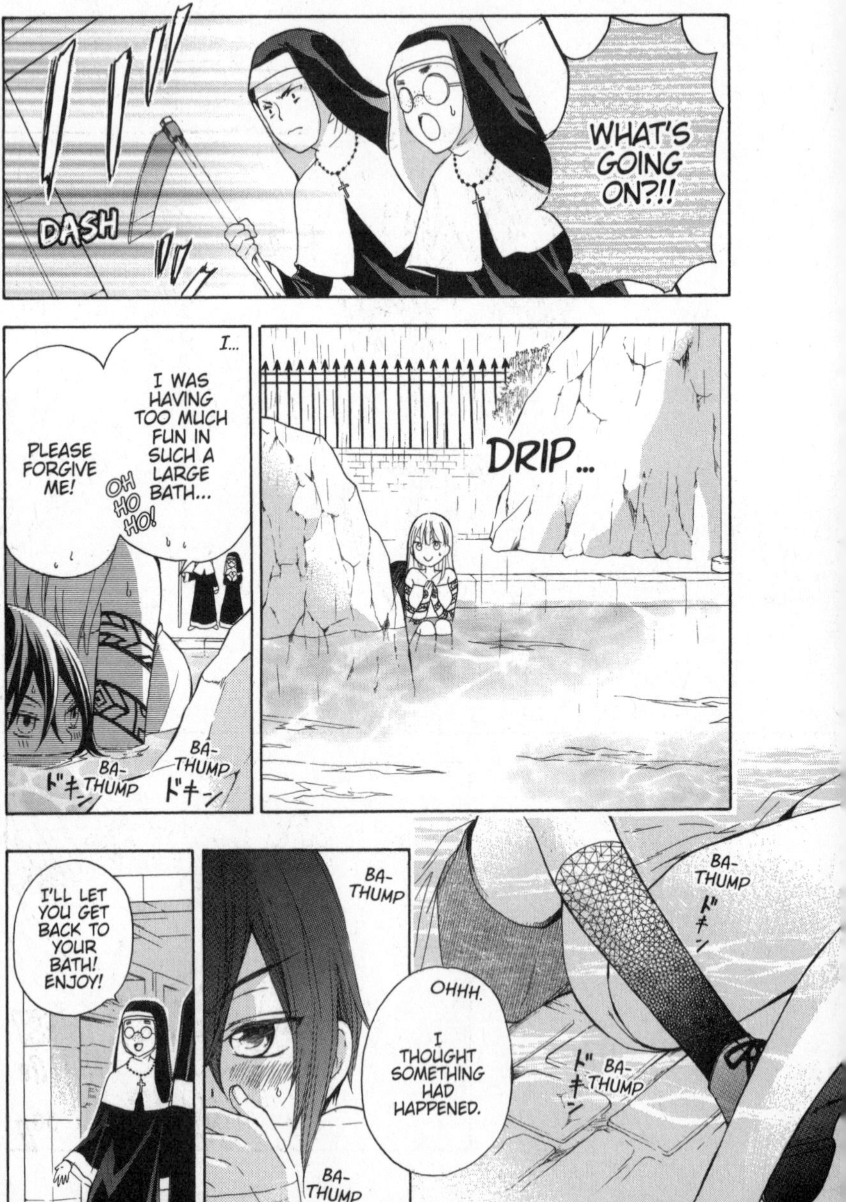
WHAT'S GOING ON?!!
DASH
DRIP...
I...
I WAS HAVING TOO MUCH FUN IN SUCH A LARGE BATH...
PLEASE FORGIVE ME!
OH HO HO!
BA-THUMP ドキン
BA-THUMP ドキン
BA-THUMP ドキン
BA-THUMP ドキン
BA-THUMP
OHHH.
I THOUGHT SOMETHING HAD HAPPENED.
BA-THUMP
I'LL LET YOU GET BACK TO YOUR BATH! ENJOY!

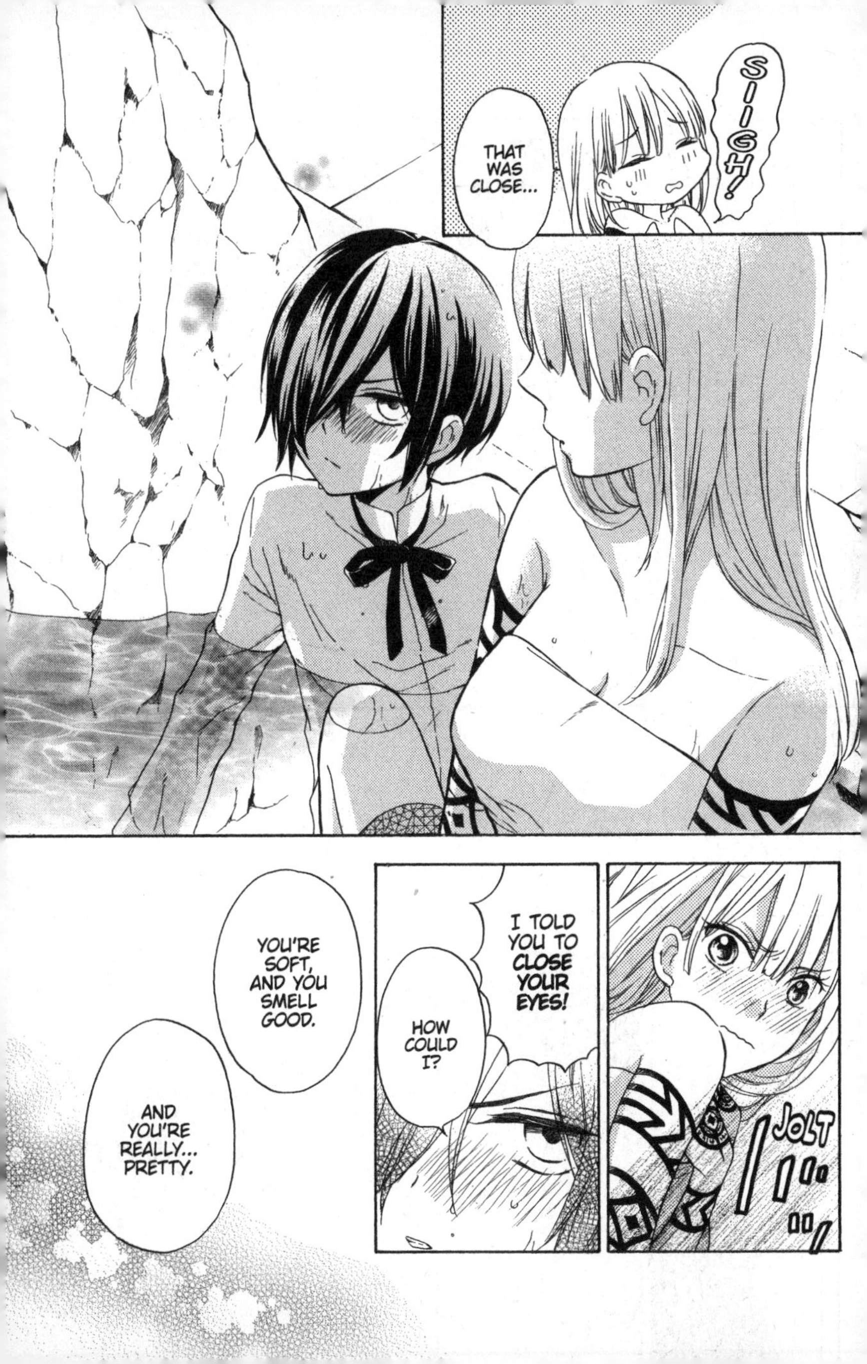
SIIGH!
THAT WAS CLOSE...
JOLT
I TOLD YOU TO CLOSE YOUR EYES!
HOW COULD I?
YOU'RE SOFT, AND YOU SMELL GOOD.
AND YOU'RE REALLY... PRETTY.

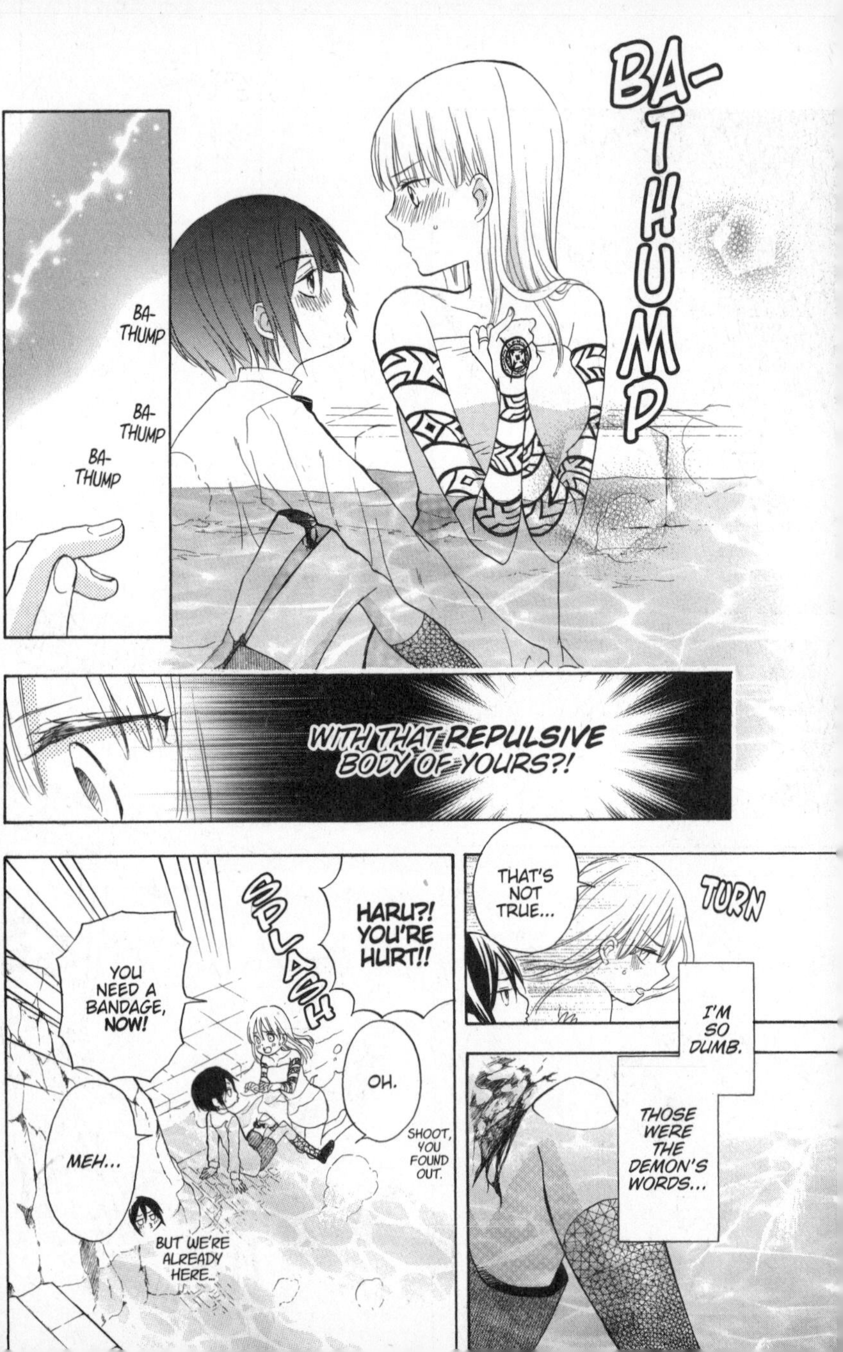

BA-THUMP
BA-THUMP
BA-THUMP
BA-THUMP
WITH THAT REPULSIVE BODY OF YOURS?!
THAT'S NOT TRUE...
TURN
I'M SO DUMB.
THOSE WERE THE DEMON'S WORDS...
SPLASH
HARU?! YOU'RE HURT!!
YOU NEED A BANDAGE, NOW!
OH.
SHOOT, YOU FOUND OUT.
MEH...
BUT WE'RE ALREADY HERE...

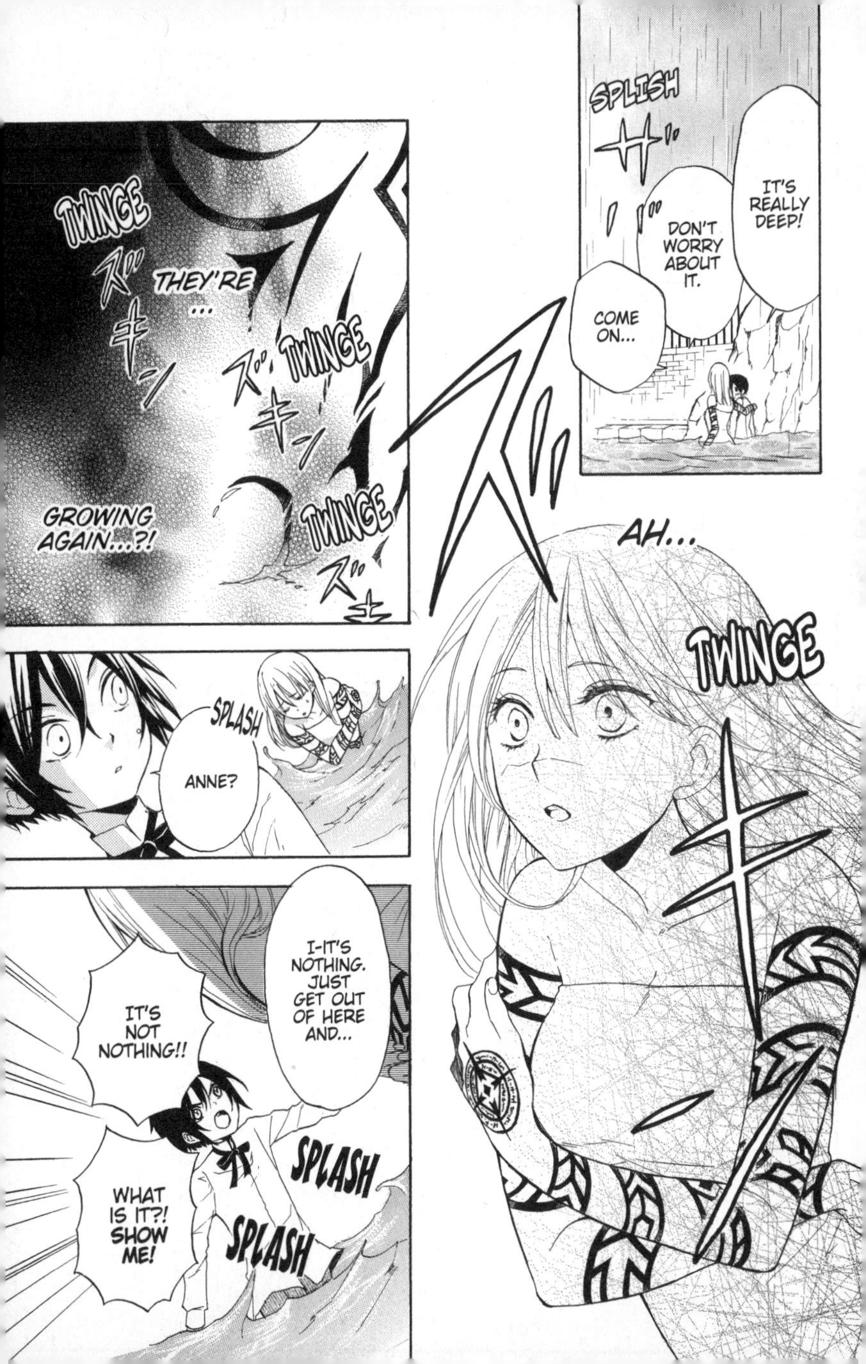
SPLISH
IT'S REALLY DEEP!
DON'T WORRY ABOUT IT.
COME ON...
AH...
TWINGE
TWINGE
THEY'RE ...
TWINGE
GROWING AGAIN...?!
TWINGE
SPLASH
ANNE?
I-IT'S NOTHING. JUST GET OUT OF HERE AND...
IT'S NOT NOTHING!!
SPLASH
SPLASH
WHAT IS IT?! SHOW ME!

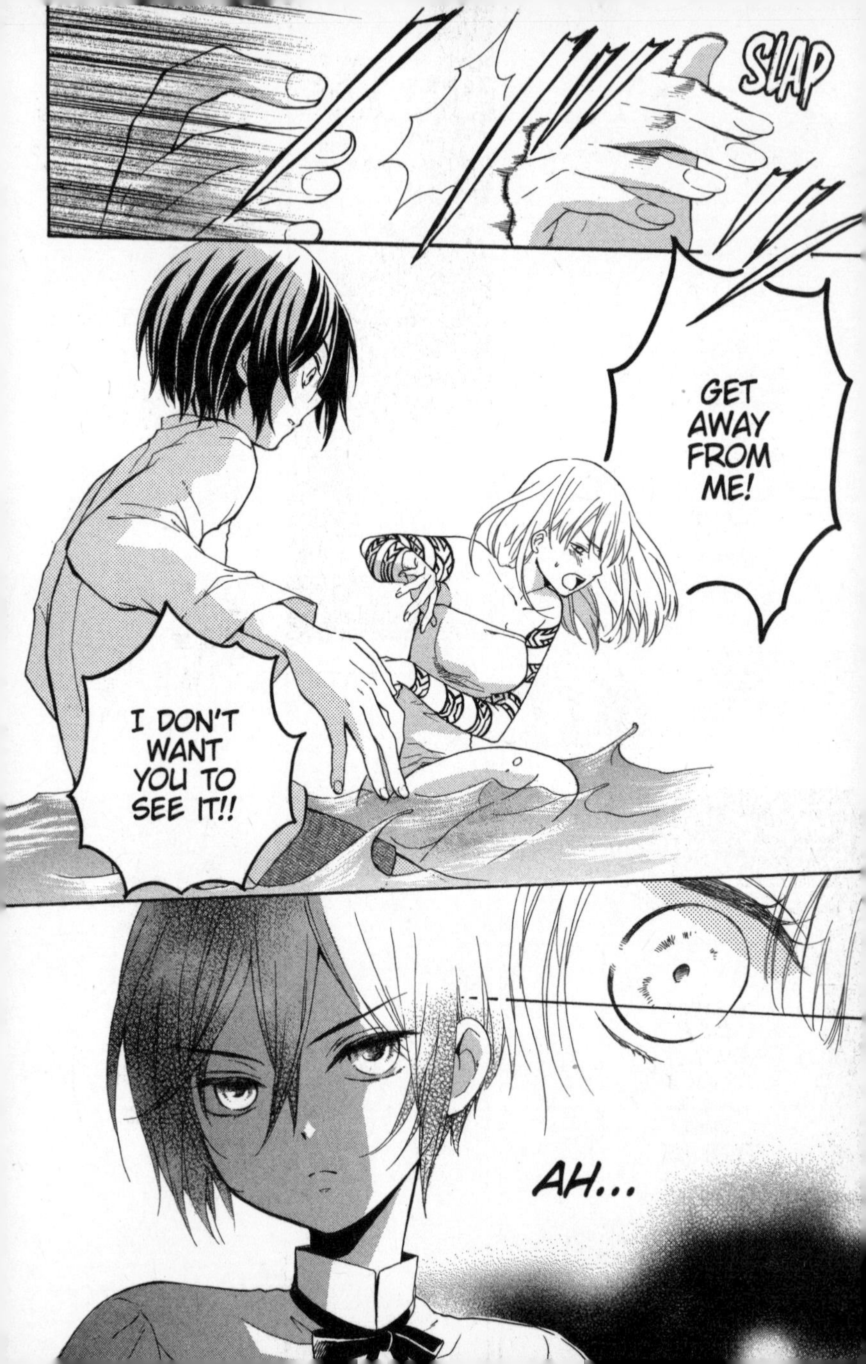
SLAP
GET AWAY FROM ME!
I DON'T WANT YOU TO SEE IT!!
AH...

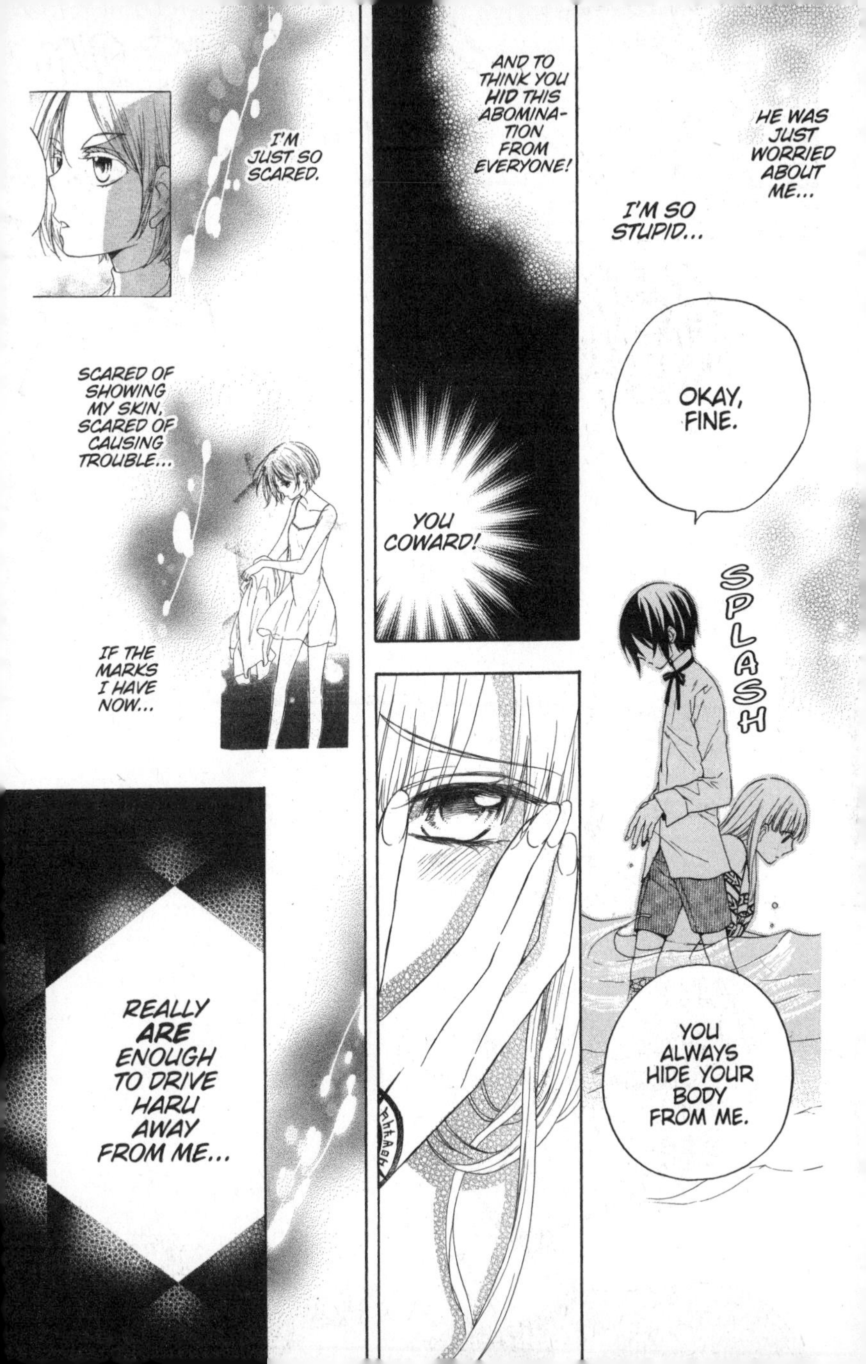

HE WAS JUST WORRIED ABOUT ME...
I'M SO STUPID...
OKAY, FINE.
SPLASH
YOU ALWAYS HIDE YOUR BODY FROM ME.
AND TO THINK YOU HID THIS ABOMINATION FROM EVERYONE!
YOU COWARD!
I'M JUST SO SCARED.
SCARED OF SHOWING MY SKIN, SCARED OF CAUSING TROUBLE...
IF THE MARKS I HAVE NOW...
REALLY ARE ENOUGH TO DRIVE HARU AWAY FROM ME...

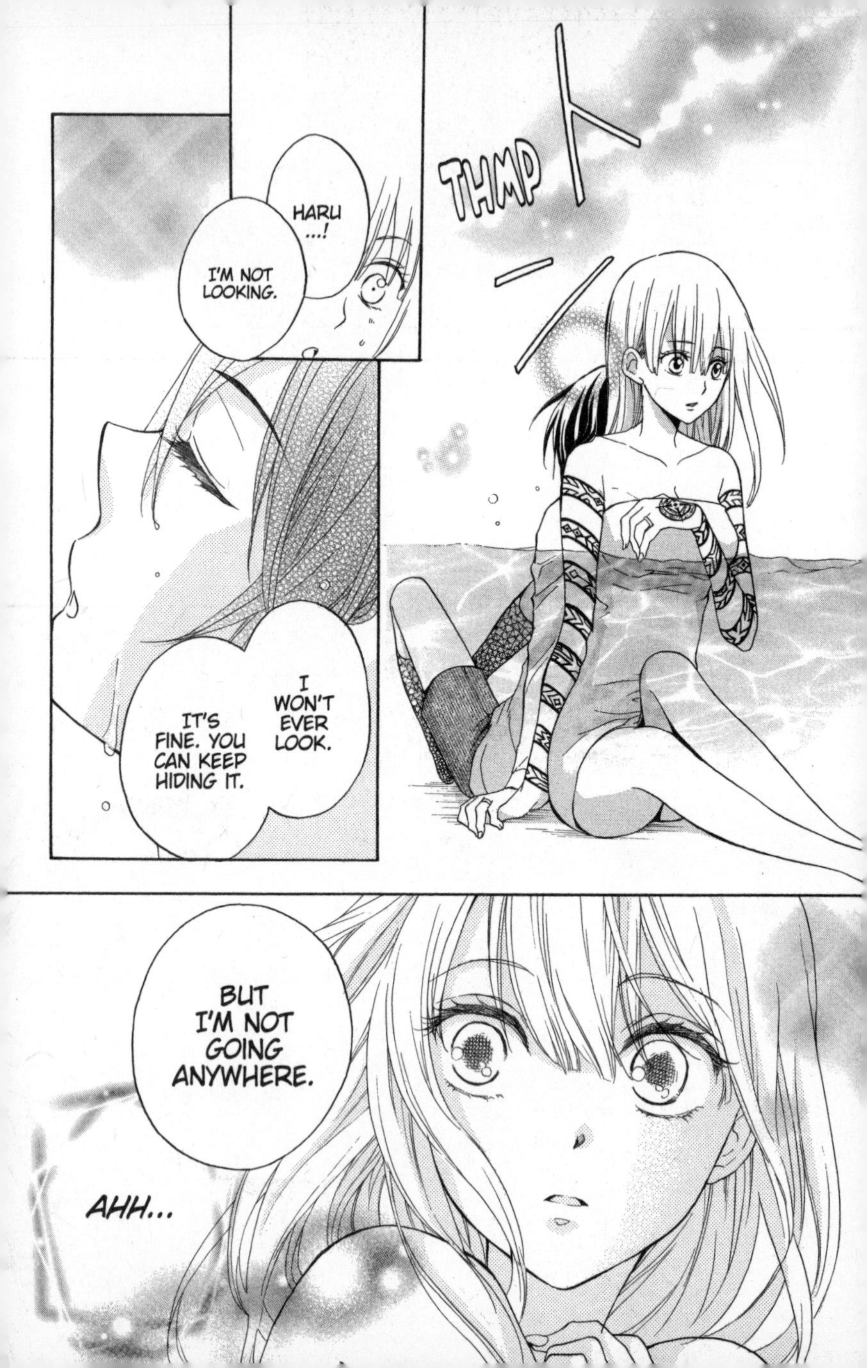
THMP
HARU ...!
I'M NOT LOOKING.
I WON'T EVER LOOK.
IT'S FINE. YOU CAN KEEP HIDING IT.
BUT I'M NOT GOING ANYWHERE.
AHH...

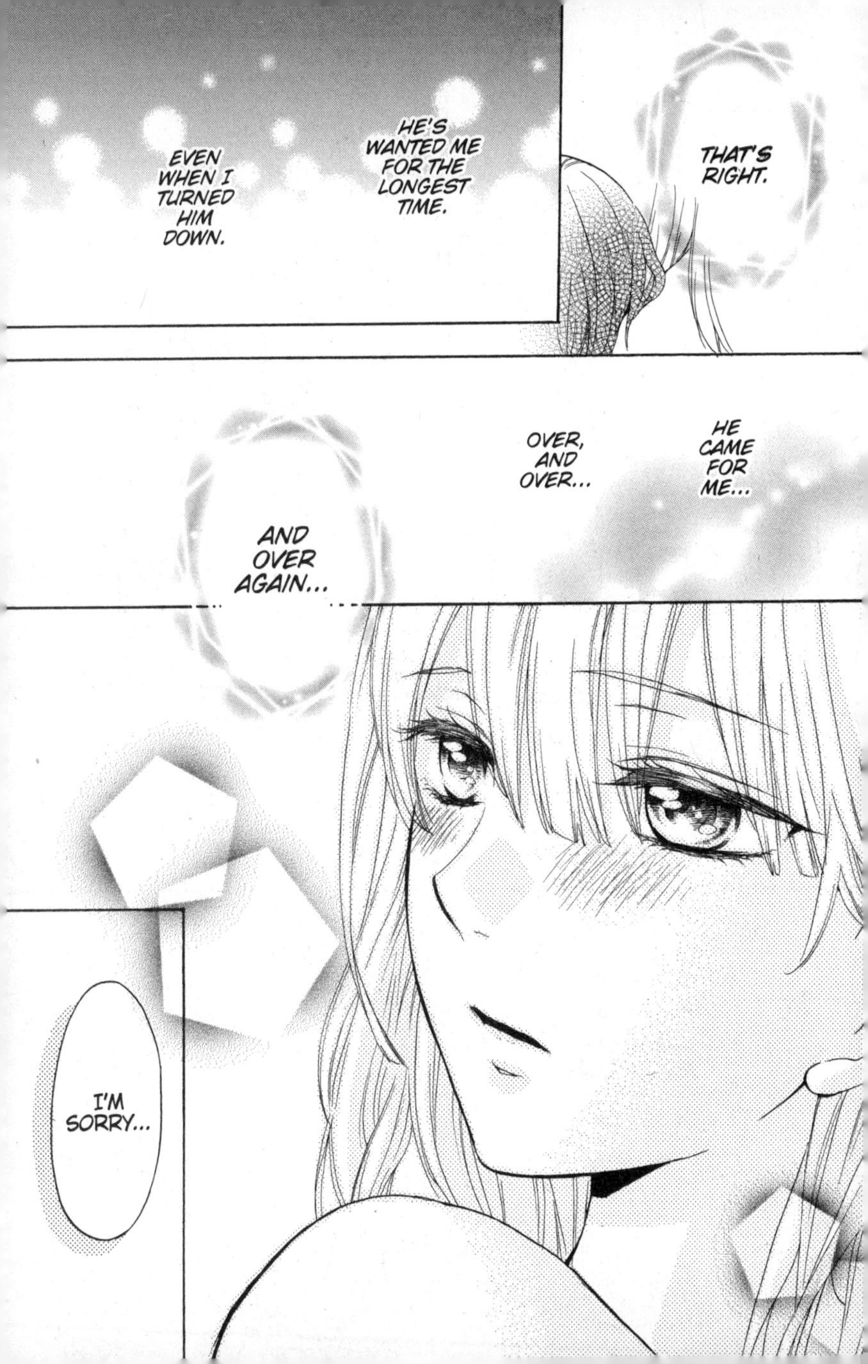
THAT'S RIGHT.
HE'S WANTED ME FOR THE LONGEST TIME.
EVEN WHEN I TURNED HIM DOWN.
HE CAME FOR ME...
OVER, AND OVER...
AND OVER AGAIN...
I'M SORRY...

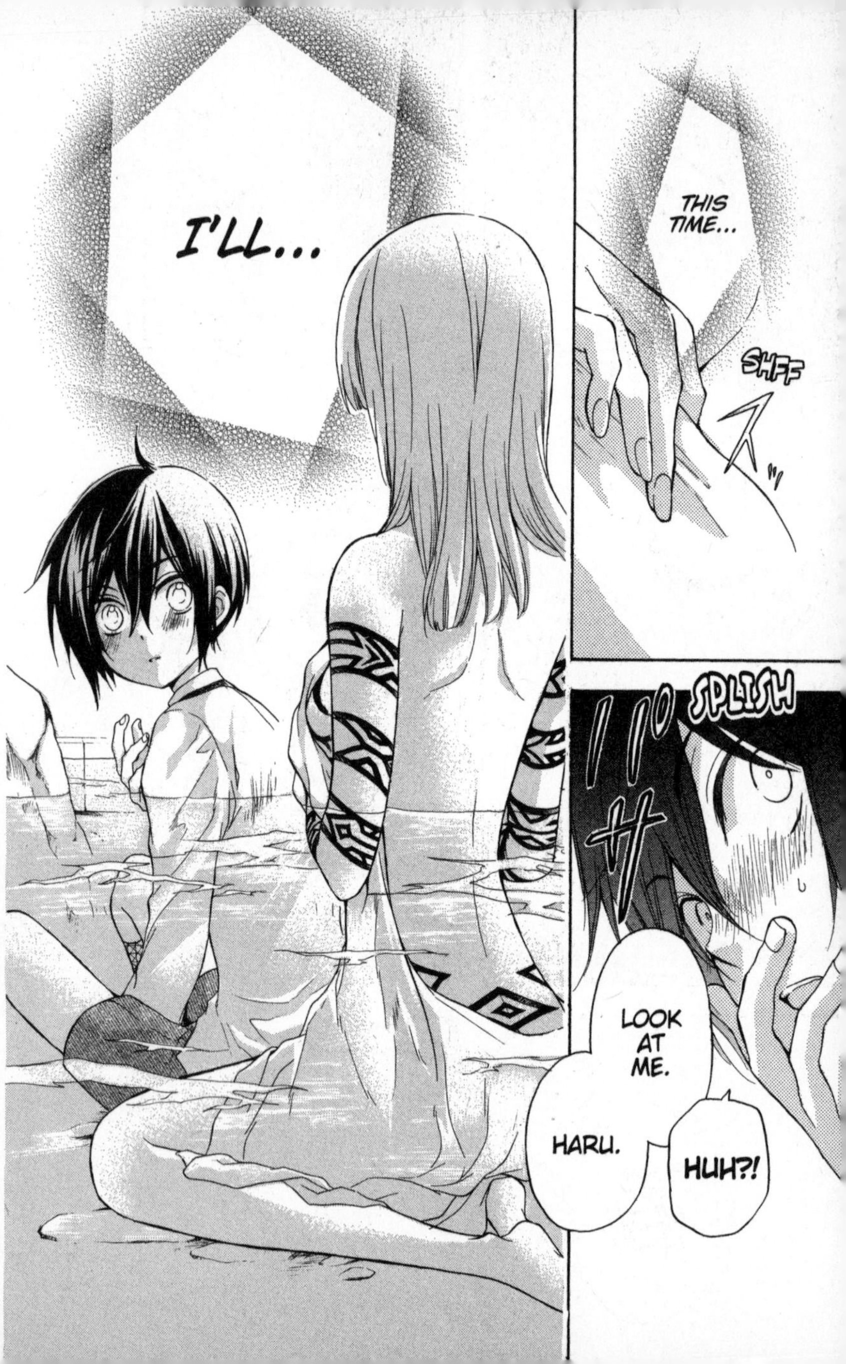
THIS TIME...
SHFF
SPLISH
LOOK AT ME.
HARU.
HUH?!
I'LL...

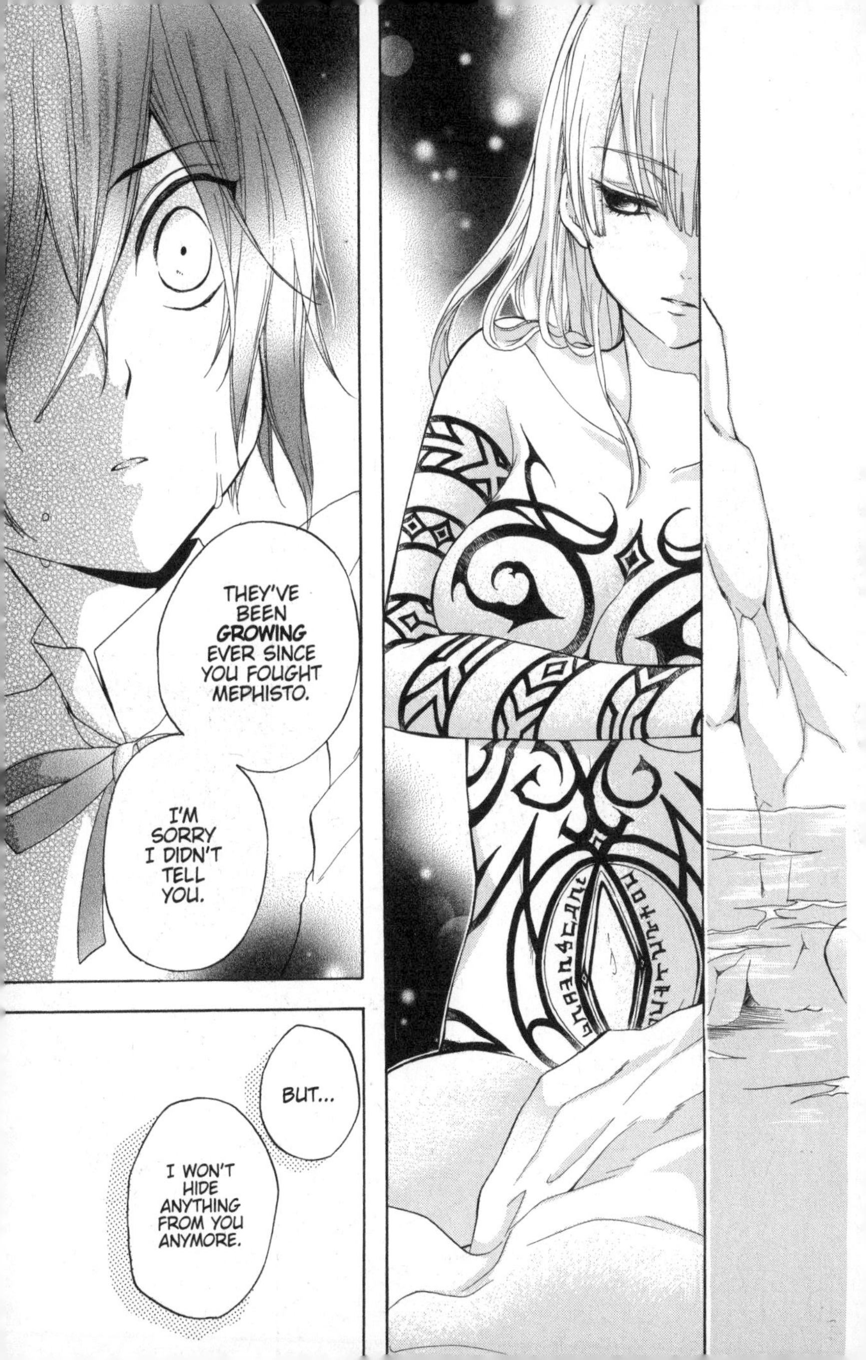
THEY'VE BEEN GROWING EVER SINCE YOU FOUGHT MEPHISTO.
I'M SORRY I DIDN'T TELL YOU.
BUT...
I WON'T HIDE ANYTHING FROM YOU ANYMORE.

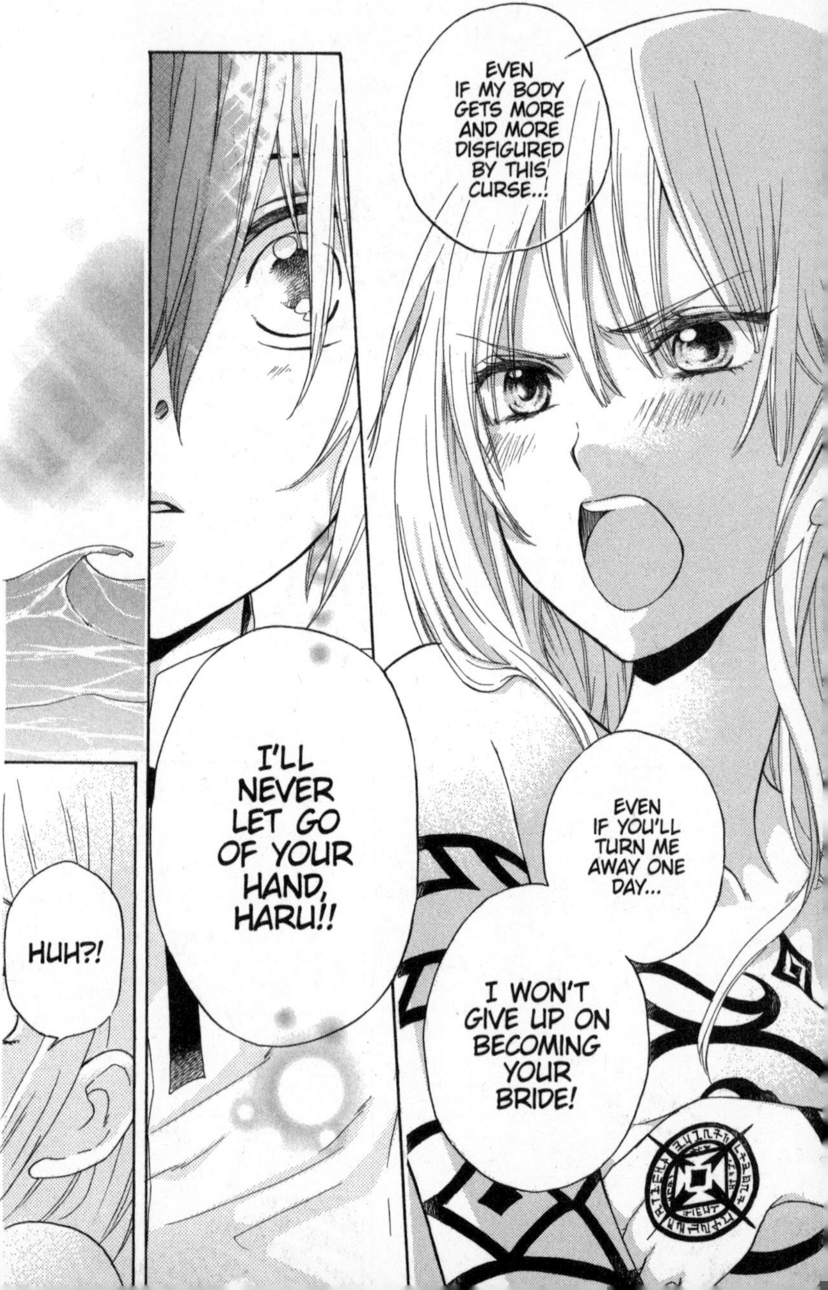
EVEN IF MY BODY GETS MORE AND MORE DISFIGURED BY THIS CURSE...
I'LL NEVER LET GO OF YOUR HAND, HARU!!
EVEN IF YOU'LL TURN ME AWAY ONE DAY...
I WON'T GIVE UP ON BECOMING YOUR BRIDE!
HUH?!

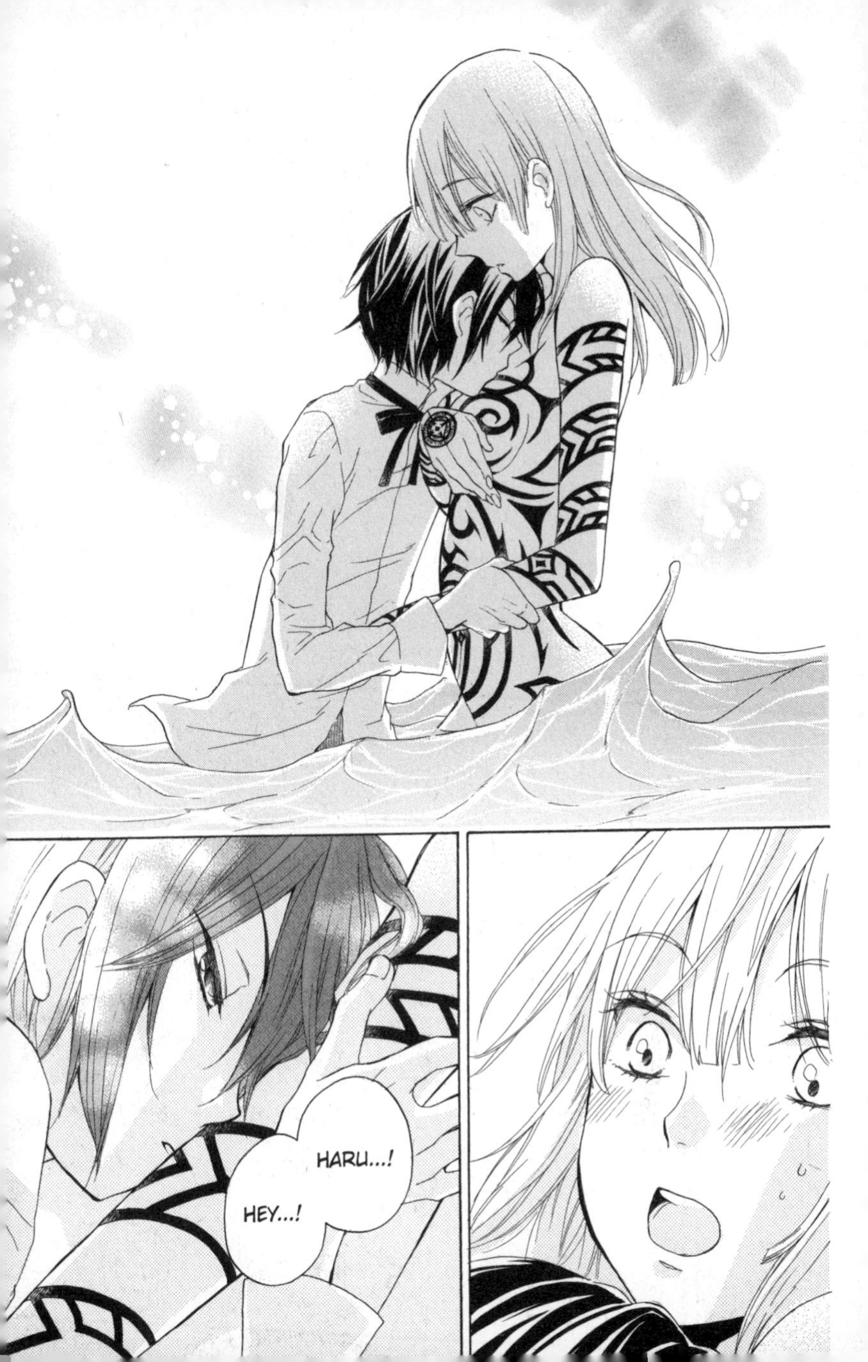
HARU...!
HEY...!

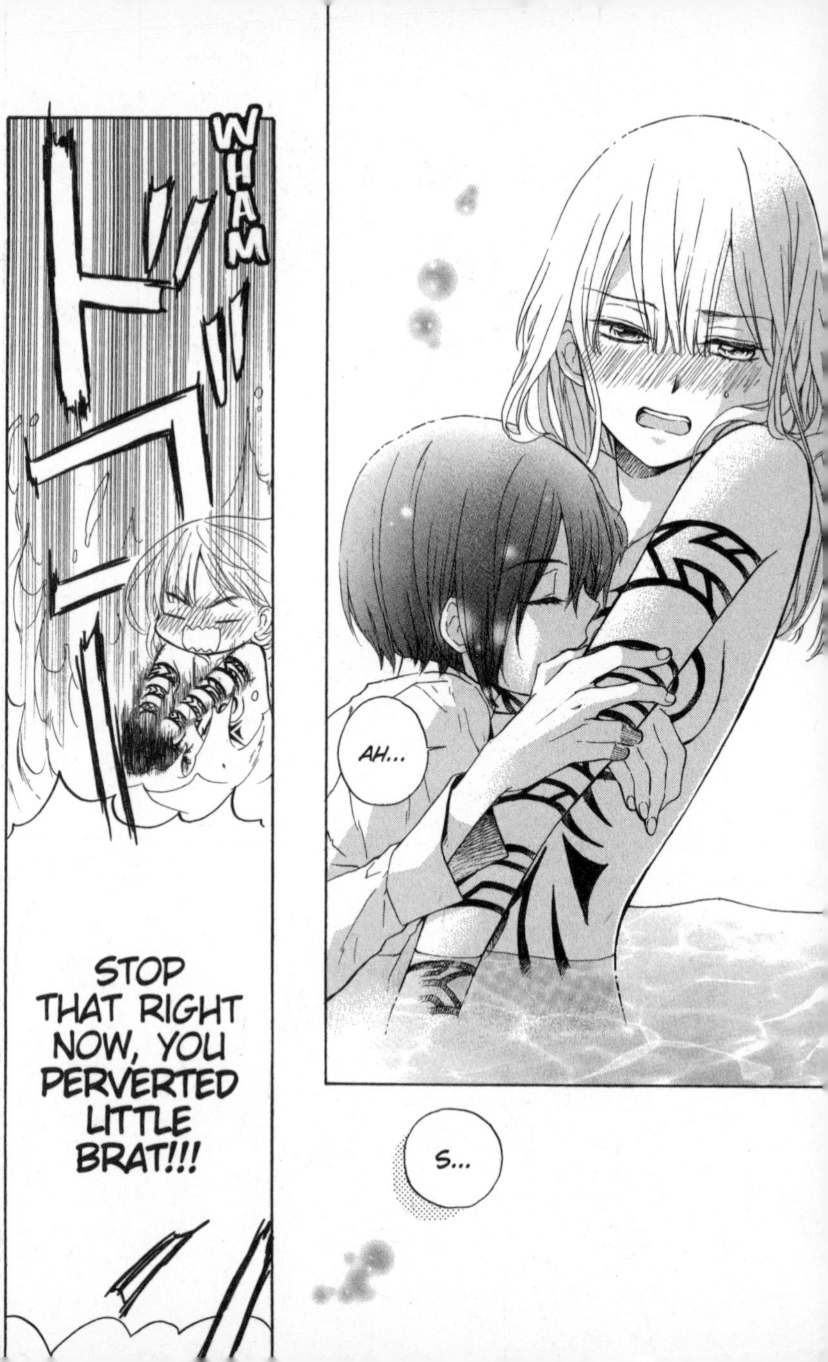
AH...
S...
WHAM
STOP THAT RIGHT NOW, YOU PERVERTED LITTLE BRAT!!!

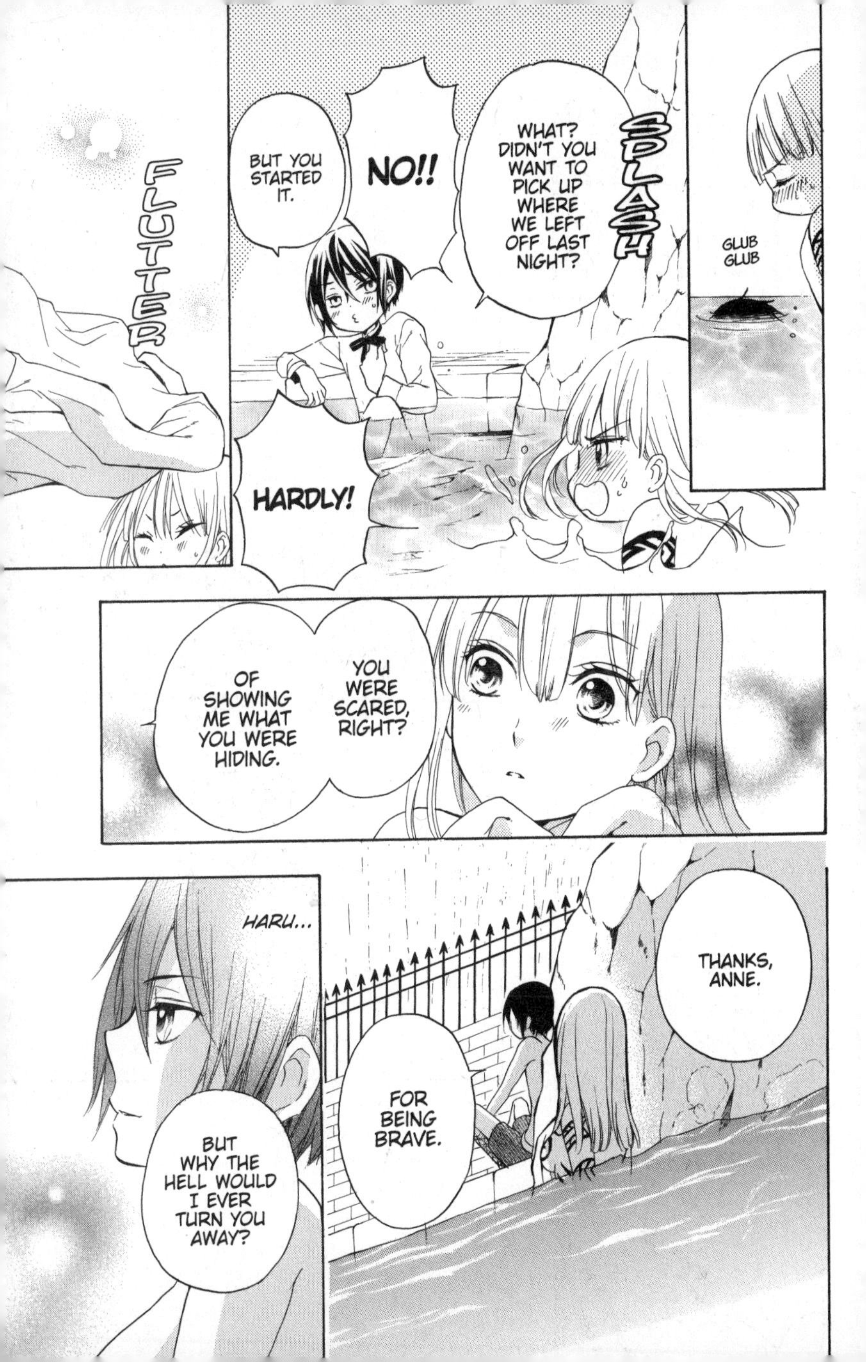
GLUB GLUB
WHAT? DIDN'T YOU WANT TO PICK UP WHERE WE LEFT OFF LAST NIGHT?
SPLASH
NO!!
BUT YOU STARTED IT.
HARDLY!
FLUTTER
YOU WERE SCARED, RIGHT?
OF SHOWING ME WHAT YOU WERE HIDING.
THANKS, ANNE.
FOR BEING BRAVE.
HARU...
BUT WHY THE HELL WOULD I EVER TURN YOU AWAY?

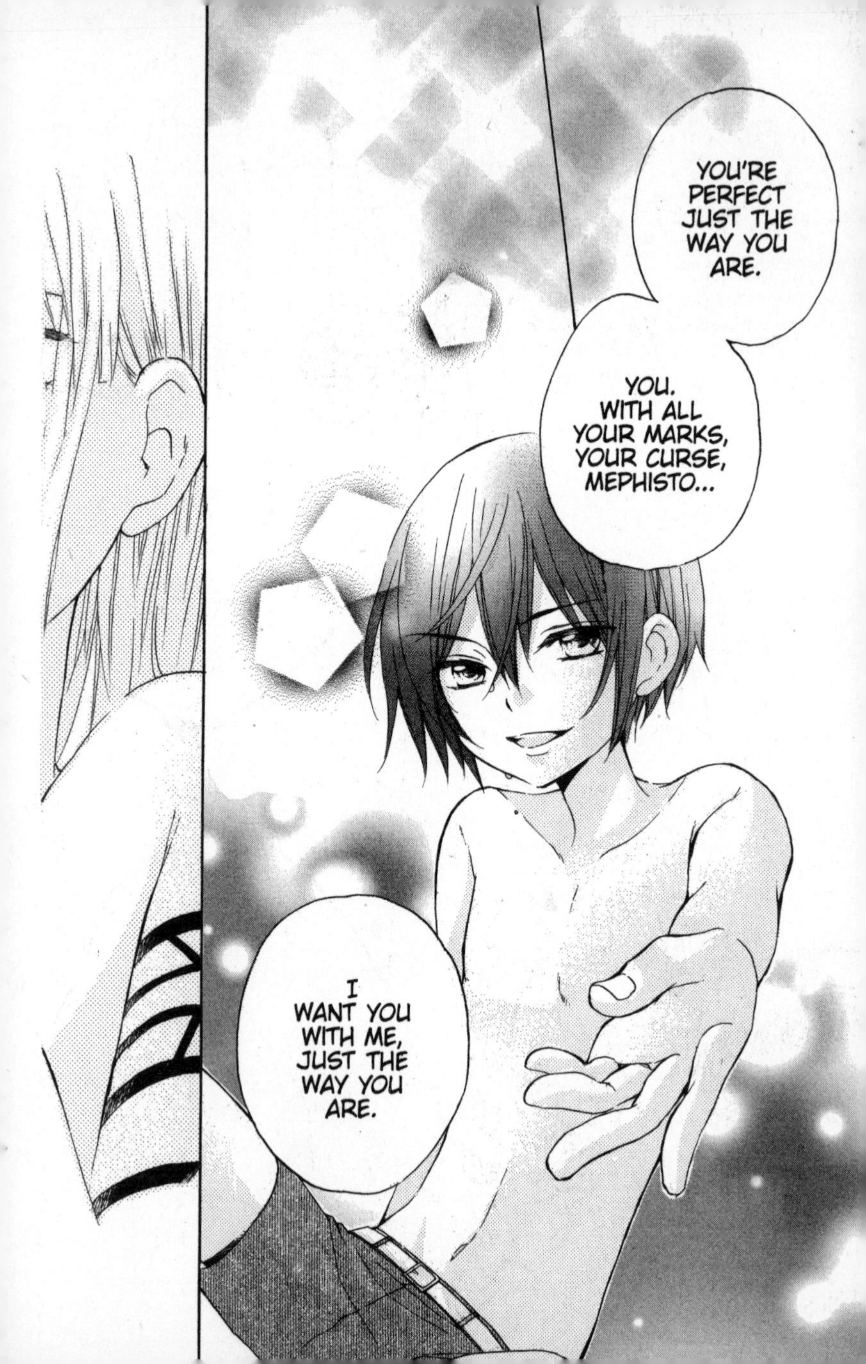
YOU'RE PERFECT JUST THE WAY YOU ARE.
YOU. WITH ALL YOUR MARKS, YOUR CURSE, MEPHISTO...
I WANT YOU WITH ME, JUST THE WAY YOU ARE.

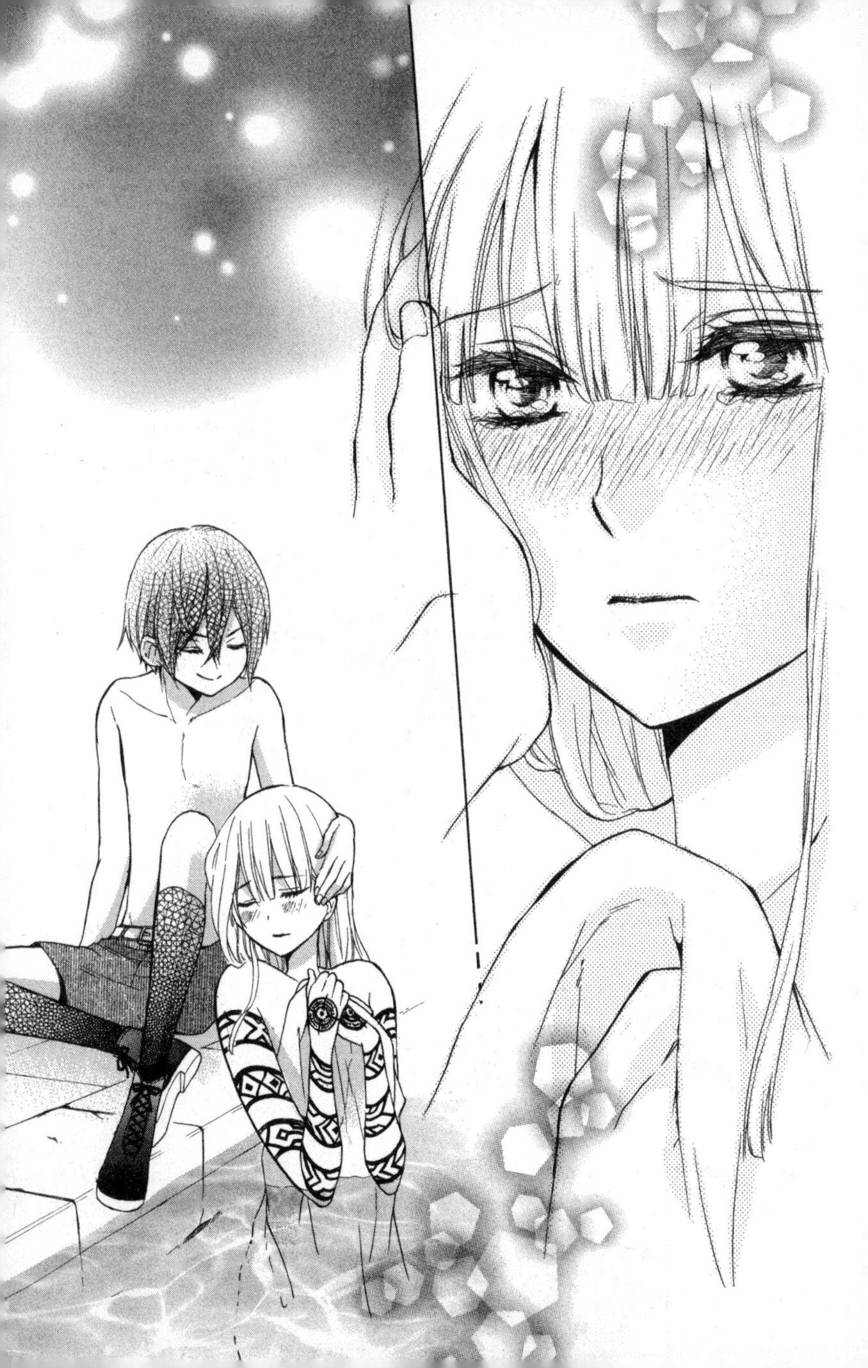

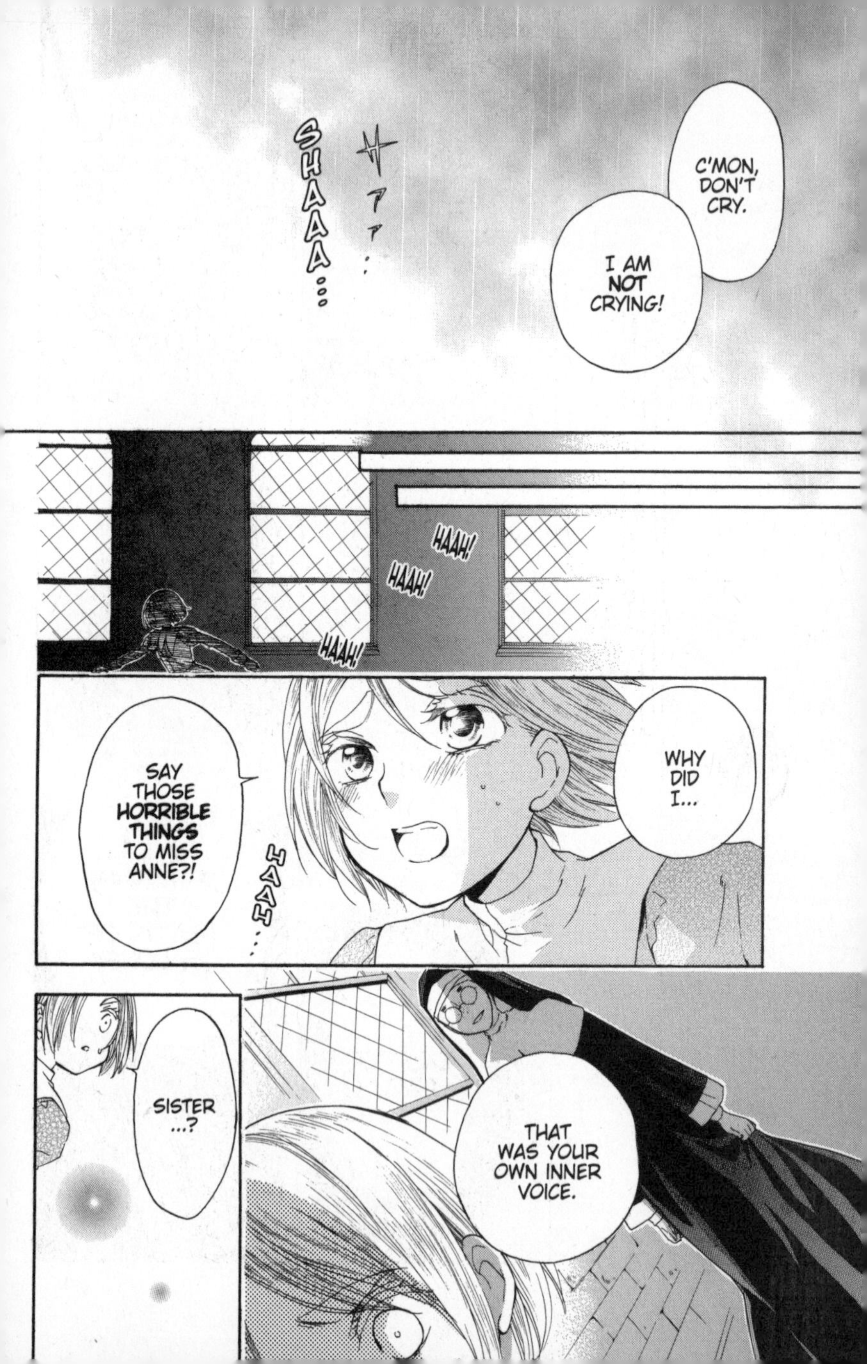
C'MON, DON'T CRY.
I AM NOT CRYING!
SHAAAA...
HAAH!
HAAH!
HAAH!
WHY DID I...
SAY THOSE HORRIBLE THINGS TO MISS ANNE?!
HAAAH...
THAT WAS YOUR OWN INNER VOICE.
SISTER ...?

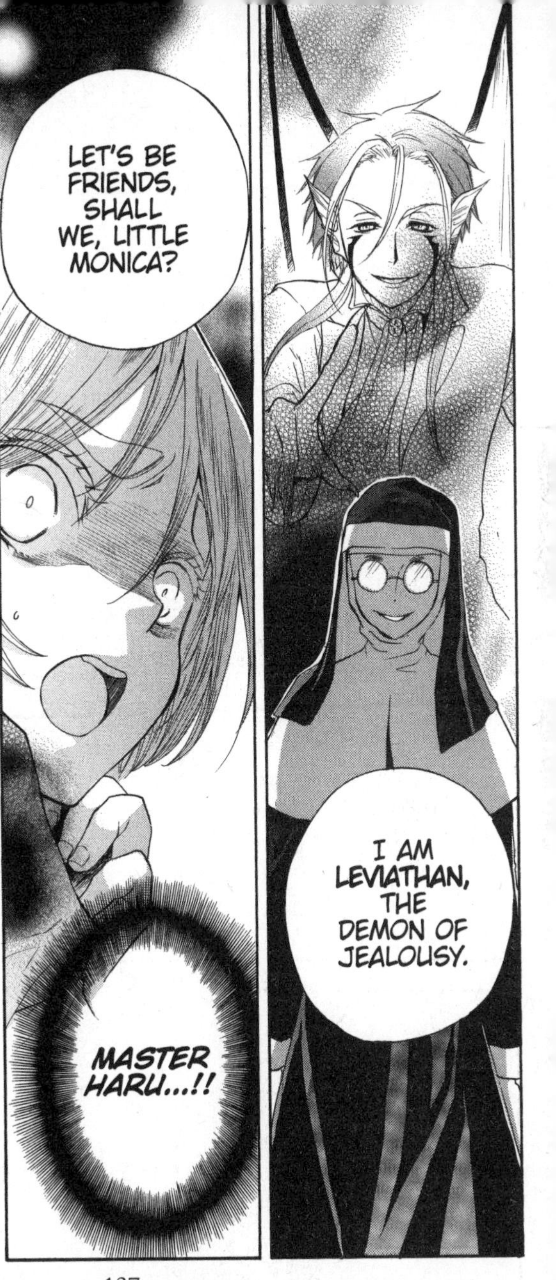
I AM LEVIATHAN, THE DEMON OF JEALOUSY.
LET'S BE FRIENDS, SHALL WE, LITTLE MONICA?
MASTER HARU...!!

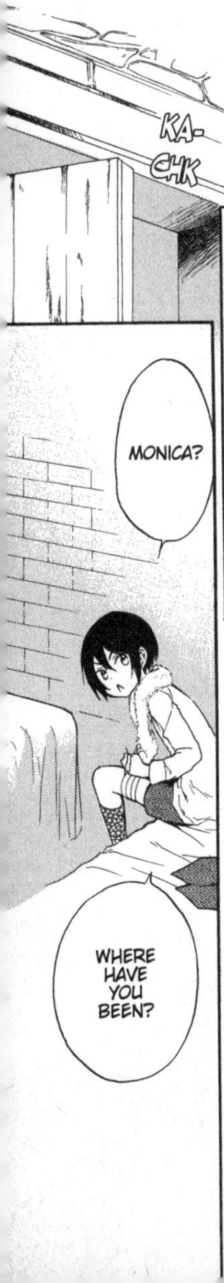
KA-CHK
MONICA?
WHERE HAVE YOU BEEN?

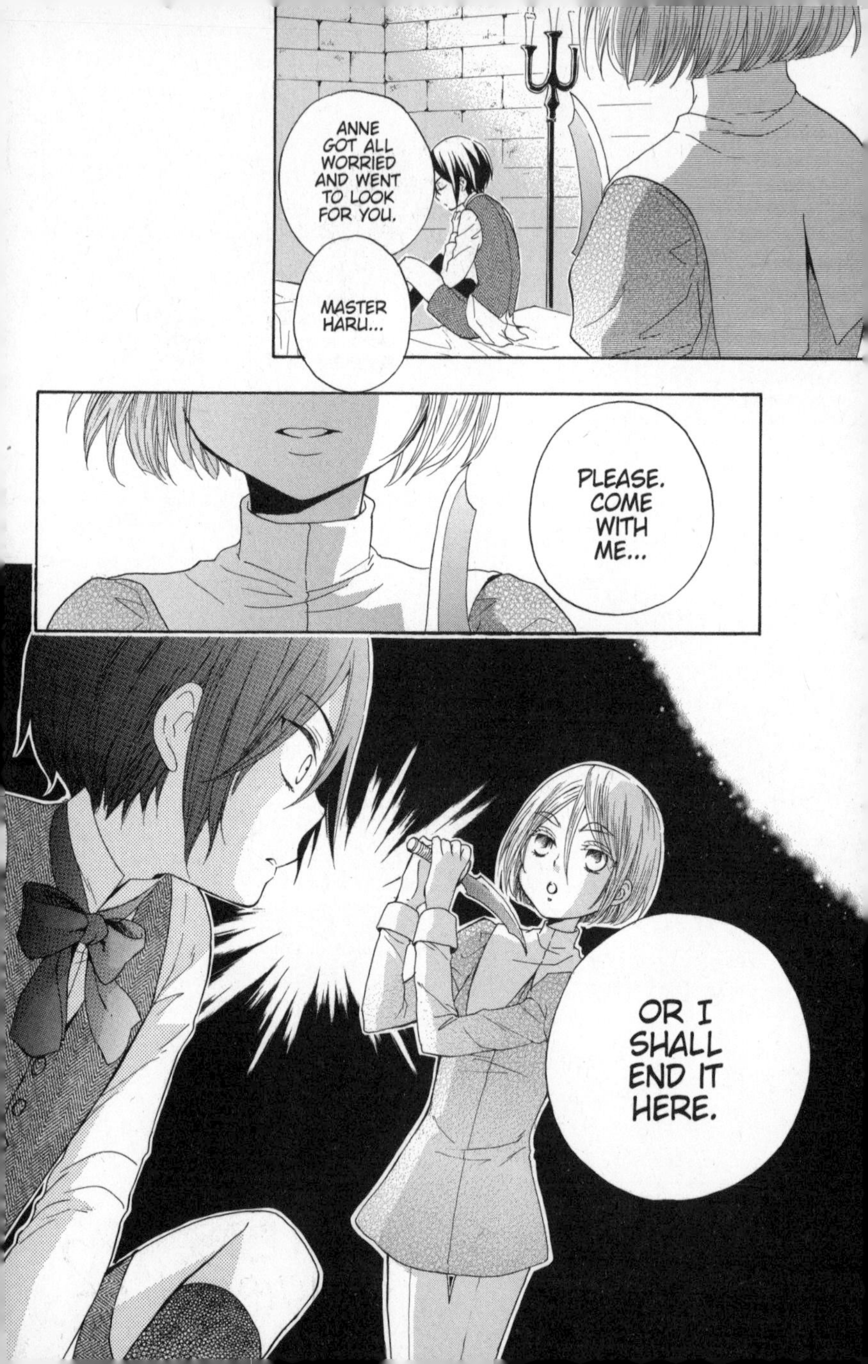
ANNE GOT ALL WORRIED AND WENT TO LOOK FOR YOU.
MASTER HARU...
PLEASE. COME WITH ME...
OR I SHALL END IT HERE.

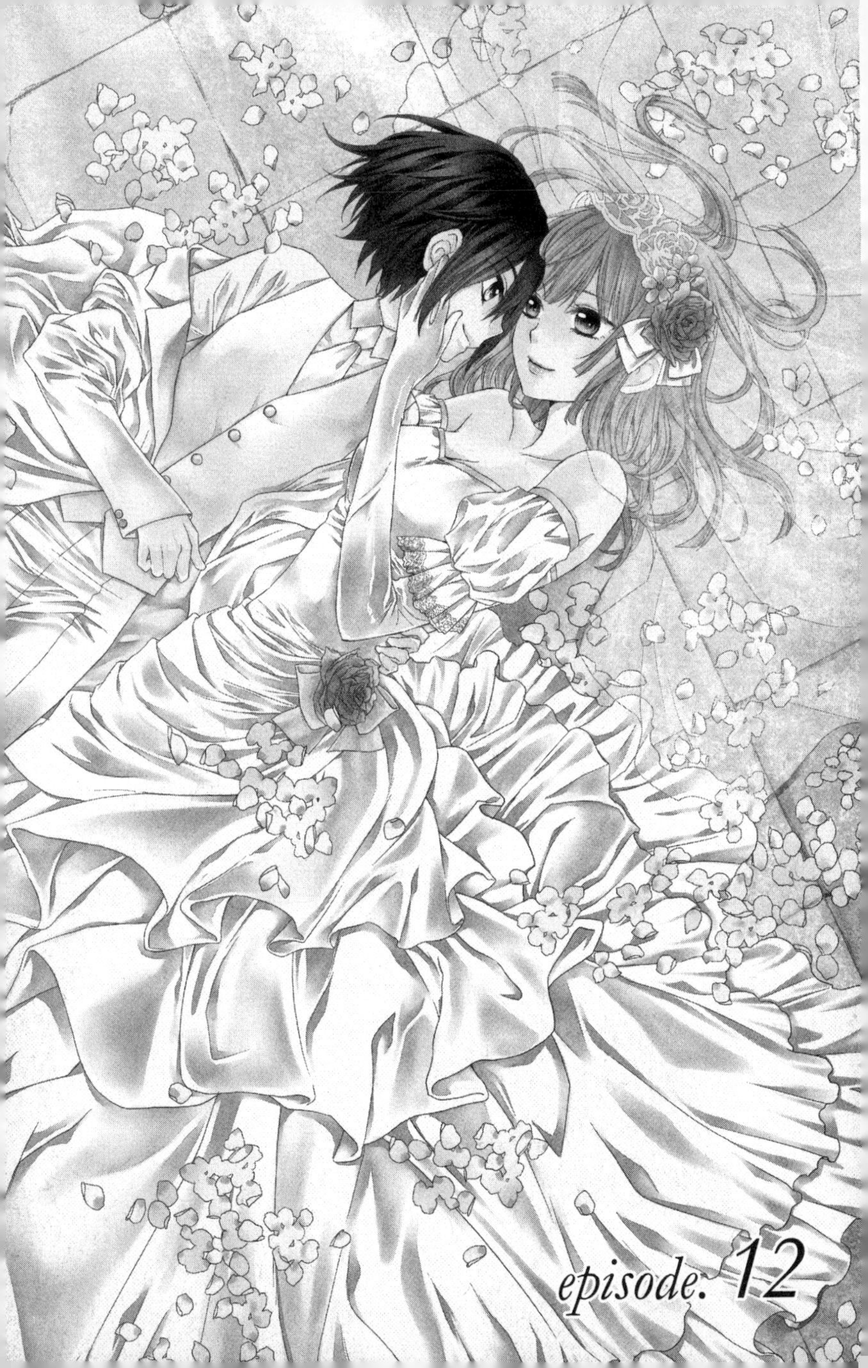
episode. 12

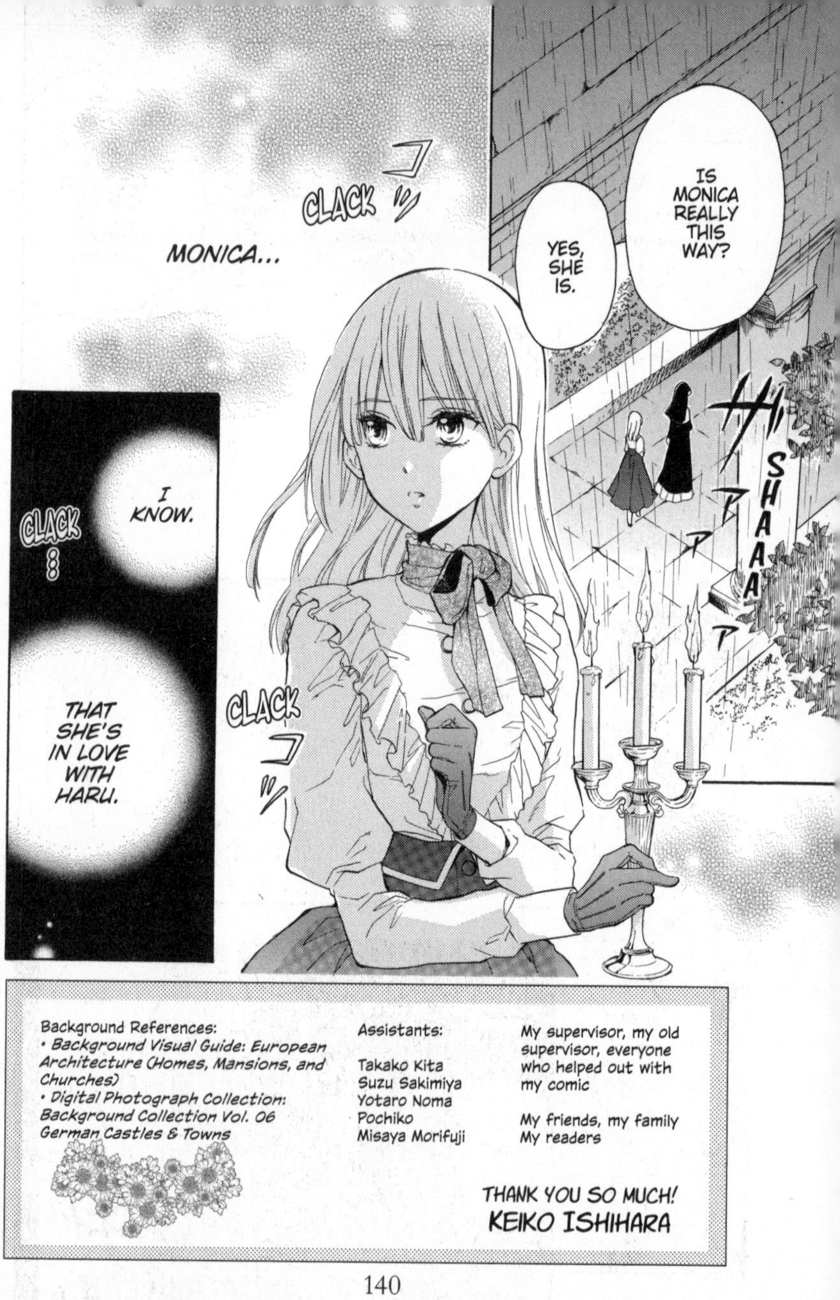
IS MONICA REALLY THIS WAY?
YES, SHE IS.
SHAAA
CLACK
MONICA...
CLACK
I KNOW.
CLACK
THAT SHE'S IN LOVE WITH HARU.

Background References:
• *Background Visual Guide: European Architecture (Homes, Mansions, and Churches)*
• *Digital Photograph Collection: Background Collection Vol. 06 German Castles & Towns*

Assistants:

Takako Kita
Suzu Sakimiya
Yotaro Noma
Pochiko
Misaya Morifuji

My supervisor, my old supervisor, everyone who helped out with my comic

My friends, my family
My readers

THANK YOU SO MUCH!
KEIKO ISHIHARA

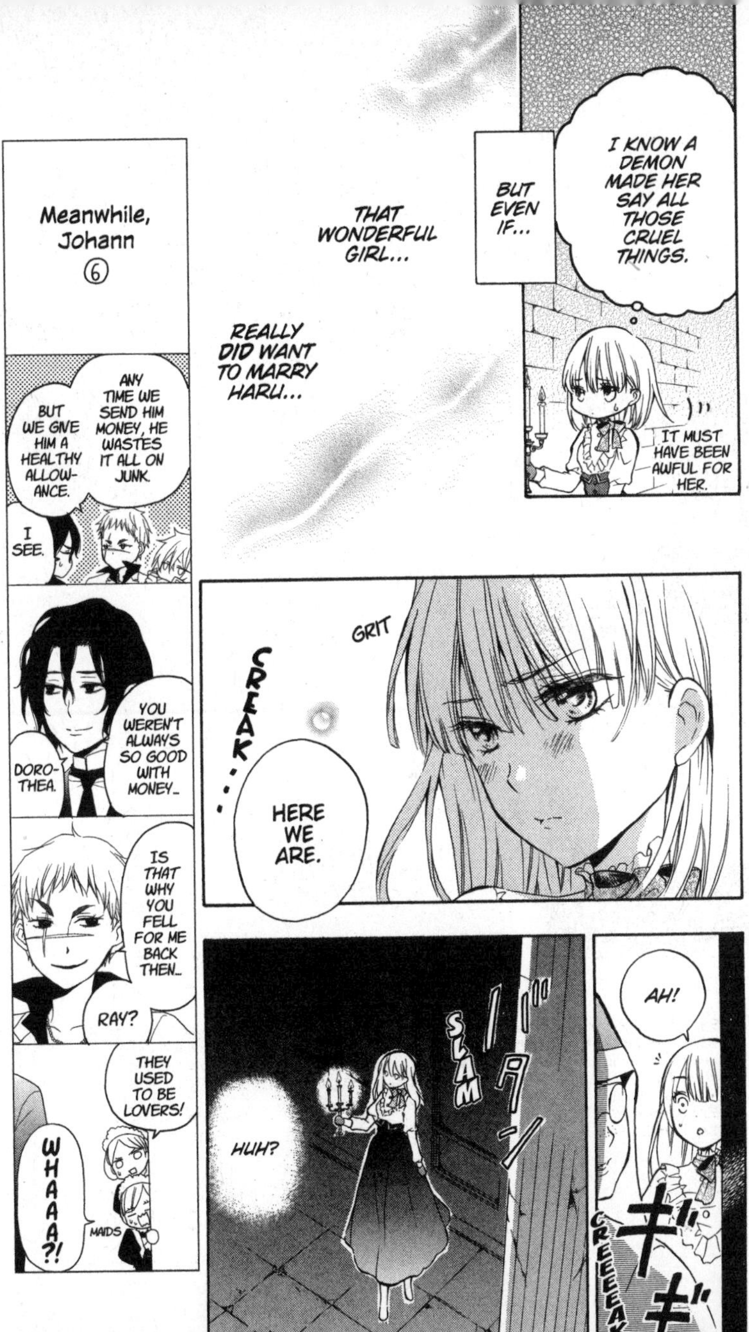
I KNOW A DEMON MADE HER SAY ALL THOSE CRUEL THINGS.
BUT EVEN IF...
IT MUST HAVE BEEN AWFUL FOR HER.
THAT WONDERFUL GIRL...
REALLY DID WANT TO MARRY HARU...
GRIT
CREAK...
HERE WE ARE.
AH!
CREEEEAK
SLAM
HUH?
Meanwhile, Johann ⑥
ANY TIME WE SEND HIM MONEY, HE WASTES IT ALL ON JUNK.
BUT WE GIVE HIM A HEALTHY ALLOW-ANCE.
I SEE.
YOU WEREN'T ALWAYS SO GOOD WITH MONEY...
DORO-THEA.
IS THAT WHY YOU FELL FOR ME BACK THEN...
RAY?
THEY USED TO BE LOVERS!
WHAAAA?!
MAIDS

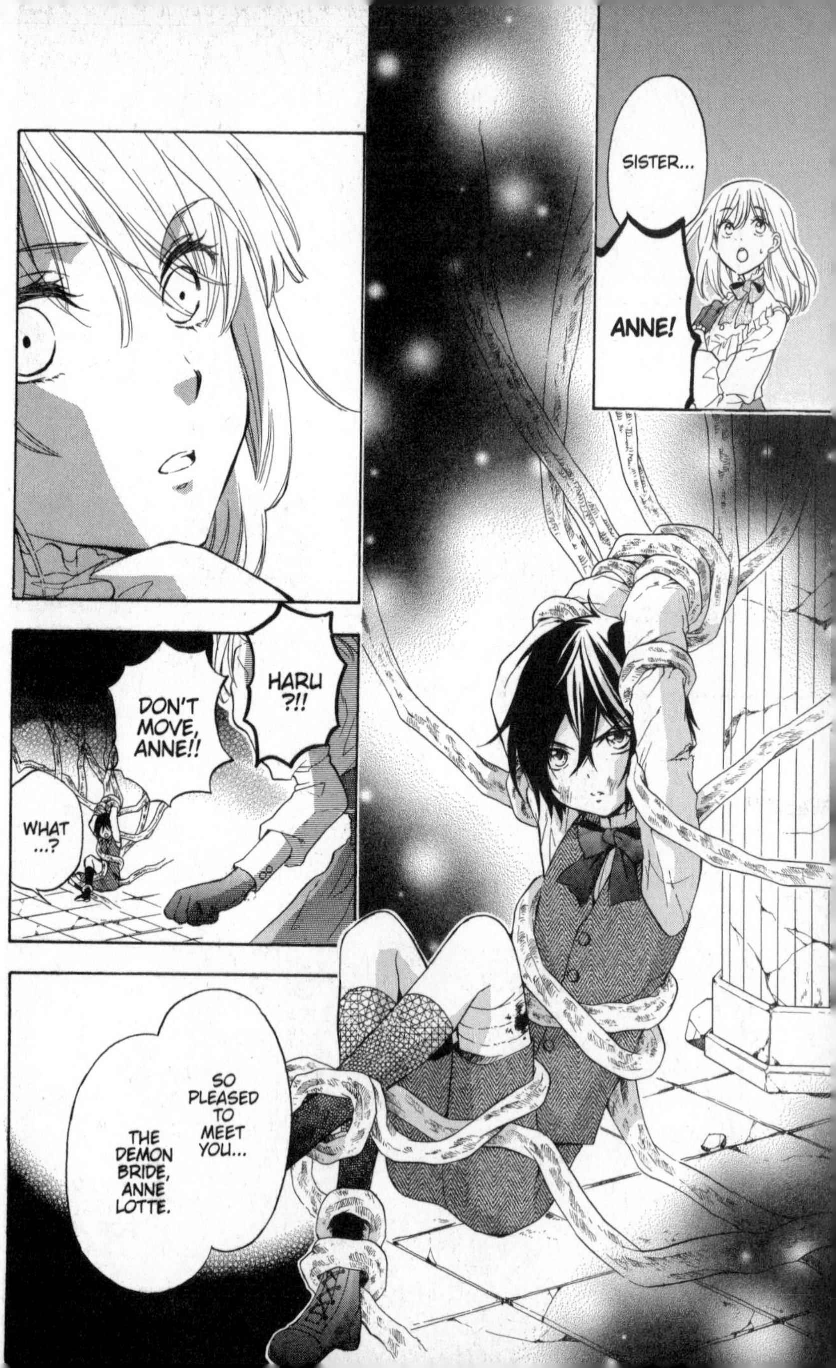
SISTER...
ANNE!
HARU ?!!
DON'T MOVE, ANNE!!
WHAT ...?
SO PLEASED TO MEET YOU...
THE DEMON BRIDE, ANNE LOTTE.

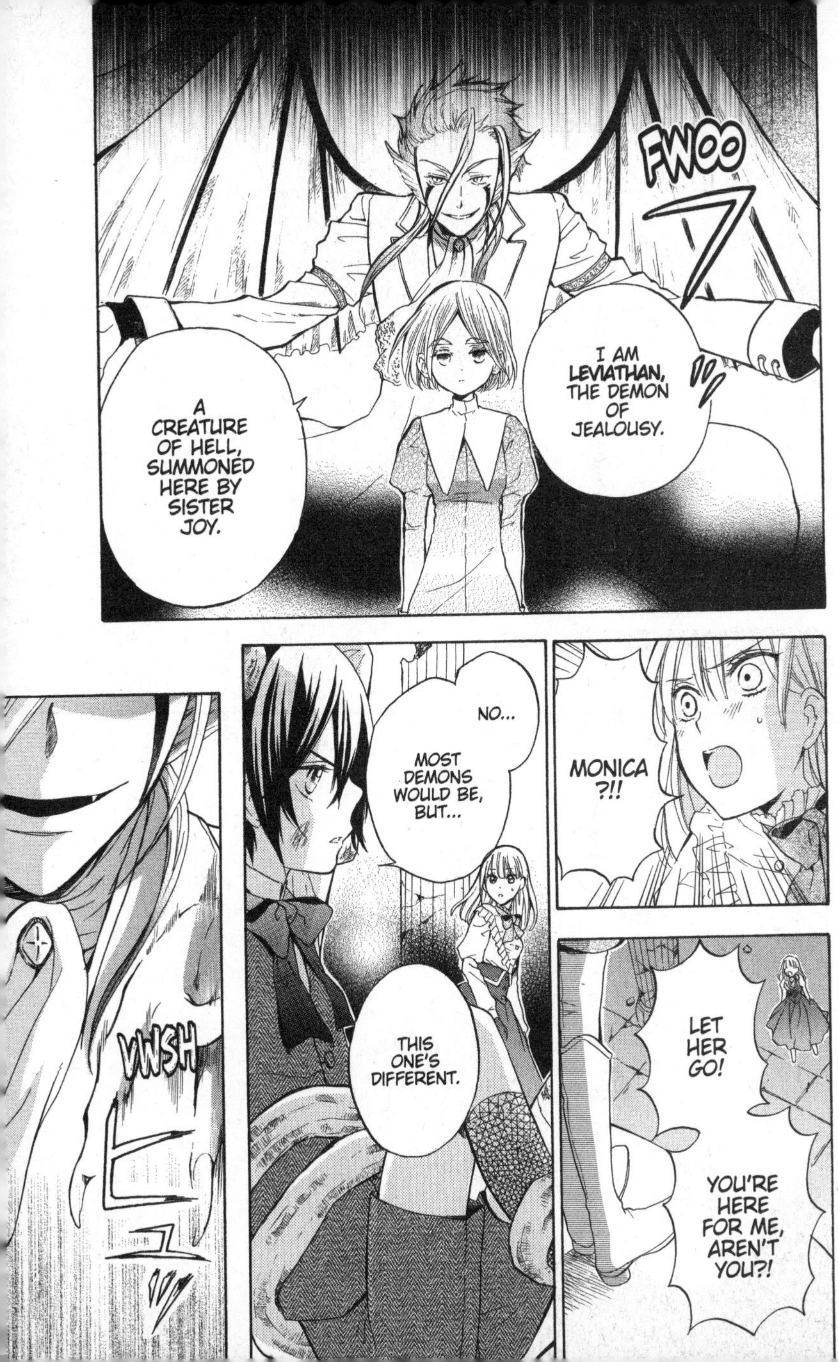
FWOO
I AM LEVIATHAN, THE DEMON OF JEALOUSY.
A CREATURE OF HELL, SUMMONED HERE BY SISTER JOY.
MONICA ?!!
LET HER GO!
YOU'RE HERE FOR ME, AREN'T YOU?!
NO...
MOST DEMONS WOULD BE, BUT...
THIS ONE'S DIFFERENT.
VWSH

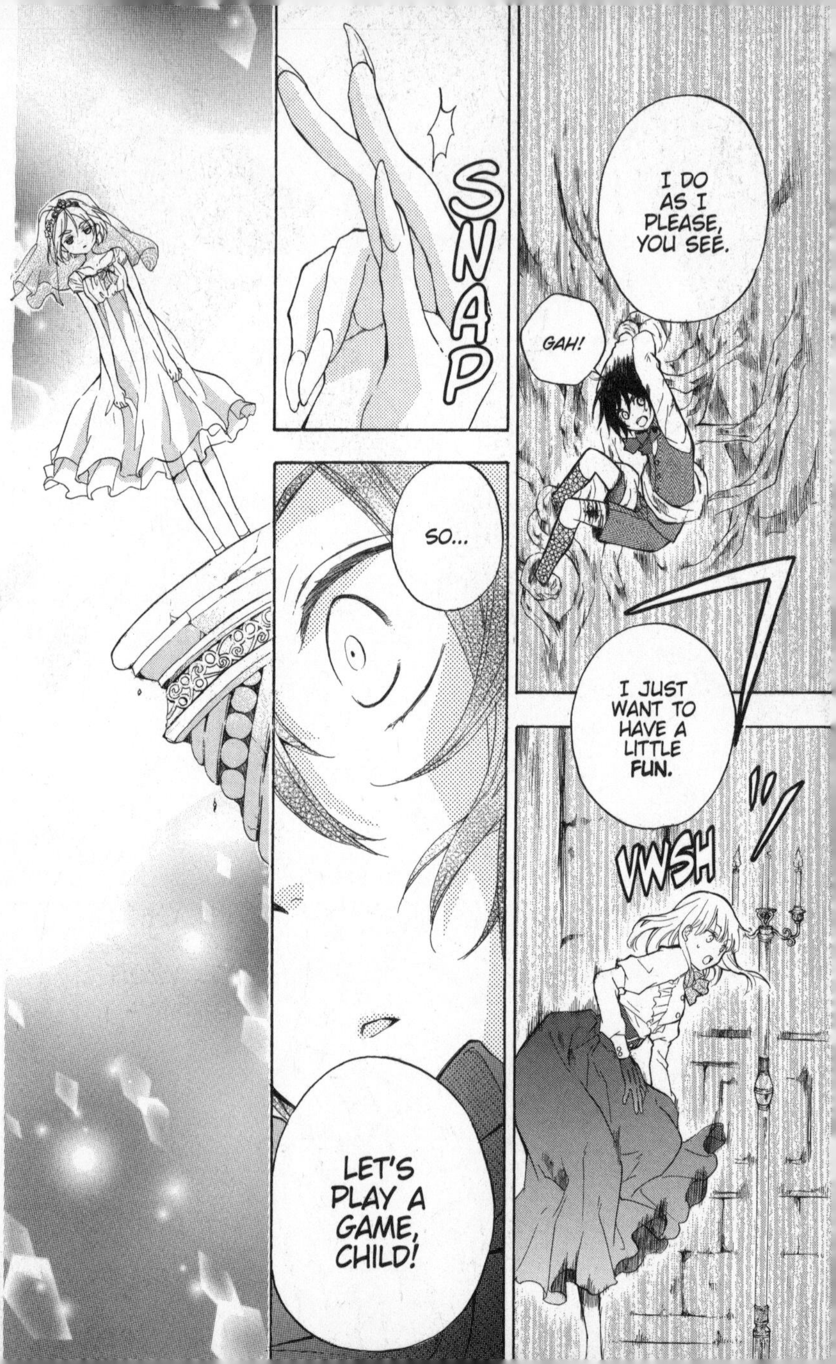
I DO AS I PLEASE, YOU SEE.
GAH!
I JUST WANT TO HAVE A LITTLE FUN.
VWSH
SNAP
SO...
LET'S PLAY A GAME, CHILD!

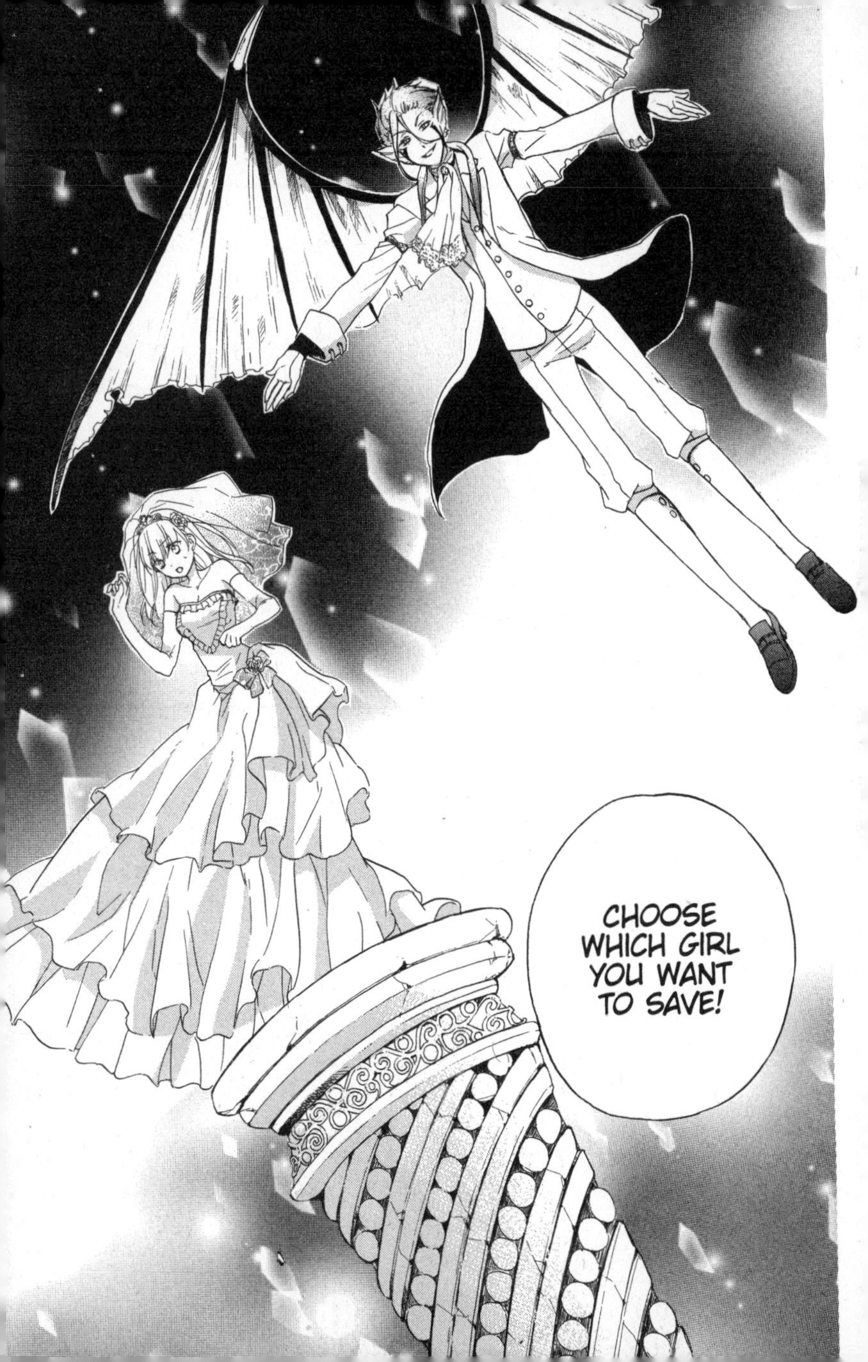
CHOOSE WHICH GIRL YOU WANT TO SAVE!

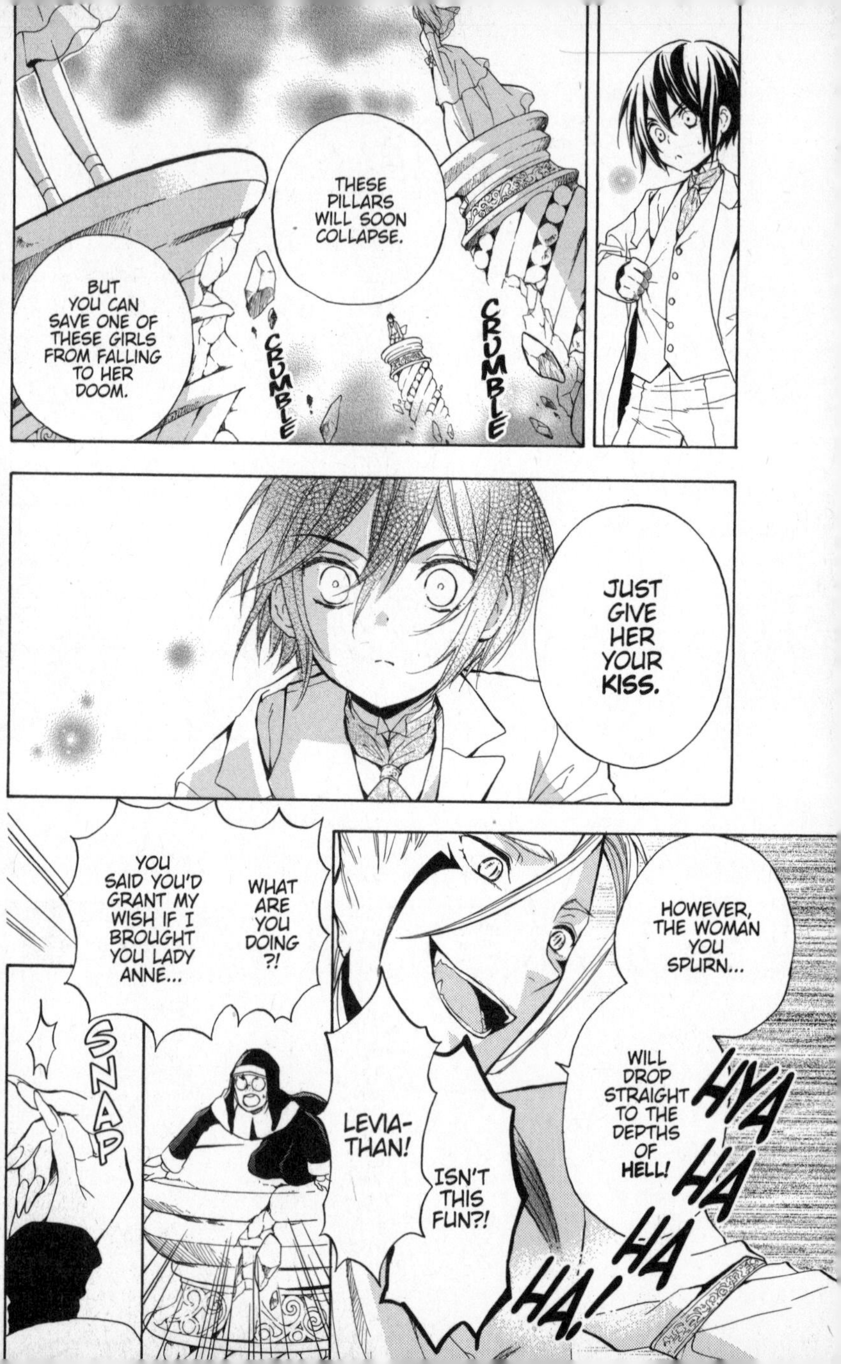
THESE PILLARS WILL SOON COLLAPSE.
CRUMBLE
CRUMBLE
BUT YOU CAN SAVE ONE OF THESE GIRLS FROM FALLING TO HER DOOM.
JUST GIVE HER YOUR KISS.
HOWEVER, THE WOMAN YOU SPURN...
WILL DROP STRAIGHT TO THE DEPTHS OF HELL!
HYA HA HA HA!
ISN'T THIS FUN?!
LEVIA-THAN!
WHAT ARE YOU DOING?!
YOU SAID YOU'D GRANT MY WISH IF I BROUGHT YOU LADY ANNE...
SNAP

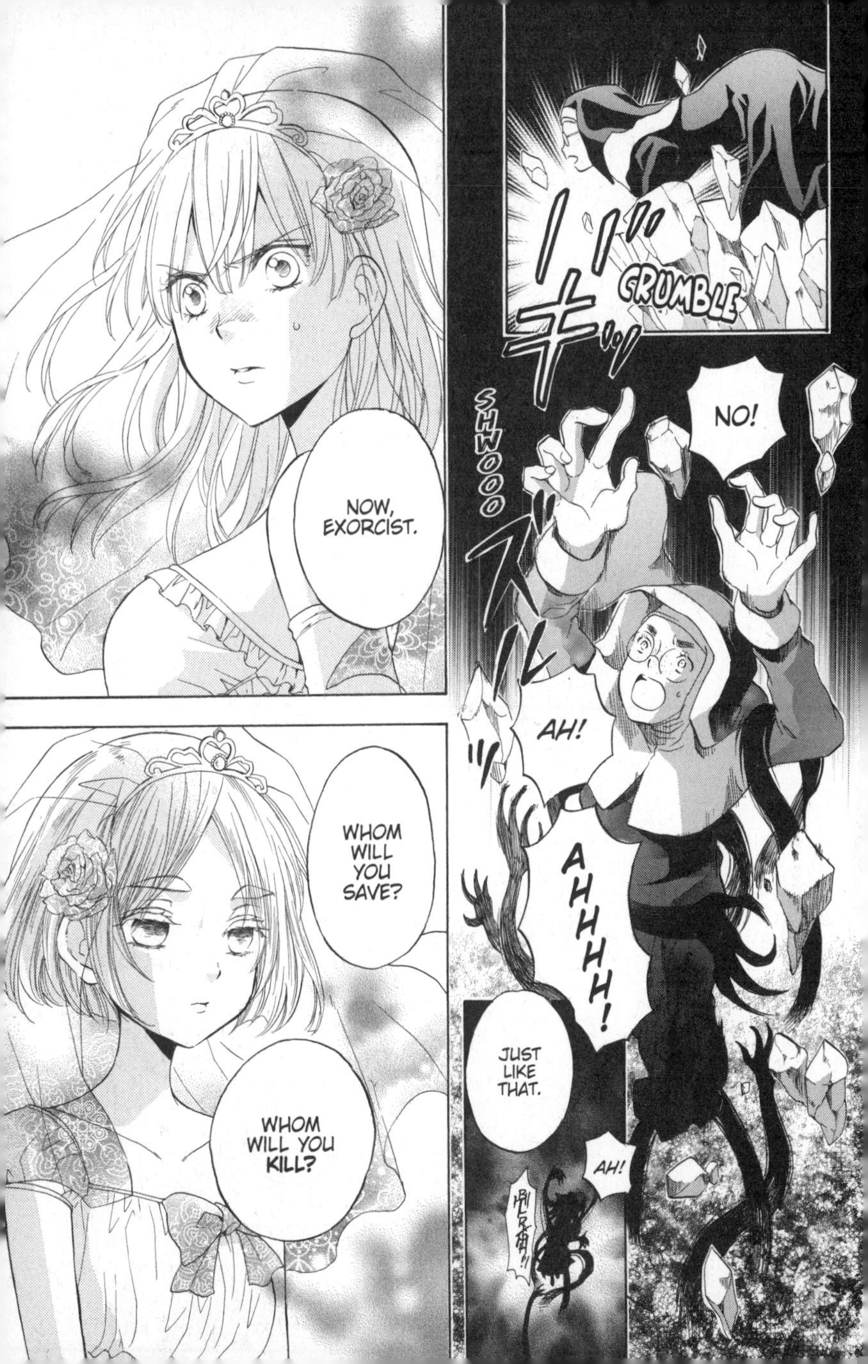
CRUMBLE
NO!
SHWOOO
AH!
AHHHHH!
JUST LIKE THAT.
AH!
NOW, EXORCIST.
WHOM WILL YOU SAVE?
WHOM WILL YOU KILL?

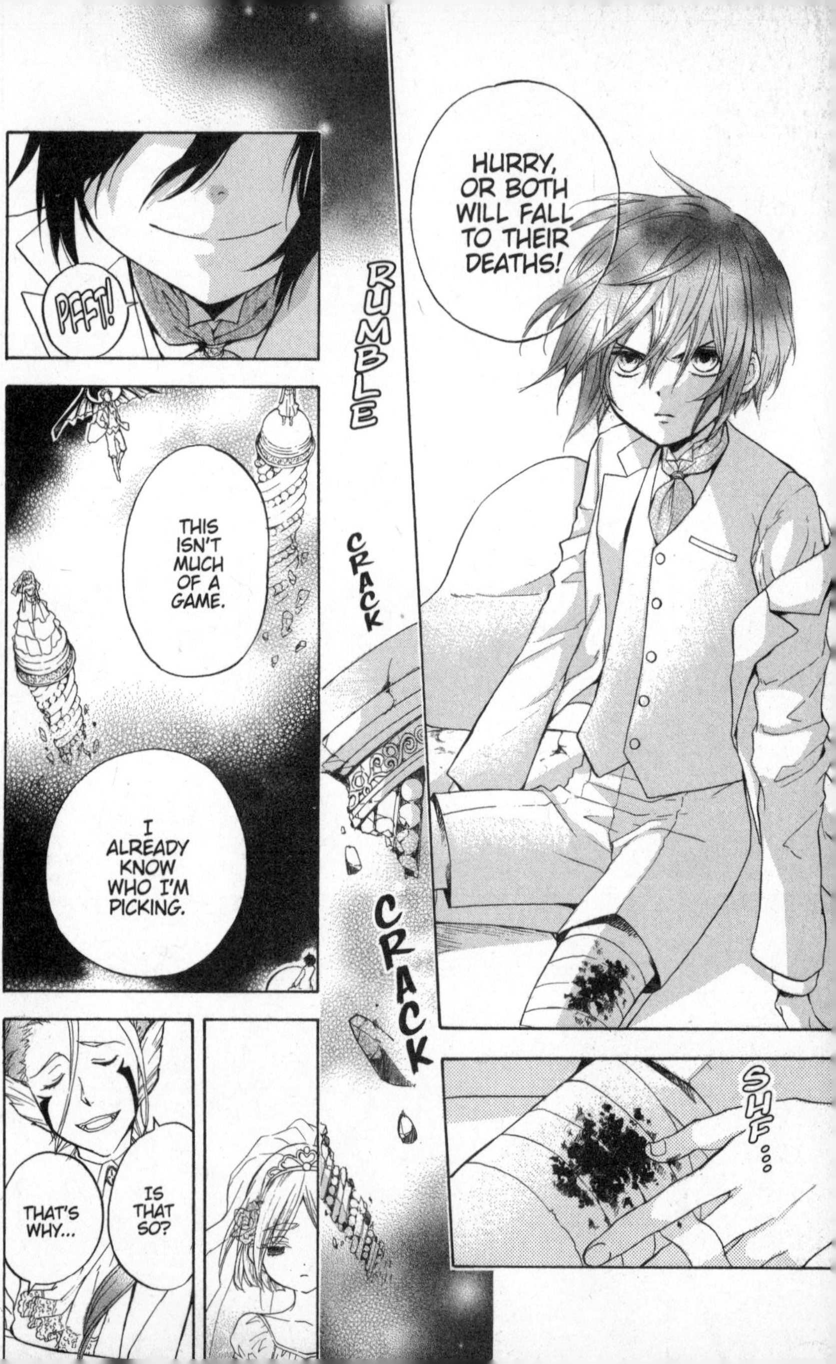
HURRY, OR BOTH WILL FALL TO THEIR DEATHS!
RUMBLE
CRACK
CRACK
SHF...
PFFT!
THIS ISN'T MUCH OF A GAME.
I ALREADY KNOW WHO I'M PICKING.
IS THAT SO?
THAT'S WHY...

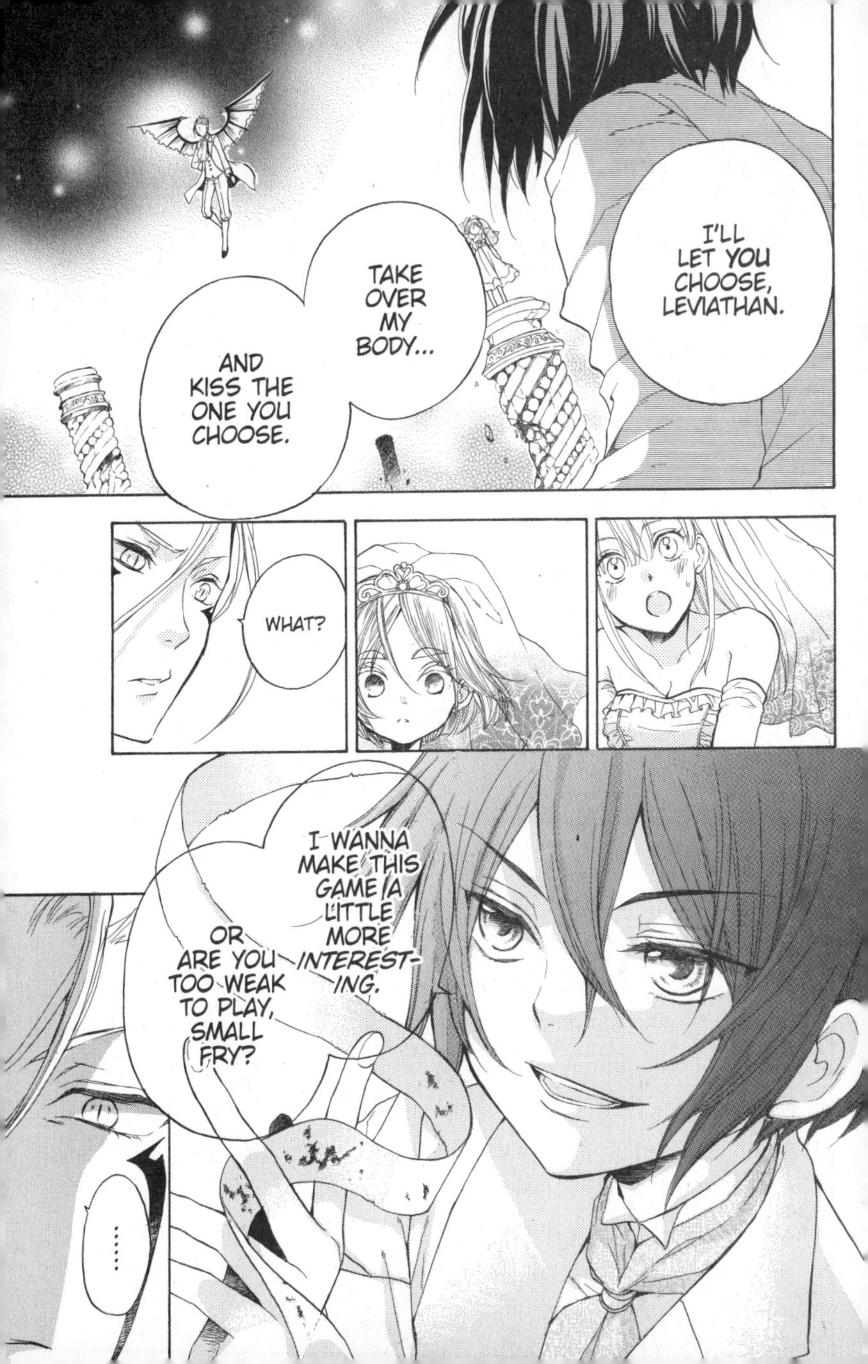
I'LL LET YOU CHOOSE, LEVIATHAN.
TAKE OVER MY BODY...
AND KISS THE ONE YOU CHOOSE.
WHAT?
I WANNA MAKE THIS GAME A LITTLE MORE INTEREST-ING.
OR ARE YOU TOO WEAK TO PLAY, SMALL FRY?
......

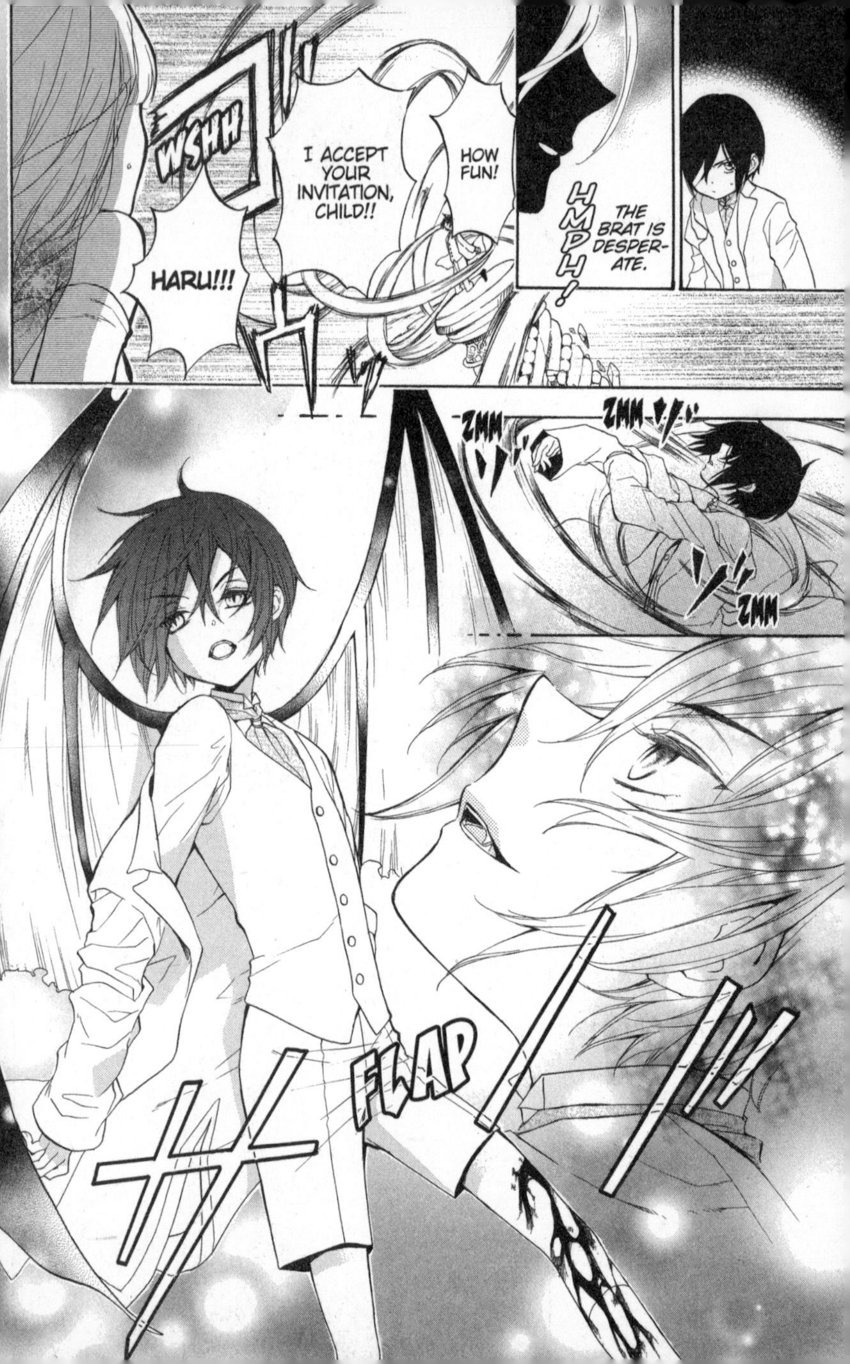
HMPH!
THE BRAT IS DESPERATE.
HOW FUN!
I ACCEPT YOUR INVITATION, CHILD!!
WSHH
HARU!!!
ZMM
ZMM
ZMM
FLAP

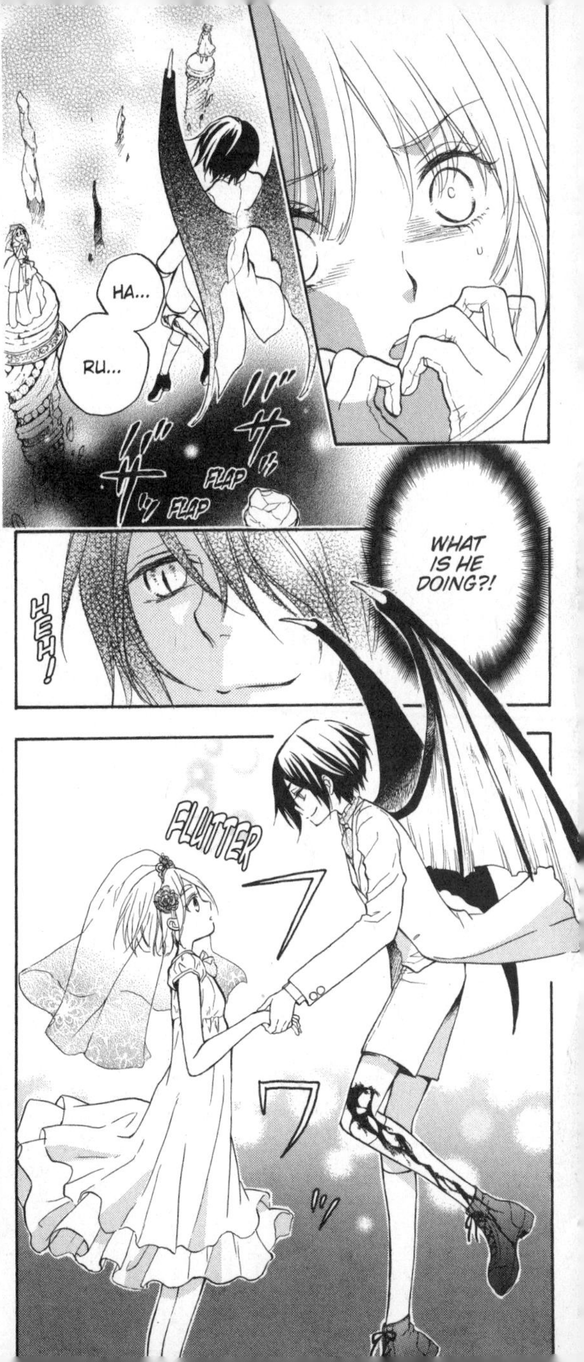
HA...
RU...
FLAP
FLAP
WHAT IS HE DOING?!
HEH!
FLUTTER

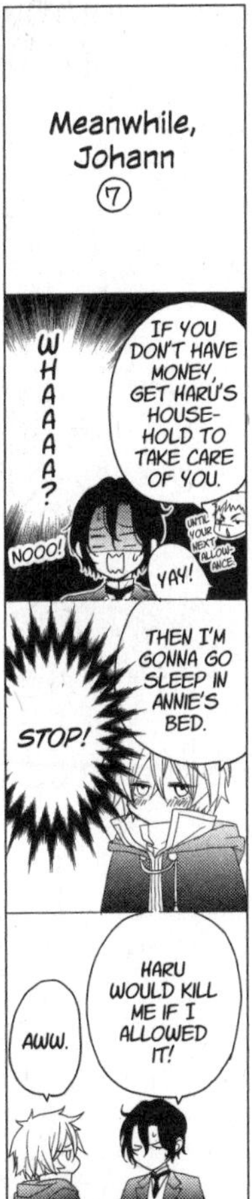
Meanwhile, Johann
⑦
IF YOU DON'T HAVE MONEY, GET HARU'S HOUSEHOLD TO TAKE CARE OF YOU.
UNTIL YOUR NEXT ALLOWANCE.
WHAAAAA?
NOOO!
YAY!
THEN I'M GONNA GO SLEEP IN ANNIE'S BED.
STOP!
HARU WOULD KILL ME IF I ALLOWED IT!
AWW.
THEN I'LL SLEEP IN HARU'S BED..
YOU NEVER EVEN CONSIDER THE COUCH, DO YOU?
TSK!

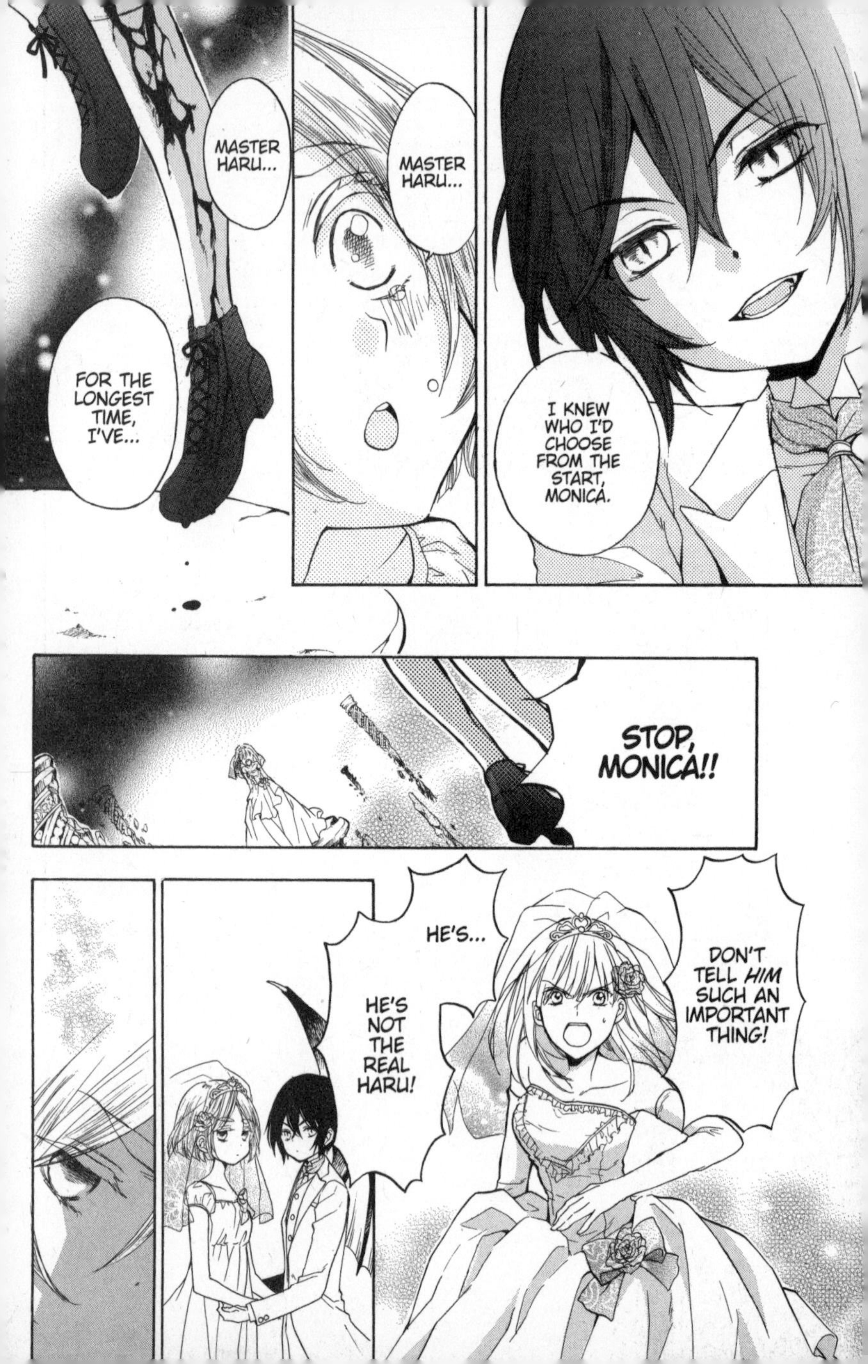
I KNEW WHO I'D CHOOSE FROM THE START, MONICA.
MASTER HARU...
MASTER HARU...
FOR THE LONGEST TIME, I'VE...
STOP, MONICA!!
DON'T TELL *HIM* SUCH AN IMPORTANT THING!
HE'S...
HE'S NOT THE REAL HARU!

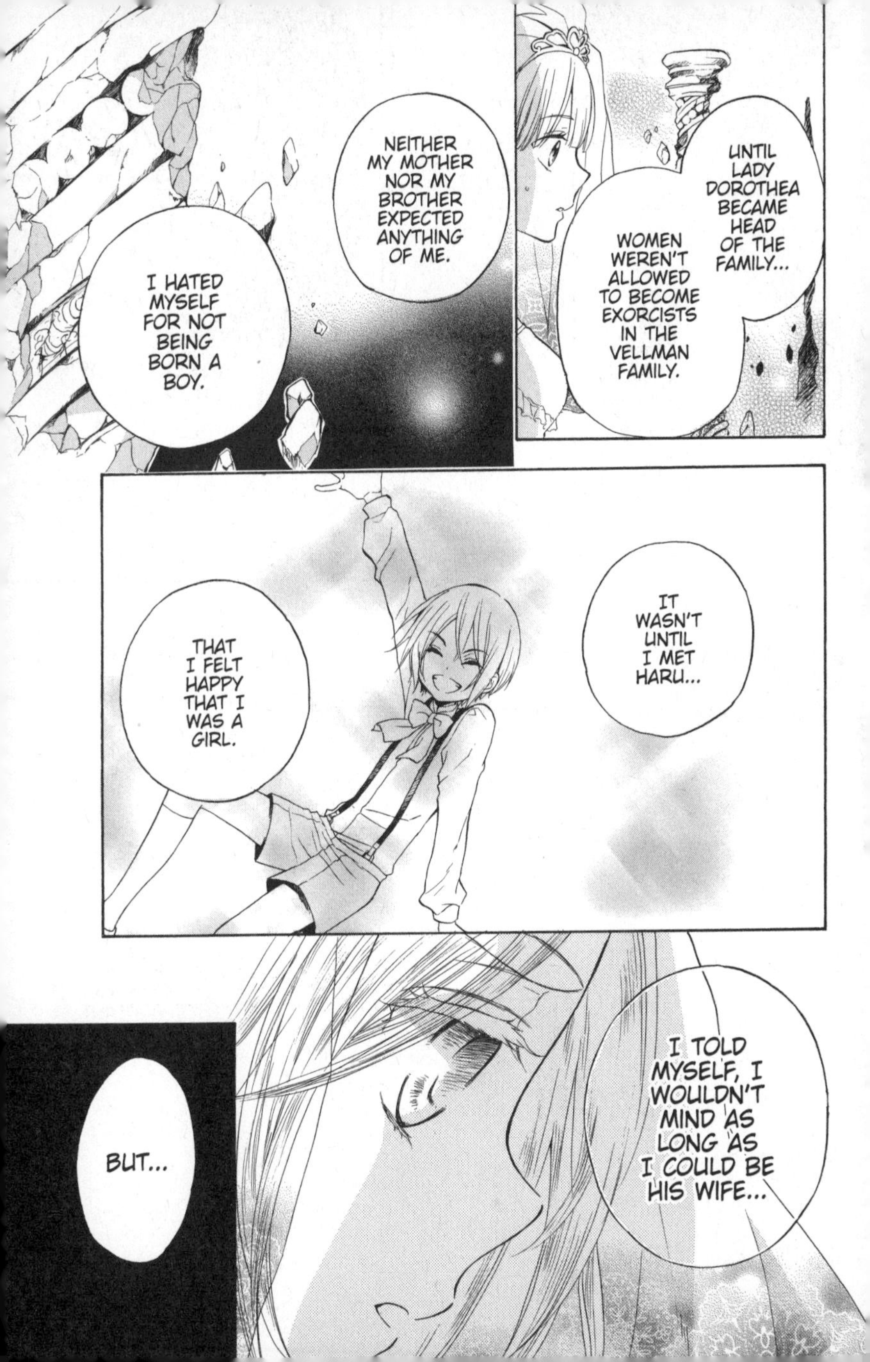
UNTIL LADY DOROTHEA BECAME HEAD OF THE FAMILY...
WOMEN WEREN'T ALLOWED TO BECOME EXORCISTS IN THE VELLMAN FAMILY.
NEITHER MY MOTHER NOR MY BROTHER EXPECTED ANYTHING OF ME.
I HATED MYSELF FOR NOT BEING BORN A BOY.
IT WASN'T UNTIL I MET HARU...
THAT I FELT HAPPY THAT I WAS A GIRL.
I TOLD MYSELF, I WOULDN'T MIND AS LONG AS I COULD BE HIS WIFE...
BUT...

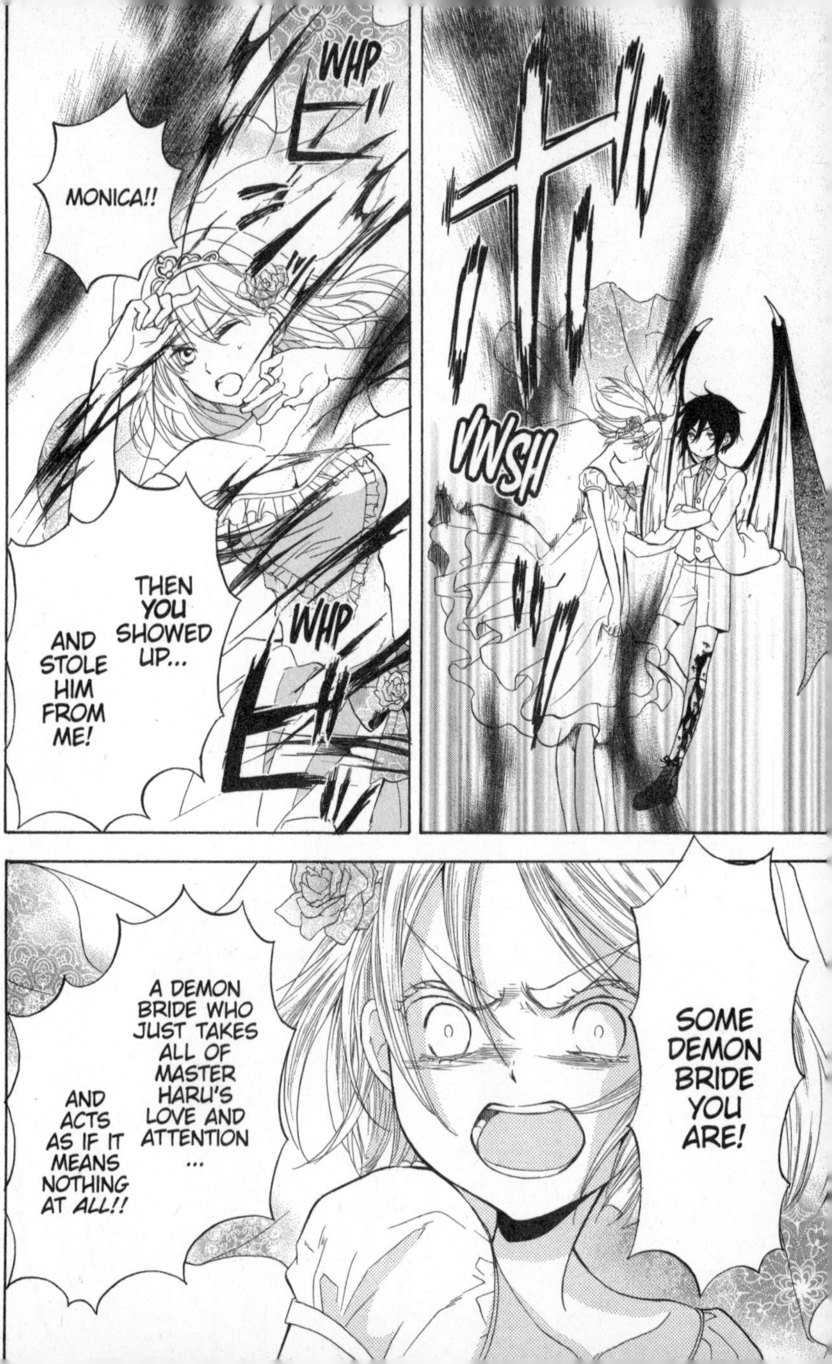
VWSH
WHP
MONICA!!
WHP
THEN YOU SHOWED UP...
AND STOLE HIM FROM ME!
SOME DEMON BRIDE YOU ARE!
A DEMON BRIDE WHO JUST TAKES ALL OF MASTER HARU'S LOVE AND ATTENTION...
AND ACTS AS IF IT MEANS NOTHING AT ALL!!

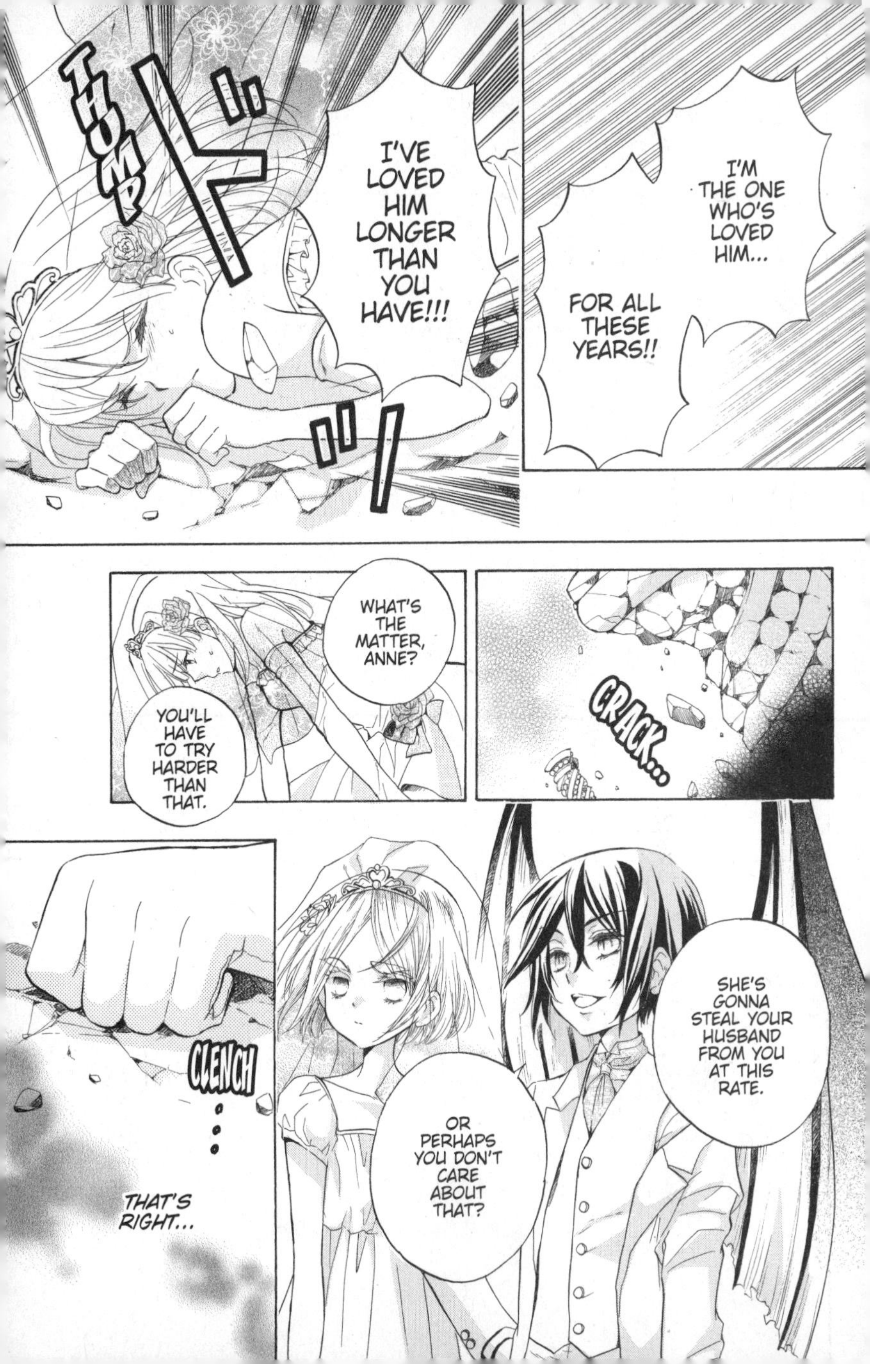
I'M THE ONE WHO'S LOVED HIM...
FOR ALL THESE YEARS!!
I'VE LOVED HIM LONGER THAN YOU HAVE!!!
THUMP
CRACK...
WHAT'S THE MATTER, ANNE?
YOU'LL HAVE TO TRY HARDER THAN THAT.
SHE'S GONNA STEAL YOUR HUSBAND FROM YOU AT THIS RATE.
OR PERHAPS YOU DON'T CARE ABOUT THAT?
CLENCH
...
THAT'S RIGHT...

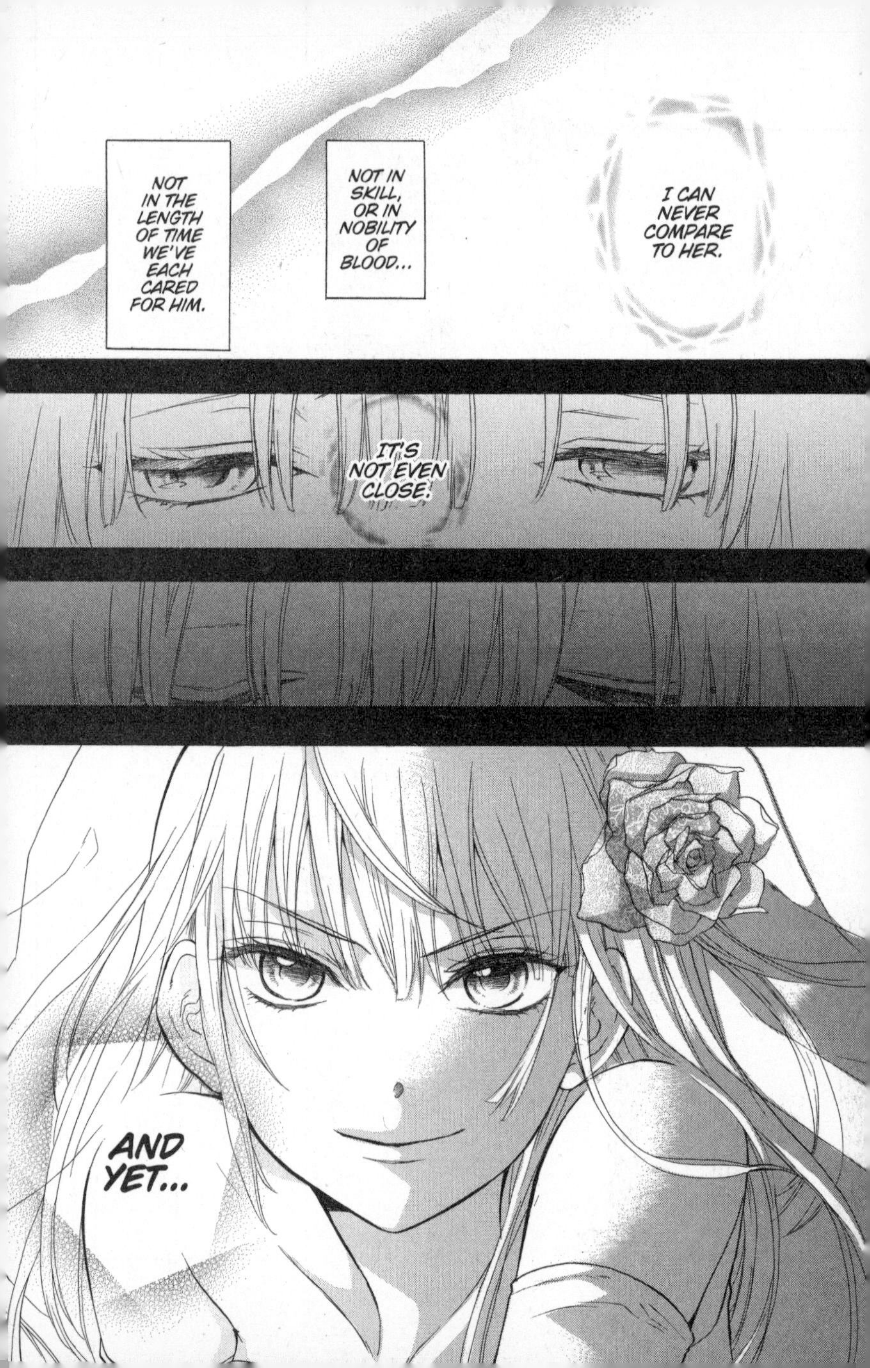
I CAN NEVER COMPARE TO HER.
NOT IN SKILL, OR IN NOBILITY OF BLOOD...
NOT IN THE LENGTH OF TIME WE'VE EACH CARED FOR HIM.
IT'S NOT EVEN CLOSE.
AND YET...

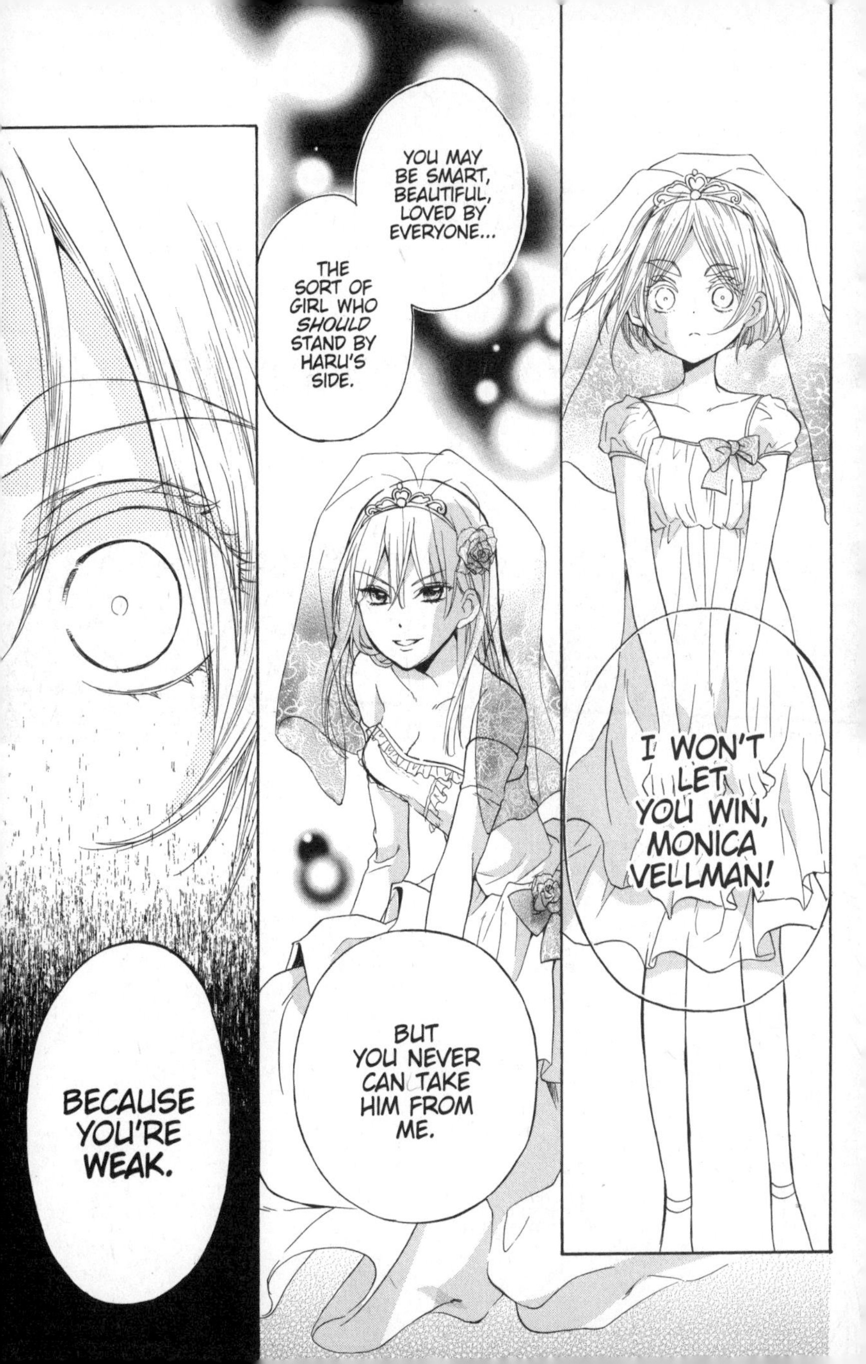
I WON'T LET YOU WIN, MONICA VELLMAN!
YOU MAY BE SMART, BEAUTIFUL, LOVED BY EVERYONE...
THE SORT OF GIRL WHO *SHOULD* STAND BY HARU'S SIDE.
BUT YOU NEVER CAN TAKE HIM FROM ME.
BECAUSE YOU'RE WEAK.

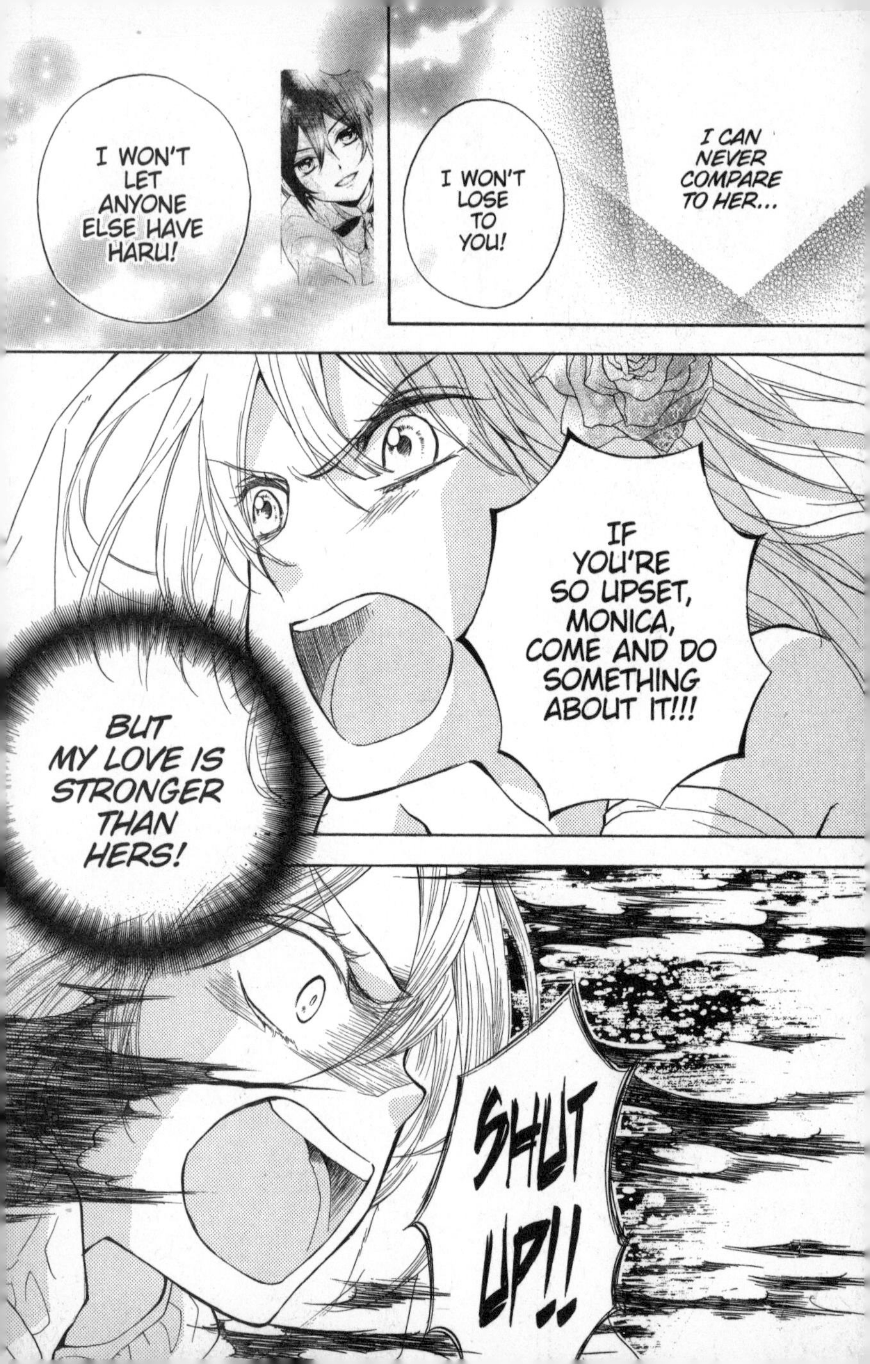
I CAN NEVER COMPARE TO HER...
I WON'T LOSE TO YOU!
I WON'T LET ANYONE ELSE HAVE HARU!
IF YOU'RE SO UPSET, MONICA, COME AND DO SOMETHING ABOUT IT!!!
BUT MY LOVE IS STRONGER THAN HERS!
SHUT UP!!

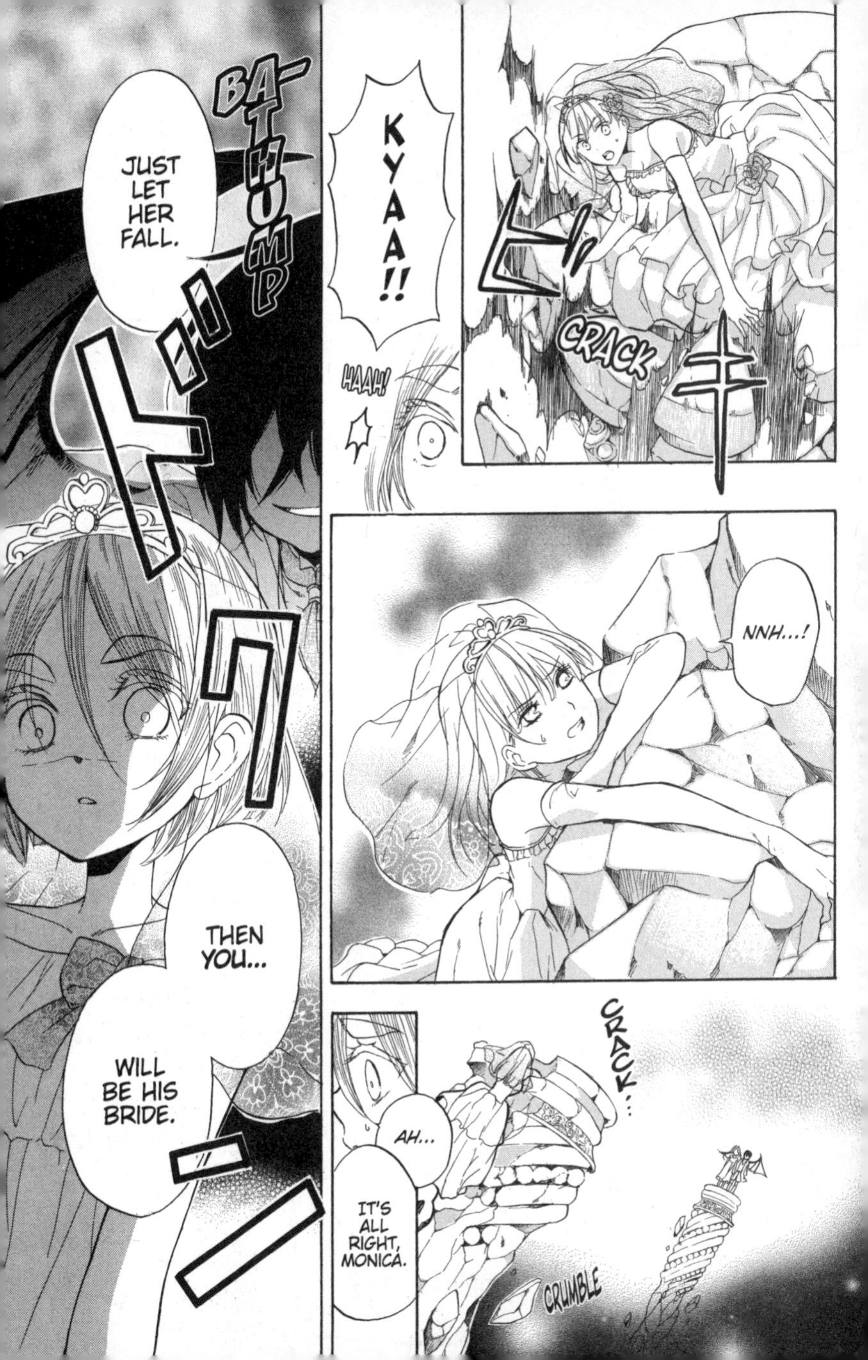
CRACK
KYAA!!
HAAH!
NNH...!
CRACK...
AH...
IT'S ALL RIGHT, MONICA.
CRUMBLE
BA-THUMP
JUST LET HER FALL.
THEN YOU...
WILL BE HIS BRIDE.

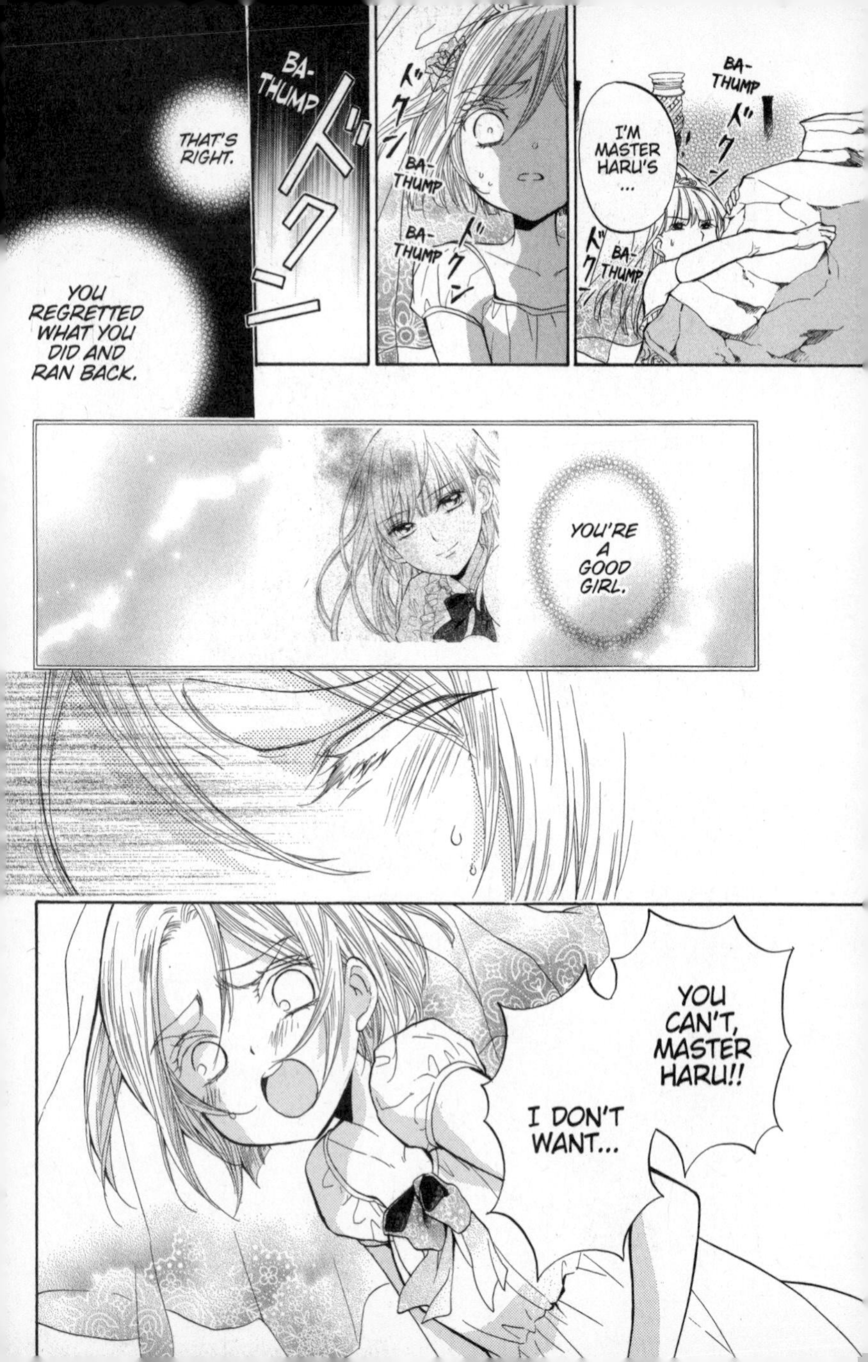
BA-THUMP
ドクン
I'M MASTER HARU'S...
BA-THUMP
ドクン
ドクン
BA-THUMP
BA-THUMP
ドクン
BA-THUMP
ドクン
BA-THUMP
ドクン
THAT'S RIGHT.
YOU REGRETTED WHAT YOU DID AND RAN BACK.
YOU'RE A GOOD GIRL.
YOU CAN'T, MASTER HARU!!
I DON'T WANT...

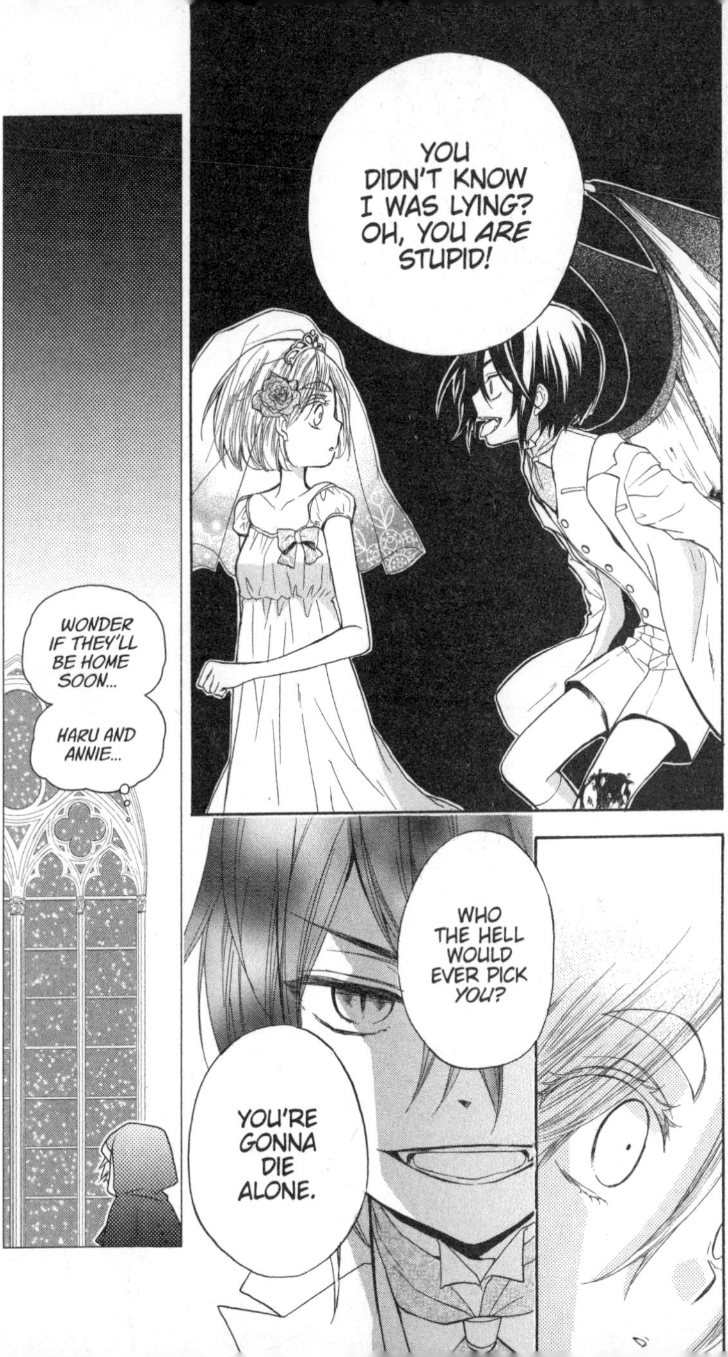
YOU DIDN'T KNOW I WAS LYING? OH, YOU ARE STUPID!
WHO THE HELL WOULD EVER PICK YOU?
YOU'RE GONNA DIE ALONE.
WONDER IF THEY'LL BE HOME SOON...
HARU AND ANNIE...

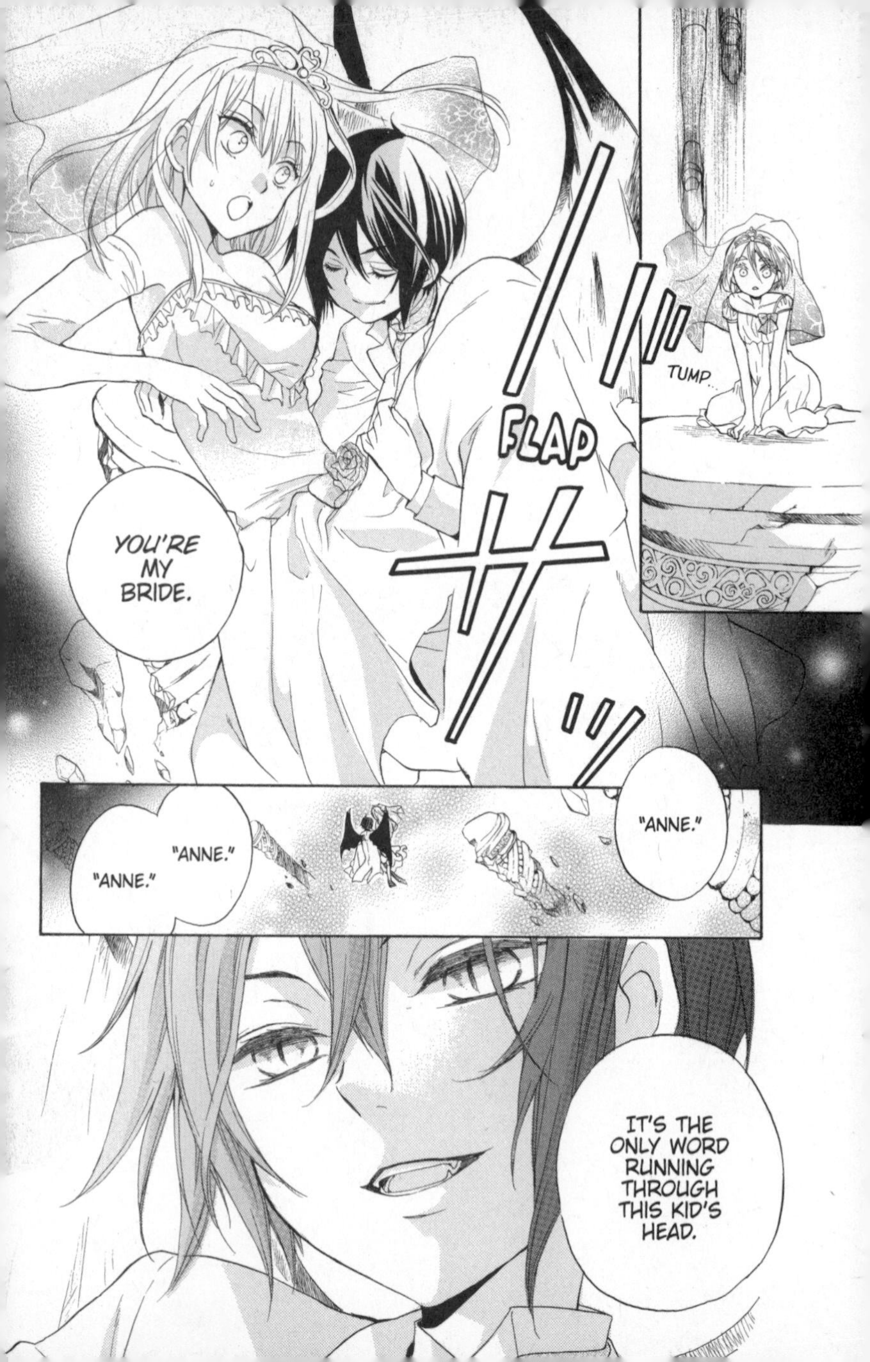
TUMP...
FLAP
YOU'RE MY BRIDE.
"ANNE."
"ANNE."
"ANNE."
IT'S THE ONLY WORD RUNNING THROUGH THIS KID'S HEAD.

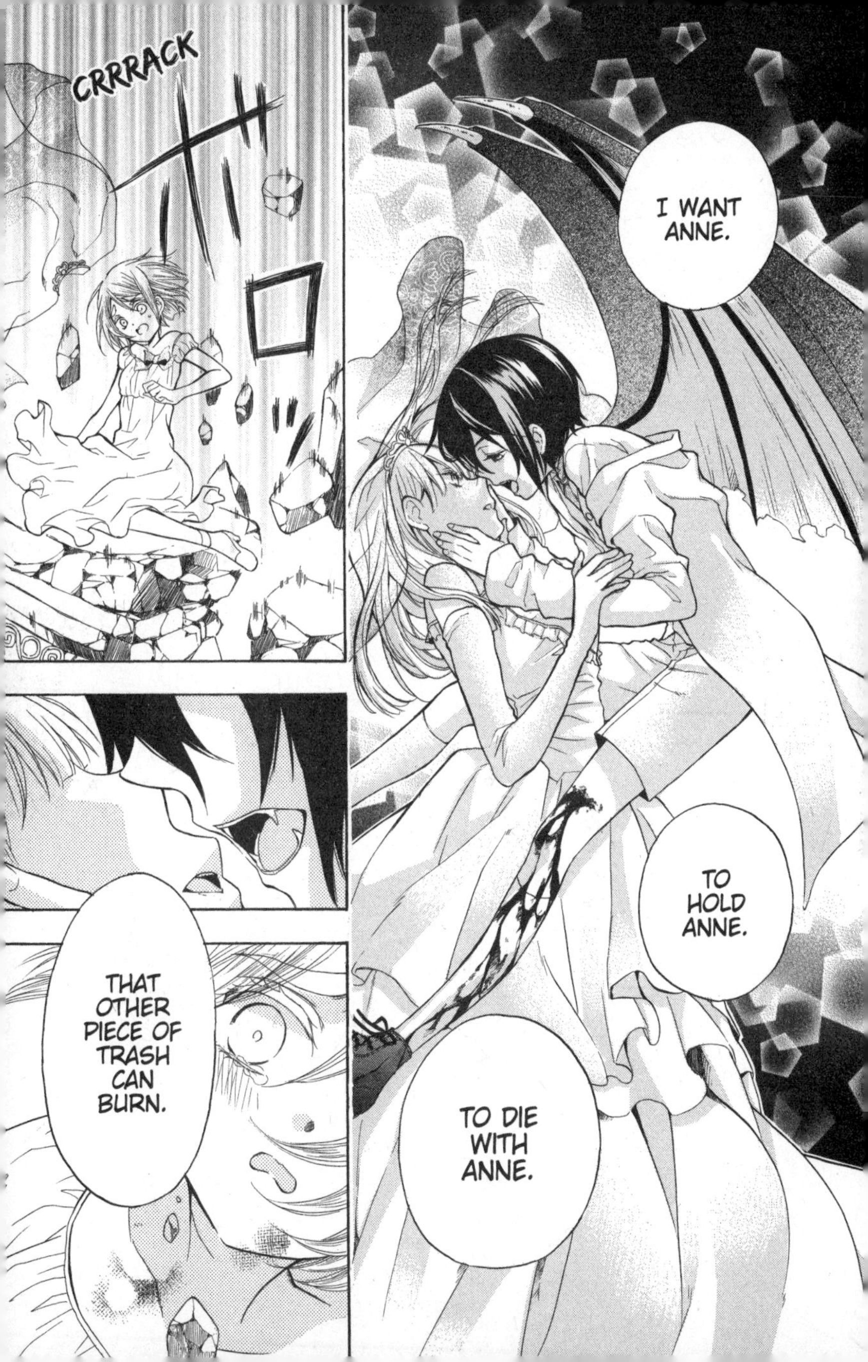
I WANT ANNE.
TO HOLD ANNE.
TO DIE WITH ANNE.
CRRRACK
THAT OTHER PIECE OF TRASH CAN BURN.

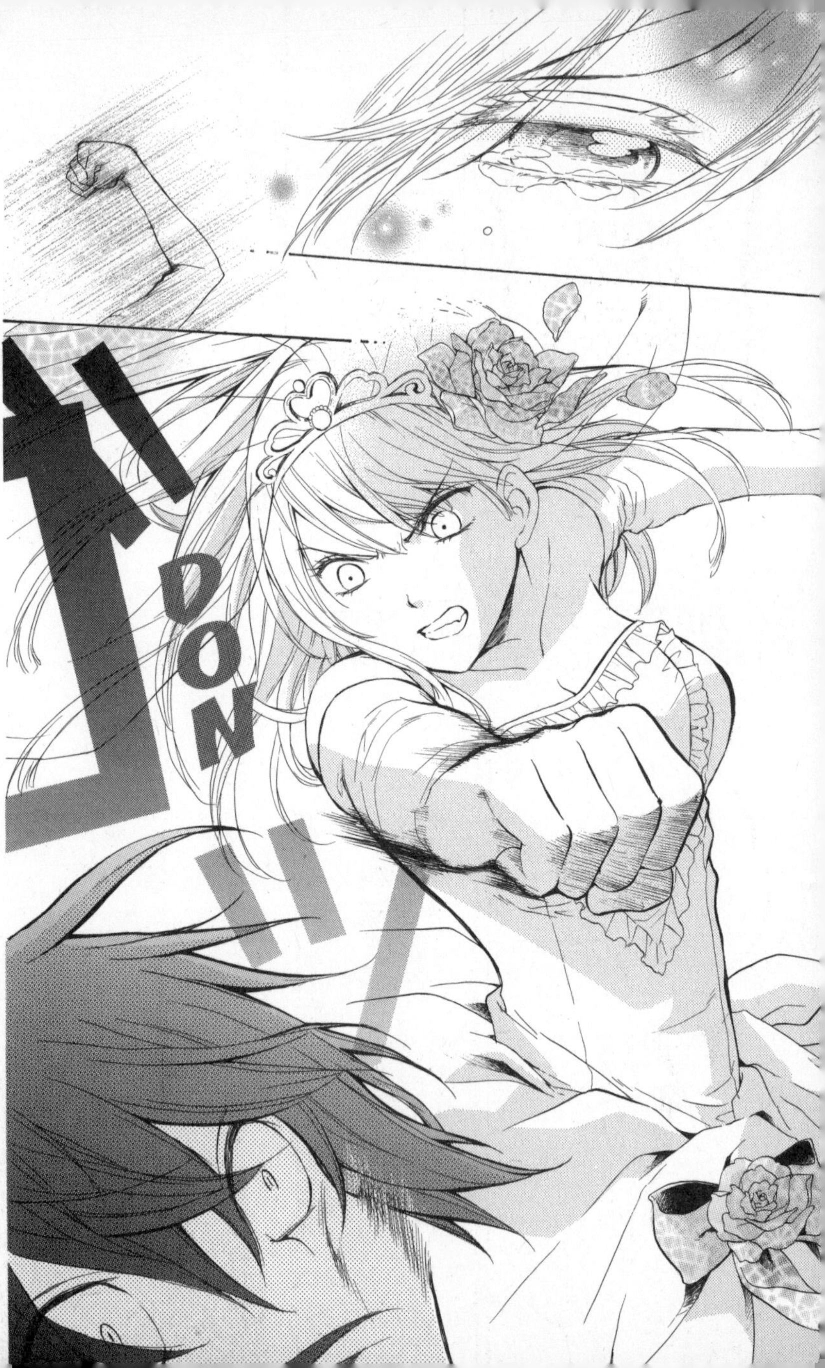
DON

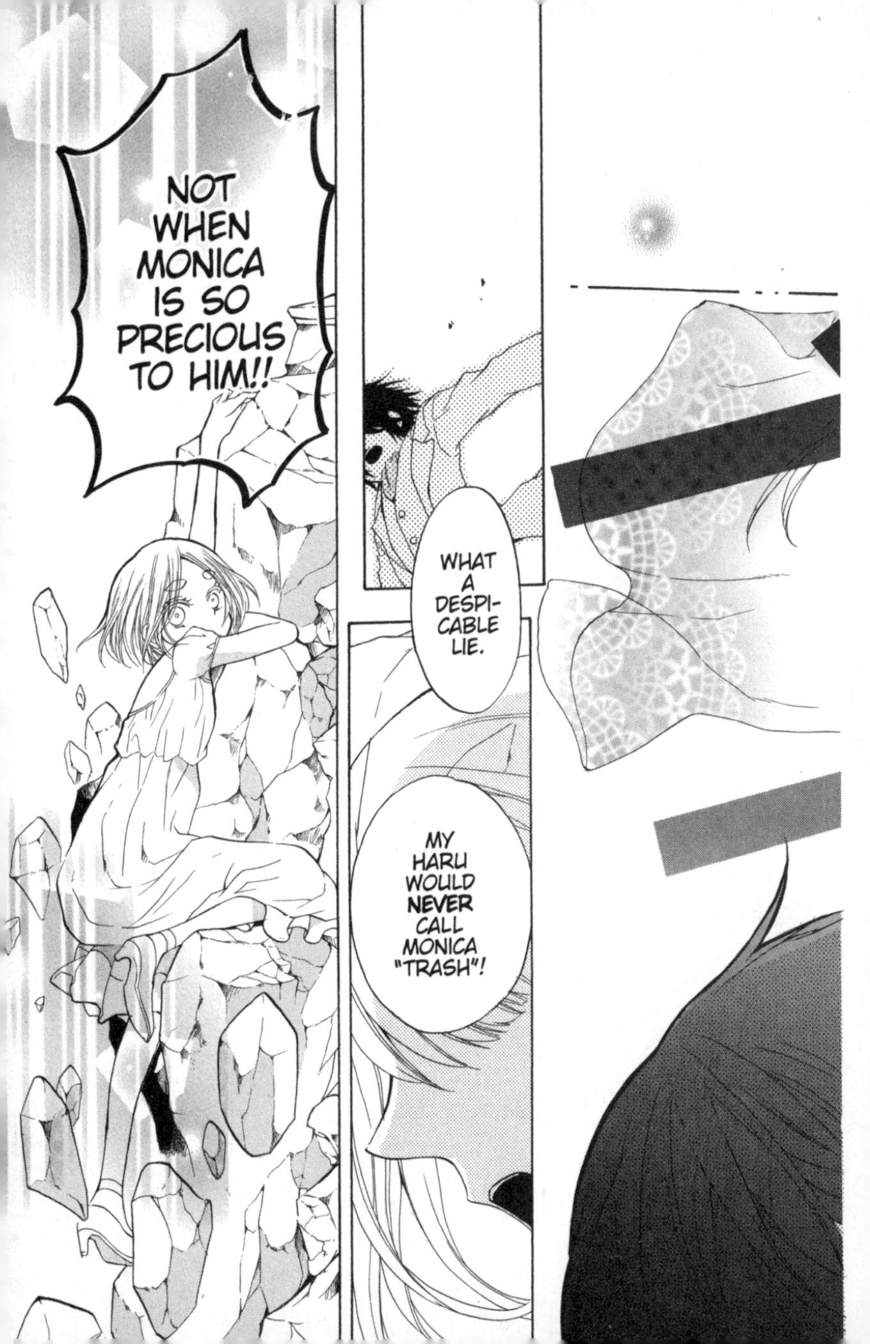
WHAT A DESPICABLE LIE.
MY HARU WOULD **NEVER** CALL MONICA "TRASH"!
NOT WHEN MONICA IS SO PRECIOUS TO HIM!!

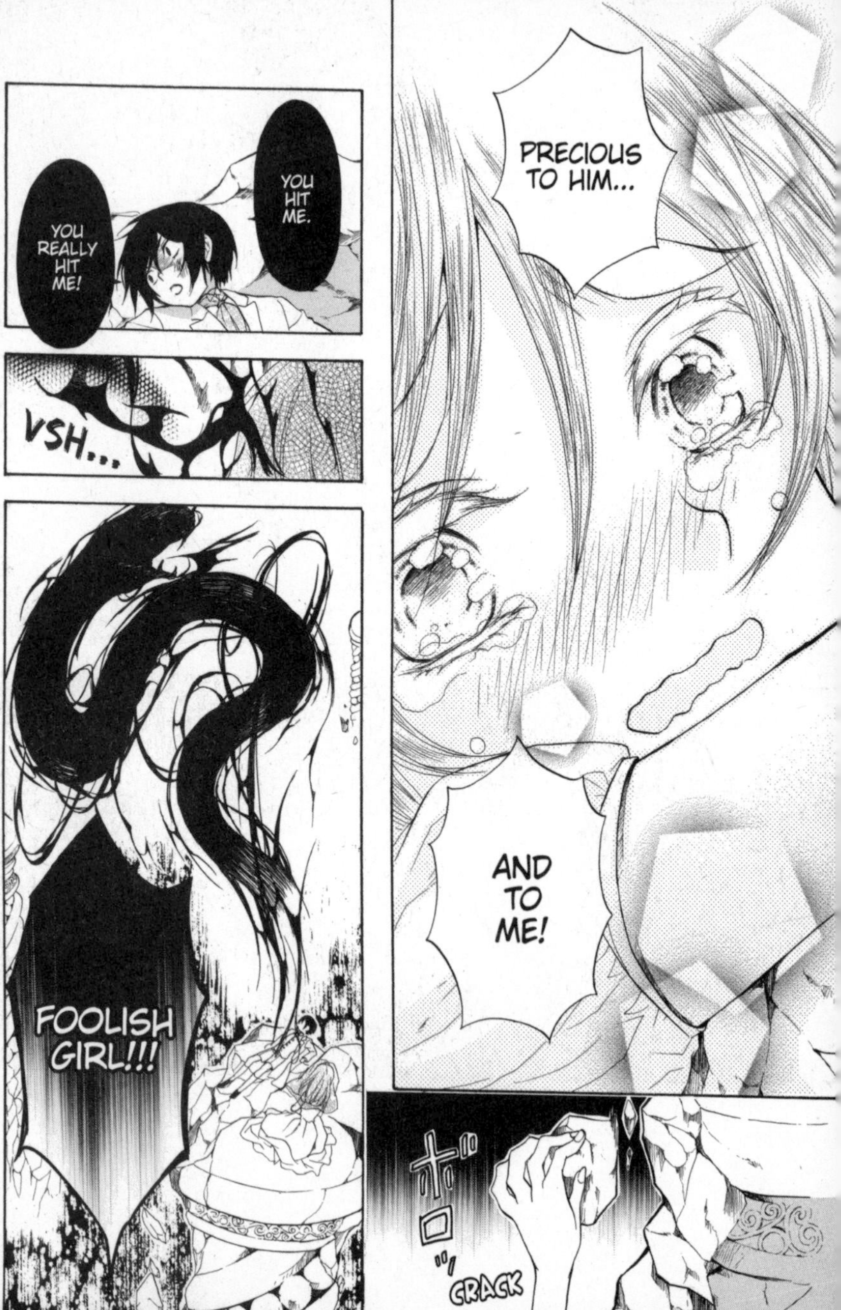
PRECIOUS TO HIM...
AND TO ME!
ボロ
CRACK
YOU HIT ME.
YOU REALLY HIT ME!
VSH...
FOOLISH GIRL!!!

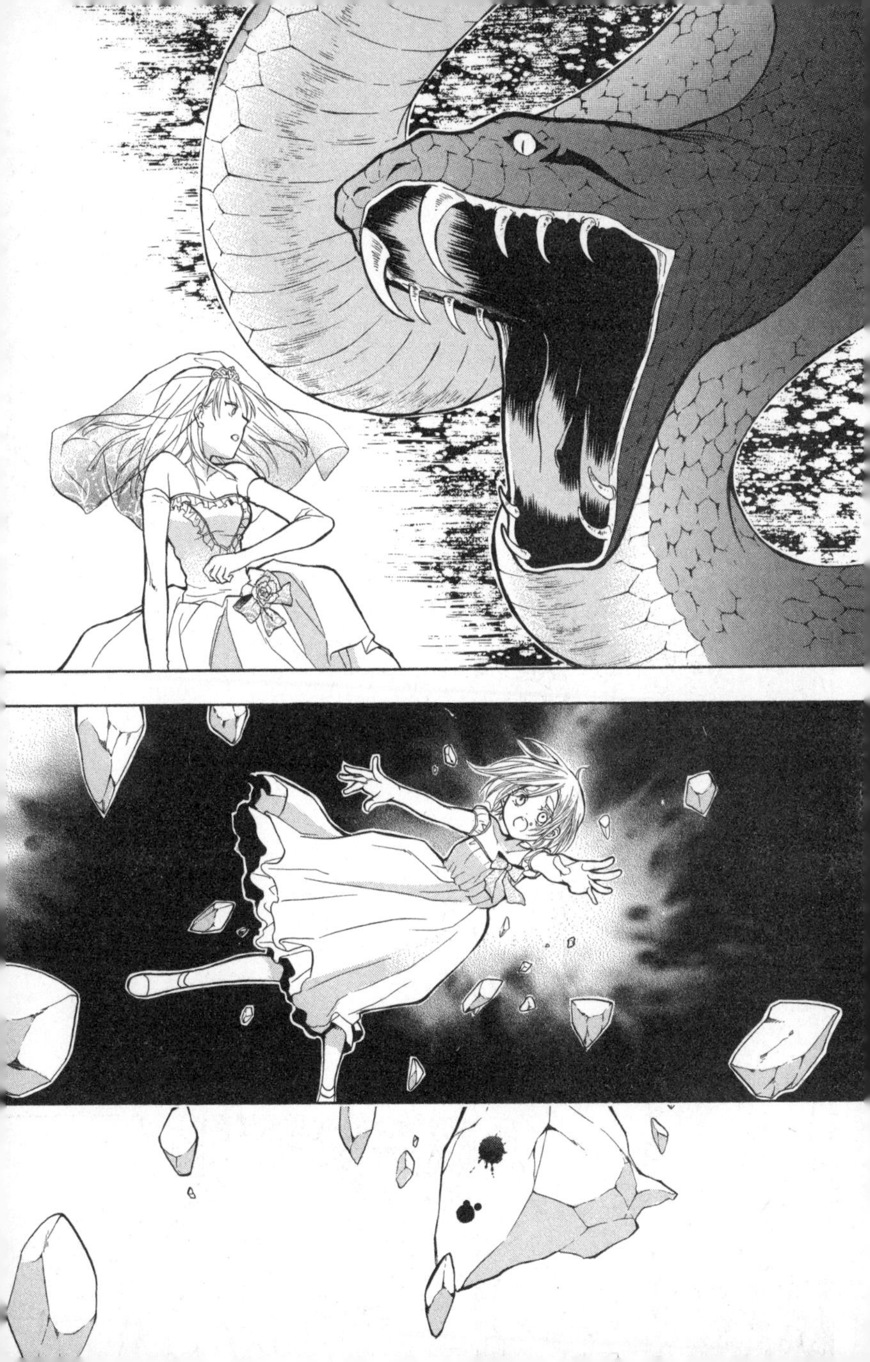

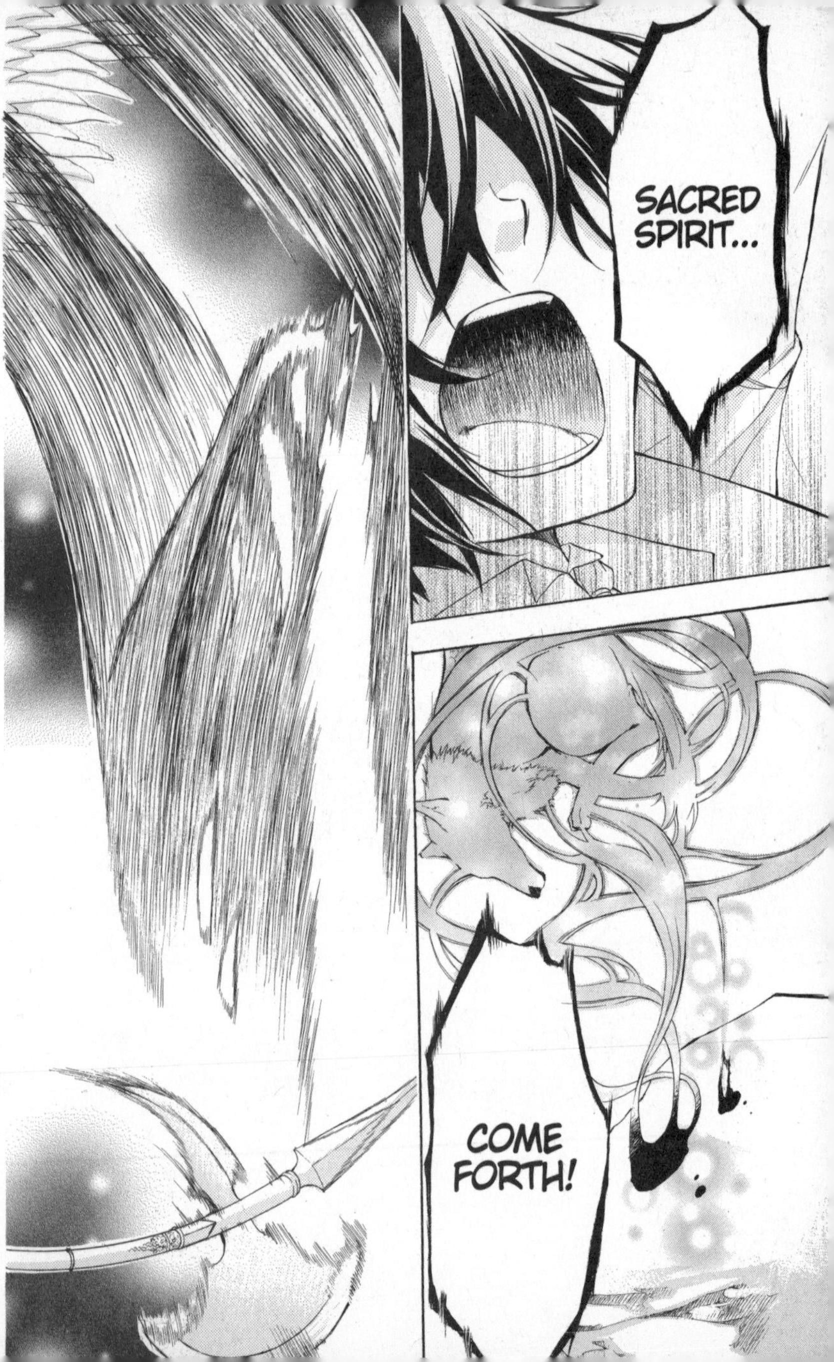
SACRED SPIRIT...
COME FORTH!

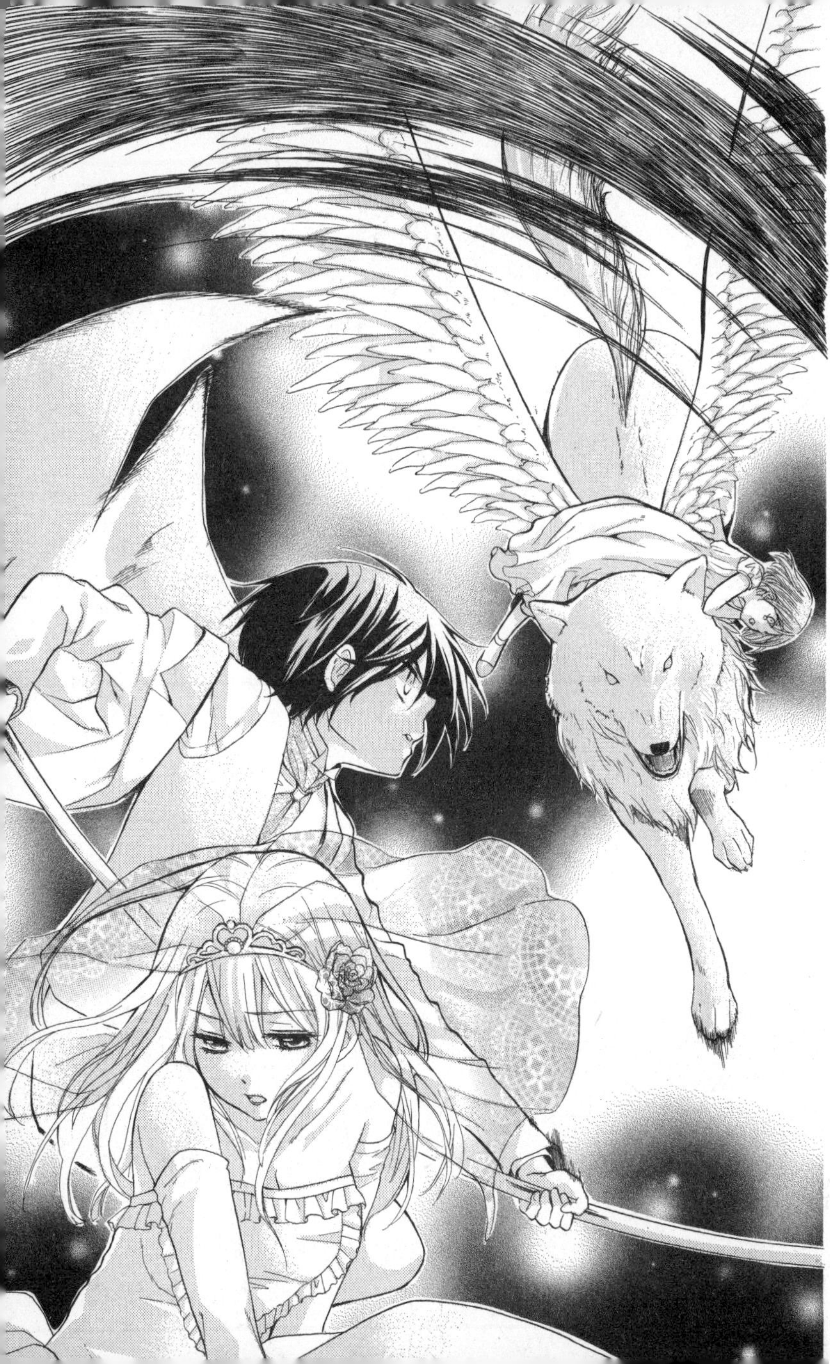

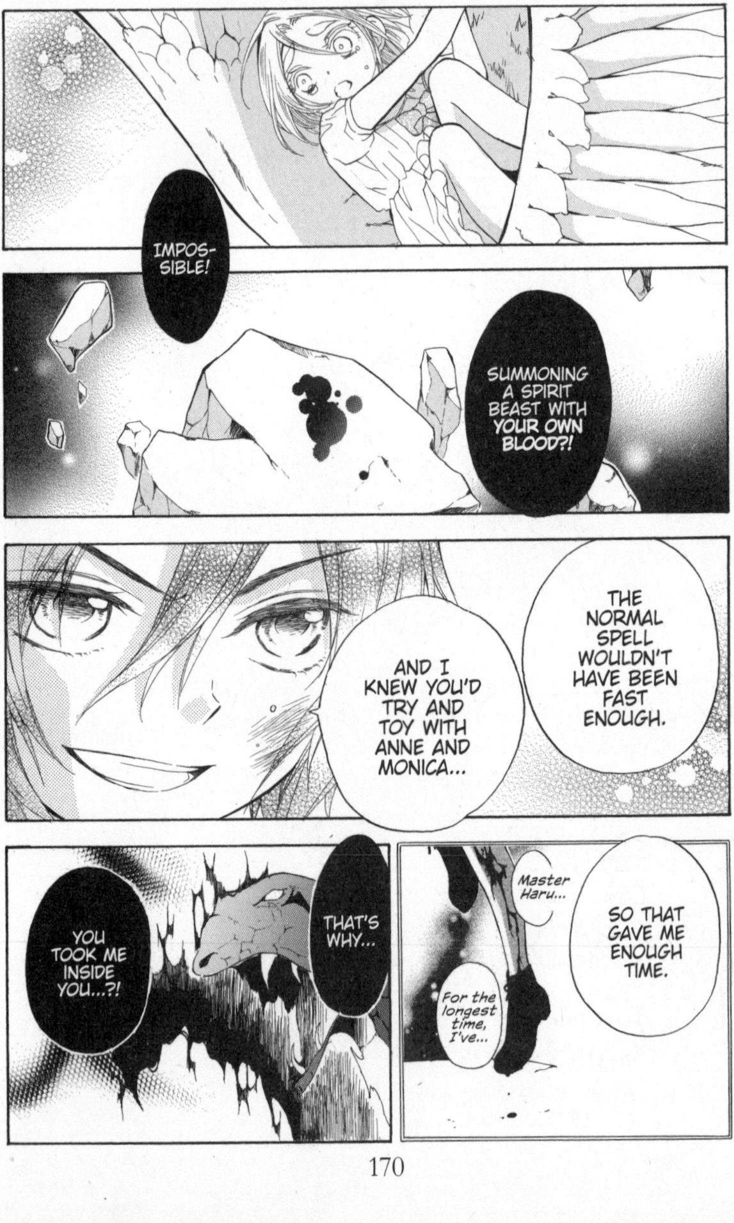
IMPOSSIBLE!
SUMMONING A SPIRIT BEAST WITH YOUR OWN BLOOD?!
THE NORMAL SPELL WOULDN'T HAVE BEEN FAST ENOUGH.
AND I KNEW YOU'D TRY AND TOY WITH ANNE AND MONICA...
SO THAT GAVE ME ENOUGH TIME.
Master Haru...
For the longest time, I've...
THAT'S WHY...
YOU TOOK ME INSIDE YOU...?!

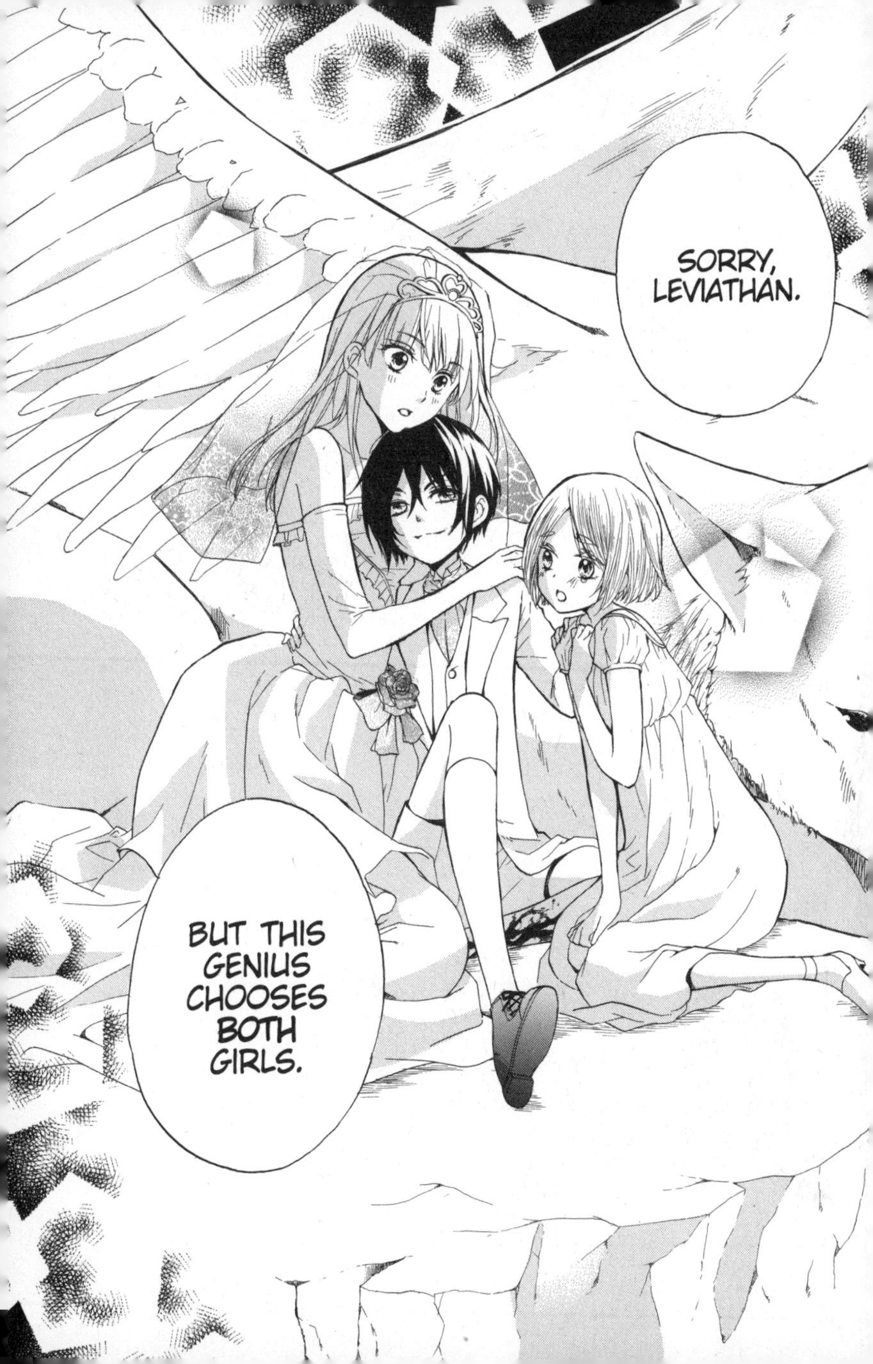
SORRY, LEVIATHAN.
BUT THIS GENIUS CHOOSES BOTH GIRLS.

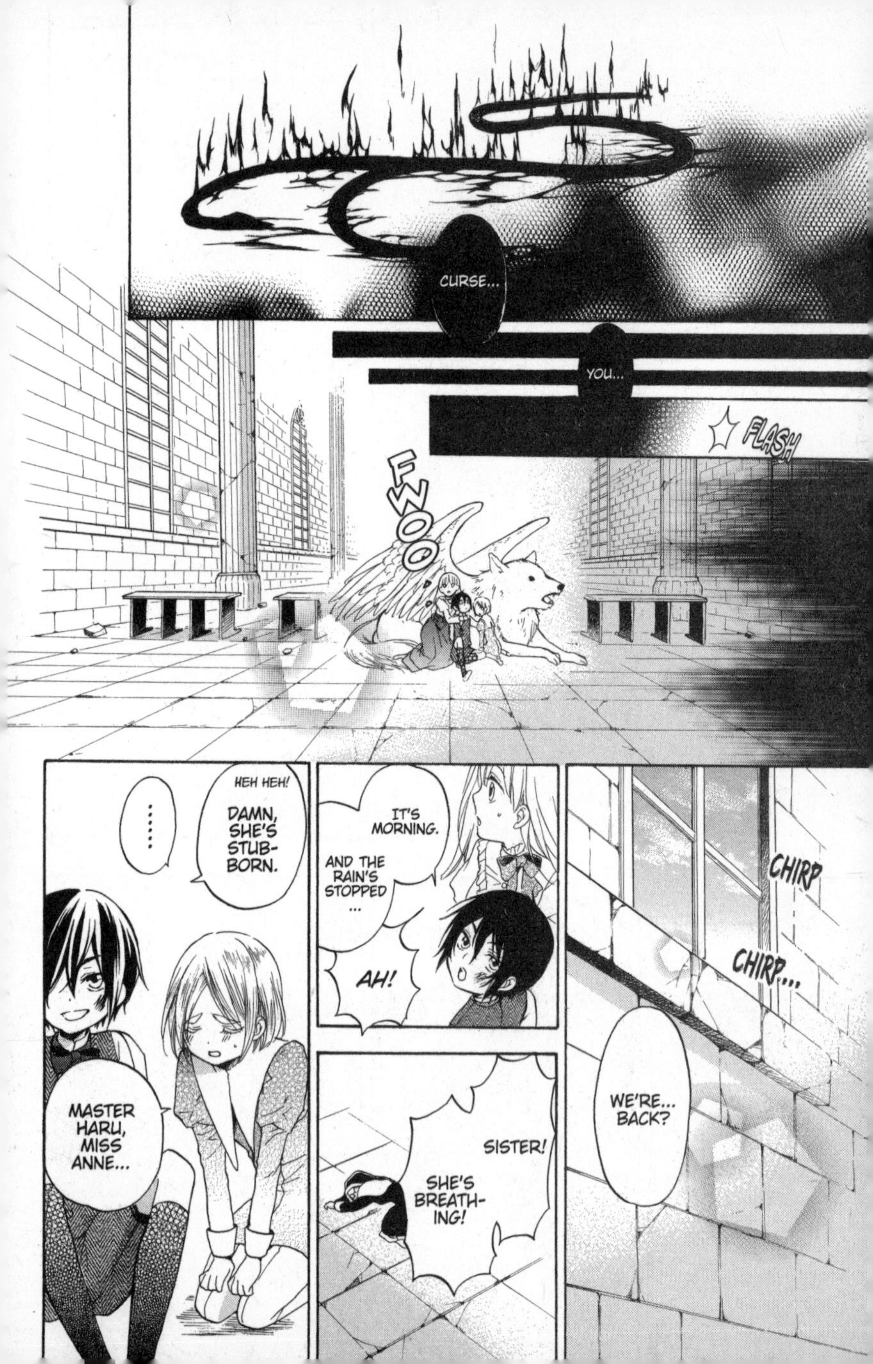
CURSE...
YOU...
FLASH
FWOO
CHIRP
CHIRP...
WE'RE... BACK?
IT'S MORNING.
AND THE RAIN'S STOPPED ...
AH!
SISTER!
SHE'S BREATH-ING!
HEH HEH! DAMN, SHE'S STUB-BORN.
......
MASTER HARU, MISS ANNE...

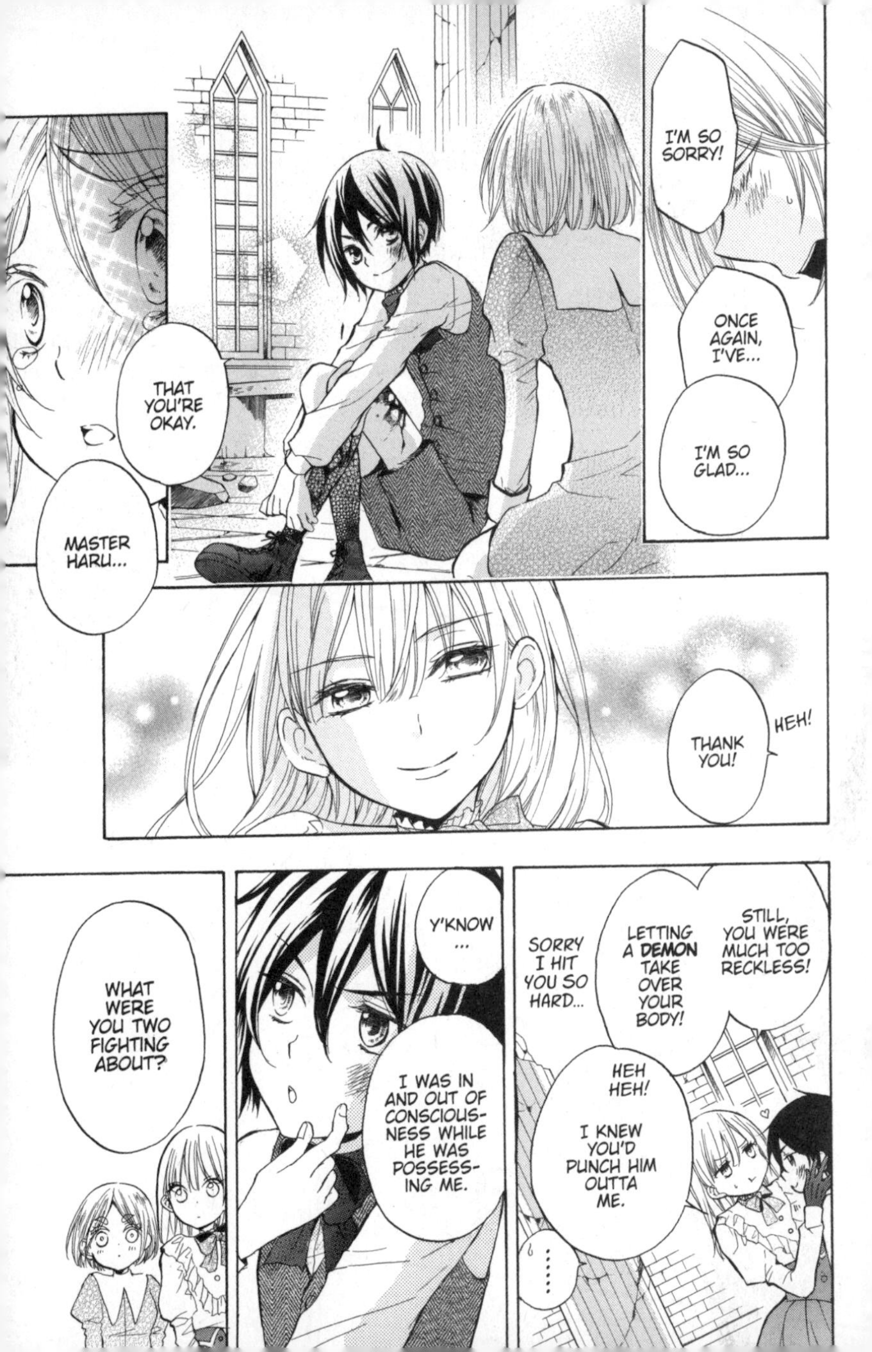
I'M SO SORRY!
ONCE AGAIN, I'VE...
I'M SO GLAD...
THAT YOU'RE OKAY.
MASTER HARU...
HEH!
THANK YOU!
STILL, YOU WERE MUCH TOO RECKLESS!
LETTING A **DEMON** TAKE OVER YOUR BODY!
SORRY I HIT YOU SO HARD...
HEH HEH!
I KNEW YOU'D PUNCH HIM OUTTA ME.
......
Y'KNOW...
I WAS IN AND OUT OF CONSCIOUSNESS WHILE HE WAS POSSESSING ME.
WHAT WERE YOU TWO FIGHTING ABOUT?

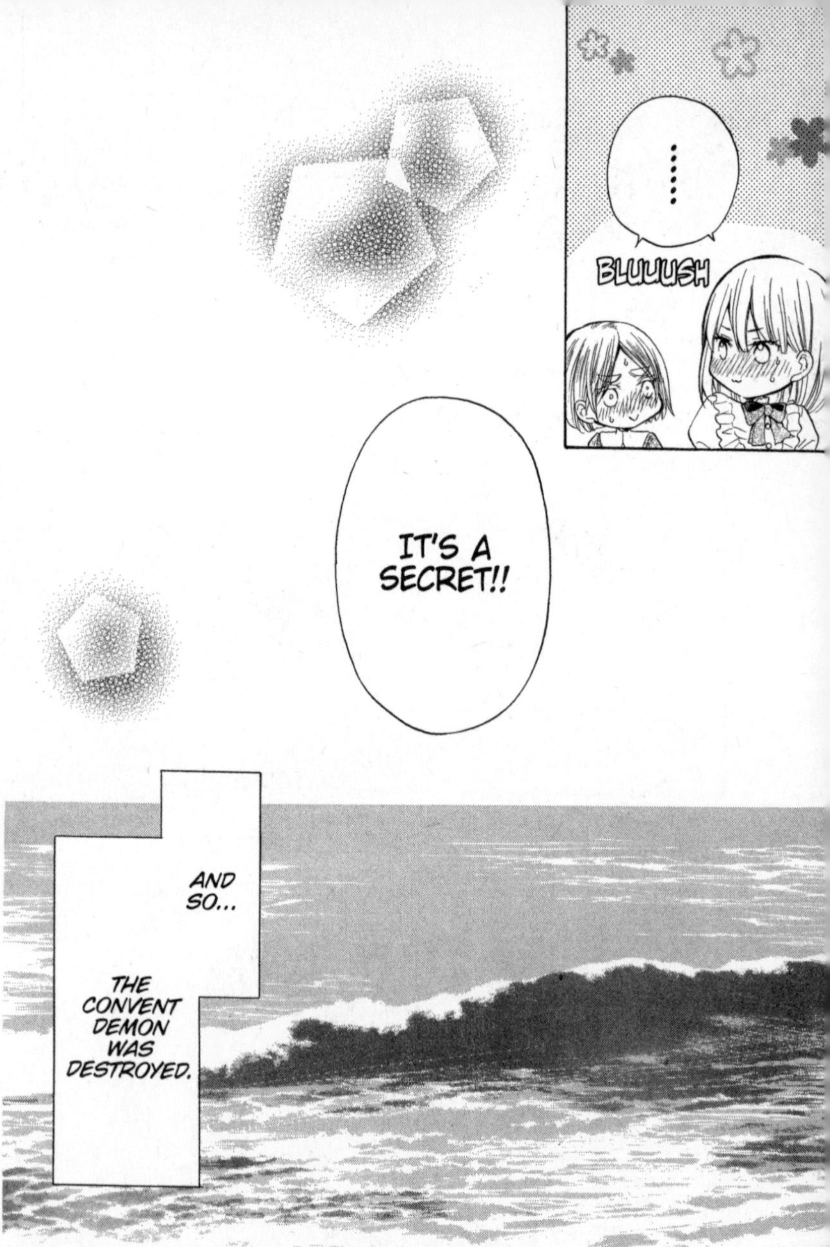
......
BLUUUSH
IT'S A SECRET!!
AND SO...
THE CONVENT DEMON WAS DESTROYED.

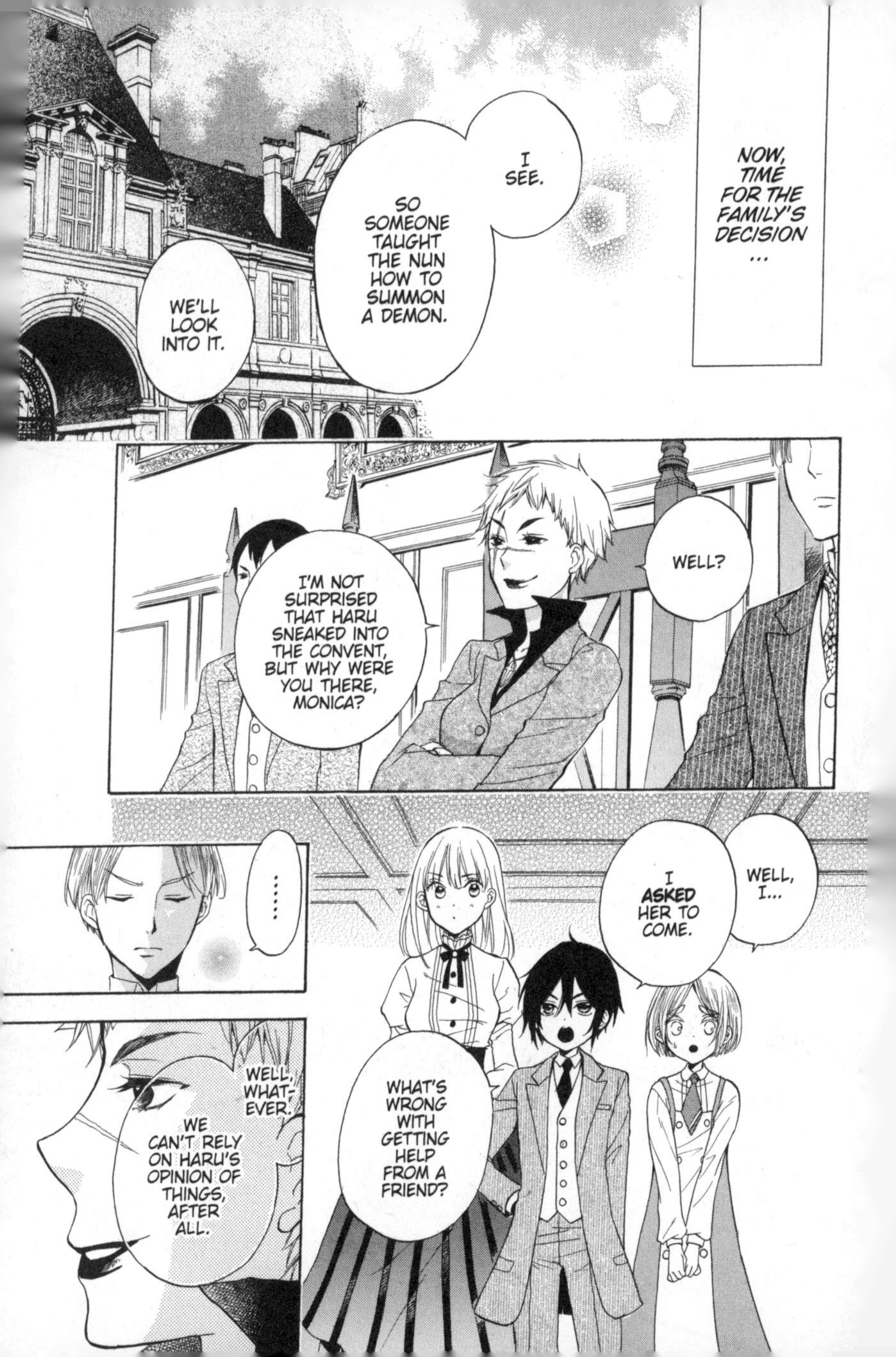
NOW, TIME FOR THE FAMILY'S DECISION ...
I SEE.
SO SOMEONE TAUGHT THE NUN HOW TO SUMMON A DEMON.
WE'LL LOOK INTO IT.
WELL?
I'M NOT SURPRISED THAT HARU SNEAKED INTO THE CONVENT, BUT WHY WERE YOU THERE, MONICA?
WELL, I...
I **ASKED** HER TO COME.
WHAT'S WRONG WITH GETTING HELP FROM A FRIEND?
......
WELL, WHATEVER.
WE CAN'T RELY ON HARU'S OPINION OF THINGS, AFTER ALL.

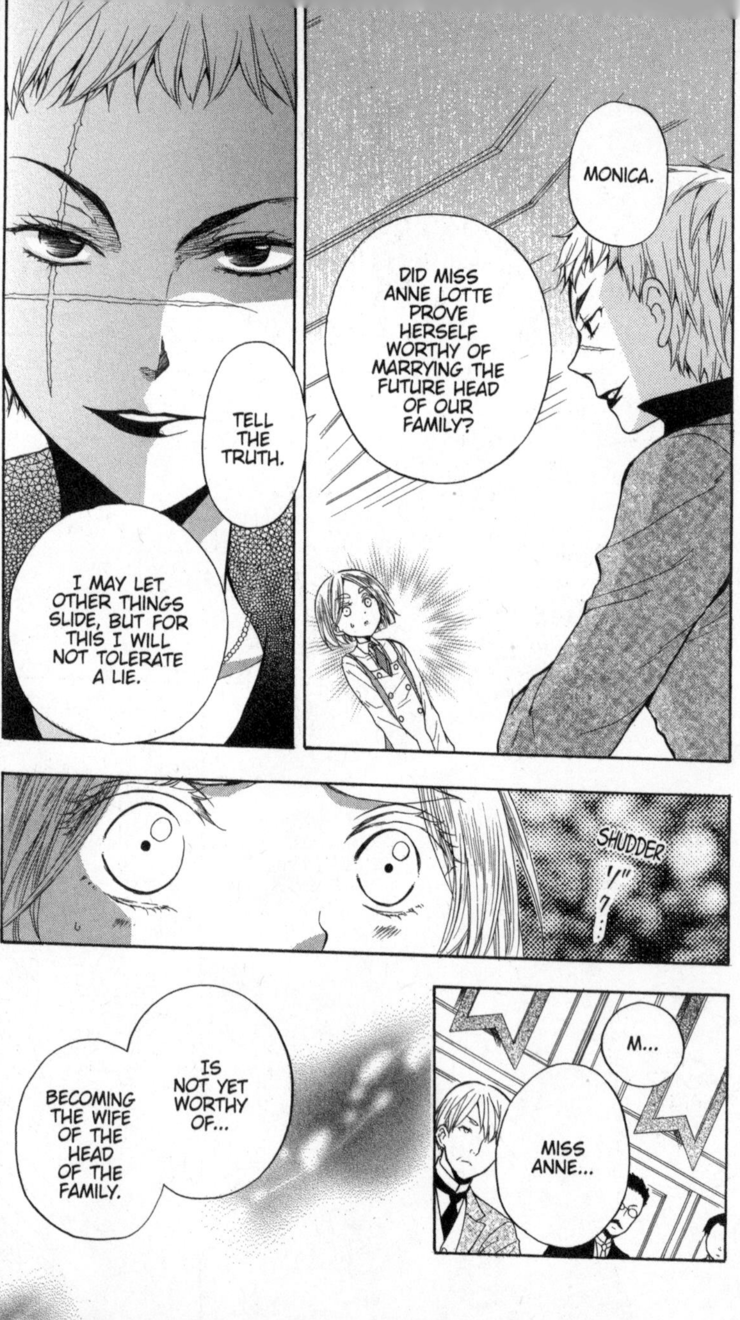
MONICA.
DID MISS ANNE LOTTE PROVE HERSELF WORTHY OF MARRYING THE FUTURE HEAD OF OUR FAMILY?
TELL THE TRUTH.
I MAY LET OTHER THINGS SLIDE, BUT FOR THIS I WILL NOT TOLERATE A LIE.
SHUDDER
M...
MISS ANNE...
IS NOT YET WORTHY OF...
BECOMING THE WIFE OF THE HEAD OF THE FAMILY.

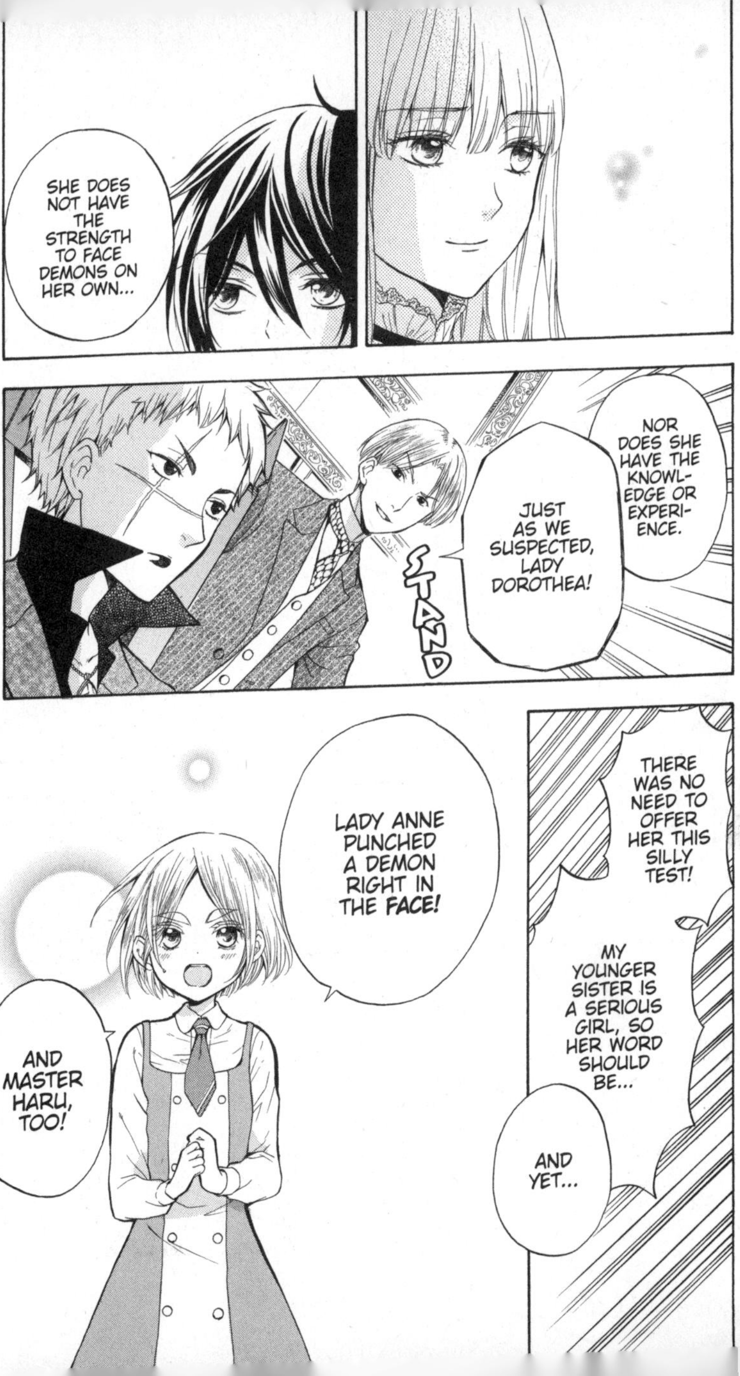
SHE DOES NOT HAVE THE STRENGTH TO FACE DEMONS ON HER OWN...
NOR DOES SHE HAVE THE KNOWL-EDGE OR EXPERI-ENCE.
JUST AS WE SUSPECTED, LADY DOROTHEA!
STAND
THERE WAS NO NEED TO OFFER HER THIS SILLY TEST!
MY YOUNGER SISTER IS A SERIOUS GIRL, SO HER WORD SHOULD BE...
AND YET...
LADY ANNE PUNCHED A DEMON RIGHT IN THE **FACE!**
AND MASTER HARU, TOO!

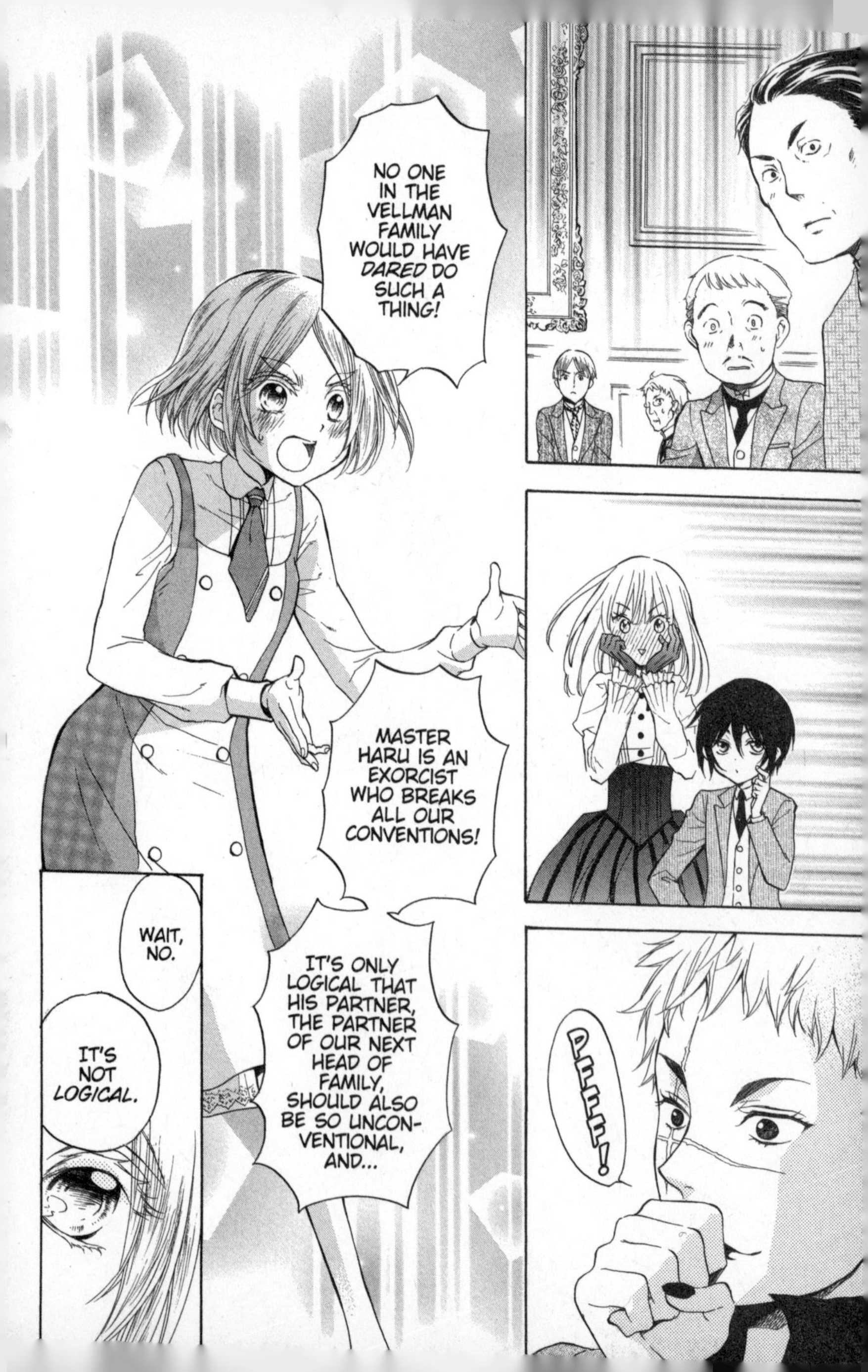
NO ONE IN THE VELLMAN FAMILY WOULD HAVE *DARED* DO SUCH A THING!
MASTER HARU IS AN EXORCIST WHO BREAKS ALL OUR CONVENTIONS!
IT'S ONLY LOGICAL THAT HIS PARTNER, THE PARTNER OF OUR NEXT HEAD OF FAMILY, SHOULD ALSO BE SO UNCON-VENTIONAL, AND...
PFFFF!
WAIT, NO.
IT'S NOT *LOGICAL.*

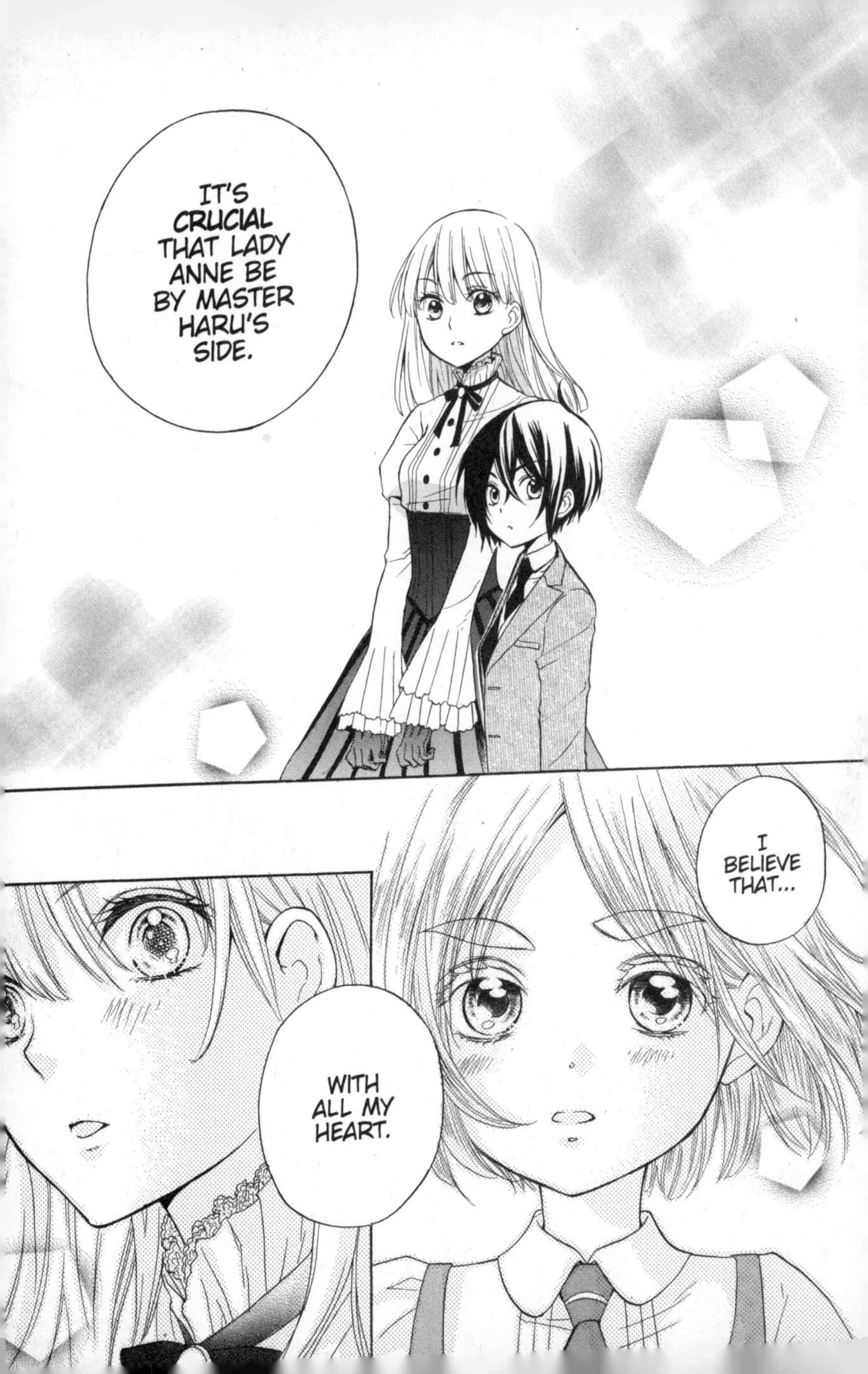
IT'S CRUCIAL THAT LADY ANNE BE BY MASTER HARU'S SIDE.
I BELIEVE THAT...
WITH ALL MY HEART.

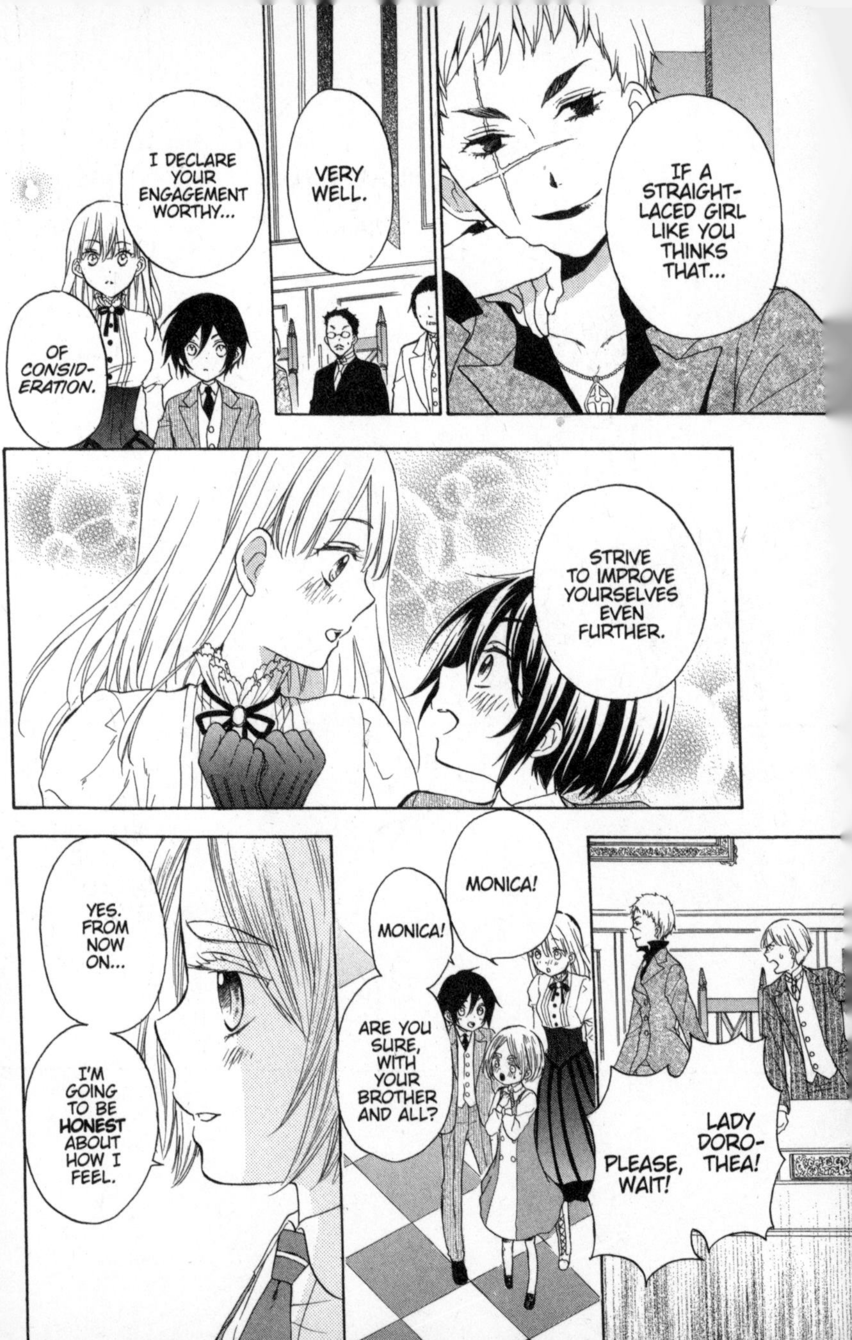
IF A STRAIGHT-LACED GIRL LIKE YOU THINKS THAT...
VERY WELL.
I DECLARE YOUR ENGAGEMENT WORTHY...
OF CONSIDERATION.
STRIVE TO IMPROVE YOURSELVES EVEN FURTHER.
LADY DOROTHEA!
PLEASE, WAIT!
MONICA!
MONICA!
ARE YOU SURE, WITH YOUR BROTHER AND ALL?
YES. FROM NOW ON...
I'M GOING TO BE HONEST ABOUT HOW I FEEL.

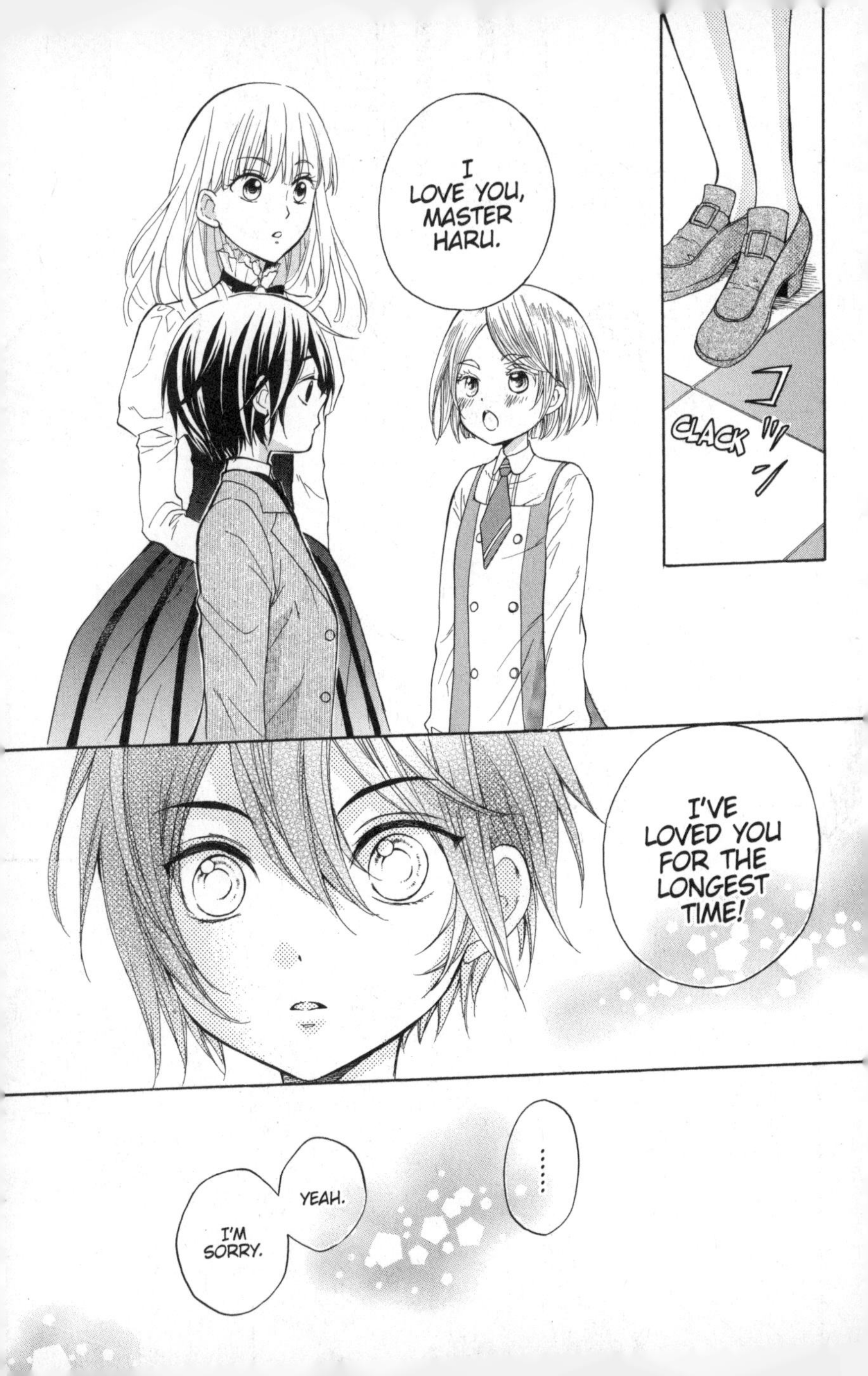
CLACK
I LOVE YOU, MASTER HARU.
I'VE LOVED YOU FOR THE LONGEST TIME!
......
YEAH.
I'M SORRY.

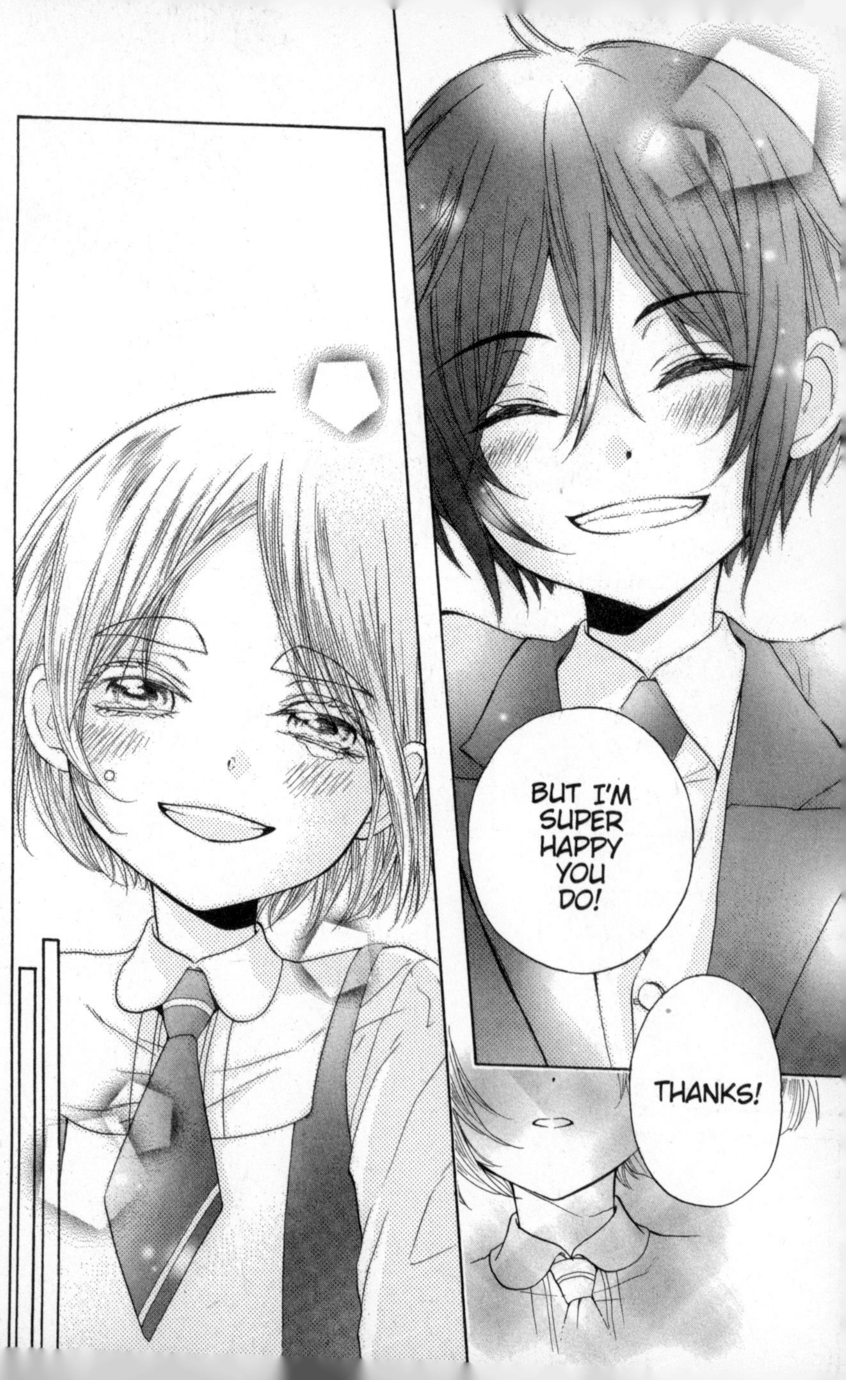
BUT I'M SUPER HAPPY YOU DO!
THANKS!

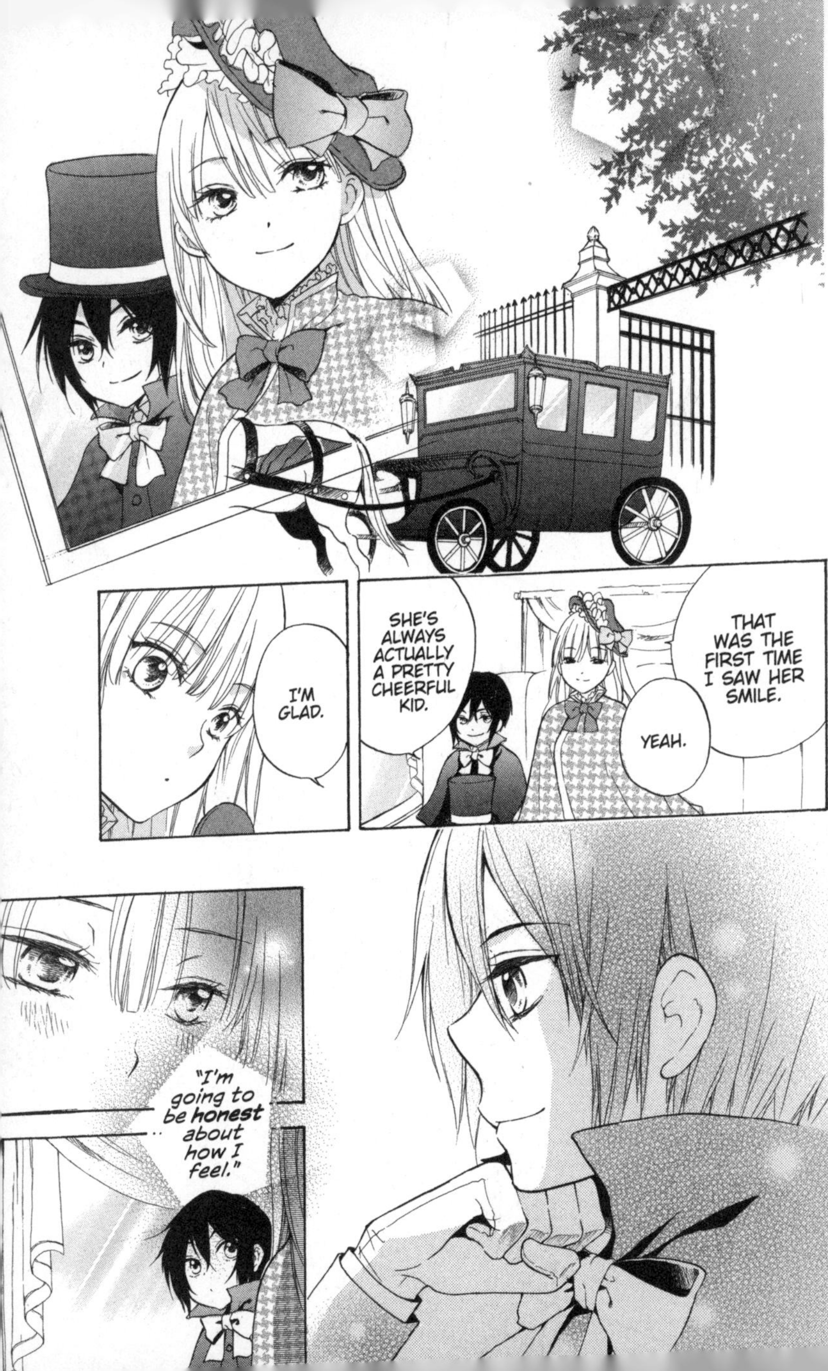
THAT WAS THE FIRST TIME I SAW HER SMILE.
YEAH.
SHE'S ALWAYS ACTUALLY A PRETTY CHEERFUL KID.
I'M GLAD.
"I'm going to be **honest** about how I feel."

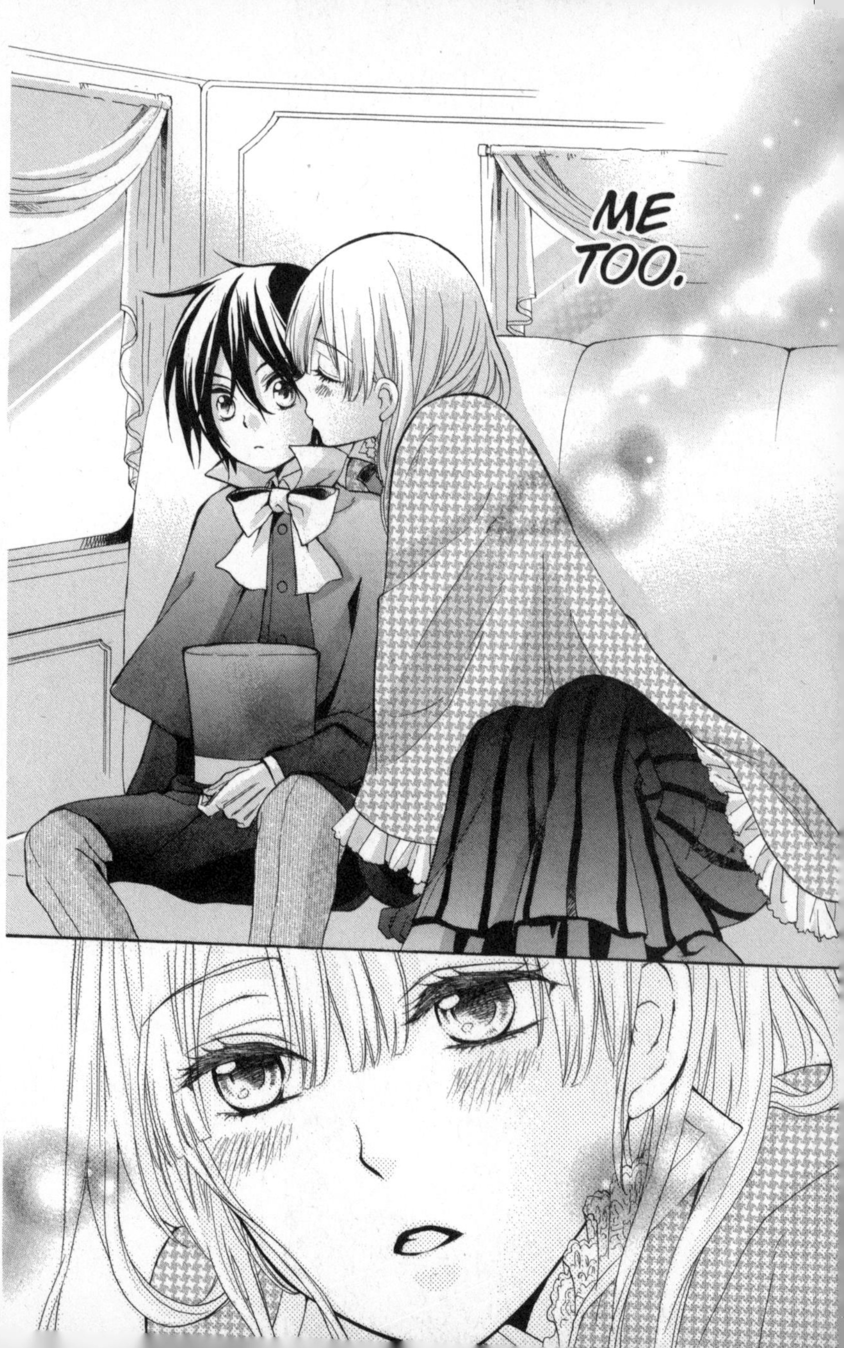
ME TOO.

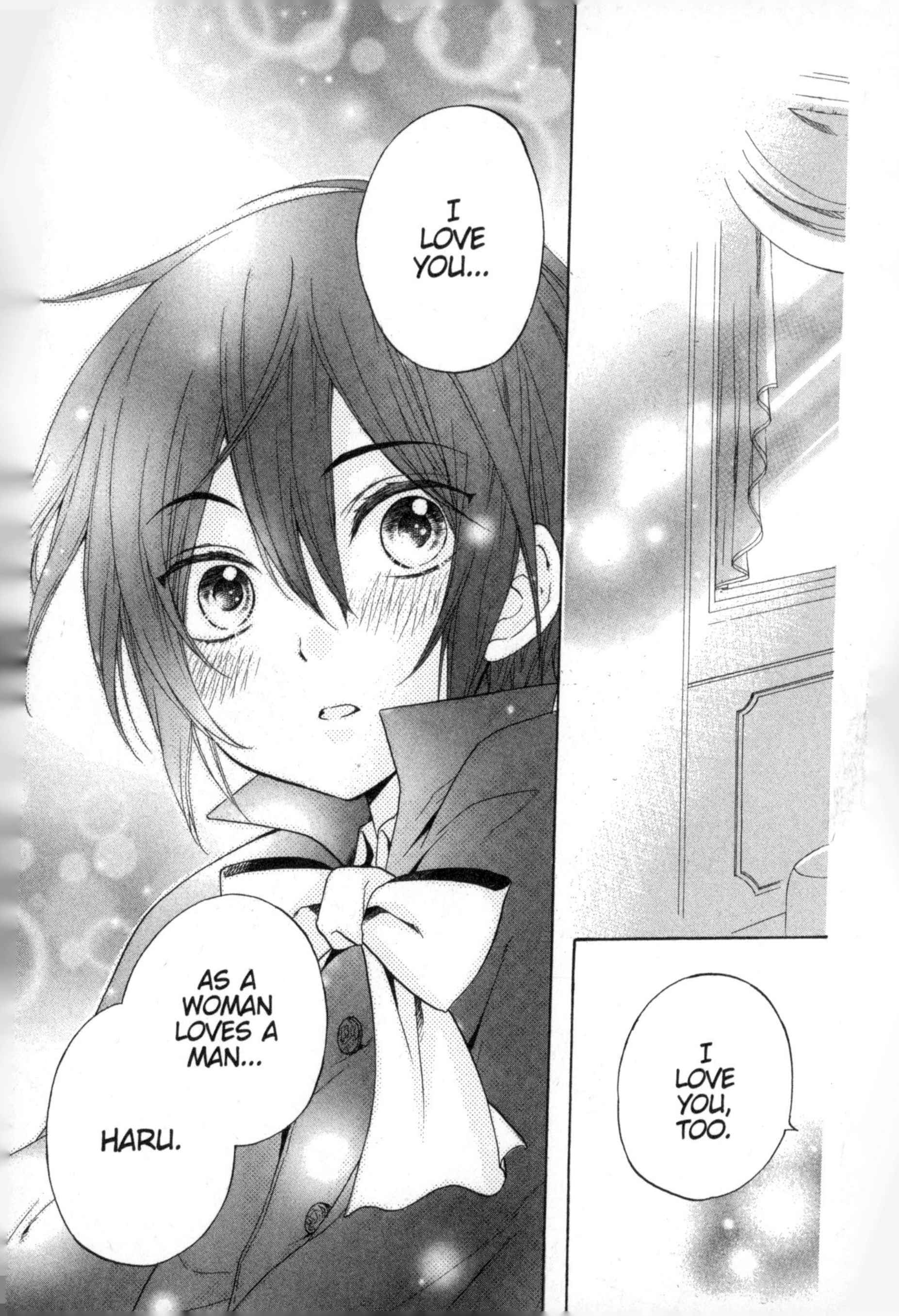
I LOVE YOU, TOO.
I LOVE YOU...
AS A WOMAN LOVES A MAN...
HARU.

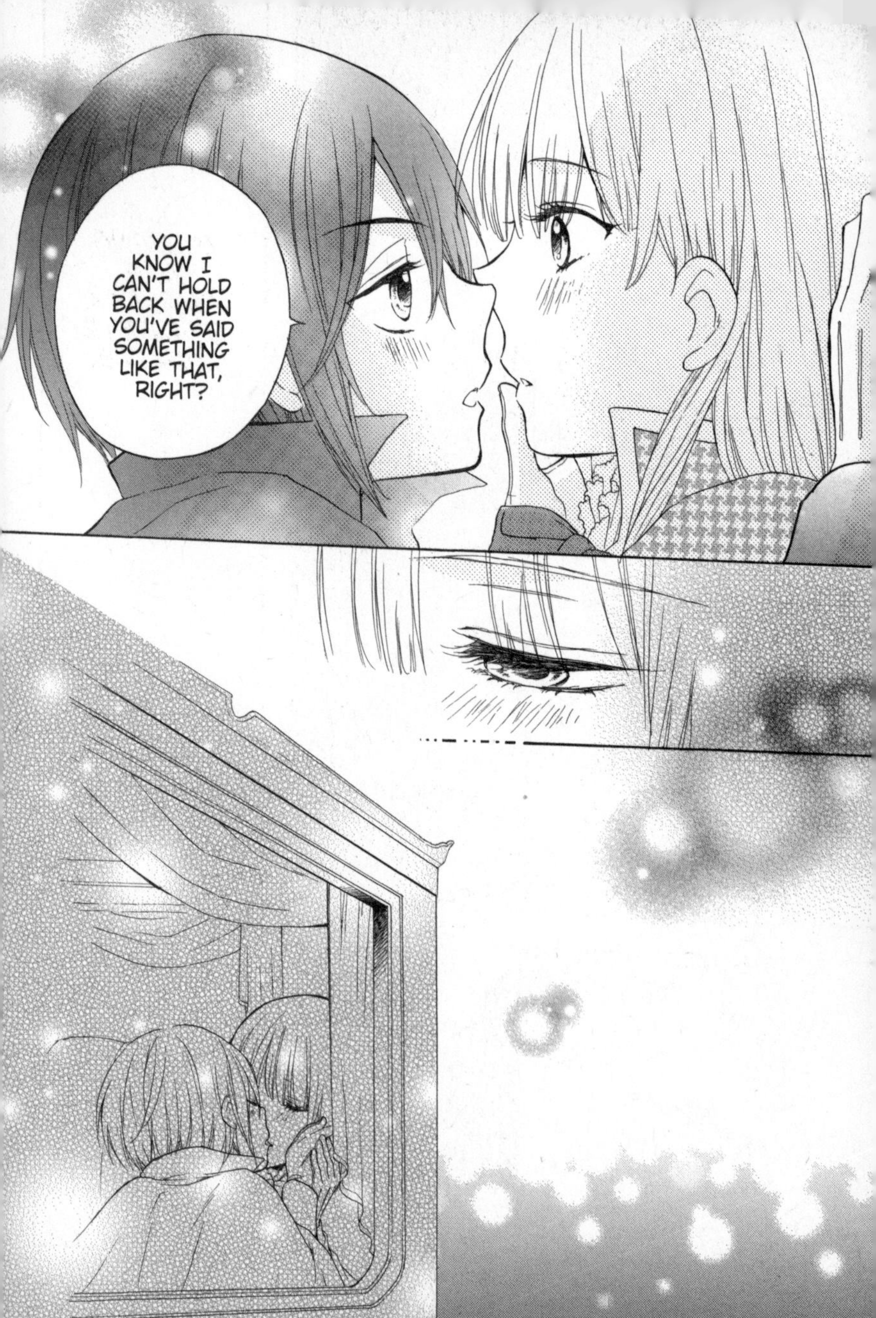
YOU KNOW I CAN'T HOLD BACK WHEN YOU'VE SAID SOMETHING LIKE THAT, RIGHT?

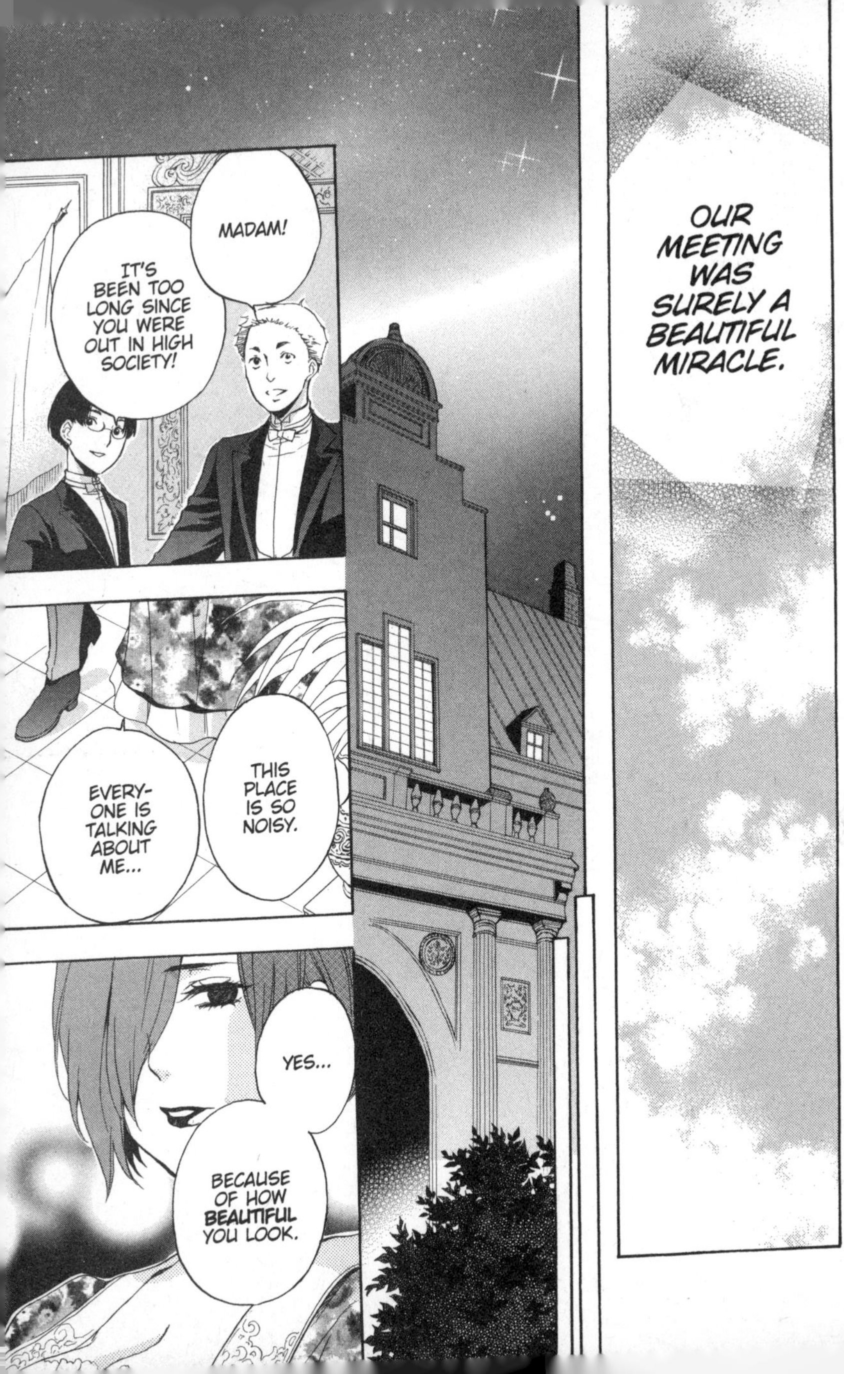
OUR MEETING WAS SURELY A BEAUTIFUL MIRACLE.
MADAM!
IT'S BEEN TOO LONG SINCE YOU WERE OUT IN HIGH SOCIETY!
THIS PLACE IS SO NOISY.
EVERY-ONE IS TALKING ABOUT ME...
YES...
BECAUSE OF HOW **BEAUTIFUL** YOU LOOK.

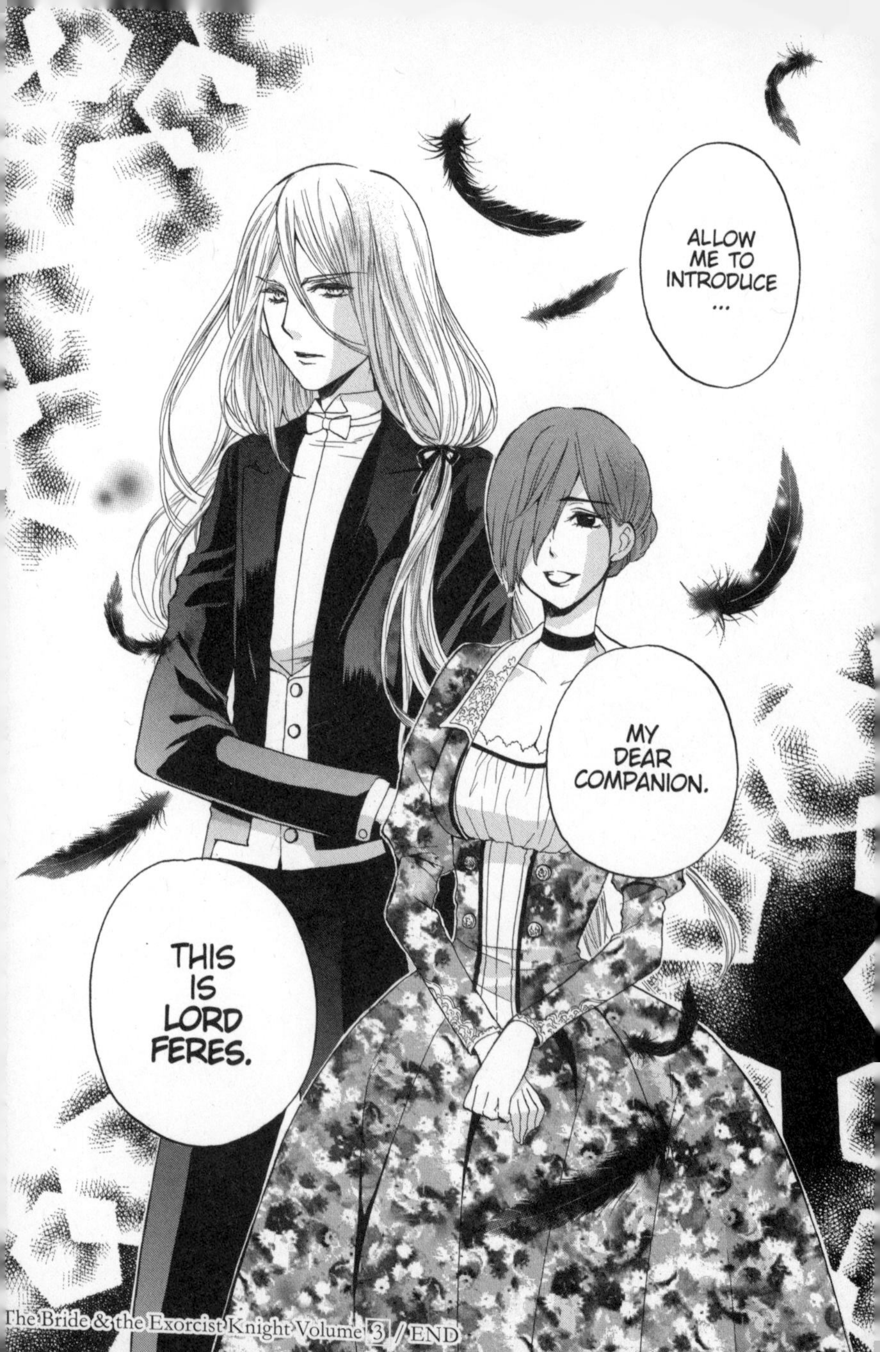
ALLOW ME TO INTRODUCE ...
MY DEAR COMPANION.
THIS IS LORD FERES.

The Bride & the Exorcist Knight Volume 3 / END

The Bride & the
Exorcist Knight

Bonus Chapter

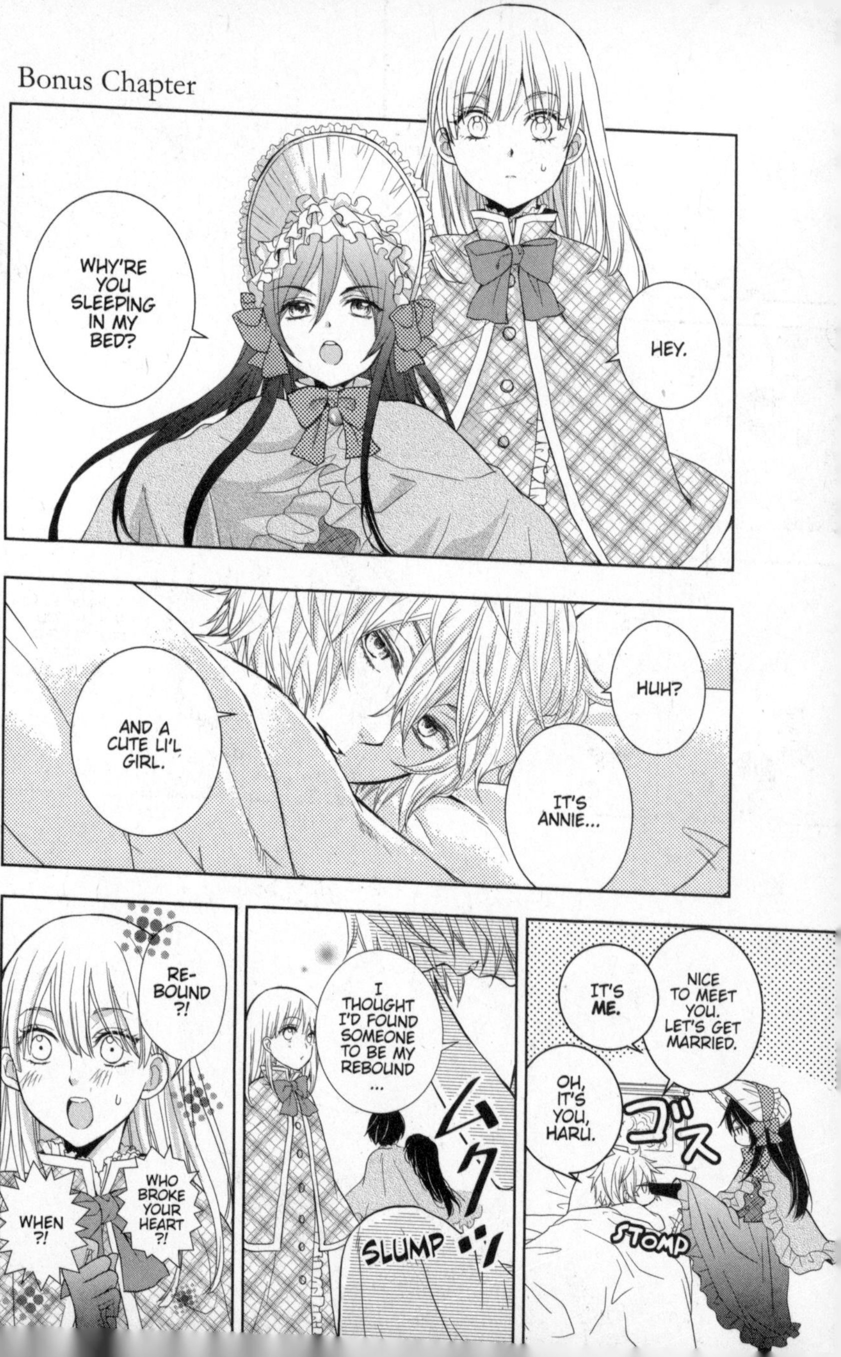
HEY.
WHY'RE YOU SLEEPING IN MY BED?
HUH?
IT'S ANNIE...
AND A CUTE LI'L GIRL.
NICE TO MEET YOU. LET'S GET MARRIED.
IT'S ME.
OH, IT'S YOU, HARU.
ゴス
STOMP
I THOUGHT I'D FOUND SOMEONE TO BE MY REBOUND...
ムク
SLUMP
RE-BOUND?!
WHO BROKE YOUR HEART?!
WHEN?!

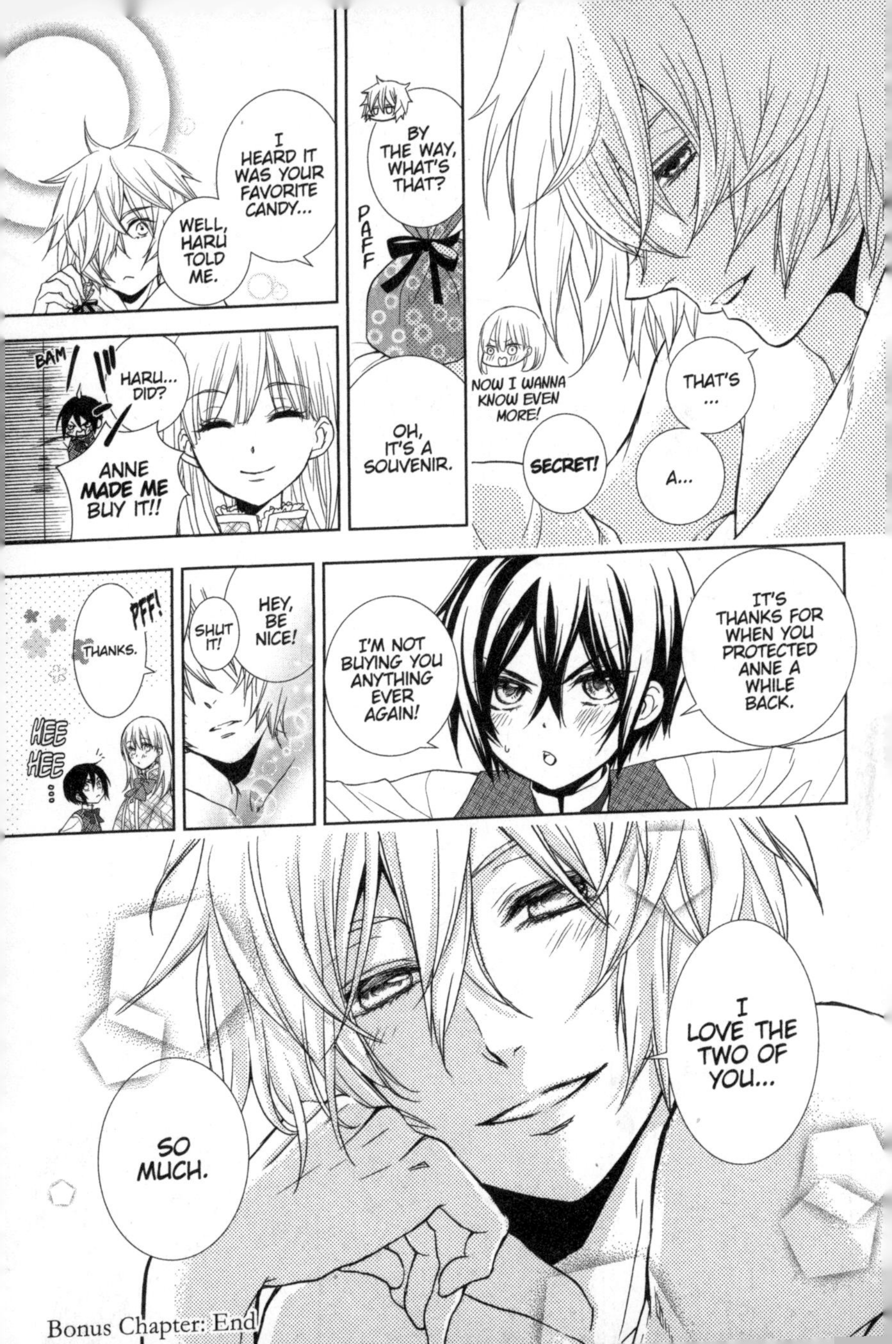
THAT'S...
A...
SECRET!
NOW I WANNA KNOW EVEN MORE!
BY THE WAY, WHAT'S THAT?
PAFF
OH, IT'S A SOUVENIR.
I HEARD IT WAS YOUR FAVORITE CANDY...
WELL, HARU TOLD ME.
HARU... DID?
BAM
ANNE MADE ME BUY IT!!
IT'S THANKS FOR WHEN YOU PROTECTED ANNE A WHILE BACK.
I'M NOT BUYING YOU ANYTHING EVER AGAIN!
HEY, BE NICE!
SHUT IT!
PFF!
THANKS.
HEE HEE
I LOVE THE TWO OF YOU...
SO MUCH.
Bonus Chapter: End

The Bride & the
Exorcist Knight

Next Volume

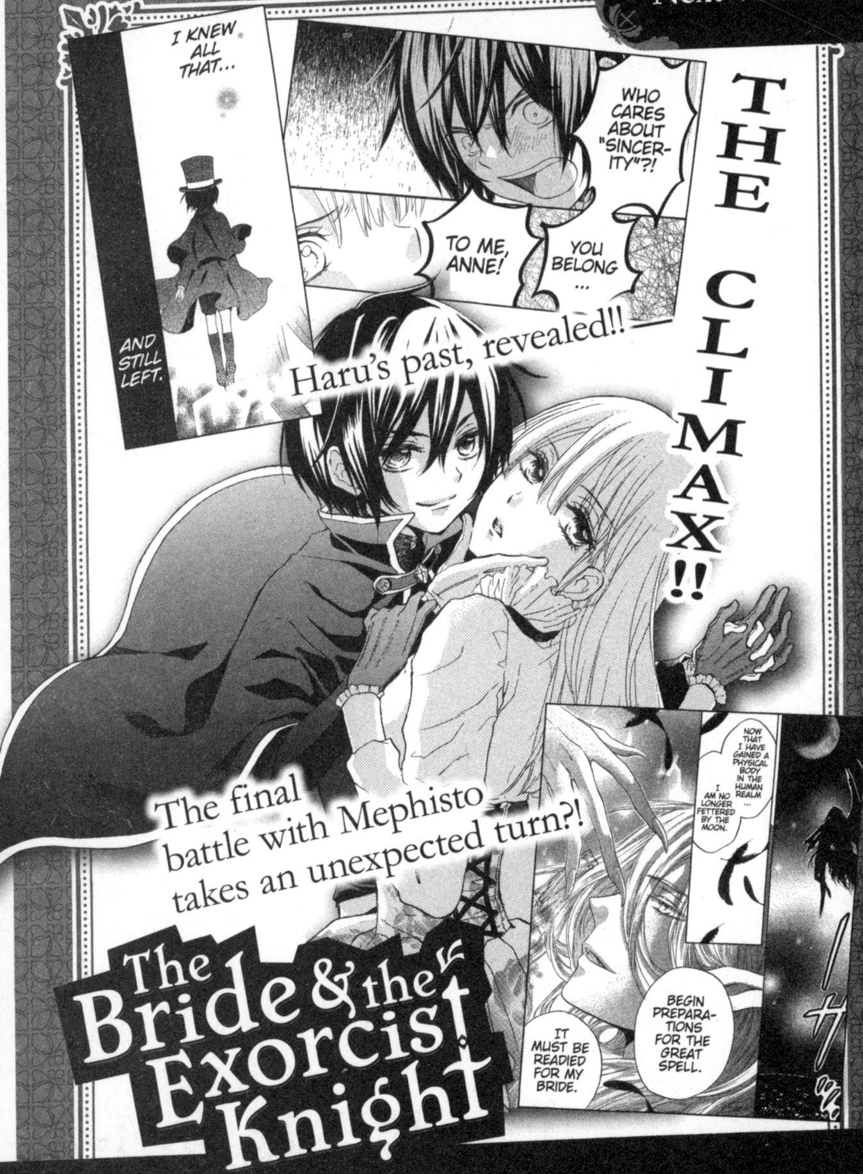
WHO CARES ABOUT "SINCERITY"?!
YOU BELONG ...
TO ME, ANNE!
I KNEW ALL THAT...
AND STILL LEFT.
THE CLIMAX!!
Haru's past, revealed!!
The final battle with Mephisto takes an unexpected turn?!
NOW THAT I HAVE GAINED A PHYSICAL BODY IN THE HUMAN REALM ...
I AM NO LONGER FETTERED BY THE MOON.
BEGIN PREPARATIONS FOR THE GREAT SPELL.
IT MUST BE READIED FOR MY BRIDE.
The Bride & the Exorcist Knight

COMING SOON!

SEVEN SEAS ENTERTAINMENT PRESENTS

The Bride & the Exorcist Knight

story and art by KEIKO ISHIHARA

VOLUME 3

TRANSLATION
Katrina Leonoudakis

ADAPTATION
Marykate Jasper

LETTERING AND RETOUCH
Lorina Mapa

COVER DESIGN
KC Fabellon

PROOFREADER
Dayna Abel
Stephanie Cohen

EDITOR
Shannon Fay

PRODUCTION ASSISTANT
CK Russell

PRODUCTION MANAGER
Lissa Pattillo

EDITOR-IN-CHIEF
Adam Arnold

PUBLISHER
Jason DeAngelis

HANAYOME TO EXORCIST
by KEIKO ISHIHARA
© Keiko Ishihara 2017
All rights reserved.
First published in Japan in 2017 by HAKUSENSHA, INC., Tokyo.
English language translation rights in U.S.A. arranged with HAKUSENSHA, INC.,
Tokyo through TOHAN CORPORATION, Tokyo.

Seven Seas books may be purchased in bulk for promotional, educational, or
business use. Please contact your local bookseller or the Macmillan Corporate
and Premium Sales Department at 1-800-221-7945, extension 5442, or by
e-mail at MacmillanSpecialMarkets@macmillan.com.

Seven Seas and the Seven Seas logo are trademarks of
Seven Seas Entertainment, LLC. All rights reserved.

ISBN: 978-1-64275-008-9

Printed in Canada

First Printing: March 2019

10 9 8 7 6 5 4 3 2 1

FOLLOW US ONLINE: **www.sevenseasentertainment.com**

READING DIRECTIONS

This book reads from **right to left**, Japanese style.
If this is your first time reading manga, you start
reading from the top right panel on each page and
take it from there. If you get lost, just follow the
numbered diagram here. It may seem backwards at
first, but you'll get the hang of it! Have fun!!

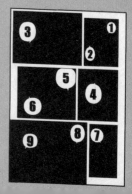